*[Handwritten inscription and signature, dated 6/19/02]*

# DEGREE OF CAUTION

by

**Sibyl Avery Jackson**

Milligan Books   California

Published and Distributed by:
Milligan Books
an imprint of Professional Business Consultants
1425 W. Manchester, Suite C,
Los Angeles, California 90047
(323) 750-3592


First Printing, October 2001
1 0 9 8 7 6 5 4 3 2 1


ISBN: 1-881524-27-2

Library of Congress Control Number: 2001135463

Publisher's note
This is a work of fiction. Names, characters, places, and incidents either
are product of the author's imagination or are used fictitiously, and any
resemblance to actual persons, living or dead, events, or locales is
entirely coincidental.

Sibyl Avery Jackson
P.O. Box 130213
Houston, Texas 77219-0213

www.SibylAveryJackson.com
SibylAJackson@aol.com

# Dedication

For my husband, Alfred, who gives me what I need.
And for Ajaye, Averi, Alex and Chris

# About The Author

Sibyl Avery Jackson earned a B.A. degree in English from Spelman College. She lives in Houston, Texas, with her husband, Alfred, and their family, where she is currently at work on a new "FBI Special Agent Monica Sinclair" novel.

# Acknowledgments

I acknowledge the living God who blesses me every day. To Him I give the glory.

Thank you to my parents, Gloria and Parnell N. Avery, M. D., for giving me life, love and instilling in me the belief that I can achieve my wildest dreams. Thanks to my sister, Natalie Avery Webster and my sister-in-law, Toni Williams, for their encouragement. A special thank you to my sister, Vida L. Avery, for burning the midnight oil with me both here in the U.S. and on the beautiful island of Bermuda.

Thank you to Dr. and Mrs. Norman Mason for continued support; to Michelle Taylor for braving frigid temperatures and the snow with me on the street of Washington, D.C.; to my cousin, actress Brenda Moore, for graciously allowing her stage character, "Ms. Lucy" to make a brief appearance in this book.

A special thank you to Bob McCormick for patiently sharing his technical knowledge and expertise.

Thank you to Dr. Henry F. Gamble, Dr. Ivan Spector, Dr. John M. Jones of Houston, Texas. Any medical errors are clearly my own.

Thank you to Sulla Hamer for sticking by me when things were dark. Hollywood needs more people like you.

Thank you to Jenna McEachern for whisking me away to the Texas Hill Country to iron out the first few chapters.

Thank you to Melanie and Ben Barnes for being there

when I asked for help.

Thank you to Edith and Coach Darrell Royal for rescuing me one weekend when I needed a quiet place to write.

Thanks to Maxine Thompson, Dr. Rosie Milligan of Milligan Books, Marilyn Emanuel, and Patricia Pollan. And thank you to Sgt. Wilbur Robinson, Jr, of the Houston Police Department.

Thank you to my sister authors, Anita Bunkley, Rev. Claudette Sims, and Margie Walker for their advice and inspiration. A special thanks to "Peat" and "Repeat". You know who you are.

Most of all, thank you to my husband, Alfred, for skillfully juggling my multiple personalities during the writing of this book. We love you. And, to Ajaye, Averi, Alex—and Chris—thank you for spurring me on by repeatedly asking, "Is the book finished yet, Mom?"

# PROLOGUE

*March 1997*

The shrill of the machine was deafening.

"He's choking!" the nurse shouted. The patient's restrained body started flinching. The doctor rushed to the bed and grabbed the nurse's arm.

"Get outta the way!" he ordered, pushing her aside. He immediately released the guardrail and began to examine the patient. "Shut that damn thing off!"

The nurse scampered to silence the alarm. She looked from the patient to the doctor, then averted her eyes.

Without saying a word, the doctor grasped the endotracheal tube in the patient's mouth and, with the tip of the suction, he drew out the fluid. The nurse quickly replaced the empty IV bag with a sterile plastic bag of medicine.

A few minutes later, the flinching subsided. The only sound in the room was the bellowing of the respirator. Like an accordion, the patient's chest kept cadence to the rhythm.

The doctor leaned over the bed and opened the patient's right eye. Using a pen light, he flickered it directly over the pupil. The pupil constricted. He got the same reaction in the left eye.

"Pressure's stable, doctor," the nurse observed, reading the monitor at the side of the bed.

"Heart rate and pulse?"

"Normal."

The doctor let out a deep sigh. He clipped the pen light to the outside of his breast coat pocket, then pulled off the latex gloves. Wiping his forehead with the back of his hand, he steadied his own breathing. Then he shook his head. *That was too damn close.*

"Doctor, I—"

"You were late administering the Haldol," the doctor admonished.

"There was an emergency with anoth–"

"He gagged because he was coming to!" he accused. "He could've asphyxiated! Keep him heavily sedated, do I make myself clear?"

The nurse bit her lips. "Yes, Doctor," she whispered.

The doctor glared sternly at the woman, then walked in front of the intracranial pressure monitoring system. Everything appeared normal. He turned around and adjusted the tube leading into the right frontal horn of the ventricle system in the patient's brain, then checked the cerebral spinal fluid bag. The liquid was clear.

He crossed his arms and stood erect over the patient. Draining tubes protruded from his body. His skin was so pale, almost translucent. His shaved head, which appeared abnormally large for the skeletal body outlined beneath the sheets, revealed a mapping of scars.

# Chapter

## 1

Monica Sinclair snatched off the tight-fitting braided wig and flung her keys onto the coffee table. Reaching for the television remote control, she punched the buttons as she surfed the channels for the evening news. The press conference had ended several hours before, but each of the Atlanta stations led with the same story—her story. After seven long months, she'd finally exposed one of the biggest cover-ups of the decade. The excitement of the day's events engulfed every inch of her 5'9" frame.

Raking her fingers through her naturally crinkly, shoulder-length hair, she plopped down on the edge of the sofa in her Buckhead home and switched to CNN just as the beginning segment aired. Sneakers, her red and white Welsh Corgi, leaped up onto the sofa next to her.

"Yes!" She balled up her fist and pulled her elbow down, then threw up the Victory sign. As if he sensed her exhilaration, Sneakers began to "yip-yip," and dance around in her lap.

"Shhh! Hush, boy!" she said, tousling Sneakers's shiny coat, eyes glued to the screen. Monica used the remote control to turn up the TV's volume.

The camera zeroed in on the anchorwoman. Staring back into the camera lens, the pretty brunette was a

Cindy Crawford look-alike complete with the distinctive mole above her left lip.

". . . Here's what FBI Director James Frasier had to say at an earlier press conference in Washington, D.C."

As the television screen quickly switched to the rebroadcast of the press conference, Monica stopped stroking the little dog and stared intently as the bare-headed man with the distinguished walrus mustache approached the speaker's podium. Adjusting his glasses, he held up his pink palms to silence the crowd of eager reporters who each sat with pad and pen in hand, and began to read his statement:

"Today, the FBI confirmed that Yreva Airlines has been cutting costs by purchasing substandard equipment from Petree Industries, which services the President's Air Force One and Air Force Two aircrafts."

Monica noticed how Frasier nervously coughed into his fist. Clearing his throat, he continued reading in a stilted voice.

"The airline has been experiencing financial trouble for several years now, forcing lay-offs of over one-third of its employees. As a result of this investigation, the NTSB has determined that the defective equipment was the major cause of three crashes in as many years—the latest of which killed more than 100 people last summer."

A loud "O" rose in the crowd, dovetailed by a chorus of "Oh, my Gods." After what seemed like minutes, but was only a few seconds of commotion, the roar of the indignation settled down to a slight murmur.

Frasier rustled his papers and went on. "Investigations into the accidents revealed each of the right engines in the aircraft experienced cracked fan blades either in the first or second stage compressors. The FAA has terminated

Yreva Airlines's license and grounded all of its aircraft. As of this afternoon, Jeffrey McNair, CEO of the airline, and two other top executives, pled guilty in a U.S. District Court on three felony counts of willfully purchasing faulty equipment for the company . . ."

He paused. "The guilty pleas could result in maximum sentences of up to twenty-five years in prison and over $2 million in fines for each of the defendants."

Once again, a furor stirred among the media.

"This is all I can say at this point. Now, I'd like to turn this press conference over to the director of the NTSB."

Camera bulbs begin to flash at once as the reporters shouted questions over one another.

"Was there a leak at Yreva?" one reporter shouted above the rest.

Frasier was responding, "A reliable source tipped us off—" when the camera cut away to a breaking-news report of a police shoot-out in another city.

"Yes!" Monica smiled, as she sat on the edge of the sofa and clicked down the volume of the television. She was the "reliable source." A retired FBI special agent—with active status—who'd spent eleven years as one of the Bureau's top agents.

Upon graduating Spelman College in 1980—after spending a year abroad as an exchange student—Monica never intended to stay when she'd first entered the agent training program at the FBI Academy in Quantico, Virginia. She'd merely considered the career detour a valuable research investment in her future as an aspiring fiction writer.

But once she'd begun the process, Monica found herself seduced by the adventure and the calculated risks—

both of which allowed her to slip in and out of worlds quite different from her own. The desire to escape from her past was the fuel firing her talent for blending into surroundings and assuming personalities totally unlike her own. As the years progressed, she became burned out from running from herself, and she retired from the Bureau seven years ago.

She was now a successful author of two mystery novels, despite the fact that she'd refused—for security purposes—to do book tours or allow photos of herself on the book jackets or in publicity packets. Coined "The Faceless Ms" by the media because of the initials she used as her pseudonym, Monica had never personally met her agent or editor and communicated with the women only by phone, e-mail, or fax. Sometimes, the urge for living on the edge stirred beyond her control and coaxed her back into the make-believe world the Bureau provided.

Monica turned the television off altogether, then surveyed the objects in front of her on the coffee table. Everything was there: The large Webster's II Dictionary sat high directly in the middle, beside it a pair of scissors, a bottle of Crown Royal and a high-ball glass. A fresh, unlit ivory tapered candle sat in a crystal holder.

Her open-planned home was located in the yuppie mecca of Atlanta, Georgia, nestled back among the trees just off of Peachtree Street. The living room was decorated with overstuffed chenille furniture, hardwood floors, and a slate fireplace. The kitchen was to the left of the living room, her home office to the right enclosed by double-french doors.

Satisfied that everything was in place, Monica poured a shot of whiskey into the glass, raised it in salute to herself, and downed the first round. She cleared her throat and reached for the matches. Just as she began to light the candle, she was startled by the ringing of the phone, chimed in by her dog's announcing bark.

"Geez, Sneakers! Do you always have to do that?" she scolded the little dog and blew out the flame, before answering the phone.

"Hello?" she said, barely catching her breath.

"Congratulations, Babe," said the familiar voice on the other end.

Recognizing her brother Michael's voice, Monica smiled as she eased down onto the sofa again.

"Everyone up here is bursting at the seams," he said louder into the speaker phone, when Monica did not immediately respond. Michael Morgan was one of the Bureau's youngest assistant deputy directors.

"I'm sure they are," Monica said, taking another sip of her drink and lighting a cigarette. "Too bad I couldn't join the celebration, being I was the 'reliable source' and all."

"Don't give us that bull, young lady," another voice boomed through the phone. "I thought I caught a glimpse of you among the crowd of reporters at the press conference this morning. You were here, weren't you?" The baritone voice belonged to Jim Frasier.

"Don't be so paranoid," Monica grinned, knowing there wasn't a snowball's chance in hell the man had seen her in the disguise she'd worn today.

"Do you actually think I'd fly to D.C., attend a press conference whose rebroadcast I could watch a million times on television, and then turn right around and fly back to Atlanta? On my dime? Besides, I could sell you a box of popcorn at a Redskins' game and you'd never know it."

"She's got you there, Jim," Michael laughed in the background.

Monica broke in. "You'd be too busy looking for me out on the field somewhere. Give up, Frasier. The only way you'd know me undercover is if I came right out and told you." Inhaling her cigarette, Monica let the smoke jet through her nostrils.

"Very funny, you guys," Jim Frasier said, without conceding they were right on the money. "On that note, I'll leave you two to finish your conversation. Just wanted to thank you again, Monica, for your help. Talk to you soon."

Monica heard the sound of the office door close.

"Jim may not have actually seen you today, Monica," Michael continued after his boss had left. "But I certainly did. That wasn't exactly a smart move, Sis. Staying out of the limelight is all a part of the job and you knew—"

Monica sucked her teeth. "Hey, cut the lecture, Little Bro."

"—the rules from the beginning when you signed on as the female version of 007 that there would be no marching bands or public accolades, once the deal was done."

"James Bond is more your role, little brother. Nothing I could pull out of my bag of tricks could make me look that white. I'm the black sheep of the family, remember?" The sudden tinge of coolness resonated in her voice, reminding them both of their family lineage. Michael became silent on the other end.

She and Michael were products of an interracial union—an African-American mother and a Jewish father—though brother and sister bore no resemblance to one another.

Monica was tall and slender with long shapely legs. She had a long Jewish nose, full lips, and striking hazel eyes. Her skin was the color of smooth caramel, her hair a dark, reddish brown. At thirty-eight, she was a beautiful woman and the spitting image of her mother.

Michael, two years younger, was muscularly built at 6'2". His eyes were the same pecan brown as his father's. His hair was straight dark brown which he wore combed back. He had the same fair skin as his father and was always mistaken for white.

"Anyway," Michael continued, ignoring Monica's comment, "I echo Frasier's sentiments."

"Which I'd like to see in the form of a fat check. I've decided to treat myself—"

"—Monica," Michael interrupted, suddenly serious. "You sure you got out okay?"

Touched by her brother's concern, she highlighted the details of the case and reassured him that her cover went undetected.

"Sweets would've loved to have seen me dressed like a 'lady,' instead of in my usual leggings and sweat shirts." Monica laughed. "Though, I'm sure our grandmother wouldn't have approved of the late-night drinking."

She heard Michael's sigh of relief. She knew he worried about her whenever she was on assignment. He'd been against Jim calling her back into the Bureau several years before when the FBI reached an impasse in a case ironically similar to one Monica wrote about in one of her books. After listening to the details, Monica convinced Michael and Frasier she knew how the crime was being committed. She'd gone undercover, used herself as bait to trap the suspected murderer—who'd abducted and killed women in five states—then led the FBI straight to the buried bodies of his victims.

"Okay, okay. I get the picture," Michael chuckled. "I promise, next time you'll sport a more desirable appearance. Which brings me to the other reason I called—"

"—Oh, no, you don't. I'm taking a much-needed vacation before I go off on another escapade for you and Frasier. A little fun and sun on the beaches in Maui. I'm gonna drink Bongo-Bongos until even I won't recognize myself."

Monica's eyes looked beyond the french doors to the manuscript on her desk.

"Besides, my deadline's coming up soon on the new book. Gotta clear this case from my head, then do some serious writing. So, thanks, but no thanks."

"This is a hot one, Monica." Michael's words tumbled out in a pitched fervor. "Could be huge, possibly affecting even you. Jim and I have started the ball rolling, but we need you.

"Tell you what," Michael continued, "why don't you meet me at Sweets's this weekend? Been promising her for weeks I'd come for a visit. Just talked to her yesterday, told her I'd try to get you to come, too. It's been almost a year since you've been home. She's dying to feed us some home-cooked meals."

Monica hesitated before responding to her brother's request. She did not want to confront a painful part of her past by going back to Amherst, Virginia, just to hear details of a case.

"I don't know, Michael," she said, slowly. "But—"

"Come on, Monica," he persisted. "Our grandmother's not getting any younger, you know. Whatta you say?"

"I don't know—"

"Come this weekend and hear me out. If you still don't want to get involved, hey, we'll get somebody else."

"Okay . . . Alright," Monica relented. "I'll call Sweets myself and let her know I'll be there on Friday."

"Great, kiddo!" Michael said triumphantly. "It'll be just like old times with the three of us together again. You know, Twig . . ." He hesitated, using his childhood nickname for her. "Talked to Dad last night, he's proud—"

"Stop right there, Michael," she snapped sharply, as if a bolt of lightening suddenly flashed through the phone line and struck her. "I don't give a damn what Ben thinks about me and you know it! Why do you insist on bringing him up?"

Releasing a deep sigh, Michael lowered his voice to barely above a whisper.

"C'mon, Monica, you're not being fair. You've never really tried to understand Dad's side or allowed anyone else to tell you. He really cares about you."

"Don't screw with me on this, Mike 'cause you won't win. You wanna relationship with Ben? I'm cool with that. Just leave me the hell out of it!" Monica snatched the pack of cigarettes from the end table beside her and lit another one, while struggling to balance the phone to her ear. Her eyes bulged wildly, each breath she took was hard and heavy and radiated like steam from a pot of boiling water.

He'd stirred the wasp's nest within her by mentioning the one name that unleashed a dark side of her she rarely saw, and she was now leading the charge. *Get a grip, girl*, Monica commanded herself, as she added another brick to the protective wall she'd constructed through the years.

"It's getting late, Mike," Monica abruptly changed the subject. She took a long drag from her cigarette, the blue puffs of smoke providing a thin hazy veil. "I need to call Sweets."

She was somewhat relieved when Michael eased the tension between them and gayly added, "Okay. Remind her to bake a couple of apple pies. And, Monica, before you go, you did one hell of a job. Thanks again."

Before Monica could say anything more, Michael hung up. She held the phone a moment, before placing the receiver back on the hook. She took a deep breath, struck another match, and lit the candle. Taking the scissors, she snipped off a braid from the wig and opened the book. Inside the hollowed opening, where pages were supposed to be, she gently placed the braid on top of the other items.

\* \* \*

MICHAEL STARED OUT the window of his Washington, D.C., office. The acrimony between Monica and their father spanned decades, with no immediate resolution in sight. Right now, he had more urgent business. He had a little more than twenty-four hours to figure out a way to convince Monica to come aboard.

\* \* \*

JUST A FEW DOORS DOWN from Michael's office, another telephone conversation was just beginning.

"Did she agree to the case?" the man's voice asked on the other end of the phone.

"Michael's talking to her now," Jim Frasier responded.

"I still don't think it's a good idea bringing Monica in on this one. It's too risky so soon after this last assignment. Michael wouldn't have gone for it either, had I told him the truth. I just don't like it.

"That's not your decision, now is it?" the voice retorted. "You wanna lose another agent? Gerald Conti never knew we were on to him and I plan to keep it that way. Our guy got in way over his head, didn't pull out when we ordered him to—a mistake that cost him his life.

"No! Do not tell Michael," the man demanded. "His knowing would only jeopardize Monica's cover."

Jim took off his glasses and pinched the bridge of his nose. He could feel the warm flush in his cheeks turning burgundy. Michael was his protege. Jim never kept pertinent information about a case from him—before now.

"I'll let you know her decision," Jim said wearily, before hanging up the phone.

He was getting too old for this job.

# Chapter

## 2

The sleek, black Silver Spur eased out of the affluent River Oaks neighborhood onto Allen Parkway and cruised towards Houston's spectacular downtown skyline. Though it was still early March, the sun blazed down and the morning air already bore the sweltering humidity more typical of a summer day.

Gerald Conti sat in the back seat looking over his day's agenda. A distinguished-looking man with wavy salt and pepper hair and a neatly trimmed mustache, he wore tailored Armani suits on his stocky, six-foot body.

"Hurry up, Bennett," Gerald barked into the intercom. "I've got a meeting with my brother in exactly fifteen minutes."

"Relax, Mr. Conti. We're just about there." A smile smirked across Bennett's dark, granite-like face as he stole a glance in the rear-view mirror at his agitated boss.

"Don't tell me to relax. Just get me there on time!"

"Yes, sir, Mr. Conti."

Gerald put the agenda aside and took another set of papers from his briefcase. Smiling to himself, he looked over the plans that would force his brother, Victor, out as head of the Conti Empire. *Not some measly wireless subsidiary president.*

The driver brought the limo to a stop in front of the forty-story building. He turned off the motor and said, "Right on time. Just like I said."

Within three minutes, the private elevator delivered Gerald up to Victor's office on the top floor.

"Good morning, Mr. Conti," Gerald heard a woman say as soon as he stepped off the elevator. He turned in her direction, and saw Victor's secretary, Sandra, standing in the doorway of his brother's office.

He nodded. "Hello, Sandra. My brother's already here, I presume?"

"Not yet, but he's on his way. Mr. Fazio's waiting in the conference room. I was just about to bring him some more coffee. Would you like a cup?"

"Please." Gerald watched as the secretary walked off. He paused a moment at the entrance of Victor's office which occupied most of the 40th floor. The floor-to-ceiling windows held a breathtaking view of downtown Houston. Gerald's eyes rested on Victor's desk, a massive mahogany Queen Anne, that had been in their family for more than seventy years.

*In just a matter of days, this will all be mine,* Gerald thought to himself, whistling as he walked in the direction of the conference room.

\* \* \*

VICTOR CONTI PUT HIS BRIEFCASE DOWN on his desk and pressed the button for his assistant.

"Right on time, Victor," Maggie Wentworth said, glancing at the Chinese clock on the wall as she walked into the room. She had been Victor's executive assistant for many years. "Your brother and Arthur Fazio are in the conference room. They got here about fifteen minutes ago and have been huddled together in serious discussion ever since."

Victor paused for a moment. He took some papers from his briefcase and headed for the door. "You coming?" He looked back at Maggie.

"Wouldn't miss it. I'll be right in once I confirm your appointments for this afternoon." She gave him a wink as she brushed past him.

Opening the door to the spacious meeting room, Victor noticed the two men abruptly end their conversation. They tried to act as if they were casually waiting for him. Instantly, his B.S. antenna went up.

"Good morning, gentlemen." Victor placed his things on the table. As both men rose to greet him, Victor shook hands with Arthur Fazio, then went to the other side of the table, embraced his brother and kissed his cheek. The public display of affection was customary among their Italian family.

Taking his chair at the head of the table, Victor noticed Arthur staring at him and then back at Gerald. Smiling, Victor shuffled some papers and asked the lawyer if there was something wrong with his attire.

"Sorry, Victor," Arthur said, with embarrassment. "Realize you guys are identical twins. But, with both of you dressed in navy suits—and the grey in the same place at your temples . . . It's eerie."

Almost on cue, Victor grinned at Gerald, knowing they were both thinking the same thing. As children, they relied on their identical likeness to play practical tricks on relatives and friends. Even now at the age of fifty-two, they were amused by the intrigued stares they got whenever they were together.

"Our situation has been uncanny, hasn't it, Gerald?" Victor asked his brother, whose wide grin stretched across his face.

"Until you ended our shenanigans by not recovering from our nasty bout with polio. We may share the same love for Italian-made suits, the same salt and pepper hair, and even the same trim mustache, but even I can't imitate that walk."

Victor laughed off the remark, but he was stung by the painful reminder of the childhood disease they'd both contracted at the age of six. Gerald recovered almost immediately. Victor had not. His right leg was permanently damaged and slightly shorter than the other, resulting in a noticeable limp. "Gimp Leg Vic," his childhood friends had taunted him.

"Nor, would you want to, I'm sure," Victor grimaced. "Let's get down to business, shall we?"

Looking straight at his brother, he continued. "Gerald, I know you've been meeting regularly with your senior staff. Where are we now with the license-renewal process for Bayou City Wireless?"

"Everything's set, Victor." Gerald loosened his tie. "Arthur's been in weekly consultation with our law firm in Washington, D.C. They're sending one of their guys down at the end of this week to go over the legalities with the vice presidents."

"Good. Let me know when it's confirmed. I want to be there."

"That won't be necessary, Victor. Everything's going according to plan."

"Every step is crucial, Gerald."

"Sure. I'll let you know," Gerald said, glancing at Arthur.

Victor turned to Arthur. "Any papers you disseminate should have the confidential-stamped seal. I don't want OmegaCom or anyone else getting their hands on our customer base, demographics, or systems analysis."

"That won't be a problem, Victor. We've never had security problems before. Except for the new VP in marketing, all of our guys have been with us from the gate."

"I agree, Victor," Gerald broke in. "We hand-picked these guys."

"Good. Normally, this would be a procedural process, but since OmegaCom has declared war to increase its market share, we have to be meticulous with every "i" dotted and every "t" crossed. We have an impeccable reputation within the industry. I'm not about to let another company come in here and change that."

Arthur Fazio had been legal counsel for Bayou City Wireless since its inception. He had been Gerald's lawyer at a communications company in Europe, before that. With his receding hairline, Arthur looked older than Gerald even though he was six years younger. His squat build didn't help matters.

Victor glanced at Maggie, who'd come in during the middle of the discussion. Her only visible reaction to the conversation was a raised eyebrow, which only she and Victor shared.

"Let's just be careful about our strategy," he repeated, leaning back in his chair.

"With the launch of the Excalibur approaching," Gerald said matter-of-factly, "I've decided to add a new position—an internal PR person. I put the public relations firm on notice, told them we needed someone inside the company."

"Good idea. Anyone in particular?"

"Not yet. Our headhunters will have a short list of candidates within the next five-to-seven days."

"Speaking of the Excalibur, any idea when the Indonesian group will be through with their testing?"

"They finished last week." Gerald beamed, straightening in his chair. "They loved it! Said it was the first piece of equipment to meet all of their needs and specifications. I closed the deal last night to ship a thousand phones to them by this time next month."

"Whoa. Wait a minute, Gerald," Victor said, suddenly uneasy that the old Gerald who made snap decisions was now manifesting himself. "We're not ready to market the Excalibur. We need time to thoroughly analyze the test results."

Victor studied the disgruntled look on Gerald's face. He continued. "Thirty days is too short a time to do the necessary checks and balances, and deliver a finished product. It simply can't be done."

"Victor, you know damn well if we're going to get a jump on everyone else in the industry, we've gotta move quickly!"

Victor's features froze as stone cold as a Noh mask.

Gerald's words began to rush out. "From what I hear, there's already a similar device—though not as elaborate as ours—already being tested in the UK. We can't pussyfoot around with unnecessary procedures. The Excalibur is sound. If it works in a God-forsaken country like Indonesia—with its mountainous terrain and monsoon season—it'll work anywhere."

Gerald gave Victor an imploring look. "You know I'm right. Bob McCormick has assured me the product approval process will be completed in time to meet our deadline. He's forwarding that confirmation on to the guys in Jakarta."

"Bob? When did this happen?" Victor asked, surprised he had not been included in the meeting with the FCC Chairman.

"Last week, while I was in D.C. The boys from Indonesia called all ecstatic about it. I met with Bob to discuss the details."

Victor remained silent.

Gerald added, "Called him this morning and told him I'd solidified the deal."

Victor leaned forward with his hands clasped together on the table. Gerald was moving way too fast. Staring straight ahead at the mirrored image of himself, Victor attempted a more neutral approach.

He measured his words. "I know you're excited about this, Gerald. In fact, you've done an exceptional job of seeing it to fruition. But I agreed to go along with letting the guys in Indonesia test it, provided *all* of the results—both here and abroad—were completely analyzed before we signed a deal."

He paused. "This is a unique piece of equipment. I'm surprised Bob would move so swiftly without more data. Perhaps I should explain to him the complex—"

"I've taken care of the situation, Victor," Gerald said sternly, his eyes squinting, as if to make a point. "Apparently, I've misjudged your confidence in me."

"We should proceed," Victor said, "with a certain degree of caution. Why don't we discuss this later? You can fill me in on the details. If there's no further business, I'd say this meeting is adjourned."

"By the way," he said, with a sudden change in thought, as the men got up from their seats, "have either of you heard from Dave Carter?"

"Not since he left eight months ago," Gerald answered, casually. "You haven't heard from him either, have you Arthur?" he asked pointedly, as he and Arthur sat back down.

"Ah . . . . No. I haven't."

Gerald turned to his brother. "What made you suddenly think of him, Victor?"

"He deserves some of the credit in the Excalibur's success, since he helped with the technical design. Also, checked in on Peters the other day, when I was at Bayou City Wireless. Wanted to see if he was settling into his job. He asked about some of Carter's notes and files he'd stumbled upon."

Victor noticed the quick glance exchanged between Gerald and Arthur. And the color draining from Arthur's face.

"Anything we need for the renewal?" Gerald sounded enthusiastic.

"Some scribbling and sentence fragments about the Excalibur. But, I couldn't make any sense out of it."

Victor continued. "So I discarded them. I explained to Peters that Carter's condition deteriorated so rapidly, he probably jotted things down to help jog his memory. He also asked for Carter's number—"

"—He didn't leave contact information."

"Carter had the most brilliant mind where electronic technology was concerned," Victor said, as though he'd not heard his twin. "I'd hope once he started medical treatment, his prognosis would be more optimistic. I expected to hear from him by now. "

"Under the circumstances, he probably just wants his privacy," Gerald sounded reassuring.

Victor shook his head. "Something's not right. He

knew I had a lot of respect for him. Rather surprised he told me about a terminal illness in a letter, instead of in person."

Gerald seemed unconcerned. "I think if anything drastic had happened, his family would've contacted us by now."

"That's odd," Victor looked at his brother with an inquisitive look. "Other than his parents—whom he said died within a year of each other—he was an only child."

Gerald cleared his throat.

"If either of you hear from him," Victor continued, "let me know. I'd like to help him in some way."

Suddenly realizing the morning was passing quickly, Victor excused himself and started to exit the room. He paused, his hand on the doorknob. He turned back to the other two.

"Don't forget to let me know about the meeting with the Washington lawyer."

Maggie followed him back to his office.

# Chapter

## 3

Monica clenched her jaw and closed her eyes as the plane raced down the runway. As much as she was required to travel, she hated to fly. The sheer burden of mentally trying to keep the plane in the air always exhausted her. On top of that, she worried about Sneakers in his animal cage. He'd gained a few pounds since the last time he was in it and she wondered if he had enough room to turn around.

It was only when the plane reached its designated altitude and leveled off above the billowing white clouds that Monica released the tension in her body. She tried to relax by focusing her mind on seeing her family again. Selectively sifting through memories of her childhood, Monica told herself, it really *is* good to be going home again. For just a few days, she would pretend there'd only been happy times when she and her family lived together in Amherst, Virginia, just outside of Lynchburg.

Monica closed her eyes and rubbed her eyelids with her index fingers, as if even thinking made her tired. Behind the dark veil, Monica conjured up her mother's presence on the shadowy stage . . . .

"Miss. Miss," a voice called out in the distance.

Monica jumped at suddenly being awakened and blinked into focus the image of the flight attendant standing over her, gently nudging her shoulder.

"Yes?"

"We're making our final decent into Lynchburg," the stewardess said. "Please bring your seat back into its upright position."

Monica nodded and adjusted her seat. Noticing the familiar Blue Ridge Mountains below in the distance, the anticipation of returning home she'd forced upon herself at the start of her trip was now replaced with a desolate sense of loss. She fingered the gold, oval-shaped locket she wore on a chain around her neck. The one with a picture of her mother as a young woman—a young woman who would never grow old.

* * *

THE MAJESTIC SPANISH OAK trees canopied the road leading up to Sweets's house. The sight of the wood frame, two-story house that had been in her grandmother's family for decades, flip-flopped Monica's emotions back again to eagerness at seeing her family. The thick denseness of the woods covered the entire seventy-five acres, while streaks of afternoon sunlight glistened through the branches of the trees.

As soon as Monica turned off the car's engine in front of the soldier-straight columns of the antebellum house, Sweets was standing inside the screened doorway, wiping her hands on her apron.

At seventy-seven, Sweets Sinclair was still beautiful. The richness of her milk chocolate-colored face glowed like fine silk. It was evident Monica did not inherit her height from her grandmother, who stood all of five foot five inches.

"I see you, Sneakers," Sweets called out to the dog from the doorway. The bluish gray tint in her hair caught the sunlight as she walked down the stairs.

Monica leaned across the seat and opened the passenger-side car door. She watched as her grandmother scooped up the little dog.

"Get on out of that car, baby, and let me have a look at you," Sweets said, putting Sneakers down and walking toward Monica with her arms extended in front of her. "Lord, child, if you aren't a sight for these tired old eyes." She took her granddaughter into her arms. The scent of fresh apples overpowered Monica as she returned her grandmother's fierce hug.

"Old? You never age, Sweets." Monica was giggling, like a child again. "You'll be around long after Michael and I have both turned to dust."

"Now, don't you go getting morbid on me, child," Sweets pretended to scold. "Stand up straight, darling, and let me take a good look at you."

Straightening her shoulders back and tilting her chin upward, Monica saw Sweets's plump face beam with pride as she looked over the top of her silver wire-rim glasses and surveyed every inch of her granddaughter's body.

"If you're not the spitting image of our Sarah," she whispered. Monica's whole body stiffened slightly at the sound of her mother's name. She slid her arm through her grandmother's and headed toward the front door.

"Did I beat Michael here?" Monica looked to the side of the house for his car.

"He's here, alright." Sweets laughed. "That silly thing arrived bright and early this morning, before I could finish my talk with the Lord. He came busting through the front door demanding his 'country' breakfast and grinning like a hyena. Why, he and his young friend almost ate me out of house and home!"

"What 'young friend'?" Monica stopped in her tracks. "This was supposed to be *our* weekend, not a get-away for Michael and one of his little girl—"

"My, my. How the beast springs forth from my little angel," Sweets chuckled, as she put her arm around Monica and guided her into the house. "Michael's guest is not a young lady. Just someone in need of a home-cooked meal and who can't wait to see *you*."

"I don't care who it is." Monica tried to disguise the jealousy her grandmother clearly detected. "Honestly, Sweets, he'd no right to invite someone to our first weekend home together in a long time. I hope you said something to him about it."

Monica followed her grandmother into the main room of the house. Slinging her large duffle bag onto the sofa near the old wood-burning stove, she turned to face Sweets with her hands on her hips and sheer disappointment on her face.

"No, child. You know I can't turn away a hungry belly." She smiled, staring over Monica's shoulder. "Besides, I thought you'd chew him out for the both of us."

"I plan to do just that. Where is he, anyway?" Monica asked, just as Michael grabbed her from behind before she had a chance to turn around. He locked her within his arms and hoisted her up into the air, amid her screams of surprise and delight.

"Gotcha!" he said, swinging a giggling Monica around as Sweets watched with amusement.

"You little sneak," Monica squealed, struggling to free herself to no avail, and enjoying every minute of it.

"So that's what you were looking at, Sweets?  You guys are too much!"

"What were you spouting off about just now?" Michael squeezed Monica tighter as he dug his chin into the back of her neck, making her laugh that much harder. "You been here five minutes and you're already acting like you're running the place.  Whatta ya have to say now, Miss Thing?  Huh?"

"I give up," Monica managed to get out between laughs. She could barely catch her breath. "I give, Mike."

"What'd you wanna tell me?"

"You win! You win!  Now, put me down, you silly thing!"

When Michael finally released her, Monica turned around and hugged him tightly, remembering the argument they had had just days before.

"It's good to see you, Mike," Monica kissed him on his cheek.

"Whoa, girl.  First, you wanna chew me out.  Now, you're smothering me with kisses. Unpredictable thing, isn't she, Sweets?" Michael returned his sister's hug, as they both grinned at their grandmother like two mischievous children.

"I'm not getting myself in the middle of one of your squabbles. I declare, you kids are going to be the death of me yet," Sweets teased, walking past them into the kitchen. "A body like mine is not supposed to have this much excitement in its old age."

Michael and Monica exchanged a glance, then swooped down on her from behind and smothered her with kisses. So engrossed in their reunion, the three were unaware they had attracted an audience.

"Uh . . . I heard all of the commotion and wanted to see if everything was all right in here." There was a sudden silence, as Sweets, Michael, and Monica turned and stared in the direction of the voice. They'd completely forgotten about their guest.

Looking somewhat embarrassed for intruding on what was definitely a family moment, a Caucasian young man in his mid-thirties with cropped red hair, freckles, and blue eyes behind horn-rimmed glasses stepped into the kitchen. The screen door slammed behind him.

"Sorry. Didn't mean to intrude. I just heard—"

"Nonsense, man," Michael said, waving an inviting hand to his friend. "Monica just got in. Forgot I'd left you out back."

Monica stood next to Sweets with a funny look on her face. Remembering what had gotten them so riled up in the first place, they broke into another round of laughter.

"Jones!" Monica exclaimed, arms spread out eagle-fashion, rushing to greet her brother's college roommate from their days at Harvard. "I was *so* excited when Sweets told me you were here." The lie came out so convincingly.

"Yep, it's me," he said shyly, returning her embrace. "Hope you don't mind my tagging along with Michael."

"Not at all." Monica suddenly oozed with charm. "You're just like one of the family." Monica saw Michael shake his head at her performance. She rolled her eyes as she swept past him, guiding Jones by the arm to the kitchen table.

"Well, now," Michael said, rubbing his hands together, "just like old times."

* * *

THE EVENING SKY WAS CLEAR as the sun faded into the night. Monica joined Sweets on the porch after dinner, watching each star as it made its appearance in the dark sky, twinkling like a sparkling diamond.

"Where's Big Red?" Monica smiled, referring fondly to the Cherokee Indian whose land abutted theirs. She always felt better knowing he was around to look after Sweets. "Thought he would've dropped by."

Sweets snickered. "That old goat went to Roanoke to pick up a part for his tractor. Said he wouldn't be back until late Sunday night."

"For Heaven's sakes, Sweets," Monica chuckled, "Red's at least seven or eight years younger than you are."

"Let him tell it, he's as old as Methuselah. Always talking about Indian spirits and all. Sometimes, when the wind is still, I hear echoes of him moaning and chanting through the woods."

"Yes. Red always did believe in the old ways."

"Hmmph. Probably putting a hex on someone he doesn't like. No wonder most of the people around here are afraid of him. I declare, when you kids were little, I always worried that some of the nonsense Red filled your heads with would give you nightmares."

"He's the master storyteller, alright." Monica smiled, fondly remembering how he had conjured up the spirits of his ancestors once, when she was ten years old, to help her fight a bully at school. "But, you must admit, the herbal medicines he made for us were more effective than any we could've gotten from the pharmacy. Remember that stuff he insisted you give us when we got those terrible coughs? Yuk! It was horrible tasting!"

Sweets threw back her head and let out a belly laugh. "Dr. Red's cough syrup—onions, wine, sugar and castor oil. That dreadful combination would clear up anything."

*So does his homemade whiskey*, Monica thought to herself. Big Red was more than her mentor on his Cherokee ancestral rituals. He'd taught her to swear, a trait he said built character in a woman. She'd been an exemplary student.

Monica still had a smile on her face when Michael and Jones joined them on the porch. Suspiciously, she eyed the backpack slung over Michael's shoulder.

"We've still got some catching up to do, Monica." Michael said, stretching his arms above his head. He looked out into the darkness beyond the lighted area of the porch. Jones sat down on the porch step.

"You children help yourselves," Sweets said with a yawn, rising to leave. "I'm going in to have my nightly chat with the Lord. Then I'm off to bed. See you children first thing in the morning."

"Not first thing, Sweets." Monica stood up to give her grandmother a  hug. "I'm sleeping in tomorrow."

"Wanna take a walk down to the pond with Jones and me and build a fire, Monica?" Michael asked, as soon as Sweets went inside the house.

"It's pitch black out there, Michael," she answered, eyeing the backpack.

"C'mon. Remember how we used to sneak out there when we were kids and watch the moon's reflection on the water?  On a full night, we could skip stones across and see them as clear as day.  Look up, Monica."

Monica looked at the shining ball in the sky smiling back at them in its full glory.

"I'd like to go, Monica," Jones said to her, reaching to help her up from her seat.

"Okay, but get a jacket," she said to him, as she repositioned the quilt around her and headed down the steps. "It's chilly out here."

* * *

"WATCH WHERE YOU'RE going, Jones." Monica tugged at the quilt he'd stepped on for the third time.

"Sorry," he said, adjusting his glasses on his nose. "I can't see shit out here."

Michael and Monica both tittered at the advantage they had over their friend. As children, they memorized every inch of Sweets's property and could find their way around the whole place blindfolded.

"Hey, you were the one who wanted to come out here, remember?" Monica took hold of Jones's arm and pulled him alongside of her.

With Sneakers in tow, the three of them walked through the heavily-wooded area for nearly twenty minutes, before reaching the clearing that gave way to the man-made pond. The moon's glow shone dimly through the trees, always staying just a step ahead of them. The night was quiet. Small creatures rustled about and scampered out of their way.

"It's still here," Michael said of the campfire site. It was located right on the edge of the pond with a sparkling view of the moonlit water. After starting a small fire, Michael took off his backpack and pulled out a medium-sized glass jug and three Mason jar glasses.

"Voila!" he said, as he uncorked the whiskey jug. "Compliments of Big Red."

"I thought Sweets said he was in Roanoke."

"He is. Caught him before he left. Told him we needed some of his special 'juice.'"

Red's special juice was a potent whiskey made from a secret family recipe which the Indians sold illegally during the days of Prohibition. Nowadays, Big Red made it for his own pleasure, and theirs.

"Was wondering what you had in that backpack." Monica rubbed her hands together and grinned. "But, I was afraid to ask in case you had ideas of us camping out here all night like we used to do."

"Believe me, the thought crossed my mind, but I didn't want to embarrass poor Jones. He's not used to toughing it in the wilderness. Rich city boy and all."

"On the contrary, Michael," Jones said, holding his glass up for some of the liquor his friend offered. "I was a Boy Scout in my youth. I probably know more about wilderness survival than the two of you put together."

"Well, that's cool, my friend, because those skills may come in handy on that little guy crawling up behind you."

Jones scrambled to his feet, turning to look at the area where Michael pointed, his drink spilling to the ground. Just as he did, Monica and Michael howled with laughter and gave each other high fives.

"Very funny, you guys!" Jones realized he'd just been the victim of a practical joke. He brushed what was left of his whiskey off of his pants leg, before taking his place back on the ground next to his pranksters.

"You set yourself up for that one, man," Michael teased, pouring more whiskey into Jones's glass as the three of them sat smiling into the seductive dance of the flames.

"Michael," Jones said, looking seriously at his friend, "I think it's time to tell Monica the truth about why I'm here this weekend." Michael nodded his head in agreement and then turned toward his sister.

SIBYL AVERY JACKSON

"Oh, brother. Here it comes," Monica said, before
Michael had a chance to speak. She took a sip of her
drink and shook her head in amusement. "Should've
known we couldn't get through the evening without discussing world peace or some crap like that. What's it this
time? Foreign policy? Alien invasions?" She held her
glass up to him after gulping the last of her drink. "Filler
up, Michael. If I get enough of this in me, I can tolerate
just about anything."

"It's nothing like that." Michael began slowly. "But,
before we go any further, Monica, I told Jones you were
back working with the Bureau."

Monica's eyes widened in disbelief. Jones knew of
her earlier career, but they'd never shared her recent stint
with anyone outside of the Bureau—except Sweets, who
was only given the simplest of details so as not to cause
her unnecessary worry. And, at Michael's insistence,
Ben.

"Don't give me that look, Monica!" Michael
exclaimed. "You know I wouldn't have done it if it wasn't
absolutely necessary. Just listen for a moment.

"Jones is here to tell you about the case I mentioned
the other day." Turning to his friend, Michael said, "Go
ahead, man."

Jones cleared his throat. "Remember the research I'm
working on for my doctoral thesis?"

"Which one?" Monica whooped. She could feel the
whiskey racing through her veins.

"Very funny. My PH.D. in Telecommunications."

Monica nodded her head, placed her glass on the
ground beside her, and folded her arms. She struggled to
keep a straight face.

"Well," he continued, "my father is a good friend of

FCC Chairman Bob McCormick. Since I'm researching the industry's license renewal process, Bob arranged for me to work in the Wireless Telecommunications Bureau. I compare information sent in by these companies to the FCC to the files the FCC keeps on them, you know, to make sure everything's in sync."

"And—" Monica patted her foot, arms still folded across her chest.

"About three weeks ago, I came across a company in Houston, Texas—Bayou City Wireless—whose license expires at the end of the year. They are a subsidiary of Conti Telecommunications, which specializes in designing and manufacturing electronic components."

Jones gave Monica the run-down on the company's history. By the time he'd finished, he had worked himself into a dither.

"I swear, Monica," he continued, "they are the goddamn giants of the industry."

"Then, what's the problem?" Monica asked dryly. So far, she had heard nothing that was of any interest to her. "Cut to the chase, will ya?"

Jones left his place in front of the fire and began pacing back and forth in front of her. "There's something fishy going on down there and I'm not sure what it is."

He took a pack of cigarettes from his jacket pocket and offered one to Monica. "There was nothing out of the ordinary, until I got to the last page of the FCC file." Jones paused, as he came back over to sit between Monica and Michael.

"Attached to the back of the last page was a handwritten list of about a dozen names, both male and female. Simply titled, The Bastrop Group. Nothing else. No addresses, telephone numbers—nothing. Just Bob's initials scrawled across the bottom of the page."

"So?" Monica asked, not sure where Jones was going with all this. "Did you ask him about it?"

"He said they were names of disgruntled customers who'd lodged minor complaints against the company."

Jones drew a deep breath.

"It bothered me for about a week because it stuck out like a sore thumb. Personal information like that was not in any of the other company files. And another thing, Bayou City Wireless's record was flawless.

"So, I did a little digging and found out that Bastrop is a town in Texas, just east of Austin, with a population of about 5,000. Since I'd copied the list of names before giving it to Bob, I called directory assistance in Bastrop to see if I could locate some of them.

"Hang onto your hat, Monica," he said. "The first five people I called on the list were either dead or hospitalized in comas. I was too shaken up to call the rest."

Jones's voice cracked.

"What? I don't be—" Monica protested.

"I called Bob again to tell him what I'd discovered. All of a sudden, he's unavailable. Yeah, right—"

"Tell her what happened then—" Michael broke in.

"Finally, last week, I burst into his office and demanded some answers. Before I could say anything about the deaths, he told me I was being reassigned to another division. He took my files I was working on, locked them in his office drawer, then dismissed me without any explanation. That was the last conversation I had with him."

Monica looked at Michael. He responded with a shrug of his shoulders.

"Wait a minute, Jones," she said, as she crossed her

long legs, unfolded her arms and leaned back on her hands. "I—"

"Before you start with the questions," he interrupted, "let me tell you what happened after that. It didn't take long for me to realize he was hiding something. After "borrowing" a copy of the key to his office, I waited one night until he left for the day and snuck into his office to check things out."

Monica raised her eyebrows. "Since when did you join the FBI?"

"I know. I know," he responded, raising his hands in defense. "I shouldn't have done it, but how else was I going to find out the truth? He surely wasn't going to tell me. When I looked into the file cabinet, I not only found the files I'd given him, but others as well—all pertaining to the same people whose names I found during my research. Only this time, there was more specific information—ages, educational and ethnic backgrounds, occupations, and more.

"According to Bob's documents, these people— twenty-eight in all—were part of a focus group organized by Bayou City Wireless to test a new wireless product called the Excalibur, supposedly the next generation in cellular phones. The trial started in 1993 and concluded in early 1995. The Excalibur is rumored to be the only one of its kind, though it hasn't been released on the market yet.

"But, get this: Bob also had medical records for each of the people on the list—dates and times when they all made doctors' appointments, what their symptoms were, if and when they spent time in the hospital. Someone was staked out in Bastrop recording all of this activity. *Why?*"

Though the wind had died down hours ago, Monica pulled the blanket more tightly around her to suppress the chills. The hairs on the back of her neck stood up. Suddenly, she straightened up and snapped her head around.

"Snea-kers!" She hadn't seen him for awhile. The dog barked in the distance. A few seconds later, he appeared out of the darkness and sat down beside her. She stroked the little dog's fur in a hypnotic motion and released a long sigh.

"It's bizarre, maybe even a little creepy, Jones," she said.

"As if that weren't enough, Monica," he continued, "twenty-five of the participants are now dead."

Monica opened her mouth to say something, but closed it again when nothing came out.

Jones continued. "Their deaths were attributed to exposure to chemicals from a hazardous waste site unearthed in Bastrop years ago. Why would the FCC have that information? I know this sounds like something right out of a Robin Cook novel. According to Bob's records, *all* of the people in the trial were healthy when the study began in 1993. What the hell is going on down there?"

Turning to Michael, he said, "Tell her, Mike, you read the file."

Michael let out a long sigh and massaged the back of his neck.

"When Jones first came to me a few days ago," he said, "I found the whole story sort of far-fetched. But, now . . ."

"Come on, you guys," Monica scoffed, "are you saying the people in Bastrop were deliberately killed? By whom?"

Michael shrugged his shoulders. "The EPA, FCC, and this wireless company are all linked to this particular group. We need to check it out. All we know for sure right now is that there was a lawsuit filed in Bastrop a couple years back against a nearby chemical company. Residents complained of headaches and dizziness. Several deaths were mentioned in the suit—some of the same names on Jones's list."

Monica stared at them in disbelief. *Stephen King, eat your heart out.* She held out her hand to Jones for one of the cigarettes he was taking from his pack.

"What the hell, Jones," she said, cupping her hands around the flame of his lighter and taking a drag from her cigarette. "With everybody mysteriously dying off, we might as well smoke the whole damn pack right here tonight. Maybe there's an epidemic spreading across the country this very minute. Ya think?"

"This isn't funny, Monica," Jones blurted out.

Monica exhaled, letting out a stream of smoke.

The woods, which had always been so inviting, now seemed an eerie place. Monica felt Michael's eyes on her, as she pulled her knees up to her chest and fumbled the blanket around her like a cocoon. Sneakers raised his head and cocked it to the side.

"Monica," Michael said, "Jim wants you in on the investigation. We've already assigned agents to the EPA and FCC. We need your help with Bayou City Wireless. I trust your instincts."

Michael shifted around and faced Monica, his eyes peering into hers in the darkness.

"I don't know, Michael . . ." Monica hesitated. "Sounds intriguing, but I have other commitments right now. I'm already behind on my new book. My editor would croak if I asked for another extension. What you're talking about involves at least six months of my time, and that's if we're lucky."

"Two months, tops." Michael held up two fingers for emphasis. "You know the Bureau will take care of the logistics. Bayou City Wireless is looking for a PR person. We'll prepare you for that."

"What's up with that? You know I don't like being out in the open." Monica was becoming irritated.

"True enough, it's a more high-profile role than you've assumed in the past, but it'll give you direct access to the company president and other top-level executives. If you turn up incriminating evidence that connects the company to the deaths of the people in Bastrop, then you're out of there and we take over. Simple as that."

"Simple as that, uh?" she repeated, her voice raising an octave. "Your ass is not the one that'll be out on the line here, Mike. There's a higher risk factor here. Besides, wireless technology changes almost on a daily basis."

"Quit stalling, Monica. We'll do what we always do—a crash course."

Michael's voice rose slightly, too. "And just when you think your pretty little brain can't possibly process another piece of high-tech information, Jim and I'll put you on a plane as the queen of communications and off to the Lone Star State you'll go!"

Monica watched the grin spread across Michael's face as though he'd just offered the invitation of a lifetime. "Now, doesn't that sound like fun?"

"Yeah, real." Monica smiled now for the first time since they'd started the discussion. There was something creepy about this assignment she couldn't shake. After weighing it against her other responsibilities, Monica decided she just couldn't do it.

"Sorry, guys. I'm gonna sit this one out." Monica shook her head adamantly. "I got bad vibes about it. Besides, I need some down time. I leave as soon as I get back to Atlanta and repack. It's tempting, but my dance card's already filled."

Michael looked crestfallen. She watched the disappointed look he gave Jones.

"Okay, Monica," Michael sighed. "I won't press you. We'll assign someone else."

Michael turned to Jones and gave him a light punch on the shoulder. "Thanks, man, for coming down to explain everything to her. You were right to bring this information to me. In the next couple of days, I'll want you to take Jim and me over everything again."

For a moment, no one spoke. The only sounds were the cicadas, the crickets, and a distant owl.

Michael looked at his watch. "Geez, it's almost midnight," he said, breaking the silence. "We should be heading back."

Monica and Jones doused the fire, while Michael poured out the last bit of whiskey from the jug, then stuffed it and the glasses back into his backpack. The three of them started the trip back to the house.

Monica walked silently between the two men, wrapped tightly within her quilt. The bottom of the fabric rustled across the dry leaves and twigs. She felt guilty for turning down the assignment. But this time, she had to consider what was best for her.

Her thoughts were interrupted when Michael reached over, put his arm around her, and pulled her close to him as they walked. Monica looked up at his shadowed face and gave him an apologetic smile.

"By the way," he said in a low tone, resting the side of his face against the top of her head, "who's your cellular-service provider?"

"Southeastern QuadCom. Why?"

He paused. "It's a Conti Telecommunications company. So is mine."

# Chapter

## 4

When the elevator doors closed behind the two men, Gerald released the restraint he'd shown during the discussion with his brother.

"Damn that Peters! Where did he get those notes? Did you know about them?" he shouted to Arthur, without waiting for answers.

"I was just as surprised to hear about them as you were." Letting out a sigh, Arthur's color returned to his cheeks. "We removed everything we needed from Carter's office right after he left."

"Apparently, you left some things behind." Gerald's face twisted with sarcasm.

"Only the files that made reference to general information all of the departments work on together. You think the notes Victor found were what we've been looking for?"

"Shut up for a minute, so I can think," Gerald snapped, running his hand over his wavy hair as the elevator doors opened and he pushed past the entering passengers.

Walking briskly across the lobby like a sprinter pushing off at the sound of the starting whistle, he didn't wait for Arthur to catch up. Outside of the building, they stepped into the car. As soon as Bennett closed his door,

Gerald immediately switched off the sound button.

"First of all," Gerald began, looking squarely at his colleague, "strike up a conversation with Peters sometime today about the renewal process. Casually mention if there's ever anything he needs to know—especially if any more of Carter's papers surface—he is to come straight to me. Give him that open-door crap about how I 'welcome the opportunity to confer with them one-on-one.'"

Arthur was paying rapt attention to Victor's words.

"Also, figure out a way to let him know I don't like my guys going around me to Victor with anything that goes on in the company. Peters may still be wet behind the ears on the company's policies and procedures, but he damn well needs to learn that I mean business where this is concerned."

Gerald paused to make sure his instructions were understood. Arthur nodded his head in agreement.

"If you're the one to discuss this with him, he won't link your conversation to the one he had the other day with Victor."

As the car entered the freeway and merged with the mid-morning traffic, Gerald leaned back in his seat and fingered his mustache again. "Damn Victor for throwing away those notes! Now there's no way to tell if they could've led to what we've been trying to find."

Arthur spoke up. "It seems now we've got more immediate problems to worry about."

"Such as?" Gerald, turning to Arthur, and tilting his head to the side.

"Your new toy. Victor may be right about delaying the shipment. You know what Carter stumbled on to."

"Goddamn it, Arthur. Carter was a fool! If I hadn't

taken matters into my own hands, he would have stopped at nothing to terminate the project."

Arthur sounded pensive. "Hell, if we didn't have Bob McCormick handling things in Washington, not to mention our "storage" at the facility, the whole project would've blown up in our faces."

Gerald's anger escalated. "Christ even now this guy won't go away. I intend to move ahead as planned. You got that? Sometime tonight—I don't care how you do it—go over Peters's office again with a fine-tooth comb. That information is here somewhere and I want it!" Gerald pounded his right fist into his left palm.

Gerald paused for a moment, but he wasn't through with his orders. "And another thing, Arthur. As far as 'agreeing with Victor,' you'd better remember who got you here in the first place. I'll not have any sonofabitch working for me who's not working *with* me. You'd better make damn sure your loyalty's in the right place."

Arthur lowered his eyes obsequiously. "Whadda you plan to tell Victor, if he finds out about our little problem?"

"Not a goddamn thing," Gerald quipped, pointing his index finger in Arthur's face for emphasis.

Arthur raised his eyes and looked into Gerald's fiery ones.

"Because he's not going to find out. He'll know only what I choose to tell him, nothing more. And you'd better follow my lead."

Arthur nodded slowly as Gerald stared at him with flaring nostrils and bulging eyes.

"I'll not let my sniveling brother's ethics get in the way of the millions of dollars we stand to gain from this project. The Excalibur is my creation. It's going to catapult me into the forefront as the real driving force behind Conti Telecommunications, not my brother."

Jerking his head away from Arthur, Gerald suddenly inhaled a deep breath, then let it out.

"As a matter of fact, I think I'll pay a quick visit to our 'storage' facility. You just do what I tell you. I'll take care of the rest." Slowly, he nestled into his seat like a child who'd crawled onto his mother's lap for comfort.

* * *

"WHAT IS IT, VICTOR?" Maggie asked. "You look a thousand miles away."

He answered her with a sigh, then gently took her hand in his and smiled wearily into her almond-colored face. Her Trinidadian accent was more pronounced. *She's worried.* Maggie had been his lover for more than seven years now.

Squeezing her hand again before releasing it, Victor got up, walked to the window, and stared out onto downtown Houston. "Maggie, something disturbs me about Gerald and the Excalibur project. I dismissed the feeling once before as a reaction to the old Gerald who always had a hidden agenda. He's moving too fast and I can't figure out why."

Maggie didn't say anything. She got up, stood behind him, and began massaging Victor's shoulders. He felt some of the tension leave his neck, his shoulders, and his chest. Victor began to voice what was gnawing at his gut.

"Did you notice how uncomfortable he was during our discussion about the project—how he appeared to be withholding something? And, then again, when I mentioned Dave Carter?" Victor turned to Maggie who now stood beside him at the window.

"Yes, I did, Victor." She hesitated. She looked as if she was going to say something more, then she stopped.

He nodded at her response, then resumed his gaze out the window. "I hope I'm wrong, Maggie." He gazed intently at his reflection in the polished glass as though he were staring into his brother's face. "I won't let anyone—including Gerald—destroy what I've spent years building."

# Chapter

## 5

The next morning, there was no mention of the conversation of the night before. Monica was relieved because she'd had a hard enough time falling asleep when she'd finally gotten into bed. The last thing she wanted was to face the whole issue again after spending a relaxing morning with Sweets.

During the afternoon, the four of them had gone into town to shop for supplies needed to make minor repairs around the house. People Michael and Monica had not seen in years sought them out.

On more than one occasion, Monica was told how much she resembled her mother and how they still missed Sarah after so many years. The well-intended remarks reignited a smoldering pain Monica had hoped to avoid on this trip home.

The feelings were further heightened on the return trip to Sweets's house when a steady stream of slow-moving headlights approached them on the two-lane highway, signaling the beginning of a funeral procession. One by one, cars in front and back of Sweets's pulled over to the shoulder and stopped. The tender gesture of respect for the dead—so rarely practiced in the city where no one stops for Death—pulled at Monica's heartstrings.

Grief overwhelmed her as she remembered another day much like this one, long ago in the winter of 1964, when they were going to bury her mother. Looking out of the window of the back seat of the limo where she'd sat with Sweets, her father, and Michael, Monica had seen the countless number of people who stopped alongside of the road and stood next to their cars. Men had removed their hats and held them over their hearts, children were positioned on their parents' shoulders and stared in silence.

How sad it was, Monica had thought at the time, that her mother could not see the outpouring of love from the people she had known or the respect expressed by complete strangers.

Now, as Monica returned to Sweets's house, she was worn out from pretending she had not been affected by the activities of the day. After unpacking the supplies, she excused herself, feigning a sinus headache and went to her room to be alone.

An hour later, as Monica lay across her bed still fully dressed, a light knock at her bedroom door jolted her. She quickly wiped away traces of moisture from around her eyes.

"Come in," she called out, as she ran both of her hands over her face and smoothed out her hair.

The door creaked open, casting a rectangle of light from the hallway, and Jones stuck his head inside the darkened room.

"Just wanted to make sure you were okay before I turned in for the night. Mind if I come in a minute?"

Monica sat up on her bed, reached over to the small skirted table next to her, and turned on the lamp. "Not at all. Come on in, Jones." She squinted her eyes to the sudden brightness in the room. She watched as he loped to the side of her bed, carrying a glass of water in one hand and a white tissue balled in the other.

"I didn't have any sinus medicine," he said softly, handing her the water glass and opening the tissue. "But I brought you some Tylenol, you know, in case you still had a headache."

Monica smiled and took the medicine from him and put it into her mouth. Throwing back her head, she chased the pills down with a drink of water.

"That was sweet of you. Thanks." Monica turned to adjust the pillows behind her back.

"Let me help you." Jones fluffed the pillows behind her. His hand lingered momentarily on her cheek, then he stood back in awkward silence.

Monica looked surprised, but she didn't say anything. She drew her knees to her chest and wrapped both arms around them. She looked up at her friend who shifted his weight from one foot to the other as he watched her every move.

"Sit down, Jones, and tell me what's happening with you. Besides your research, that is." Monica chuckled, watching Jones slide into the chair across from her.

"Not much to tell, really. I don't seem to have much time for a social life these days."

"Aren't you dating anyone?"

Jones smiled a lop-sided grin, his face turned beet red as he lowered his eyes. "Here and there." He looked back at Monica shyly. "Haven't found Ms. Right, yet." For a few seconds he was silent, wringing his hands in his lap.

"You will. You're a good man, Jones."

"I mean I've found her, but—"

"But what?" Monica felt amused, although she didn't

want to admit it to herself.

Finally, after nervously clearing his throat, he looked pointedly at her and blurted out, "I really care about you, Monica. Always have. I was wondering—You think there's a chance we could . . . uh, you know . . . go out together sometime? It'd be a long-distance relationship, of course, but I'd be willing to give it a try, if you were."

Monica had known for years Jones had a crush on her. Although she was aware of his adulation, she didn't feel the same way about him. But the last thing she wanted to do was to hurt his feelings.

"Jones . . ." She held out her hand which he hesitantly accepted. "I'm flattered, really I am. You're probably the sweetest guy I know and a very good friend. I love you dearly, but not in that way."

Jones looked up with milquetoast eyes.

Darnnit, Monica thought, why hadn't she ever developed feminine wiles? She tried to pick her words as tactfully as she could manage for her "shoot from the hip" personality.

"We've known each other a long time. Being with you on a deeper level would sort of be like dating Michael."

"Ouch," he said lightly, giving her hand a squeeze.

Monica tried to clean it up. "C'mon. You know what I mean. You're family. Besides, my personal life is so screwed up right now, I couldn't give you—or any man—what you need. You deserve someone special, someone who doesn't carry around a lot of excess baggage. Anything other than a caring friendship between us could jeopardize the close relationship we already have. I wouldn't want that to happen, would you?"

Jones adjusted his glasses and smiled. "I guess not.

But it took me a long time to work up the courage. Couldn't go any longer without telling you how I felt. Listen, don't tell Michael about this, okay? I don't want him to know I made a complete jackass out of myself."

"You did not." She laughed again. "And, no, Michael doesn't need to know. Let's just keep it between us, okay?"

Still holding her hand, Jones stood up, leaned over the bed, and kissed her lightly on the cheek. "Remember, anytime the load gets too heavy, I'll always be here for you." He paused for a second and then, with a sheepish grin, he said, "Goodnight, Sis."

"Night, Bro." Monica smiled, watching him as he walked to the door. As he reached for the glass door-knob, she called out to him. "Jones?"

"Yeah?"

"Thanks."

"Anytime."

# Chapter

## 6

"Did you find anything in Peters's office?" Gerald barked into the phone, guzzling the last of his Hennessey. He had been impatiently waiting all day for the call from Arthur.

"Nothing," Arthur said. "I don't know where Peters found those notes he gave Victor, but there sure isn't anything left of them now. This is the second time this weekend I've searched the office. It's clean."

"Don't give me that shit, Arthur. I know Carter hid that information somewhere. And, dammit, I want it."

"Has the doctor tried questioning him again?"

"Doesn't do any good. Carter still hasn't said a word. I don't know if the drugs have really affected his mind or if he's faking it. Either way, I'm not taking any chances."

Gerald clinked his ice cubes in his empty shot glass, glumly contemplating the future.

"That information is the only incriminating link between me and that goddamn study, and I intend to find it. Until I do, Carter stays right where he is. There is one thing I plan to do first thing in the morning, though." Gerald took a sip of the melting ice and bland Hennessey. "I think it's time to announce the tragic news."

"What 'tragic' news?" Arthur asked in surprise.

"Quite a shame, really. How I just got word of

Carter's unfortunate death and cremation. I think a memo would be appropriate, don't you?"

"I guess that'll put a stop to all the questions about his condition."

"Poor Victor will be so upset. Besides, it's almost the truth—as soon as I find what I'm looking for, it's bye-bye Carter. Have a good evening, Arthur."

Gerald roared with laughter and hung up the phone.

* * *

MONICA FOUND HERSELF thinking about the events of the weekend as she drove from the Atlanta airport to her home in Buckhead. She'd been unable to get the case out of her mind. Michael and Jones had tried one last time before she'd left Sweets's house to talk her into reconsidering taking the case. Monica had stood her ground. "I've got to take some 'me' time."

On her trip back to Atlanta, for the first time she noticed—really paid attention to anyhow—the number of people with cellular phones affixed to the sides of their heads like natural appendages. They were every-where—in the airport, on the streets, driving past her on the freeway. She even hesitated a few moments before picking up her own car phone to place a take-out order at a Chinese restaurant. Monica laughed it off, but she'd been more than acutely aware of how quickly she had ordered her meal and hung up.

* * *

MICHAEL AND JONES WERE SILENT as they began the two-and-a-half hour trip back to Washington.

59

Staring out into the vastness of the green farmland and mountain tops, Jones retraced his steps in his mind to see if there'd been something he missed. He always came back to the same place: the Bastrop Group. How could he find out more? Jones must have muttered the words out loud.

"What?" Michael asked. "Did you say something?"

Jones stared back at his friend with a puzzled look, then let out a heavy sigh.

"I was saying," he answered, "how can I go back to work tomorrow and act as if everything's okay?"

"Easy. Do whatever you were doing before, keep your mouth shut, and your eyes and ears open. Leave everything else to me."

"I was thinking, Mike," Jones said, turning in his seat and staring intently at Michael, "what if I snoop around a bit more? Every company that plans to release a new product has to submit test results to the FCC for approval. Maybe, I could find out about them. Better yet, I could go to Houston and —"

"No way," Michael said. "You've always glorified the jobs Monica and I have, but this is not some game we're playing. This is for real—dangerously real."

"But—"

"But—nothing. Experienced agents have gotten killed doing what we do. Hell, I worry about Monica every time she goes on an assignment, and she knows her stuff. I don't need you making some stupid mistake that'll get your ass killed. If you hear anything else about Bayou City Wireless, act like you didn't, then call me from someplace other than the office."

"Don't you see, Michael?" Jones protested. "I've studied this company. I know more about it than anyone else you could assign."

Pulling the car over to the shoulder, Michael pressed on the brake so hard that both he and Jones bounced in their seats. Before Jones could ask what was going on, Michael lit into him.

"Listen to me, Jones," Michael shouted. "Don't screw with this, man. You don't have the faintest idea of how fast you could wind up dead, poking your nose where it doesn't belong. I told you I would handle it and I will.

"In the meantime, you take yourself back to work and don't even mention Bayou City Wireless. When you see Bob McCormick, chat it up about dear old dad, the weather—anything you can think of that'll assure him you've suddenly gotten amnesia about the company. Understand?"

Jones could not believe how angry Michael had suddenly become.

"Okay, Mike." He threw up his hands in a "I give" manner. "Don't work yourself into a lather. Just offering my help, that's all. You wanna do it your way, fine. I'll mind my own business from here on out."

"Make sure you do, Jones. I'm not kidding. We're going to nail this bastard McCormick, and he's gonna have some explaining to do."

"Okay, buddy. Relax. I hear ya. Just trying to help. Now," he said pointing to the road in front of them and quickly changing the subject, "you think you can get me back to Washington in one piece? I've got to get some sleep before I take my know-nothing ass back to work tomorrow."

Michael stared at him long and hard, before steering the car back onto the highway.

As they rode the rest of the trip, Jones made up his mind he had a job to do, too. And it did not include sitting back and doing nothing.

# Chapter
# 7

Jones's first week back at work after the trip to Virginia seemed set at warp speed. He'd talked to Michael only once and learned the investigation of the wireless communication's case was underway.

As promised, Jones had gone back to work and hadn't uttered a word about Bayou City Wireless. He'd run into McCormick once on the elevator and was shocked to find the man in a jovial mood. It was as though the incident with the Houston company never happened. Swept under a rug, out of sight, out of mind.

Jones had almost decided that maybe it would be best to let Michael throw back the carpet and expose the dirt when, quite by accident, Jones encountered one of the guys he'd worked with on the renewal process. It was early morning, and Jones had just gone into the break-room for some coffee.

"Hey, buddy," Terry Eckland said. "We miss you back in the division."

"You know how research can be . . . " Jones picked his words carefully, just in case he was being setup. "Never know where it'll take you next."

"Probably just as well you left when you did." Terry lowered his voice. "All hell's broken loose on one of those renewals. The old man himself  took the project from us. It doesn't make sense."

"What?"

Terry looked over his shoulder and continued, sotto voce. "That only happens when there's a problem. That company was squeaky clean. The scuttlebutt is the president of the company is flying in tomorrow night to meet with the Chairman. We're not supposed to know about it, but you know how the rumor mill is around here."

Jones flashed one of those "I-know-what-you-mean" kind of smiles, as he poured himself a cup of coffee. "Really? Which company?" he asked nonchalantly, stirring cream into his coffee. "There were several of them that didn't seem to have a problem. Maybe, there was something we overlooked."

"No way, man. You remember that Texas firm, don't you? The one down in Houston? Clean as a whistle. Then, all of a sudden, the division chief walks in one day and asks for all of the information we were working on and tells us he's taking the files to Bob McCormick to be reviewed. No explanation. No nothing.

"Next thing we hear, Rita—you remember Rita, don't you? The brunette I went out with a couple of times?"

Jones nodded.

"Anyway, Rita overhears McCormick's secretary making arrangements for an evening meeting between him and Bayou City's president." Terry threw Jones a suspicious look. "Say, Jones. You didn't ask to be transferred because you knew there was trouble going down with that company, did you?"

Jones wanted to continue being noncommittal, but he had to say something to throw Terry off the track. "Nah, man. You said yourself the company was unblemished. I just needed to move along with my research. I'm sure they're just tying up loose ends. Who knows, maybe the guy is just passing through."

Jones was on a fishing expedition now.

"I don't think so. Rita said Mr. Conti was meeting McCormick in his office at 9:00 p.m., and, judging from the secretary's tone on the phone, this is no social chat. Rita said the secretary was very upset when she finished talking to Mr. Conti. In fact, Rita said the girl was on the verge of tears."

*Interesting,* Jones thought, as he cleaned up his mess. The breakroom filled with people and the last thing he needed was to be seen talking with a colleague from his old division. If someone had gone through the trouble of watching every move the people in Bastrop, Texas, had made, they were surely keeping an eye on him now.

"Hang in there, Terry," Jones said, heading for the door. "I'm sure it'll all blow over soon."

"Hope so, man. See you around. Hey, Jones? Why don't you meet some of the guys and me for drinks after work one day this week?"

Jones was already down the hall and he didn't look back. His mind was racing with the news of the scheduled meeting. When he got back to his desk, he shuffled some papers about and stared at them as if he were actually interested. Instead, he was making a mental note to call Michael later that evening.

Then, just as that thought entered his mind, it was quickly shoved aside by another. What could Michael do at this point? Without tangible evidence? Not a damn thing! Suddenly, something else occurred to Jones. He smiled to himself for not thinking of it sooner. Nodding his head slowly in approval of the plan now taking shape in his mind, Jones decided there were a few things he would do himself, before making that call.

He was going to catch a fat rat and he'd use more than cheese as bait.

# Chapter

## 8

It took Jones only a few moments to devise the plan, but more than twenty-four hours to implement it. Once he'd decided to record the conversation between Gerald Conti and the FCC Chairman, there'd been no turning back.

He sneaked into McCormick's office to hide the recording device, when McCormick and the other employees had gone for the day. Beforehand, Jones had mentally considered a list of possible hiding places. He'd finally settled on the eight-foot silk Ficus tree, located directly to the right of McCormick's desk. It was perfect. The only place in the office that would not be disturbed, should it take Jones several days to retrieve it.

Jones had planted the recorder underneath the moss, just inside the large Oriental pot. The trunk of the tree was intertwined with real wood bark that sprouted branches just at the base that allowed only the recording area of the device to be exposed.

Jones positioned himself now on top of some storage boxes in the small closet to the left of Bob McCormick's office. The room was used for storing disks and other preserved documents, and had an air vent that blew dry, cool air into the room to keep the moisture out. It also flowed directly into the Chairman's office.

At precisely 8:55 p.m., Jones heard the ring of the elevator and then the sound of heavy footsteps coming his way. From what he could determine from the pattern of the steps, there were at least three people in the group.

They stopped just outside of McCormick's office and knocked lightly on the door. Jones waited for the sound of the Chairman's voice, which would indicate how much of the conversation Jones would be able to hear clearly from his position. He was excited when the voice, though somewhat muffled, was clear enough to understand, as the Chairman called out for the men to come inside the office.

* * *

GERALD CONTI WALKED INTO the room with Arthur Fazio and another one of Gerald's men, and closed the door behind him. After greeting McCormick, he took a seat across from the massive oak desk and crossed his legs. He did not like the idea of being "summoned" to Washington, especially since he was the one calling the shots.

"What's so important, Bob," he said, eyeing the Chairman crossly, "that you had me fly up here in such a hurry? Wouldn't a telephone call have taken care of it?"

"Not this time, Gerald," McCormick responded without blinking. "When's the exact date the first shipment is expected to leave the country for Indonesia? The paper work is just about completed."

"Relax, Bob. The phones go out the end of next month. We've gone over all this before—I don't understand what's the big deal."

"The deal is, Gerald," McCormick answered with a

slight edge in his voice, leaning forward in his seat, "I want that equipment out of this country as soon as possible. There have been a couple of hitches that I've personally averted. I don't want any more screw-ups."

Gerald motioned to Arthur to give him a cigar and a light. McCormick clenched his jaw and grit his teeth as he watched the fire ignite and burn the tip of the cigar. Arthur Fazio and the other man joined Gerald in lighting their own cigarettes.

Gerald looked up at McCormick and grinned. He knew tobacco smoke irritated the older man's allergies, but he wanted to remind the Chairman who was still in charge. One of his men walked over to McCormick's side, by the Ficus tree, and blew smoke in his direction. Gerald smiled in amusement.

"It's not like you, Bob, to get so nervous," Gerald continued. "Have you forgotten how much money is in this deal for you?"

"I have not," he replied, gingerly. "That's my retirement money—my ticket to get as far away from you as possible. But, I haven't forgotten the casualties along the way. When you first said you needed the perfect test site, I helped you find an undetectable cloak of deceit. When the results were in, I turned my head. An isolated incident, you said.

"And it's still not over!" McCormick dug through some papers on his desk and snatched out a manila envelope. Opening the document, he pulled out its contents and threw them to the edge of his desk in front of Gerald. "You told me months ago, it was over. Explain to me, Gerald, how it's still going on."

Gerald looked at him suspiciously as he reached for the papers. Glancing over the first page, he stared back at McCormick in surprise.

"Where'd you get this?"

"You didn't think I'd just walk away from that little situation down in Bastrop and not follow-up on my own, did you? I kept one of the guys down there, to make sure it was over. But it isn't, is it?" McCormick pounded his fist on the desk. "This situation is out of control."

"You're getting worked up over nothing, Bob," Gerald said coolly. "This is just a coincidence, I tell you. What happened was necessary."

Gerald continued without emotion. "The Indonesians needed special equipment and Bastrop was the perfect place. With its heavily-wooded pine trees and its proximity to Houston, it was vital for monitoring purposes. It's no big deal."

Gerald had not told Bob of his plan to release the product in the States. And he wasn't about to tell him now.

"Really? Then why don't you tell Victor? Let's see if he'll see it the same way."

McCormick hit a raw nerve. Gerald felt his nostrils flaring.

"Because this is my goddamn project, you sonofabitch!" Gerald flared angrily back at him, stubbing his cigar out in the empty coffee cup on McCormick's desk. "I am the one who's going to get the credit when news of this deal breaks. Not Victor.

"So, quit whining like a school boy, Bob. We're talking about nobody hicks from the backwoods of Texas. We cleaned up behind ourselves, didn't we?"

Gerald spat out the word 'we' to remind McCormick of his involvement. Smiling, he went on. "And you conveniently kept that little fact out of our files to the tune of $5 million. So don't get high and mighty with me, you double-standard weasel.

"So, relax. When all this is over, we'll drink to your retirement and to my success." Gerald began to chuckle, and as his men joined in, laughter filled the room and echoed through the air vents.

* * *

ENJOY YOURSELVES NOW, Jones bristled. The only toasting you'll be doing when I get through with the two of you will be out of tin cups, in a jail cell, right before they fry your asses!

It was time for him to bail out and hope the entire conversation was caught on tape. All the questions had not been answered, but it was another piece of the puzzle to take to Michael. He would sneak back into the office before dawn to get the recorder.

Jones prepared to leave the small room, slipping down from the stack of boxes. He left his stake-out position moments too soon.

* * *

REACHING FOR THE CIGAR he'd forgotten he'd stubbed out earlier in the coffee mug, Gerald again motioned to Arthur to light him another one. Instead of waiting for it to be brought to him, Gerald walked over to him, took the cigar and lit it, puffing fiercely. As if to irritate McCormick even further, he flicked the ashes into the Oriental pot that contained the Ficus tree. Laughing at McCormick's bewildered reaction, Gerald looked down to see if he'd hit his target when something caught his eye. He reached slowly into the pot and moved the moss to the side.

"What the hell?" Gerald scowled, as he snatched the recorder and waved it at McCormick. The tape was still rolling. "What the fuck is going on here?" he shouted, as he stopped the tape, pressed the rewind button, and then replayed the last few seconds of the conversation.

Bob McCormick jumped from behind his desk and brought a finger to his lips, motioning with his free hand to Gerald's bodyguard to take a look outside the office. The man unfastened his jacket, withdrew a gun from its holster, and slowly opened the door. As he looked outside the room, he heard a door close at the end of the hall.

"Someone just went down the stairs," the man said to Gerald, who immediately ordered him to follow.

* * *

JONES WAS UNAWARE of the commotion in the hall. But when the door to the stairwell opened a level above him several seconds after he'd closed it, he knew to haul ass. He never saw who was after him, didn't see the gun that fired the fatal bullet that struck him in the neck. It was over in a flash, the sound of the shot muted by a silencer.

* * *

GERALD AND McCORMICK bolted down the two stair levels and looked over the dead body lying at the bottom of the landing. Gerald was the first to see Jones's face when his bodyguard turned the body over. Gerald only shrugged his shoulders and stepped aside.

"You know him?" he asked McCormick, when the expression on his face registered that he did.

"Yeah," he responded with remorse. "One of those little 'hitches' I mentioned earlier."

"Well, now, he's not a problem anymore," Gerald said coldly, as McCormick continued to stare at Jones's lifeless body and the stream of blood flowing from the wound.

"Get rid of him, boys," Gerald ordered his men. "And clean up this mess when you're done. I don't want a trace of blood left." He looked back at a stunned McCormick who had not moved from his position.

"Get a grip on yourself, Bob," he ordered, taking charge of the situation and starting back up the stairs. "It's over. Let's go back to your office and have a drink, while we discuss how you're going to handle this little incident."

Without uttering a sound, McCormick turned around and walked like a zombie back up the stairs to his office.

# Chapter

## 9

Monica stretched her exhausted body as she drove the remaining distance to her house. It was 8:20 p.m. Jet lag from the ten-hour flight from Hawaii was starting to kick in. Almost immediately after turning onto her street, she noticed a strange car in the distance, parked in front of her house. Suddenly, Monica was wide awake.

She pulled over to the curb two houses down from hers, turned off her lights, and switched off the ignition. She peered through the darkness, watching her house for a few moments until she caught a glimpse of a shadow, moving across her front porch. Opening the armrest compartment next to her, she reached inside and took out her six-shooter, which lay hidden beneath a clutter of paper. Eyes fixed on the silhouette of a man sitting on the edge of her porch, Monica turned off the inside light switch, then eased open her door and slid out of the car.

Crouching down and moving quickly, Monica sprinted to the back of the house next to hers and came back around to the other side closest to her house. With her arms extended in front of her holding the gun in place, she slowly crept up to the edge of her house. She counted to three before jumping from her hiding place.

"Get up slowly, asshole! I've gotta gun," she shouted

to the startled figure, her gun clearly visible in front of her. "Hands in the air where I—"

"Put that damn thing away before you kill somebody, Monica," the man shouted back.

"Michael?" Monica called out, walking toward him, still holding the gun in position.

"No. Your neighborhood stalker. Now put that thing away before one of us gets hurt."

"You scared the shit out of me!" She trembled at the thought of how close she had come to shooting her own brother. "What the hell are you doing here?"

"Let's go inside before someone starts screaming for the police."

Putting the safety latch back on the gun, Monica tucked it into her waistband, then took her keys from her pocket and unlocked the door. Once inside the house, she punched in her alarm code, switched on the light, and waited for her brother to close the door behind him. Something was wrong. Michael never came to Atlanta without calling.

"What took you so long to get home?" Michael's face furrowed into a frown. He took off his leather jacket and threw it onto the sofa before walking into the kitchen. "I've been waiting for you for almost two hours."

"My flight was delayed." Monica watched Michael as he took a bottle of Bordeaux from the rack and uncorked it. She wondered why her brother was acting so irritated. True enough, she'd almost shot him, but he knew that was her job. What did he expect, creeping around her house at night?

Michael poured two crystal stemware full to the brim with wine. Keeping his eyes on Monica, he handed her a glass. His glazed stare bothered Monica, but she didn't know what to say. Suddenly, her stomach began to quake. Something was wrong, but what was it? Hands trembling, she gulped down her first drink.

Finally, Michael spoke up.

"Jones is dead, Monica."

Monica gulped for air as if she'd been punched in the stomach.

"What? What are you talking about?" Her voice sounded like it did whenever she went swimming—as though her ears were plugged up. This all seemed so unreal, it felt like she was swimming under water or wading through a river in a dream. Except this was a nightmare.

"They killed him. Made it look like an accident. But I know fucking well he was murdered." Monica stared at Michael in shock.

"Start at the beginning, Michael." She bit her bottom lip, holding back tears. "Who is 'they'? Who killed Jones?"

"The day we left Sweets, Jones told me he wanted to snoop around some more. I warned him not to, that I'd handle it. I hadn't heard from him since his first day back and decided to check on him. Using the name of one of our classmates, I called his office and was told he no longer worked there."

"What?"

"He never returned any of the messages I left on his home phone, either. That's when I called his parents. His father told me what happened. Or, rather, what he was told had happened."

"What did Mr. Jones say?" Monica lowered her voice, seeing the pain in her brother's eyes and feeling the sudden loss of their friend weighing on her own heart.

"The police told him Jones had walked upon a shoving match between two men after leaving work late two nights ago. When he'd tried to intervene, the aggressor drew a gun and shot Jones in the neck. The two men fled, left Jones on the side of the street. He died almost instantly. The police don't have much to go on because it was too dark and the one witness who saw the fight can't give a description of either of the men. His story sticks. Questioned him myself."

"So you think Jones was killed because of what he told us in Virginia?"

"I can't prove it, but my gut tells me he must've stumbled onto something and was killed in the process. There are too many unanswered questions."

"Like what?"

"First of all, I can understand why the shooter left the scene. Why would the other man—who was an alleged victim himself—run away, unless it was a front? And why would Jones be out walking at ten o'clock at night when his car was parked in the FCC garage? It was still there the next morning when his father went to the office to collect his things."

"Did you mention Jones's suspicions to his father?" Monica took a long sip of her wine.

"What good would that have done? I don't have any proof. But, believe me, I'm gonna find some. I feel responsible."

"That wasn't your fault, Michael. Jones brought the information to you, *if* that's what got him killed."

"Yeah, but I got him all worked up about it, even asked him to help try to convince you to get involved with the investigation. Guess he figured since he'd snooped around the first time without getting caught, he could do it again. I should've *known* when he agreed too easily to back off, that he might try to make something happen. Jones had a lot of book sense, Monica, but no street smarts."

Monica poured her brother another glass of wine and they both sat quietly for a few moments. Stung by the news of Jones's death, she instantly thought of the private moment they had shared their last night together at Sweets's house. In a way, she too, felt some responsibility for his death. Maybe, if she had agreed to take the case in the first place, he would still be alive. . . .

"Have our guys found anything at the EPA?"

"Not yet." Michael took another sip.

"The funeral's tomorrow afternoon in Washington," Michael continued. "One of my guys is bringing Sweets up in the morning."

"Michael," Monica started slowly, "I finished the revision on my book while I was in Hawaii." She looked over at her brother, who stared miserably into his glass.

"Jones is dead, possibly murdered, and all you can think about is your book?" Michael sounded annoyed.

"I didn't mean it like that." Monica gave Michael a sad smile. "It's just that now it looks as if I'll have a little time to help out with the Bayou City Wireless case. That is, if you and Frasier still want me."

Michael stared back at her. The beginning of a smile curled his lips.

"That's great, Monica." His words belied his weary tone. "I'd hoped you'd finally come around. Wish Jones hadn't been killed in the process."

Suddenly, as if he had just been injected with multiple B-12 shots, Michael sprang from the chair and reached for his jacket.

"Where're you going?" Monica put her hand on her hip.

"To the airport. Get your things. If we hurry, we can make the ten-thirty flight to Washington."

"Now?" She followed her brother into the kitchen and watched him pour the last of his wine down the drain. "You don't even know if there are seats available."

Michael reached into the inside pocket of his jacket and pulled out two Delta Airlines tickets. Tossing them to Monica, he said, "I'm one step ahead of you, big sister. Just pack something for the funeral. You can buy whatever else you'll need later—at the Bureau's expense, of course. Now, get your ass up and let's go. I'll fill you in on what we've planned for the case so far."

"Geez," Monica sighed, "poor Sneakers is gonna think I've abandoned him for good. Give me a sec to call Sweets and let her know he'll be staying a while longer."

Monica reached for the phone, but put it down when she saw the sly look on her brother's face.

"Don't tell me you've taken care of that, too?" She tilted her head to the side.

Michael nodded.

"Honestly, Michael, what would you have done, if I'd said 'no'?"

"Never crossed my mind," he said, checking the windows and doors to make sure they were secure. Monica dashed to her bedroom to pack a few things.

Resetting the timers on the lights and punching in her security code again, Monica paused a moment by the front door and thought about Jones. With a wry smile, she winked an eye, as though he were standing in front of her.

"This one's for you, Jones," she said aloud, as she closed the door and started on her journey.

# Chapter
## <u>10</u>

The organ music piped through the Washington Cathedral in a brisk tempo, signaling the end of the service. Monica, Sweets, and Michael walked stoically behind the grieving parents, as the couple said their final farewell to their only son.

Monica was relieved that the service lasted only forty-five minutes. She hadn't been to a funeral since her mother's and was grateful Jones's parents had insisted on a closed-casket funeral. She thought she would smother being so close to the bronze casket covered with a large spray of orchids and roses, as she sat with Sweets and Michael on the pew directly behind Jones's parents. She could not stop the tears from flowing and was annoyed by the idea of even trying to. Unlike the funeral service for her mother, where the entire congregation was African American and outwardly expressive in their emotion, the people attending Jones's funeral were most-ly white and more reserved.

Now, that she was finally outside, Monica decided she would not attend the grave-site service.

"You go ahead, Michael," she said softly, pulling him aside after he and the other pallbearers had loaded the casket into the black hearse, parked with its motor idling in front of the church. "I can't take anymore. I'll wait for you and Sweets at your place, then I'll drive Sweets back to Amherst."

"No, darling," her grandmother broke in before Michael could answer. "I don't think I'll go to the burial either. It's already three-thirty and I want to be home before dark."

"You sure?" Michael asked them both, his eyes glistening with tears.

"Positive." Monica attempted a wan smile.

Michael shook his head and gathered them in his arms. Monica thought her heart would break at his grief. When she pulled from his clench, she noticed him staring off in the distance behind her.

"Wait here a minute," he said, wiping his eyes with his hand and brushing past them.

Monica turned her head and saw a man leaning against the back door of a black limousine, his hands in his pockets, his head fixed in their direction. She had not seen him in more than twenty years, but as she gulped in a deep breath and felt every muscle in her body constrict, she knew the tall man with broad shoulders was her father.

Monica watched as Michael went over to him and the two embraced. Though she stood at a distance, it astounded her to see how much father and son really looked alike as they stood facing one another. Aside from the age difference and the gray that streaked the edges of Ben's temples, the two men were like a silhouette of one person, cut out and joined at the nose.

"I'm going to the car, Sweets," she announced, turning to walk away.

"Wait, darling." Her grandmother gently took Monica's arm. She had also seen Ben. "Don't you think you should go over and speak to your father?"

"I've nothing to say to him, Sweets." Her eyes flashed angrily. "You go if you want. I'm going to the car."

Monica had been sitting in the car for about ten minutes, smoking a cigarette, when Michael tapped lightly on the passenger window.

When Monica let the window down, he hesitated before speaking. In a tentative voice, he ventured, "Dad's getting ready to go back to Hartford . . ." He took a deep breath. "He'd like to talk to you before he—"

"Don't start, Michael," Monica cut him off, turning her head away from him to blow smoke out of her window.

"He's just a few feet away. Couldn't you just—"

"No. Now, if you don't mind, please tell Sweets it's time for us to get on the road."

Michael studied her long and hard, before finally turning to leave.

Monica leaned her head against the headrest and took deep breaths. It was only then that she realized she was shaking.

\* \* \*

IT WAS 6:30 P.M., WHEN MONICA pulled the car up to the front door of Sweets's home. She could hear Sneakers barking from inside the house as soon as she and Sweets stepped from the car.

Monica went straight to her room and changed her clothes. She knew her grandmother was upset with her, but she wasn't in the mood to deal with it now. Jones's funeral, and then seeing Ben so unexpectedly outside the cathedral, brought out too many deep-seated feelings.

She took two Tylenol capsules from her purse and popped them into her mouth, chasing them down with water. When she opened the door to her room, Monica heard Sweets in the kitchen humming to herself.

Convincing herself she'd feel better once she had some fresh air, Monica slipped out the front door and headed towards the woods. She didn't know where she was going, but she moved with the hurried, long strides of a person on a mission. Unaware of how long she walked or of the direction she'd taken, Monica stopped abruptly when she found herself standing at the entrance of the old family cemetery.

With her body trembling, her heart pounding, Monica gripped the handle of the dingy, white wooden gate. She had not been there for many years, denying to herself that it even existed. She wanted to turn around and run as far away from the core of her pain as she could. But now, standing face-to-face with her past, Monica knew if she left this very minute, she would never have the courage to get this far again.

Thrusting her hands in her pockets, Monica took a deep breath and entered the sacred area. She blinked back the tears, then walked slowly to her mother's grave and fell to her knees. Placing one hand on the tombstone, she carefully traced the boldly-written name of *Sarah Adele Sinclair* with the fingers of her other hand. For the first time in years, Monica allowed herself to succumb to her grief. Once the tears began to well up in her eyes, she could not stop them from flowing. Her cries were so loud, she did not hear the footsteps behind her.

"I was hoping I'd find you here, darling," Sweets said softly, taking her granddaughter into her arms. "You have yourself a good cry. You've needed to do that for a long time."

For ten minutes, Monica sobbed uncontrollably, shoulders heaving, until finally, there were no more tears left to shed. For the first time in decades, the painful memories she kept buried rushed through her mind: The tender moments she and Sarah had shared at bedtime when reading Psalm 23 from the family Bible; the scent of her mother's Chantilly perfume that had lingered behind and comforted her long after Sarah turned off the light and left the room; the way they'd played "chopsticks" together on the upright piano, increasing the tempo, and crescendoing until they'd giggled themselves silly.

*Oh, God . . . help me.*

Now, stepping back from her grandmother, Monica wiped her eyes with the handkerchief Sweets handed her. Sniffling, Monica tried to find her voice.

"I'm sorry, Sweets." She blew her nose into the handkerchief. "Everywhere I turned today reminded me of Mama."

"There's nothing to apologize for," Sweets said gently, as she smiled into Monica's tear-stained face. "Your mother was a special person. She deserves to be remembered and mourned. You haven't let yourself do that. Why?"

"It's too painful, Sweets. Even the good memories haunt me. She was so young. How could she have had cancer all that time and not known it? Maybe if she had felt something earlier, she could have been saved."

"You can't think like that, baby. The doctors told us then that breast cancer could exist for a long time without a woman ever knowing it. When your mama found that lump, the cancer had advanced so rapidly she was given less than a fifty-fifty chance to live."

"I know women who have beaten breast cancer—how come you didn't try to save her?"

Tears flooded Sweets's eyes. She heaved a deep sigh before she continued. "It was too late. Ben and I were devastated."

Monica turned away from her grandmother at the mention of her father's name. "Right," she scoffed bitterly. The lava of pain simmered inside of her.

"So devastated was he," Monica blurted out, "that before Mama was cold in her grave, he took Michael and moved back to Hartford, the child who could pass for white. He left the little darkie behind. Where was his love then, Sweets? Ben was ashamed of us, can't you see that? A man from a powerful, wealthy Jewish family, who kept his black mistress and his bastard children neatly tucked away in the hills of Virginia, where no one would find out about us. When it was time for him to step up to the plate and claim his children—both of us—he only wanted the one who looked most like him. I'll never forgive him for that!"

Before Monica could take another breath to continue, Sweets slapped her across her face. Even when they were children, she had never laid a hand on them. Stunned, Monica blinked back the tears as she grabbed her stinging face.

"Don't . . . you . . . ever . . . !" Sweets's voice trembled as she enunciated each word for emphasis. Her eyes narrowed into pinpoints of rage. "They were both fine people. They adored each other and loved you and Michael even more. Can you honestly say you have no memory of the happiness our family shared? You were not so young then that you can't remember it now."

She took Monica's hands and pulled her down to sit with her next to Sarah's grave. "I've loved your dad like one of my own since he was ten years old and spent a couple of summers here when Mr. and Mrs. Morgan went to Europe. Ben and Sarah became best friends.

"Years later, when they fell in love, I knew it would be dangerous for them. I was the first to say it wouldn't work. Ben wanted to move your mother to Connecticut with him, which would have been disastrous. The last thing the Morgans wanted was a black daughter-in-law—called Ben a disgrace to his family. They threatened to disinherit him if he didn't end the relationship."

"I don't wanna hear this."

"You need to know what they were up against. Ben told them Sarah was the woman he wanted to spend his life with, that no amount of money was worth him losing her. That convinced Sarah and me of his commitment to her, though Sarah insisted he continue his career in Connecticut. Reluctantly, he agreed. His parents thought it was over.

"Sarah stayed with me, teaching music and acting at Amherst School. Ben came every Friday, stayed until Sunday when he caught the last train back to Hartford. You don't think that was love? Not many people would've gone through the trouble."

"He never married her."

"Remember, interracial marriages were against the law. I supported them with all my heart because I knew the good Lord wouldn't have brought those two young people together, if He had not wanted it to be so."

"How come his name isn't on *my* birth certificate?"

"Your mother insisted you and Michael keep her last name. In case the Morgans found out and made trouble."

Sweets pursed her lips and wiped her eyes with the edge of her apron.

"Everything was wonderful until Sarah noticed a lump on the outside of her right breast. You were about five then. Sarah was tested and we found out she had breast cancer that had spread to her lungs."

Sweets stopped talking for a moment. She turned her head in the direction of Sarah's grave and blew a gentle kiss. Turning back to Monica, she took her granddaughter into her arms. With her head buried in Sweets's shoulder, Monica quietly cried. Sweets then spoke in a soft voice.

"Look at me, child." Sweets hooked her index finger under Monica's chin, then lifted her granddaughter's face to hers. "Before she died, Sarah asked Ben and me to make her a promise. You listening, baby?"

Monica nodded. She plucked up a blade of grass and toyed with it. She glanced over to her mother's tombstone a few feet away. The crickets sang their night songs as she turned back to Sweets.

"She wanted us to promise her after she died that Ben would take Michael back to Hartford. She'd always worried about him because he looked more white than black. She knew there would be problems, once he was old enough to go to school."

"She didn't have to separate us."

"It would've been impossible for Ben to raise a black daughter in a white world. Sarah was adamant about it. Finally, Ben and I both relented."

"Michael was my baby, too! Didn't anyone think about how I'd feel?"

"Oh, darling, we did. Lord knows I didn't want that baby to leave! After Sarah's funeral, Ben stayed with us for a few weeks. He was heartbroken. When it was time for him to leave with Michael, we both tried to explain the situation to you."

"The first year after Mama died is still a haze."

"How do you convince a six year old that it's not her fault her mother's dead, and now her father and brother were going away without her? Once you'd made up your mind Ben was leaving because he didn't love you, you were determined to believe it."

"So he took my only brother away from me and changed his name?"

"He wanted to change your name, too, remember? He tried to talk to you about it, you didn't want any part of it."

"So what did he tell his great white parents when he came home with Michael?"

"That the child's mother was dead. Nothing more."

"Why didn't he come back to see me?" Monica heard her voice crack. She bit her bottom lip to keep from crying again.

"He did, but you wouldn't see him. When he called, you wouldn't come to the phone. He was so hurt, but he held out hope that with time, you'd understand."

"I don't remember him coming at all."

"Well, he did . . . you must've blocked out the memory. After about a year and a half, he decided it would be best for you if he didn't stay when he brought Michael to visit. By the time you were in junior high school, he stopped coming altogether."

"He missed all of my life, Sweets."

"He *always* knew what was happening with you. Michael told him, too, when he was old enough. Ben knew about your first date, what you wore to the senior prom, your accomplishments in school—I sent him pictures of you every year."

"Big deal. A picture's not the same—"

Sweets held up her hands, cutting her off. "He watched both your high school and college graduations from the back of the auditoriums—much like he did today at Jones's funeral. He didn't want to ruin your day by having you see him, but he wanted to be there just the same.

"Monica, Ben never stopped loving you. Even now, he hopes and prays you will love him again like you did before your mother died."

Wiping her eyes, Monica stood up from Sweets and walked a few steps away. She pulled out a pack of cigarettes from her pocket and lit one. Everything Sweets just said swirled around in her head like leaves caught up in a whirlwind. All she'd ever remembered about him after her mother's death—until now—was anger and hurt.

Now, the haze was clearing. She saw herself sitting in her swing, refusing to look at his face. She remembered the catch in his voice, his choking back tears when he'd begged her to understand that he had to honor her mother's wishes. It had started to rain then. Much like the tears that fell from both their eyes.

"Ben's not the person you've chosen to believe he is, darling," Sweets continued. "He's simply a man who loved a woman beyond all obstacles. And who loved and tried to raise his children as best he could."

There was a struggle tugging inside of Monica now. It was easier to hate someone she'd detested most of her life than accept someone she'd just been introduced to. The one thing Monica knew she needed to do at this moment was make amends with her grandmother.

As she stubbed out her cigarette, Monica walked back to Sweets who was standing against a live oak, patiently waiting for her. Monica reached out for her and pulled her close.

"I'm sorry, Sweets," she said softly, wrapping her arms around her grandmother's thick waist. "Mama meant the world to both of us. I had no right to say such awful things about her. I don't believe, however, the relationship would have lasted if she'd lived."

Sweets smiled at her for a moment. Closing the gate to the cemetery behind them, she linked her arms in Monica's and headed for the house.

"Think about it, Monica. Ben's a successful lawyer, who can afford to live anywhere in the world, have any woman he desires. Instead, he's chosen to stay in Hartford and live alone, in the same house where he raised Michael."

"I don't buy that malarkey."

"I've watched your daddy grow from a child into a fine man," Sweets said knowingly. "He loved your mama. Yes, it would've lasted forever."

"I'm glad you believe so, Sweets. I'm just not so sure."

"Call your father, Monica, and talk to him."

"I can't, Sweets. Not yet. Too much time has passed."

"Sometimes we spend our lives thinking we have all the time in the world to right our wrong. Open your heart. You'll see the love that's yours."

"I already see and feel it—from you and Michael." Monica took her toe and kicked a rock into the brush along the path. "That's enough for me."

# Chapter

# <u>11</u>

Bayou City Wireless was located in the Galleria area of Houston. The fourteen-story building faced Houston's busiest freeway and the harried pace of the passing motorists reflected off of the mirrored front.

The top floor housed a slew of legal counsels and Gerald Conti's office. Cramped into the southwest corner of the building, in a space less elaborate than his brother's, Gerald's office was too small for his taste.

The floor-to-ceiling windows provided a view of the freeway and wrapped around to the swampy Buffalo Bayou. The inside of the office included a huge desk, a conference table with chairs, a sitting area, and an openly displayed bar on the lighted, mirrored bookshelf. Two large Hunter fans hung from the ceiling, off-white french doors led out to a terrace. Whenever he smoked his Cuban cigars, he opened the doors and turned on his fans.

Smoking was a violation of the City of Houston's fire code and he knew it, but didn't care. None of his employees dared to report him. He was a man who played by his own rules.

It had been almost two weeks since Gerald's meeting in Washington and he'd already forgotten about the little incident at the FCC building. He concentrated his efforts on more important things. As he usually did with things he didn't want Victor to know, Gerald kept his meeting with the FCC Chairman to himself. As far as Gerald was concerned, he had everything under control.

Sitting behind his desk, Gerald locked both hands behind his head and reared back in his chair. A smile played at his lips. If he could just hang on for the next few weeks, he was going to make telecommunications history and become head of Conti Telecommunications in the process. That was his plan all along, to produce a product so big he could oust Victor as head of the corporation. Nothing would stand in his way.

Despite initial obstacles, the Excalibur was a success in Indonesia. Because of the dense population and over-crowding of streets, a vast number of Indonesians worked in the field and still traveled about the country on foot and/or bicycle. In regions where land-line phones were not practical, a more mobile type of communications was needed.

Cellular had been introduced during the last few years and, though successful, there were still problems getting the signals over the highest mountains and through the dense forests. The monsoon season created another problem, because the rain-soaked leaves absorbed the frequency signals transmitted by cellular, making it virtually impossible to connect calls over an extended area.

The Excalibur was the remedy for all of that.

Gerald let out a sigh of contentment. He was steamrolling ahead.

A knock on the door interrupted his thoughts. It was Sunday afternoon and, aside from the weekend engineering crew, Arthur was the only one who knew Gerald was in.

"C'mon in, Arthur."

Arthur walked into the room. "The new PR girl starts tomorrow," he said, handing a dossier to Gerald. Taking a seat across from his boss, Arthur watched as Gerald reviewed the documents.

"I assume she's been properly screened?"

"Just like every other top-level position. Did the usual background check. Everything's in order. She's a graduate of the University of Georgia; got her first job at a major telephone company right out of college; worked her way up through the years and became spokesperson of the company five years ago."

"I still don't like the idea of a woman speaking on the company's behalf. They never seem credible to me."

"You want credibility, Gerald? Or someone we can control? She's good-looking and has an excellent reputation for working with the media and the public. I think she'll work out fine."

Gerald grunted.

Arthur continued his spiel. "We've got all males in the top positions, as it is. We can influence how she disseminates information outside of the company without her knowing exactly what's going on in the inside."

"You'd better be right, Arthur. Did you get her office set up?"

Arthur nodded his head. "It's right next door to Peters's. Her furniture's being arranged now and I've assigned one of his secretaries to her. You want to meet with her in the morning?"

"No. Let her get situated first. I'll talk to her after lunch, then introduce her to senior staff in the afternoon."

Arthur stood up to leave. He gave a tight smile.

"Okay. Anything else before I go?"

"No. I'll call, if I need you."

After Arthur had closed the door, Gerald settled back in his chair and put his feet up on the desk. Taking the resume from the documents with one hand and bringing a cigar to his lips with the other, he studied the credentials of his newest employee.

Everything was coming together just fine.

# Chapter

## 12

Monica scanned her new office and decided it would do nicely for the thirty days she would occupy it. When Jim Frasier had accelerated the time line for the assignment, she'd almost reneged on her commitment, knowing it would take her at least three times as long to infiltrate a company the size of Bayou City Wireless. Jones's death warranted immediate closure to the case.

She reported to work an hour early to meet with Arthur Fazio and to get her office together before starting her first day at Bayou City Wireless. The two boxes she brought with her had already been unpacked, their contents meticulously arranged in their places. She slapped her hands up and down in a "Job Well Done" sign.

It had taken less than thirty minutes to get the office in shape. Now that she had another fifteen minutes to kill before everyone else came in, she sat down to catch her breath.

Picking up the name plate on her desk, Monica stared at the bold white letters on the black background: TAYLOR LEBLANC. She and the Bureau had chosen that name for her to use on this assignment. Almost immediately upon her arrival in Washington for her briefing a week and a half ago, she began using it. She studied the terminology; the differences between processing a cellular phone and a land line phone call; the meaning of mobile, portable and transportable phones; the difference between an analog system as opposed to a digital system. The whole process drove her crazy.

During her crash course, Monica learned more than she cared about the industry, but committed everything to memory. She had watched numerous slides on the key executives in the company and had taken notes and memorized their roles.

Monica paid particular attention to the film clippings the Bureau had on Gerald and Victor, carefully studying the demeanor of both men. There was something unsettling about Gerald. She also noticed Arthur Fazio was present in every photo and film clip of him. Monica made a mental note to study their relationship.

In addition to the information she learned about the company, Monica memorized information on herself, as well. The photo on her desk of her 'family' was a picture she took with a Justice Department employee's real family. The degree and achievement plaques neatly arranged on her wall were counterfeits. Her new identity's resume reflected the career background of the public relations position posted by the company.

Unknown to Bayou City Wireless and other unsuspecting companies, the executive search firm the company used was a legitimate company established by the FBI many years ago to place agents all over the country when investigations into the corporate world were warranted.

Monica's birth certificate and social security number had been replaced with that of the fictional Taylor LeBlanc, as were her fingerprints, credit cards and credit history, driver's license and banking information. The small, two-bedroom white cottage with black shutters near the Village just off of Kirby Drive, where she would live for the next month, had also been leased in the name of Taylor LeBlanc and had been furnished and decorated while Monica was in Washington. In addition, the Bureau had installed an alarm system, with carefully hidden video-monitoring equipment.

A connoisseur of disguise, Monica's appearance had been altered. Her natural shoulder-length crinkly curls were cropped and relaxed, and parted on the right side. Monica's eyes were now dark, enhanced by a pair of walnut brown contact lenses which blended well with the darker shade of hair.

Monica took in a deep breath and slowly exhaled it upon hearing the hustle outside of her office. The first of the employees had started to dwindle in. She had lost track of the time and now it was time for her to get busy.

"Okay, Taylor LeBlanc," she mumbled under her breath, pushing her chair back from her desk and heading toward the door. "You've got only thirty days to do your thing, so let's get started. It's show time."

Outside her office, Monica looked around and saw the heads above the cubicles before her. She glanced slightly to her right and spotted her secretary's desk. The woman's back was turned to her. Monica walked the short distance to make her acquaintance.

"Hi," Monica greeted the woman. "You must be Suzanne. I'm Taylor LeBlanc, Bayou City's new communications liaison."

Monica fought an urge to laugh out loud, when she saw the secretary visibly jump. The startled woman swiveled her chair around and struggled to hide the make-up mirror in her hand.

"Uh . . . hi," the woman giggled, stuffing the mirror into her pocket before extending her hand to Monica. "Yeah. I'm Suzanne James. Pleased to meet ya, Miss LeBlanc."

Smiling, Monica shook Suzanne's hand, as she studied the fidgeting woman whose tight-fitting dress appeared to be at least two sizes too small—emphasizing her sculptured breasts—and was much too short for office attire. Her makeup was heavily applied with contrasting shades of blue eye-shadow, black eyeliner, and candy-apple red lips. Suzanne's hair was long, blonde, and wild. The "I-just-woke-up" look instantly reminded Monica of Dyan Cannon.

"Please, call me Taylor," Monica insisted, trying to make the young woman feel at ease. "We're going to be working closely with one another, so I'd like for us to be on a first-name basis, if that's okay with you."

"Sure. I'd like that," Suzanne gushed in an East Texas drawl. "Is there somethin' I can get for you, Miss—uh, I mean, Taylor?" She pronounced "Taylor" with heavy emphasis on the first syllable and an "a" at the end.

"As a matter of fact, I could use a cup of coffee. Care to show me where I could get some?"

Monica followed a sashaying Suzanne through the maze of cubicles. It was after eight o'clock now and most of the employees had settled into their daily routines. Suzanne stopped along the way to introduce her new boss to a few of them. By the time they reached the coffee room, gotten their beverages, and made their way back to Monica's office, Suzanne had told her little tidbits of personal information about almost all of them.

The young woman's strong Texas accent and excessive talking were beginning to grate Monica's nerves. Just about the time Monica thought she would  never get to work, a figure appeared in her doorway and knocked on the door.

"I don't mean to interrupt," the man said to Monica, "I just wanted to introduce myself to you before going into a meeting for the rest of the morning."

Suzanne looked up and managed a nervous smile. She quickly excused herself, telling Monica she would be at her desk if she needed anything else. The man walked into the office and offered his hand to Monica.

"I'm Larry Peters, vice president of marketing.  My office is right next door."

"It's a pleasure to meet you, Larry. I'm Taylor LeBlanc. Come on in."

"No. I can't stay. I'm on my way to a nine o'clock meeting with my staff.  Just wanted to stick my head in and say hi."

"I'm glad you did." Monica remembered him from the slides. He was an expressionless, hard-to-read kind of guy with dark hair, receding hairline, and dark eyes. He was average height for a man and about twenty pounds overweight. His serious face made him look much older than his thirty-something years. According to the information she'd learned about him in Washington, he stayed mostly to himself and did a good job.

"If you have a moment later today," Monica made sure her voice sounded friendly but authoritative, "I'd like to find out what's happening in your department. It'll take me a while to learn everything that's going on in this company, so I might as well jump in now."

"I understand." Larry glanced down at his watch.

"I've been here almost seven months and I'm still learning my way around. Come by my office this afternoon. We'll talk more then."

Larry had only been gone for about two seconds before Suzanne popped back into Monica's office.

"Gosh. He probably talked more to you in the last few minutes than he's talked to me the whole time he's been here," she whispered in a surprised voice. "He's a strange guy. Hardly ever smiles."

"I hear he's good at what he does." Monica looked back down at the stack of papers on her desk, hoping Suzanne would get the hint that she was too busy for another one of the woman's long-winded conversations.

"That's true," Suzanne conceded. "Things are so different around here with him in charge of Marketing after someone like Carter . . ." Her voice trailed off during the last few words so that it was barely audible. Monica looked up and noticed a sad look on the secretary's face.

"I'm sorry, Suzanne. I missed the last part of what you were saying."

"I just meant Mr. Peters is totally different from the guy who had the position before him. Dave Carter was a fun person and he made it fun for all of us. I used to work for him."

"Did he leave for another company?"

"No. He died a couple of weeks ago."

Monica rapidly flipped through the pages of her mind and drew a blank on an employee named Dave Carter who had died. She had no information on him whatsoever and wondered why she'd not been told of him during her briefing. She did not like surprises.

"Was he sick?" Monica perked up, suddenly interested. "He was when he left about seven or eight months ago. Then two weeks ago, we got a memo about his death. We never found out what was wrong with him."

"Interesting." Monica spoke the word under her breath.

"Anyway," Suzanne continued, "Mr. Peters came a month or so after Dave left. He's a little stale, if you ask me."

"I'm sorry about your former boss, Suzanne," Monica said, committing Dave Carter's name to memory and making a mental note to ask Michael about him. "But, if we don't get to work soon, the day'll be over before we know it."

"You're right. Holler if you need me to do somethin' for ya."

"Thanks. Please pull the door a little on your way out, Suzanne."

*She can't possibly be real,* Monica thought to herself, shaking her head in amusement. Whatever was going on here, Suzanne James would be of no help. She certainly would not be a threat to Monica's mission—unlike the person she was due to meet later that afternoon.

* * *

AT FIVE MINUTES TO ONE, Monica stood outside of Gerald Conti's office and identified herself to his secretary. After buzzing him on the intercom and announcing her, the woman told Monica Gerald would be with her momentarily. Monica took a deep breath and considered what her first reaction would be to the man whom she knew held the key to all of her questions. She knew he was a pro and suspicious by nature, so she would have to be extra careful in her dealings with him.

102

The phone on the secretary's desk rang again, and this time, Monica was told Mr. Conti would see her now. Rising from her seat, Monica adjusted her suit and waved a hand over her hair, as she walked the few steps to the door leading into the office. When she stepped into the room, she was momentarily caught off guard.

Standing at opposite ends of the large leather sofa were both Gerald and Victor, who each rose to their feet as she approached. At the sight of the two men together, Monica drew in a deep breath, but retained her composure. She was not surprised, however, to see Arthur Fazio lurking in the background. It was obvious to Monica by the coy looks on the men's faces, they were all anticipating her reaction to seeing Gerald and Victor together for the first time. Walking toward the twin figures, Monica extended her hand to Victor first.

"Hello, Mr. Conti. I'm Taylor LeBlanc," she said, shaking his hand firmly. Before he could utter a response, Monica withdrew her hand and then offered it to Gerald, who was now standing next to Victor.

"And you must be Mr. *Gerald* Conti," she said, feeling the strong pressure from his hand lessen at the emphasis on his first name. She smiled pleasingly at both men as they looked from one to the other in astonishment. Victor was the first to speak, as he smiled broadly at the confident woman in front of him.

"Well, Ms. LeBlanc," he said, offering her a seat in one of the chairs across from the sofa. "It is a pleasure to meet you, indeed. I must say that you have made an incredible first impression. Wouldn't you agree, Gerald?" Victor pivoted on one foot towards his brother whose face registered annoyance rather than amusement.

"Yes," Gerald responded unenthusiastically. "How

were you able to tell us apart?"

"It's simple, really," she said matter-of-factly, enjoying the idea that she had beaten them at their own game. "There's always that little difference that gives twins away. Sometimes, it's the intonation in their voices or the way they pronounce certain words. Or, sometimes it's the way they hold their heads or gesture with their hands. But, with you two, it's something a little more obvious."

Monica paused before continuing, knowing they were hanging on to her every word.

"And what would that be?" Gerald asked.

"That little pin, Mr. Conti," Monica laughed, pointing to the small, round sterling silver pin on Gerald's lapel with the letters "BCW" engraved in gold.

"My secretary told me as soon as I got in this morning that if I ever encountered the two of you in the same room at the same time, the surest way to identify the company president was to look for the one wearing the Bayou City Wireless pin on his left lapel. I was told that you wear it *religiously* everyday."

Victor boomed with laughter and slapped his thigh. Arthur followed next with a stifled chuckle that exploded into a laugh as loud as Victor's. Gerald couldn't help but join in.

"'Touche,' Ms. LeBlanc," he finally conceded. "I guess my employees are more observant than I give them credit for."

"Please, call me Taylor," she said. "Ms. LeBlanc sounds so formal."

"We'd like you to do the same," Gerald said, looking to Victor who nodded in agreement as he rose to leave.

"By all means," Victor grinned. "I see you've picked

a winner, Gerald."

Turning to Monica, Victor reached to shake her hand again. "I'm afraid I must get back to my office. I only wanted to stop in and introduce myself to you. Should you ever have a need to meet with me, please feel free to give me a call or just come by Conti Towers." Turning to the lawyer, he said, "Arthur, could you come with me for a moment? I'd like to speak with you about the renewal process." With that he hugged his brother and the two men left the room.

Monica noticed Gerald's back grow rigid when Victor extended the invitation to her. His disposition changed once Victor left and he'd retreated to the chair behind his desk. In fact, he was completely relaxed as she noticed him glance more than once at her legs as she crossed them at the ankles. She also noticed him staring at her now.

"Have we met before, Taylor?" Gerald asked.

"If we had, Gerald, I'm sure I'd have remembered." Monica wondered what could have given him that impression.

"There's something about you that seems vaguely familiar." He stared at her a moment longer and then, suddenly, straightened up in his chair.

"Now that we're past the formality of introductions," Gerald changed the subject abruptly, "how about we get down to business? Your resume is very impressive. I think you're going to fit in very nicely here at Bayou City Wireless. Are you comfortable with your office?"

"Yes, thank you."

"You'll be working directly for me." Gerald looked at Monica, then turned away. He did not hold direct eye contact long, she noticed.

"I meet every Tuesday morning with my senior staff to go over the week's agenda and address any concerns or problems. I expect you to be there tomorrow morning at seven-thirty sharp. I know I don't have to tell you, Taylor, that everything we discuss in those meetings is completely confidential."

Suddenly Gerald's voice took on a hushed tone. "We decide during that time what information will be shared with the rest of our employees and how we're going to present it to them. You and I will talk more frequently, since you will be communicating with the media and the community. It's important that we are in agreement on how information is disseminated. How we are perceived by our customers depends largely on how we position what we have to say. Don't you agree?"

"Absolutely," Monica said. "That's what public relations is all about, influencing the way people think. The more positive they feel toward the company, the more profitable and productive we are."

Monica almost laughed at her little speech, which could have come straight from the pages of a PR 101 textbook. She knew she'd chosen the perfect response when she saw Gerald's eyes gleaming like a child's coveting a shiny, red fire truck in the window of a toy store. She knew the bottom line with him was making money— and lots of it.

"I've asked the other members of the senior staff," Gerald continued, looking at his watch as he talked, "to assemble in the main conference room in about ten minutes. I want to introduce you to them. You'll be expected to meet with them weekly on your own to keep abreast of what's going on in their departments.

"After we meet with the others," Gerald continued,

"I'll brief you on the major projects you'll be working on." Checking his watch for the second time, Gerald pushed his seat back and walked around his desk toward the direction of the door to his office. "Ready to meet your new colleagues?" he asked, as he stood in the doorway.

"Just lead the way." She smiled, noticing out of the corner of her eye the way he looked at her. *I'm ready for just about anything.*

\* \* \*

TWENTY MINUTES AFTER SHE WAS introduced to the vice presidents of the company, Monica returned with Gerald to his office to go over the details of her job. Aside from the normal press releases, community newsletters, she was filled in on her responsibility of collecting information for the license renewal. After Gerald finished his instructions, he walked over to his file cabinet and removed a black, leather tote that looked a lot like a 35mm camera bag. Placing it on the table in front of Monica, he sat on the edge of the table beside it and stared intently at her.

"Our latest development." Gerald tapped the bag lightly with his hand. "Devising a PR plan for it will be your top priority. Only a handful of people here know about it, so be careful not to discuss it with anyone, except those people whom I identify. But first, a demonstration."

He motioned to Monica to open the tote. She eyed him suspiciously, then unzipped the top portion of the case. Monica held her breath in anticipation, as she looked inside and saw the black, hand-held wireless phone. She gently removed it and looked back at Gerald, whose face boasted a broad grin.

"What's this?" she asked, coyly.

"This, young lady, is the Excalibur. Conti Telecommunications' newest product—and secret weapon."

"Secret weapon against who?" Monica raised a brow.

"The rest of the industry, who else? The name of the game is always competition and this little baby is what's going to skyrocket Conti Telecommunications light years ahead of the rest."

"What makes this phone so different? It looks like a regular cellular phone."

"Ah . . . but, it's much more than that. Push the latch on the side of the keypad and display screen, and flip it open."

Monica did as she was told and was taken aback when she saw a hand-held computer with large screen, keyboard, and function buttons. The whole thing couldn't have weighed more than a pound, though it was not too bulky. Speechless, she looked back at Gerald, who was amused by the amazed look on her face.

Continuing to examine the product, Monica thought it was the perfect time to ask Gerald a few questions.

"Isn't it a beauty?" Gerald asked, beaming. "Designed it myself. It's the only one of its kind in the whole world. Soon, it will become the most sought after wireless phone ever. And, it will only be manufactured by Conti Telecommunications."

"What does it do, exactly?" Monica studied the phone more closely.

"Just what you see. It's a cellular phone and computer, complete with calendar and other applications. All of your communications needs rolled into one; access the Internet in the morning, write business reports on the computer in the afternoon, send e-mail and fax messages at night."

"Other wireless phones have similar capabilities. What exactly makes this so unique?" Monica treaded slowly. She did not want to raise suspicion.

"No." He was emphatic. "There is nothing on the market to compare to the Excalibur. Let me show you something." He walked back over to his cabinet and withdrew another black tote, identical to the one Monica had in her hand. Taking out another Excalibur phone, Gerald switched on the operating switch. He then told Monica to close the phone she was holding and do the same.

"Watch your display screen," he said, with a mischievous smile, punching in a series of numbers. A few seconds after he'd entered the final number, Monica's phone began to ring. "Press the 'send' key," he instructed. She did and was amazed to see Gerald's face appear on the screen in clear, vibrant color. Smiling into the phone, Gerald continued with his instructions. "Now press the 'spkr' key and talk to me."

Monica held the phone in her left hand, pressed the button with the index finger of her right hand, and stared into the display screen.

Putting the phone to her ear, she spoke into the mouthpiece "Testing one, two, three—" Monica stopped, when she heard the echo of her voice coming through the speaker of Gerald's phone.

"Do you still think this is 'just a cellular phone'?" Gerald said into his speaker. Holding the phone in her hand, Monica continued to stare at Gerald's image on the screen. She had never seen anything like it.

"Not at all," Monica answered, turning off the device and placing it on the table. She looked up at Gerald and saw the look of satisfaction on his face at his successful presentation.

After a few moments of silence Monica finally said, "I'm impressed . . . it's absolutely amazing."

"More than that. It's colossal! Can you imagine the impact it's going to have on the market? The public's going to eat it up."

"When is the launch date?" Monica tried to sound casual.

"In the next few weeks. I haven't determined the exact date, as of yet."

"Won't it be too expensive for the average consumer? Cellular phone prices have dropped tremendously over the past few years. With all of its unique capabilities, this phone is sure to be too high for most people to afford."

"Just under $1000, but that's a small price to pay for all of the features it provides. A laptop costs more than that."

"True enough. Still," she said, playing the devil's advocate, "the average person may be reluctant to spend that much on a new product that doesn't have a proven track record, yet. What about product reliability? How are you going to convince the public this phone will meet all of its expectations?"

Gerald stiffened in his chair. When he glared at Monica as if he had just been insulted, a warning bell went off in her head. She tried to ignore the spasms in her stomach.

"Taylor, this company prides itself on product reliability. We have conducted extensive testing on the Excalibur and it has *exceeded* all of our expectations.

Peters will share with you the results of the product study we did with one of our focus groups, and you'll see then what I'm talking about."

"Well, that's wonderful," Monica said, enthusiastically. "I can include statements from some of the participants in our media—"

"There's no need for that," Gerald interrupted, curtly. His expression had suddenly changed from raving accolades about the product to alarm. "Everything you'll need can be found in the trial summary you get from Peters."

"Don't you think that it will add more credibility to include testimonials from actual users of the product?" Monica asked cautiously, careful not to tip her hand.

She watched as Gerald tightened his jaw and shot a warning look at her.

"This company's reputation is credibility enough. We can successfully market this product without comments from those people. The company's success does not depend on them. Your job is to put together an outstanding public relations campaign for this device. Our ties with the participants are over."

Monica started to press further, but decided she had gone far enough for the first day. There would be time to find out more. At least she had seen the actual product.

"I suppose you're right," she conceded more cheerfully. "I'll review the study and then arrange a meeting with Engineering first thing in the morning. Anyone in particular I should talk to?"

"Cameron Maxwell," Gerald said in a lighter tone. "He's the best engineer around."

Once again, Monica noticed how swiftly his attitude changed, like a chameleon who'd leaped from a brown limb of a tree and landed on one of its lime-green leaves.

"Cameron Maxwell, it is," Monica responded, as she stood and extended her hand to Gerald. "Enjoyed our visit. I'm sure I'm going to like working here."

"Likewise," Gerald shook her hand, then walked her to the door.

After Monica left, Arthur Fazio entered the office. Closing the door behind him, he walked over and took a seat across from Gerald's desk.

"Well? How'd it go?" he asked Gerald, who was rubbing a finger across his mustache.

"Fine. She asked too many goddamn questions, though. Even suggested getting in touch with some of the study participants to get their response to the Excalibur."

"You persuaded her otherwise, didn't you?"

"What do you think?"

"How'd she respond?"

"She got the message. I don't think she'll be a problem, but keep an eye on her."

# Chapter

## 13

The next morning, Monica glanced over her notes for her nine o'clock meeting with Cameron Maxwell. She had gotten a good look at the Excalibur, but so far, there was nothing visible about it that suggested it could cause the type of health problems the Bureau suspected. Yesterday, after she left Gerald's office, she had gone straight to Larry Peters and asked for the trial study.

She chewed the inside of her cheek as she perused the papers. Just as she had anticipated, the study included specific information about the product use and only generalized information—about a paragraph long—that stated the participants' satisfaction with the device. No mention of deaths or illnesses or dissatisfaction of any kind graced the pages. Monica hoped Cameron Maxwell could provide some answers.

She stepped from behind her desk and walked outside to look for her secretary. Suzanne was nowhere to be found. Sighing, Monica turned around and walked back into her office. Just as she entered the room, the pen perched behind her right ear dropped to the floor. Monica stooped down to pick it up and was startled by a voice behind her.

"I wouldn't bend over like that, girlfriend," the male

voice said. Monica snapped her head around and stared up into the grinning face of the prettiest man she'd ever seen, standing with his hands on his hips. He was pushing what resembled a shopping cart.

"Excuse me?" Rising from the floor, she lifted one eyebrow.

"Don't get defensive," he said, handing her a stack of mail. "I'm Jazz, the company mailman. I came by yesterday to meet you, but you weren't here. Taylor LeBlanc, right?"

"That's me," Monica said, pulling at the skirt of her creme-colored suit. She studied the young man. Though his flawlessly smooth face resembled that of a teenage boy, years away from being introduced to a razor, he was probably more than twenty years old. About five feet eight, reed-thin, dressed in perfectly creased blue jeans, he wore a starched, white, long-sleeve dress shirt, and a multi-colored tie that would have been too conspicuous on someone else. Monica guessed by his accent, olive complexion and curly black hair, that he was of Latin descent.

"Jazz . . ." She repeated the name, savoring its sound. Her eyes focused on the wisp of black strands swooped across his forehead that never moved, no matter how much he shook his head. "What an unusual first name."

"Made it up myself." He took his hand and rubbed his chest in a circle. "After seven kids, my Puerto Rican mother lost all her imagination when it came time to name me. Jasper Lopez didn't quite cut it. Jazz had more creative appeal."

"For what?" Monica jerked her head back, waiting for an answer.

"Fashion, girlfriend. I am a . . . designer!" He waved

a snapped finger across the air in front of him. "Or, at least I will be, once I have enough designs to foot the bill. Then, I'm off to New York to give Adrienne Vittadini, Chanel, Victor Costa and the lot a run for their money. In the meantime, I am destined to lead a drab existence behind this cart, hoping to save at least one fashion-unconscious lost soul around this place."

Monica laughed out loud. He was definitely the most flamboyant person she had met in a long time. "What type of clothing do you design?"

"The most creative and fabulous of them all, honey— women's fashion. Gowns, suits, dresses, pantsuits—everything the fashion-conscious woman needs to express who she is." Jazz paused, twisting his mouth to the side, squaring his hands before him as if to form a frame.

"Take you, for example. That creme-colored suit you're wearing, accentuated by the double strand of pearls and clip earrings exude elegance, and says you're a woman of sophistication who's confident and sure of herself."

Monica chuckled, wondering what he would say about her closet full of over-sized sweaters, tee shirts, and leggings.

"Then, take that secretary of yours," he continued in distaste, dropping his voice a decibel or two, looking around to make sure Suzanne was not within hearing range. "Call the fashion police on that one. Buys all of her clothes from Fredericks of Hollywood. That's no exaggeration; I know because I deliver her packages. Suzanne adds a blazer to dresses and skirts too little for Barbie and calls it office wear."

Monica gave a tight smile, but her eyes danced with laughter.

"I'll bet you she wears her make-up to bed and just reapplies it in the morning. That girl is a cross between Charo and Bozo the Clown. A couple of hours with me and I could do wonders with her."

He paused for a moment, then changed his mind. "On second thought, two weeks would be more realistic."

Monica let a tiny laugh slip out, but to control herself, she glanced at her watch. Suddenly she realized she had to hurry or else she would be late for her meeting.

"Nice talking to you, Jazz," she said, ending the conversation as she grabbed her purse, and a pad and pencil from her desk. "I've got a meeting with Cameron Maxwell at the PCSC in fifteen minutes."

"Now, there's a man with GQ style—and a great ass," Jazz added. "Check you later when I make my afternoon rounds. Let me know if I can show you the ropes around this joint." Leaning his head back into her office, he whispered, "I know most of the gossip before it hits the rumor mill. Hell, I start a few rumors myself, just to keep things exciting around here. I like you, Taylor LeBlanc. You and I are going to be great friends." Winking, he flashed a grin and headed his cart down the hall.

* * *

THE PCSC, PERSONAL COMMUNICATIONS switching center, was inconspicuously located in an office park and warehouse area, just a short drive from Bayou City Wireless's corporate office. The brain, connecting all of the company's cell sites and tying them into the local telephone company, was a two-hundred foot tower. Projected above the two-story building, it provided the perfect landmark for Monica, as she navigated her Ford Explorer among the endless blocks of office buildings.

Turning into the driveway that led to the PCSC, she pulled up to the front and parked her truck. Once inside the small waiting area, she pushed the button on intercom to announce herself and waited for the security lock to signal she had been cleared to enter.

"Hi. Taylor LeBlanc to see Cameron Maxwell," Monica said to the receptionist, seated behind a desk in a room not much bigger than the small reception area that she'd just left.

"Yes, Ms. LeBlanc. He's expecting you. If you'll follow me, I'll show you where to go." The lady punched a series of numbers into the keypad on the wall outside of the door to her right and pulled it open. "Cameron's office is at the end of the hall." The lady stepped aside to let Monica pass.

Monica marched down the narrow hallway and knocked lightly on the closed office door. A deep, masculine voice called out for her to come in. As she opened the door, she realized she had interrupted a meeting.

"I'm sorry," she apologized to the three men who were engrossed in conversation, huddled together at a small round table in the corner of the office. "I must be early. I'm Taylor LeBlanc. I have a nine o'clock meeting with Cameron Maxwell." Monica was not sure exactly which one he was.

"That's me," a dark-skinned man said, as he stood up, walked to the door, and invited her into the office. "I'm the one who should apologize to you, Miss LeBlanc, for letting this meeting run overtime. Give me a couple of minutes to wrap things up and I'll be right with you."

As she watched him walk back to the table, Monica

lowered her head to conceal a smile. *Jazz was right,* she thought. *Cameron definitely has a great ass.*

After the other two men had gone, Cameron shook Monica's hand. She liked the firmness in his grip.

"Have a seat, Ms. LeBlanc." Cameron pointed to a chair at the table after the other two men had gone.

"Call me Taylor," Monica said.

"I was just about to get some coffee. Can I bring you back a cup?"

"Thanks. Black, with sugar."

Monica looked around the modest-sized office to get an insight on what kind of person Cameron Maxwell was. On the wall behind his desk was a framed degree from Stanford University, and several citations, along with three Outstanding Achievement Awards presented to exemplary company employees. Monica gathered from the set of clubs sitting in a worn, leather golf bag in the corner of the room, that he was an avid golfer.

"Do you play?" Cameron asked, handing her a Styrofoam cup.

"Play?" Momentarily, Monica was at a loss. She didn't have a clue what he meant.

"Golf? I noticed you were staring at my clubs."

"No." She was embarrassed that he had caught her checking out the room. "Never found the time."

"You should try it. It's very relaxing." He took a sip of the coffee and leaned back in his chair. Grinning, he added, "So, Taylor, you're the new PR person."

"That's right." Sipping her coffee, she looked up. "You sound as if you're surprised."

"Frankly, I am. I wasn't expecting a woman—a black woman, that is."

"Oh?"

"This company doesn't have much of a track record in hiring black executives. There's only one female director, three female managers, and none of them is black. All of senior staff is white. In fact, I'm the only black director in the company. So, when I heard Gerald was looking for a new spokesperson, I naturally assumed he was going to get another one of his boys. You're a welcome surprise. And a beautiful one at that."

He continued to stare at Monica, which made her a little uncomfortable. Cameron Maxwell was a handsome man, in a rugged sort of way. Espresso in color, he was about six feet tall with bold shoulders. His thick eyebrows arched over dark brown eyes, and his freshly shaven face showed tiny lines around the mouth. His hair was coarse and cut very short.

"I assume," Monica continued, trying to keep the conversation on a business level, "your secretary explained why I wanted to meet with you."

"Not before Gerald called and told me himself," he answered. "What's your impression of him?"

Monica was surprised at the direct question. "Sharp. Concise. Very sure of himself. Why?"

"Gerald's a cool cat, but you have to watch yourself with him. He's tough as nails and he wouldn't hesitate to chew you up and spit you out like yesterday's chewing gum, *if* you're not one of the big boys."

"Are you 'one of the big boys'?"

Leaning forward with his hands clasped together on the desk, he grinned, "Let's just say I know how to play the game. I suggest you learn pretty fast how to do the same, if you want to stay around here for awhile."

"I'll keep that in mind." Monica took her pad and pencil from her purse. "Tell me something. Exactly what

119

does a field network director do?"

He laughed in a rich baritone which made Monica tingle inside. "There are days when I ask myself that same question. The title would seem to encompass just about everything. Basically, it's two-fold: I head up a team of technicians and engineers who maintain the system out in the trenches, and I monitor the activities of the NMS."

"NMS?"

"The network management system that lets us monitor each point site to see how they're functioning. If there's an error of any kind, we know about it automatically."

"You do all that from here?"

"Yes, ma'am," he said, "and a lot more. The NMS is staffed twenty-four hours a day, seven days a week. My team watches the network more closely than the airline guys in a control tower. I could show you around, if you'd like."

"That'd be great. But before you do, tell me about the Excalibur. Gerald showed it to me yesterday and, quite frankly, I was impressed."

"It's really a fascinating piece of equipment." Cameron put his hands behind his head, rearing back into his seat. "It was several years in the making and has posed quite a challenge for us in getting the network ready for it."

"Why's that?"

"For starters, we hadn't yet converted to digital. We were still using an analog system."

"And the Excalibur is a digital communications device, right?"

"Right," he said. "The analog system is a constantly

varying transmitting signal. Digital systems are more accurate. They turn the human voice into Os and 1s of computer language, before you transmit. The benefits of digital technology are that you can more precisely define what the information is that's being transmitted, which has everything to do with voice transmission. It becomes even more important if a product is going to do data and video, which happen to be the two prime features of the Excalibur.

"So, we basically had to go into the system, and replace the analog circuit cards with digital circuit cards for the transmission and receiving side of the operations. Of course, after that, we introduced a number of digital phones which created other problems that we had to overcome, like fine-tuning the voice transmission. So, when Gerald first told us about the Excalibur concept and that it was already being manufactured at Bayou City Wireless's plant in Mexico, I was skeptical as to whether he would be able to pull off such a sophisticated device."

He took a deep breath. "I'm excited as hell that he did. The system should be ready soon to handle the initial capacity of Excalibur customers."

"I'm sure there are always a lot of risks involved for any company when introducing a new product."

"There certainly are. Especially when that product is a complex piece of equipment like the Excalibur. Other wireless manufacturers have tried and failed before the product even made it off the assembly line. But, that was never one of my concerns—product reliability, I mean."

"What do you mean?

"As an engineer, I was more interested in the increased frequency level of the Excalibur and staying within the safety standards set by ANSI."

Monica stopped writing and looked up from her tablet. She remembered Frasier had touched briefly on the American National Standards Institute during her briefing. It was the safety standard for radiation exposure which had been adopted by the FCC.

"I don't understand."

"Think of the cellular phone as a radio that transmits radio signals. Radio-frequency radiation is electromagnetic energy emitted in the form of waves. Cellular phones transmit voice messages by sending electronic signals from an antenna over radio waves at frequencies between 824 and 894 megahertz, that's millions of pulses per second. These signals are a form of radio-frequency radiation."

"Could you elaborate?"

"According to ANSI's standards for radiation exposure, devices operating on 7 or less watts of power at 1,000 megahertz will not produce immediate thermal effects. Portable cellular phones operate well below 7 watts of power. They use up to a maximum of 0.6 watts of power—less than the amount of power required to light a flashlight bulb."

"And the Excalibur?" Monica's interest perked.

"Since it's the next generation of cellular phones—a personal communicator, to be exact—its functioning capabilities require a higher radio-frequency level. My initial concerns were that it would emit too much electromagnetic rays that could cause health concerns."

"Such as?"

"Interfering with medical equipment in hospitals, affecting heart pacemakers, hearing problems, headaches—"

"Cancer?" Monica interrupted, as she scrutinized his face closely for the slightest change in expression. She could not detect any.

"Now, that's the million-dollar question. There are some scientists who think it's possible, but there's been nothing to substantiate it. The NIH—National Institutes of Health—is studying the issue now, as are an industry-funded group of scientists, but to be quite honest, Taylor, nobody knows for sure. It will be several years before the results of those studies are known." Cameron looked at her for what felt like moments, but was actually just a few seconds, before continuing.

"Anyway," he sighed, "my concerns about the Excalibur were short-lived, because Gerald and Carter found a way to keep the power and frequency level safely within the recommended levels. How they did it, I can't tell you."

Monica thought for a second. *Why was a vice president of marketing involved with the technical side of the product?*

"Gerald told me you helped with the design."

"I did, *after* Gerald and Carter worked out the configurations."

"If the product had been unsafe, surely the FCC would have detected it during some phase of its testing, right?" Monica pumped for more information, yet tried to keep her tone from sounding overly nosey.

"They didn't do the testing. We did. We always have our own people conduct equipment tests, then send the results to the FCC for approval. Gerald is close to the Chairman, so everything is usually processed pretty quickly."

That explains how McCormick was involved, but Monica still couldn't understand Carter's role.

"Wait a minute," she said, "I thought Dave Carter

was head of the Marketing department. Why would he have been involved with engineering?" Monica was getting signals, but she wasn't sure, at this point, what they were.

"Carter was an engineer who switched to the product development side of the business. The way he described it, he wanted to track the product after it was released to see how it progressed. Anyway, he worked with Gerald to design the Excalibur and spent a lot of time in the Mexican plant."

Cameron flexed his fingers. "When it was finished, Carter conducted the product study in Bastrop with the people he'd assembled to test the product. You know about the study, right?"

Monica shook her head. She wondered how much *he* really knew.

"Carter visited Bastrop often during the testing," Cameron continued, "meeting with the people and collecting the data. It didn't surprise me one bit when he suddenly became ill after the trial ended. I don't know how he was able to keep up the pace, traveling back and forth daily to that town. Spent most weekends there, too. The responsibility was too much for one person."

"I heard about his death from my secretary." Monica tried to make her comment sound casual. "What was the matter with him?"

"I'm not sure. The word around the company was that he was in the beginning stages of Alzheimer's when he resigned. He did seem a bit distracted and somewhat aloof during those last days, but I don't have any experience with the disease, so I only know what they told us."

"Alzheimer's . . ." Monica repeated. "I didn't realize he was an older man. Judging from the age group of senior staff—early 40s—I naturally assumed he was a younger man."

"Thirty-nine to be exact," Cameron added, as Monica grew even more suspicious.

"That's too bad." She decided that she really needed to talk to Michael about this. Changing the subject, she said, "I heard the Bastrop Study went well and the participants were pleased with the Excalibur."

"Everything worked out okay," he said, reflectively. "Although there was one time, after the study ended, when I thought the Excalibur project was history." Cameron put his elbows on the desk, interlocked the fingers of both hands, and brought them up to his mouth.

"Carter and Gerald got into a big shouting match outside of Gerald's office one evening. I had gone to Gerald's office to talk with him about something else when I overhead him and Carter shouting to the top of their lungs behind the office door. I couldn't detect exactly what they were saying, but I do know that Carter was screaming about the Excalibur and some kind of complication in Bastrop.

"Before I could get a fix on what he was raving about, the door flew open, hit the wall behind it, and Carter stomped out in a rage. I don't even think he saw me. Gerald called after him and then yelled at him to keep his mouth closed or Gerald would close it for him. But Carter was gone and didn't look back. I waited about five minutes before knocking on Gerald's door. I didn't want him to know that I'd overheard part of the conversation." Cameron looked up at Monica and realized he'd rambled on too long.

"Did you ask Carter about it?" Her voice came out softly.

"Didn't have the chance. Two days later, he was gone." Cameron rose from his seat. "Why don't we go take a look at the NMS, now?"

Monica hesitated a moment, wanting to know more about the dispute between Carter and Gerald, then put her purse on her shoulder and followed Cameron down the hallway. They came to a locked door with a digital keypad Monica recognized as the kind which had to be reconfigured after every use. After entering a security code, Cameron opened the door and they were met with a blast of cool air.

Cameron must have noticed Monica's shudder at the sudden change in temperature. "Sorry. I should have warned you. We have to keep the thermostat turned low because there's so much machinery crammed into such a small area, they tend to cause overheating."

Monica looked around the room and saw several people stationed in front of computer monitors, other equipment lined the back of the room. There were charts and maps on every wall. Cameron made the introductions and then led Monica to a workstation in the corner.

"This is RISC," he said, sitting down in front of a computer and motioning for her to take the chair next to him.

Monica gave him a puzzled look.

"A reduced instruction set computer. The software is a package produced by Alternative Computing that uses a program called NMS/6000 which collects not only calling detail used for billing purposes, but it's used for QoS, quality of service measurements."

"That's incredible."

"You see," he continued, "it's very important for us to look and see what the transmit and receive power is, because if we start to lose power in the circuit cards in the personal communications point, PCP, then we need to immediately dispatch a team of technicians to fix the problem."

"Don't you have a backup?"

"Sure. We have utility power, then we have UPS— uninterrupted power supplies that are the batteries and generators. It's just a temporary backup that kicks in until we are able to return the system back to its original level of function."

Cameron's gaze returned to the screen. "Here, let's take a look at one of the points in north Houston. You'll get a better idea of what I'm talking about."

Monica stared at the screen and took notes as Cameron went through the demonstration. As she tried to concentrate on what he was saying, she found her eyes repeatedly drawn to the question mark she'd made next to Carter's name.

\* \* \*

"WHY DIDN'T YOU TELL ME about Dave Carter?" Monica blurted out as soon as Michael answered the phone. It was 10:00 p.m., and she had been calling his townhouse in Georgetown every thirty minutes since she'd gotten home from work shortly after seven.

"I'm fine, Monica. How are you?" Michael sounded exhausted.

"Sorry, Mike. This is important." She lit a cigarette, drawing a long puff from it.

"Who's Dave Carter?" Michael repeated.

"The guy who helped design the Excalibur and left the company after the study ended. He wasn't mentioned once during the whole briefing and his photo was not in the batch you guys showed me."

"Slow down. What are you talking about? Everyone important to the case was in the files. I've never heard of a Dave Carter and Frasier hasn't said anything about him."

"Weren't you listening?" Monica snapped impatiently. "Dave Carter was the vice president of marketing who helped Gerald with the design of the Excalibur, the equipment used in the study in Bastrop. He resigned from the company shortly after that, stating in his resignation letter that he had a terminal illness."

"And?"

"He was only thirty-nine years old and was believed to be in the beginning stages of Alzheimer's. He was also the sole person in charge of the Bastrop people. I also found out that two nights before he left his resignation letter, Carter had an explosive argument with Gerald about the communications device which ended with Carter storming out of the office and Gerald cursing after him about 'keeping his mouth shut.'"

"And you think that argument was connected to the people who died in Bastrop?" Michael suddenly sounded interested.

"Could be. The employee who told me about it wasn't able to hear the whole conversation. Guess what else?"

"What?" Michael's excitement leaped through the phone.

"There were initial concerns that the device would be too powerful and would end up exposing people to too much radiation frequency."

"Can you get your hands on one of the phones? Maybe our guys could take a look at it."

"I've only seen two of them and Gerald has them both under lock and key. The demos for the execs won't be available for another two weeks, so I'll see what I can do about it then. I'm beginning to think Dave Carter has the answers."

"You just said the man was dead, Monica." Michael sounded weary. "Don't go off chasing ghosts in the night. Let's stick to finding out what we can about this Excalibur. You can't get answers from a corpse."

"Maybe not," Monica conceded, "but I can find out if he left any clues behind. Dig around a bit up there, Michael, and see what you can find out about him. The days are flying off the calendar and I'm looking in every direction I can for answers."

"Alright. Talk to you later."

# Chapter

## <u>14</u>

Jim Frasier was momentarily startled when he heard the question. He had been anticipating it, but not this soon. As he picked up the mug of hot coffee and blew into the rising steam, he knew what he had to say.

"Well?" Michael asked again, waiting for an answer.

"We didn't include him because he had already left the company before Monica accepted the assignment," Jim simply answered, before bringing the cup back up to his mouth.

"Monica said he helped with the design of the Excalibur," Michael countered. "Did you know that he's dead?" Michael repeated what Monica told him last night.

"We found out right before Monica came in for her briefing, checked it out and found nothing suspicious about it. I didn't think it was necessary to include him, since it was too late for him to add any value to the investigation. What's important is for Monica to find out if there's a connection between the phone and the deaths of those people in the study."

With the skill of an Indy 500 driver, Jim seamlessly steered the conversation away from Dave Carter. The less said, the better. "We've already shortened the time we can spend on this case because we don't know when

Gerald Conti is going to make his next move. Did she say if she found out anything we could use?"

"Not yet," Michael answered. "She did say that Gerald Conti gave her a demonstration of the Excalibur. She also mentioned that Bayou City Wireless conducted its own testing of the equipment and sent the results in to the FCC. Apparently, the company had been approved years ago to conduct its own testing." Hissing through his nose, he added, "No doubt Bob McCormick had a hand in that."

"Let me know the minute she finds out anything." Jim abruptly ended the conversation. "I've got some important calls to make this morning, Mike. Do you mind?" He motioned for Michael to close the door when he left.

"Oh, sure," Michael said, staring back at his boss like a child who had just been dismissed.

Jim heard Michael's footsteps pause on the other side of the door once the young man had closed it. After a long silence, he heard him slowly walk away. Jim could tell Michael thought he was being evasive, but those were his orders. He shook his head and slowly picked up the phone.

"Michael just left." Jim cupped his hand over the receiver as he spoke into the phone. "He asked about Dave Carter."

"What'd you tell him?" the Attorney General asked, breathing heavily into the phone.

"What do you think I told him?" Jim shot back, unable to restrain his anger. "I don't like lying to him."

"It's necessary right now, Jim. We've discussed that. What about Monica? Is she suspicious?"

"Not yet. From what Michael says, she's just curious

as to why we didn't tell her about Carter from the beginning."

"Make sure he keeps her head clear. We don't want her tipping Conti off. We've gotten too far to have this case backfire now."

Before Jim could respond, the man on the other end had hung up the phone. No good-byes, no assurances, only a subtle warning—"Your ass is grass if this fails." Jim stood staring into space for a moment, as the information settled into his bones. Suddenly, a chill caterpillared up his spine.

"Right," Jim said, slamming the phone into its cradle. He hoped for all of their sakes he wasn't making a grave mistake that would put Monica's life in jeopardy.

* * *

MONICA WALKED OUT OF HER OFFICE and almost collided with Cameron in the hallway.

"Goodness!" Monica stumbled to keep her balance as Cameron caught her by the shoulders.

"You okay?" he asked, still holding onto her. "Should have sent a warning signal ahead of me to let you know I was coming."

"No big deal." Monica stepped back out of his grasp. The attraction she felt from his touch startled her. "I should pay more attention to where I'm going. What brings you to HQ?"

"I'm on my way to Bastrop," he said. "The NMS got a signal this morning that there was an unusually high rate of failure with one of the PCPs up there. I'm not sure what's causing it. It may just be a bad temperature sensor that's not getting enough cooling. Won't know for sure, until I check it out." He turned away, then pivoted around on one foot as if it was a spontaneous idea. "Thought you might like to go along, to get a first-eye view of what I was talking about yesterday."

Monica hesitated. "Let me think for a second, Cameron," she said, trying to see her day's agenda in her mind. At the same time, she noticed how handsome he looked dressed in charcoal pants, crisp white shirt with burgundy tie, and suspenders. "I'm doing an on-camera interview with Channel 13 at four o'clock this afternoon about the phones we're donating for the annual Muscular Dystrophy telethon. Would we make it back in time?"

He checked his watch.

"Let's see, it's eight-ten now. It's an hour and forty-five-minute drive to Bastrop. Depending upon the severity of the problem, it shouldn't take me more than an hour or so to assess the situation and then fix it." He saw her hesitate and flashed a winning, white-toothed smile. "After that, we could grab a bite to eat and be back here by three o'clock sharp. How's that?"

Monica's face twisted to the side in indecision. She didn't say anything.

Cameron put his right hand over his heart and held up his left palm. "I promise, I'm an excellent driver. You'll be in good hands."

Monica felt the corners of her mouth tugging into a smile. She considered the offer. This would be a great opportunity for her to see the town and find out something about the study.

"Okay," she finally relented, getting her purse. "Let me tell Suzanne I'm leaving."

"Great. I'll meet you on the first floor of the parking garage."

Fifteen minutes later, they were driving west on I-10 to Bastrop. Monica gazed out of the window of Cameron's Toyota Land Cruiser as they left the city limits. It was a hazy morning and the roads were damp from the storm the night before. For the first half hour, neither spoke. The only sounds in the car were the uninterrupted tunes that played on Sunny 99.1 FM radio station.

"How about some coffee?" Cameron said, breaking the silent spell.

"Sure. But, I wouldn't want to delay the trip by stopping to get some."

"Do me a favor." He grinned. "Grab that bag off the back seat for me."

Monica unbuckled her seat belt and reached around the side of her seat to get the plastic grocery bag. Placing it in her lap, she opened it up and found a large, metal thermos, two Styrofoam cups, spoons, and a zillion small packages of sugar.

"Are you always this prepared?" Monica laughed, unscrewing the top of the thermos.

"Always." He smiled confidently.

"You take sugar?" she asked, then realized from Cameron's broad grin that he'd found the question suggestive. "In your coffee, I mean."

"Nope. Straight black."

Monica handed him a cup and then poured some for herself.

"I didn't get a chance to ask you yesterday where you were from."

"Born and raised in Georgia."

"Let me guess. Spelman woman, right?"

"Wrong. University of Georgia. My parents couldn't afford the tuition at Spelman, so I went to UGA instead."

"Grew up right here in Houston, myself," Cameron offered, without waiting to be asked. "In the Cuney Homes projects in Third Ward. Right by Texas Southern University. You know where that is?"

"No. Don't think so."

"It looks a lot better now than when I lived there. My father died when I was eight. My mom raised me by herself."

"Must've been hard on you. Without a dad."

"Mom did the best she could on her wages as a cook at TSU, but it was never enough. I got my first job when I was eleven, pumping gas at a service station on the corner of Scott St. and N. MacGregor. The area was mostly Jewish back then, but, there were a few black doctors and lawyers who lived in the mansions on North and South MacGregor who stopped by once a week to get their cars serviced.

"Dr. Edward Parnell took a special interest in me. He was the first black surgeon I'd ever known. One day, he asked me what I wanted to be when I grew up. I told him I didn't know exactly, but that I liked to take things apart to learn how they worked, then put them back together again.

"Dr. Parnell told me, 'Son, what you want to be is an engineer and I'm going to help you.'"

"Sounds like he became a surrogate father to you," Monica interjected, encouraging him to continue talking.

"He did. He changed my life. I'd never heard of that title before, but from that day on, I had one goal: To be the best damn engineer, ever. And you know what? Dr. Parnell was true to his word. He took me under his wings and hired me to do odd jobs around his mansion on N. MacGregor. I was mesmerized. I'd never been inside a house so big."

"That had to be quite an experience."

"It was. Talk about synchronicity. Dr. Parnell had a passion for tinkering, too. He had a train set he'd built that occupied half of the second floor, and featured everything from caves to tunnels to bridges, the whole nine yards. He taught me everything about electrical circuits, power, and energy. I was in hog heaven. Together, we installed an alarm system throughout the house. We even built two-way radios. I became the child he and his wife never had."

"How nice."

"When I graduated high school, Dr. Parnell told me about Stanford University's Electrical Engineering Program and told me he'd pay my tuition on one condition: That I promised to study hard and make something out of myself. That's exactly what I've done."

Cameron didn't look at Monica when he'd finished his story. He stared at the road in front of him and remained silent.

Leaning her head against the headrest of the truck, she asked, "Where is Dr. Parnell now?"

"Died about a year ago." Cameron's tone became morose. "A massive heart attack. Mrs. Parnell is in a nursing home. I go by to see her once a week."

"And your mother?"

"Mama died while I was at Stanford," he said, sadly. "That's my only regret. She never got a chance to see how her son turned out."

Monica sighed and thought of her own mother. She understood all too well Cameron's last statement. She often wondered if Sarah would have been proud of the person her daughter had become.

"Enough about my life," Cameron said, his voice perking up. "What about yours?"

"Nothing as exciting as yours."

She told him the family history the Bureau had concocted for her.

"Do you visit them often?" Cameron asked, when she had finished.

"Couple of times a year."

"I take it you're not very close to your family?"

Monica threw him a quizzical look. "What makes you say that?"

"Just by the way you talk about them. You seem so detached."

It made Monica uncomfortable how blunt and astute Cameron was. When he looked at her, it was as if he could see the things she tried to keep hidden.

"It's just your imagination." She adjusted her body in the leather seat, giving him a look that said the personal talk was over. "I just don't like to talk about myself, that's all."

"Okay, I know when to back off." He suddenly smiled. "You just won't give a brother a break, will you?"

Monica laughed. His directness and humor reminded her of Michael. They rode in silence as they turned off I-10 onto 71 West.

"How much farther?" Monica asked, noticing for the first time that the flat farmland had turned hilly.

"Oh, about another thirty minutes or so."

"You know, Cameron, I was thinking that it would be great to include statements from some of the participants from the Excalibur focus group when we announce the product in our press conference and newsletters."

"It'd probably add a personal touch to our collateral

pieces."

"Exactly," Monica agreed. "I looked at the study results and was surprised that we didn't have any of their names or addresses. They were only identified by gender and numbers, like jurors in high-profile criminal trials being shielded from the media. Did you ever meet any of them?"

"Nope. Carter and I usually went to Bastrop at different times. Whenever we did go together, I was always too busy working on the sites to go with him to the meetings. Gerald can tell you who they are."

"That's just it. I asked him about it, and he didn't seem to like the idea. He said we didn't need their input. Frankly, I don't see a problem with it."

Cameron's disposition changed as he turned his head and looked straight at Monica.

"Let me give you some advice, Taylor," he said. "Don't get off on the wrong foot with Gerald. I told you yesterday, he's a tough dude. Whatever he says, goes. Victor's the only one who goes head-to-head with him."

"What's the harm?" she persisted. "I pulled out other brochures and newsletters of earlier product releases and they included testimonials. The Excalibur's hotter than anything the company's ever introduced. Why wouldn't Gerald want to use that leverage?"

Cameron was silent.

"Unless," Monica hesitated, "the study was not as positive as it appears."

Monica examined Cameron's face closely and saw him wrestling with his next words. His gaze never left hers, but she knew he was not totally looking at her. His eyes squinted slightly and the veins in his temples protruded from his hickory skin.

"I'm not saying I disagree with you, Taylor," he finally said.

Without realizing it, Monica leaned her body to the edge of her seat, hoping Cameron was about to reveal something important.

"Quite the contrary, I think using personal statements would have an impact. But," he continued, "Gerald calls the shots. It's his ship and he steers it into whatever waters he chooses."

"I thought Victor was the captain," Monica said, playing the devil's advocate. "Maybe, I should ask his opinion."

"Going around Gerald to Victor is the surest way to get yourself fired," Cameron warned. "They may be brothers, but there's fierce competition between them. Look, I may be talking too much here, but I like you. . ." He stopped as if he had to ponder his next words.

"And—"

"You'd better listen to what I'm saying. When I made the statement yesterday that I 'know how to play the game,' I wasn't kidding. If you want a future in this industry, you do your job and know the score. No matter what you see or hear, it's Gerald's way or the highway."

He turned his eyes back to the road in front of him and said, "So, as far as talking to the people in Bastrop, that's out."

Monica said with a sigh, "Guess I don't have much of a choice."

* * *

"JUST AS I SUSPECTED," CAMERON said to Monica, stepping inside the small personal communications point, or PCP, located in a fenced area behind the

Bastrop Fire Station on Chestnut. A green, eighty-foot stealth tower loomed in the background and blended in with the trees beside it. "It's too hot in here."

The windowless, prefabricated building was no bigger than a closet and was compacted with stacks of computer equipment. A low hum buzzed in the background as Monica watched Cameron adjust the temperature controls.

"This shouldn't take long at all." Cameron threw the remark over his shoulder, not looking back at Monica.

"Why did you choose this location for a PCP?" she asked innocently. "I sort of expected the site to be in a more isolated area."

"We have points all over the rural area." Cameron opened his canvas bag that contained his supplies. "But since we were testing a product locally, we needed a site that was centrally located. This was the most logical place since the station already had an existing tower for emergency management services. We worked out a deal with them that allowed us to tear down their old communications tower and reconstruct a taller, more durable one we could share with both fire and police radios."

"Oh?" Monica interjected, her ears peeled back.

"Bayou City Wireless financed the project, but, technically, the town owns it and leases the space to us. It was a deal that worked well for everyone." Cameron turned back to Monica. "Listen, you don't have to stand here while I do this. Why don't you look around town? Main Street is just a block up the street."

"You sure?" Monica lifted her eyebrow. She didn't want to seem too eager, but she was dying for a smoke anyhow.

He winked one eye and flicked his hand with a "I've-got-your-back-Sister," sign. "There are a lot of historical buildings and several specialty shops and restaurants. It's really interesting looking, gives you the impression that you've just stepped onto the set of an old Western movie."

"Okay. What time do you want me to meet you back here?"

"Tell you what. There's a place on Main Street that has great bar-b-que. The Bastrop Bar-B-Que & Meat Market. I can meet you there at eleven-thirty. That'll give me enough time to run several tests on the system and call back into the office and make sure everything's functioning properly. Sound good to you?"

"Great."

Downtown Bastrop looked exactly like Cameron had described it. Main Street was a narrow, two-way street that had angled parking spaces that practically led right up to the shop doors. Most of its historic buildings dated back to the mid-1800s to early 1900. Their sandstone fronts had been restored and were linked together like row houses commonly seen on the East Coast. A unique blend of the old and the new, the quaint town was snugly situated on the banks of the Colorado River and filled with loblolly pines neatly bunched together.

The once cloudy skies had cleared and the sun warmed the brisk morning air as Monica strolled through the shops, exchanging pleasantries with people she passed along the way. Looking into their weathered faces, she couldn't help but note they were probably friends or relatives of the mysterious participants in the study. She had already tried to reach the last three people on the list of names—the ones that had not been labeled dead. All to no avail. She hadn't been successful in reaching a single one. Two of them were in the hospital, and the third was out of the office. Frustrated, Monica abandoned all hopes of finding someone who could give her some information about the study.

After browsing through the Old Main Bookstore, Monica walked the few steps toward Chestnut Street to the two-story, brick Meat Market where she was to meet Cameron. She'd paused briefly to glance at a painting in the window of the art gallery next door, when, from her peripheral vision, came a familiar sight. She gasped as she turned and saw a man walking a Welsh Corgi with the same red-and-white coat and white paws as Sneakers. Smiling with delight, Monica walked toward the man and excitedly bent down to pet the little dog.

"I can't believe it!" she said, rubbing the dog's head as he scampered around her feet, tangling himself within his leash. "What's your name, little guy?" Realizing she was over-indulging herself with the dog and had not bothered acknowledging its owner, Monica stood up and introduced herself to the Caucasian man who was just a few inches taller than she was.

"I'm Taylor LeBlanc." She stuck out her hand. "I got so excited when I saw your Welsh Corgi, I completely forgot my manners."

The man shook it and smiled.

"No problem," he said in a low voice, his handshake weak. "It's nice to see someone who recognizes the breed. Not too many people around here do. I get asked a dozen times a month about him. His name's Patch."

"Patch," Monica repeated, looking down at the dog who appeared to be full grown, although he was smaller than Sneakers. "I have a friend who has a Corgi with the same coloring, even the white paws. His name is Sneakers."

As they engaged in conversation about their love for the sheep-herding dogs, Monica noticed the man had not offered his own name. His eyes were shielded by dark sunglasses worn under the bill of a baseball cap. Though there was a crispness in the morning air, it did not warrant the leather bomber jacket the man wore zipped up and snapped around his neck. His face was thin, his low cough gave Monica the impression that he was probably recovering from a cold.

"I can tell from your mid-Western accent," she remarked, "you're not a native Texan."

The man smiled and wiped his mouth with a handkerchief he retrieved from his coat pocket. "You've got a good ear. I'm originally from Nebraska. Came here a few years back to open a veterinary hospital. What about you? You don't sound like you're from Texas either."

"Georgia. Though I just recently accepted a new job in Houston."

The man said in a low tone, "I get that way quite often, these days. In fact, I'm going there this afternoon. Maybe, I'll bring Patch with me on one of my visits, so he and Sneakers can get acquainted."

"I'd like that." Monica whipped her business card from her purse. "Only Sneakers and my friend live out of state. But call me anyway. Here's my work number. Sneakers has a skin allergy that drives my friend—"

Monica stopped when she saw the man stare at the card she held out to him. In fact, he withdrew his hand as soon as he glanced at it. Looking back at her, his friendly demeanor changed like a day suddenly growing dark.

"It's time for Patch and me to leave," he said, tightening the dog leash around his wrist. "Nice talking to you."

"Wait. I didn't get your—" Monica didn't get the chance to finish her sentence. The man had already spun around and slowly ambled across the street, his steps carefully measured. Her business card still positioned between her fingers, she stood there looking after him, wondering what had made him leave so abruptly. Monica didn't see Cameron when he walked up beside her.

"I see you found your way around." Cameron still held his bag in his hand.

"Did you see the guy I was just talking to?" Monica asked, nodding to the man who was almost at the end of the street. "Over there with the dog."

Cameron looked to where she stared.

"I've seen him a few times. With Dave Carter, I think. Why?"

*So that's why he left in a hurry!* Monica thought to herself. *The company name on my card scared him off.* She realized then that he was probably the doctor on the list she had tried to reach earlier.

"It's nothing," she lied. "A friend of mine has the same breed of dog and I wanted to ask him where he got his."

"Funny-looking little thing, isn't it?" he laughed. "Ready to get something to eat? I'm famished."

Monica stood there for a moment, staring at the man as he turned the corner and disappeared from her view.

\* \* \*

AT EXACTLY THREE O'CLOCK, Monica stood in the doorway of her office. As she and Cameron said their goodbyes, they were both taken by surprise when they saw Gerald coming in their direction.

"There you are, Taylor." Eyeing them both suspiciously, Gerald's voice sounded like ice cubes clinking against each other. "I was just coming to see you. I trust you and Cameron have been putting your heads together on the Excalibur project."

Before Monica could speak up, Cameron answered for both of them.

"Absolutely, Gerald," he said, taking charge of the situation. "Taylor's a quick study. I think you're going to be pleased with the PR plans she's come up with."

Turning to Monica before leaving, he said, "Let me know if you need additional information. See you later, Gerald."

After Cameron walked away, Gerald followed Monica into her office and watched her as she put her purse beneath her desk.

"Well," he said, casually, "I see you've made a friend in Cameron."

"I hope so," she said coolly, matching his tone. "With all the work I've got to do, I could use all the friends I can find."

"I'd like to hear about those plans Cameron just mentioned. How about tomorrow afternoon? Two o'clock okay with you?"

Monica knew he was trying to trip her up and she was ready for him.

"Two o'clock's fine," she answered assuredly.

"Good. See you then."

When he left, Monica put her hands on her hips and shook her head. She didn't know if she was more angry at Cameron for putting her on the spot or at Gerald for calling their bluff. Just as she sat down to look over her notes, she heard the sound of Jazz's squeaky cart wheel and the brief exchange that passed between him and Gerald.

"Whew!" an exasperated Jazz said, as he came into Monica's office and plopped down in a chair opposite her desk. "What did you say to get him in a tizzy, girlfriend?" He tossed a hitch-hiker's thumb over his shoulder in the direction Gerald had gone.

"What do you mean?"

"His royal pain-in-the-ass looked supremely pissed when he left your office. I swear, that man has the personality of Dr. Jekyll and Mr. Hyde. One minute he's oozing with charm, the next he's downright nasty. Wanna know what he just said to me?"

"Really, Jazz," Monica started to protest. "I don't have time to—"

"He said," Jazz continued, as if he had not heard her, "that his mail was getting to his office too late in the morning and that I should locate his first, then deliver it to him before each of my runs. Do you know how much mail goes through this place everyday? He's crazy as hell. If he's not careful, Jazz may just decide to buy him an admission ticket to that nut house he gets so many letters from."

Monica had tuned out most of the conversation, but Jazz's last sentence got her attention.

"'Nut house'?" she asked, watching Jazz's lips curl up at the ends.

"I told you before, Jazz knows everything that goes on around here," he said, grinning like a Cheshire cat. Without waiting for her to ask him again, he leaned forward in his seat and lowered his voice.

"For the last several months, Gerald has been getting a lot of mail from this funny farm down in Hilton Head,

South Carolina."

Stretching his long neck around to see if anyone was within hearing distance of Monica's door, he turned back to her and whispered.

"I know the place because my mother's sister works for one of the resort hotels there. I visit her sometimes during the summer, when I take my vacation. Anyway, Gerald gets a letter from this sanitarium once a week. Not any of those advertising brochures with pretty pictures, but letter-size, hand-addressed envelopes. I didn't pay much attention to them when they first started coming. But when they started arriving every Wednesday morning, certified, and from the same doctor—his name is always on the return address—I figured Gerald and Victor had some kooky relative locked away there. Got another letter today. Who knows?" Jazz hunched his shoulders. "With his personality changes, I wouldn't be surprised if Gerald himself has a couch there with his name personally engraved right on the—"

"Taylor," Suzanne interrupted, startling both Jazz and Monica by her sudden appearance outside of Monica's doorway. "Mr. Davis from Channel 13 Eyewitness News is here to see ya."

"Geez, Suzanne!" Monica snapped, slamming her pen down on her desk. "Couldn't you have buzzed me first? Go out to the lobby and tell him I'll be right there."

"Uh . . . he's waitin' by my desk."

Monica cocked her head to the side and saw a male figure with pad and pencil in hand. To his right, was another man holding a television camera. "Well, offer him something to drink, Suzanne, and tell him I'll be right out."

Monica was almost seething when the secretary left the room. The woman's timing could not have been worse. "Damn," Monica said. "Is she always so ditzy?"

"Twenty-four seven," Jazz chuckled. "Everything in that little brain of hers could fit on the head of a stick pin."

He then flashed a devilish grin and whispered to Monica before leaving, "You know, I think I'll check to see if I can get a group rate for Suzanne and Gerald in Hilton Head."

Monica was not amused. Her radar was locked onto what Jazz had said before Suzanne's interruption and wouldn't let go. Now, she'd have to wait until after her meeting to figure out just what it was that bothered her.

"Damn!" Monica whispered again before composing herself, as she walked out of the office.

* * *

THE MAN WATCHED with considerable interest as the pretty woman spoke into the camera. His nurse at M.D. Anderson Cancer Center had just turned on the television when the 6 p.m. news segment came on about Bayou City Wireless's donation of phones to the Muscular Dystrophy Association. He became disgusted when the reporter talked about the company being a pillar in society, coming to the rescue of various Houston charities with its donations of cash and use of wireless phones. With every ounce of energy he had, he fought to keep his blood pressure from rising to the cuticles of what little hair he had left on his head. This was his last chemotherapy treatment and he didn't need the aggravation to prolong his stay.

His eyes became transfixed on the now familiar face that suddenly reappeared on the television. The audio was low, the woman's words of no importance to him. What he saw on the screen was more important than any sound uttered from her lips. He squinted to get a better focus of her face. There was something different about her, so unlike the others he'd known. When her name appeared on the bottom of the screen, he struggled with a shaking hand to reach the small pad and pencil on the table beside his bed.

He repeated the name over and over in a whisper, so it would not slip from the shallowness of his mind, until at last, he'd written out the one name that was his last hope.

Exhausted, he let his scrawny body sink back into the bed and closed his eyes. When he opened them again, he turned his head and watched the chemotherapy drip slowly into the IV needle leading into his vein. Before drifting off to sleep, he whispered the name again. *Taylor LeBlanc.*

# Chapter

## 15

The taxi pulled up to the curb of Manny's, a brightly lit night club in Montrose, and slowed to a halt. The stunningly-dressed woman inside reached over the front seat, handed the driver a ten-dollar bill, and told him to keep the change. She could hear the jazz music and feel its vibration beneath her sling-back pumps, as soon as she stepped out of the cab and stood within a couple of feet from the entrance.

The night air felt cool upon her bare shoulders. Tilting her chin upward and shaking the blond strands from her eyes, the woman sauntered through the front door, the short gold lame dress hugging every curve in her body like a peel on an orange.

The club was crowded for a week night, Monica thought, as she glided her sleek legs through the maze of bodies. Gratefully, none of the faces looked familiar.

With the music blaring above the muffled conversations, she claimed a seat at the bar and ordered a Jack and coke.

"Here ya go, doll," the bartender said, setting a glass down on the counter in front of her.

"Merci," Monica replied with a seductive smile. Holding her head at a Lauren Bacall angle, she whipped out a cigarette from her small, gold clutch purse. On cue, the bartender drew a lighter from his pocket and leaned over the bar. Cupping one hand around his, she lit the tip of the cigarette on the flame and exhaled a long stream of smoke.

"You're new around here, aren't ya, doll?" The bartender studied her.

"Mais, oui. From France." Monica smiled inwardly at her heavy French accent.

She spoke three foreign languages and had a natural knack for them. Gracefully, she extended her hand to introduce herself.

"I'm Dominique. Dominique Deflore." He shook her hand and held it a nano-second longer than Monica would have liked.

"Sam Davis."

Without a word, she gently slid her hand from his.

"Ah . . ." She flashed a knowing smile, pointing her cigarette at him. "Like Sammy Davis, Jr., the great American singer."

The bartender laughed at the comparison. "Something like that. Listen, doll, need anything else, just raise ya glass."

"Merci." Monica smiled as she watched him move to the other end of the bar. She shook her head and felt the weight of the long, platinum blond wig she wore bounce against the back of her neck. The shimmery reflection of the dangling gold earrings bounced off the mirror behind the bar and drew Monica's attention to it. She stared at the long, fake eyelashes layered with black mascara, which lay like individual fans against her eyes.

Her eyelids were exaggerated with dark eye shadow. An abundance of burgundy blush outlined her high cheekbones and matched the shade painted on her lips.

She smiled to herself and wondered what Cameron would think of her—dressed like a call-girl in a pick-up bar.

The thought of Cameron jolted her back to reality. Ever since they'd returned from Bastrop earlier in the day, he invaded Monica's thoughts when she least expected it. She couldn't push him from her mind, though she wasn't really sure she wanted to, and that frustrated her. Annoyed with herself, Monica reached for another cigarette and accidentally knocked her purse to the floor. As she slid from the barstool and reached down for it, she heard a woman's deep voice behind her.

"I told you about bending over like that, girlfriend," the deep, sexy voice said to her.

Monica froze in her crouched position for a few seconds, then stood up and turned around in the direction of the comment. *It's about time.*

"Pardon?" She stared into the face of a gorgeous young woman, elegantly dressed from head to toe. The woman flashed a brilliant smile, her pearly white teeth sparkling like diamonds.

"You don't fool me one bit," the woman said, wagging her finger. "I'd know that delicious body a mile away. Though, I must say, that French accent is good."

"There must be some mistake." Monica avoided the woman's gaze as she watched the stunning beauty slide onto the bar stool next to her.

"No way, girlfriend." The woman threw her head back and gave a throaty laugh. Then dropping her voice an octave lower, she added, "Jazz never makes mistakes like this, *Miss Taylor LeBlanc.*"

Monica snapped her head around and pretended to scrutinize the flawlessly made-up face. Beneath the perfectly-blended foundation, the carefully shaded brown eyes, crimson lips, and a head full of glorious long black curls, Monica saw a hint of recognition. When Jazz winked in satisfaction, Monica's eyes feigned surprise.

"Jazz!" she exclaimed, as her new co-worker shook his head slowly in the affirmative. They both burst into a fit of laughter. When they finally got control of themselves, Monica was the first to speak.

"Okay, Jazz. You got me."

"Sh-h!" He spoke in a hushed voice, with a finger to his lips. "In here, I'm Jazmeen." Looking around the room, he eyed a small table in the corner. He motioned to Monica with a crooked finger. "Get your drink and let's move someplace more private."

When they were seated, Jazz took a sip of his gin and tonic, and stared at Monica. "I knew there was something about you I liked from the moment we met," he said, rhythmically stirring his drink to the beat of the music.

"What's that?" Monica reared her head back, as if surprised by the question.

"In a way, you're just like me."

"Oh?"

"Look at us. You're dressed like a Parisian harlot and I'm in drag. I spotted you when I first got here." He gulped down another sip of his drink. "Drawn to that exquisite dress like a moth to a flame. Versace, right?" Monica nodded her head.

"I knew it was, girlfriend." Jazz looked as though he marveled at her transformation. "He has fabulous designs. It wasn't until you bent over that I knew for sure it was you."

Monica tilted her head to the side, but didn't say anything.

"Your ass is a dead giveaway. The only reason I

revealed myself to you is because I realized I wasn't the only one with something to hide."

Monica chuckled at his deduction and wondered if Jazz had any idea how right he really was. She felt satisfied with herself tonight at her success in finally locating him. That had been her plan when she'd called Michael earlier in the day and asked him to run a check on Jazz. Time was crucial to her investigation and she wasn't about to leave her next discussion with Jazz to chance. When Michael had called back and told her that Jazz sometimes cruised the club scene dressed as a woman, Monica had created Dominique. Three bars in just as many hours, she finally found him.

"Why do you do it, Jazz?" Monica knew she was only half playing the part, because the other half of her really wanted to know his answer. "Dress like a woman, I mean?"

Jazz shrugged his shoulders and tightened the chiffon pashmina that concealed his Adam's apple. His facial expression suddenly turned sad.

"It started out as a game, you know, to test my designs." He turned his palms up facing the ceiling, staring into his glass. "I'm an unknown in the fashion world and I thought if I could get the reaction of other women who saw my creations, I could get a feel for what they really wanted in evening wear. What I hadn't counted on was all the attention that I'd get from other men." He then looked up and stared into Monica's eyes.

"I feel good about myself when I'm Jazmeen, Taylor." His eyes burned through her like the sun scorching paper through a magnifying glass. "I'm beautiful and the men love me. They wait on me, treat me like a piece of fine porcelain."

Jazz let out a deep sigh. "Don't get me wrong—I don't go around dressing like this to pick them up. Hell, I can do that as Jazz. It's just that the people I meet when I'm Jazmeen treat me better than they do when I'm Jazz, and I like how that makes me feel."

Monica lowered her eyes and took a sip of her drink to force down the lump that had grown in her throat. She understood only too well Jazz's questioning of self-worth when he was out of character, because, sometimes, she felt the same way when she came off an assignment or completed a book she'd written. She was more confident, more willing to expose herself as her alter egos, than she ever could be in real life.

"I understand, Jazz," Monica finally said, after they had been silent for too long. "I feel that way too, sometimes. Tell you what." She cheerfully raised her glass in the air. "You keep my secret, I'll keep yours."

Jazz looked up and smiled. Raising his glass, he clinked it against hers. "Deal. Wouldn't the guys at the office be shocked if they could see us now?"

"Speaking of the office, Jazz," Monica ventured slowly, glad that he'd brought the conversation around to Bayou City Wireless, "you said something today that got me kind of curious. Remember telling me about the letters Gerald gets from Hilton Head?"

Jazz nodded.

"Why do you suppose Dr.—"

"Dr. Blackburn."

"Blackburn." Monica repeated the name as though Jazz had mentioned it before. "Why do you think Dr. Blackburn keeps writing Gerald each week?"

"Beats me, honey." Jazz shrugged his shoulders again. "Like I said before, maybe Gerald and Victor have a looney relative stashed away or something."

"I guess you could be right." Monica rested her chin on her palm, thoughtfully. "Though, I wonder why Gerald would risk people finding out about his connection to the institution by having the letters sent to the office."

"No one sees them, but me." Jazz sounded certain. "When they come in, I take them straight to Gerald. He issued that order months ago when they first started coming in. It's one of those nice-looking nut houses, really."

"Really?"

Jazz nodded. "Even has a small, lush green golf course on the grounds and everything. Ever hear of crazy people playing golf? Unless you knew about Port Royal Meadows—like I did when I saw the letters— you'd never know what it was."

*Port Royal Meadows*, Monica thought to herself, filing the name away.

"Bayou City Wireless seems like a crazy house, sometimes." Monica chuckled. "I can't seem to get anyone to tell me about that product study in Bastrop."

She looked off to the side, but caught Jazz's image out of the corner of her eyes. If he knew about the sanitarium, maybe he knew something about the study.

"Ah, yes. The secret weapon. That was Carter's territory."

"So I've heard. Early stages of Alzheimer's forced him to resign, right?"

"That's what they said. Don't believe a word of it, myself."

"Really? Why not?"

"Because I knew Carter pretty well." Noticing Monica's arched eyebrow, he quickly added, "I don't mean like *that.* We were friends. He was the only one of the high-level executives who didn't act like I disgusted him. I don't believe for one minute he had Alzheimer's."

When he became silent, Monica gave him a little push. "Go on."

"He was a technical person. Technical people are always a little off-beat. But, a lot of what he said made sense and that's what always bothered the other Bozos."

"Bozos?"

"The other vice presidents. He told me that one evening before he left. I'd walked past his office at the end of the day and saw him staring at a large diagram spread across his desk."

"Then what happened?"

"He then looked up at me with a hollow expression and didn't say anything at all. He looked kind of sad, like he was upset about something. He told me to come on in and visit for awhile."

"Had he done that before?"

"We usually shot the breeze during the day whenever I delivered his mail, so his invitation to come into his office was not unusual. When I sat down, I could smell the faint scent of Tangeray on Carter's breath, me being a gin man, myself. He'd been at it for awhile because his speech was a little slurred.

"Anyway, he asked me how I liked working for the company, if I liked my job and all. I was caught off guard by the formality of the conversation, thought maybe someone had complained about me so I told him every-thing was cool. He then asked me what I thought about the products the company was selling."

"What did you say?" Monica waved her hand and gave Jazz a look, which implied that he had all the juice on everyone.

Jazz perked up. "I made a joke and said something like I thought they provided a more entertaining option to sitting in traffic and shooting the finger out the window at the idiot in front of me who'd just let the eighteen-wheeler in front of him. He usually laughed at my jokes. This time he didn't. He just pointed to the diagram and asked me if I ever wondered how much power was in one of 'these little guys.'"

"What was it?" Monica interrupted.

"Beats me. Some kind of wireless phone. Not that I could tell by the drawings because they were upside down with pieces of equipment scattered all over the page in different stages of development: the antenna in one place with math equations like we learned in high school and the body of the phone in other places."

"And?"

"The name Excalibur was written across the top of the page. Anyway, I looked at the paper, shrugged my shoulders again and waited to see where Carter was going with the conversation. He then babbled on about the unknown dangers with increased frequency levels, antennas, and something about a ratio of a thousand-to-one."

Jazz polished off the last of his drink.

"I didn't know what the hell he was talking about. But he got my attention when he said that they would kill him to make sure no one ever found out about it."

"Who is 'they'?"

"That's what I asked him. He seemed sort of paranoid to me."

"And?"

"Carter just gave me a dark, sad smile and took a

drink from his coffee cup. When he finally spoke, he told me to pay no attention to the rambling of an old engineer, delving into the mystics of modern technology. He then pulled the bottle of Tangeray out of his desk drawer and told me to close the door on my way out. I stared at him for a few moments more, then finally walked out, closing the door behind me."

Jazz looked back over his shoulder. He trembled, as he held on to both of his elbows. "Girlfriend, I stood outside of his office scared shitless. I mean I was as white as Casper. I had planned to ask him about it the next day, but when I saw Carter again, he acted like the conversation never took place. The next week, Gerald's secretary gave me the memo to circulate to the employees about Carter leaving the company."

"Did you ever find out what Carter was talking about?"

Jazz shook his head. "Nope. But, believe me, after that weird conversation, I'm content with listening to the radio when I'm stuck in traffic."

Monica lit another cigarette and propped her elbow on the table.

"Jazz . . ." She blew smoke out the corners of her mouth. "Tell me about Port Royal Meadows."

# Chapter

## 16

"Mr. Peters just got in, Taylor," Suzanne whispered into Monica's office. Monica had been waiting all morning for Larry Peters to return from his appointment outside of the office.

"Thanks, Suzanne." Monica pushed her paperwork aside to concentrate on the approach she'd take when talking to the man who did not engage in idle conversation like the other employees.

Monica pushed her chair back and walked out of her office. Turning the corner that led to Peters's office, she stood in the doorway and watched him as he stood behind his desk, unpacking his briefcase.

After knocking lightly on the door, she stuck her head inside. "Hey, Larry. Got a few minutes?" she said cheerfully.

"Can't it wait until this afternoon, Taylor?" He never looked up, as he took some papers from the briefcase and filed them into his cabinet. "I just got in and I need to salvage some of the morning."

"Gerald wanted me to get with you this morning to go over your marketing strategy for the Excalibur," Monica lied, knowing Peters would never double-check with their boss.

Peters looked at her for a beat of a second, then

snapped his briefcase shut and waved a hand for her to come in. "Okay." He sat down behind his desk and folded his arms.

Monica slid into a chair across from his desk. "What's the next step after the press conference?"

Peters cleared his throat. "We'll run several 'teasers' in the *Houston Chronicle* everyday the week before the press conference. After the announcement, we'll run two, full-page ads on Wednesday and Sunday, half-page ads the other days. We'll have a four-week flight with twelve, thirty-second slots per day on cable and the national networks, with our heaviest impact during prime time and the news lead-ins." His voice droned on. "There will also be thirty-second segments on five radio stations, as well as billboards strategically selected throughout the city and Internet advertising.

"My people are working on the collateral pieces, which will include brochures and fact sheets. That's about it." He looked at her matter-of-factly and waited for a response.

Monica bit the inside of her jaw to keep from laughing. Peters had rattled off everything like a robot who'd been programmed to speak on command. It took less than thirty seconds.

"Wow." She almost giggled. "You sure have everything already figured out. Dave Carter must have left some heliuva 'notes'."

"Hardly." He chuckled for the first time since Monica had met him. "If you can call that mumbo-jumbo stuff he wrote 'notes.'"

"That bad, huh?" She smiled along with him.

"Most of his old files were either sent to storage or destroyed after he left because they were undecipherable. Couldn't make heads nor tails out of what I did happen to come across, so I passed them on to Victor." Looking back down at the stack of papers on his desk, he said to Monica. "If that's all, Taylor, I need to get back to my work. I'm behind as it is."

"Sure, Larry." She walked toward the door, then turned back around. "Oh, I almost forgot. Do you have head shots of senior staff? I may need to use them in my publicity packets."

Peters pulled open the drawer on the side of his desk, fingered through the files, pulled out a large white envelope, and handed it to Monica. "Keep it. I'll get it back later."

* * *

"WHAT'CHA LOOKIN' AT, TAYLOR?" Suzanne asked, leaning forward on Monica's desk.

"Photos of senior staff. I'm thinking of using a few of them with some of the press releases." Monica sighed, tossing the stack of photos on her desk in frustration. She had hoped there would be one of Dave Carter in the pile. There wasn't.

Suzanne picked up the picture of Larry Peters and giggled. "He looks like such a dork, doesn't he?" She turned the picture around for Monica to see. Suppressing a laugh, Monica agreed.

"Dave Carter took a great picture," Suzanne continued, still staring at the black and white photo of Peters. "He was so handsome."

Monica looked at her. She kept her tone casual. "What'd he look like?"

"Oh, tall and blond with blue eyes like Robert Redford. Had a great body—big shoulders, small waist, sort of like a football player." Suzanne's eyes lit up. "He lifted weights and jogged every mornin' before coming to work. He had a neat smile. Had a little strawberry mole on his forehead I thought was kinda cute." She then grinned at Monica. "Wanna see a picture of him?"

"You got one?" Monica was genuinely surprised.

"Kept an extra one when we had them made. I was crazy about him, but never told him. I knew he wouldn't gimme the time of day. Hold on a minute. I'll be right back."

*Well I'll be damned,* Monica thought to herself, with a grin. When the secretary returned with the photo, Monica studied it carefully. She took special note of the strawberry birthmark on Dave Carter's forehead. *The girl's finally come in handy for something.*

\* \* \*

THE TELEPHONE RANG ON MONICA'S desk just as she returned from her afternoon meeting with Gerald. She held her breath before picking it up, hoping he wasn't calling her back for additional information. When she glanced at the phone and saw the display indicating an outside call, she let out a sigh of relief and picked it up.

"This is Taylor."

"Is this Taylor LeBlanc?" the man said on the other end in a low, raspy voice.

"It is. May I help you?" Monica strained to hear past the heavy breathing, wondering whether it was a crank call.

"You don't know me, but I talked with you briefly the other day in front of the market." The man spoke with difficulty. "My name is John Smith. I really need to speak with you. Could you meet—"

*The market?* Suddenly, Monica's mind shot to the man with the Welsh Corgi in Bastrop. Remembering the recording device she'd discovered on her phone the first day she'd arrived at the company, Monica grabbed a pencil and interrupted the man's speech. "I'm sorry, Mr. Smith, I can hardly hear you. If you'll give me your phone number, I'll call you right back."

"No! I must see—"

"Mr. Smith—" Monica's voice was urgent—"I can barely hear you. Give me a number where I can reach you and I promise I'll call you right back." She was aware of the passing seconds. Wherever he was, she didn't want him hanging on the line long enough for the call to be traced.

"I'll only wait ten minutes. The number is . . ."

Exactly four minutes later, after she'd hurried to the pay phone in the snack bar in the basement, Monica dialed the number Mr. Smith had given her.

When the same raspy voice answered on the first ring, her heart ka-thumped. "Mr. Smith?"

"Glad you called back, Ms. LeBlanc."

"Sorry about the interruption. My phone's had a lot of static all day. I had to move to another line."

"I understand." His voice sounded weak. "Ms. LeBlanc, could you meet me this afternoon? Now, if it's possible."

"What's this about, Mr. Smith? My schedule's full for the rest of the day."

"Not on the phone. I'm going back to Bastrop this evening. I must talk to you before I leave. Please, Ms. LeBlanc. It's very important."

Monica glanced at her watch. It was three twenty-five. "Tell me where you are."

# Chapter

# 17

"Taylor got a suspicious call from a man identifying himself as John Smith," Arthur said, short of breath. Security had alerted him to the call just as it was being completed. He rushed right over as soon as he listened to the tape.

"John Smith?" Gerald asked, snapping his head up at Arthur.

Arthur told Gerald what he had heard on the tape. The conversation only lasted a few seconds and there was no time to trace the call.

Gerald's temples began to throb. "Was there a problem with her phone?"

"No. Clear as a bell. It was as if she intentionally shut him up before he could say anything."

"Dammit! Local or out of town?"

"Here in Houston."

"Did she call him back?"

"The guys just finished checking the tapes. If she did, she didn't use one of the phones on the network. She was gone from her office by the time I got there. Her secretary said she'd left for a meeting at the *Chronicle*."

Gerald walked over to the window in his office and began pulling on his mustache. He didn't need this crap, things were going too well for him to be haunted by the past.

"Do you think it was one of *them?*" Gerald sounded eerily calm.

"I don't know." Arthur shook his head and took a seat. "Could be. The man's voice sounded weak and frail."

Neither of the two men spoke for awhile. Arthur crossed his right leg over his left, nervously bouncing his foot.

"What do you want me to do about it, Gerald?"

"Find out which one of the Bastrop people was in Houston today. That shouldn't be so hard. The last report said that the remaining three were near death." Gerald cracked his knuckles, as he paced the floor. "Of course, that was a few weeks ago. Apparently, one of them has made a miraculous recovery. Temporarily, that is."

Gerald stopped pacing for a moment. "As for Taylor," he added as an afterthought, "keep an eye on her. From now on out, I want to know every phone call she makes or receives."

* * *

MONICA WALKED INTO the McDonald's across from St. Luke's Episcopal Hospital in Houston's world-renowned medical center, and immediately scanned the room as she approached the take-out counter and ordered a small coffee. Hearing her name called out in a low voice from across the room, she turned her head slightly to the right and saw a man sitting in a booth, staring at her from beneath the front of a Houston Astros baseball cap. His face looked more gaunt and thin than Monica remembered, his eyes the size of golf balls. His body appeared scrawny in the baggy clothes that Monica suspected had once fit him properly. She paid for her coffee and walked to where he sat.

"Mr. Smith?" she asked.

He nodded. "Sit, Ms. LeBlanc," he said slowly. "Thank you for coming so quickly."

"Please, call me Taylor. You said it was an emergency, Mr. Smith, though I'm a little curious as to why you didn't talk to me when I saw you the other day."

"My real name is Jack Stevenson. I panicked when I saw the Bayou City Wireless name on your business card. Didn't know what to say at the time. I realize now that I have no choice. I must talk with you before it's too late. I promise not to waste too much of your time."

Monica stared at him and nodded her head. "Go ahead. I'm listening."

Jack Stevenson took a deep breath and released it slowly. "I was one of the participants in a focus group your company conducted several years ago. You know about the Bastrop Group?"

"I'm familiar with it, but that study concluded before I came to work for the company."

"There were twenty-eight of us in the group." His face grimaced as if he was in pain. He struggled for breath. "I'm the only one left."

"I don't understand."

"What I'm trying to tell you, Taylor, is those phones we tested have already killed twenty-seven people— well, twenty-five, at least. Two others are hospitalized in comas and aren't expected to recover. I'm the last surviving member and I don't have much longer to live."

Monica wanted to blurt out the hundreds of questions that had accumulated in her mind since she'd first heard of the case. "Mr. Stevenson—"

"Jack."

"Jack, what you're saying is impossible." Monica hated sparring with him on something so serious. "There's no scientific—"

"That's what the FCC Chairman said when I confronted him. So did your company president. But I know differently. Nobody believed me when I said the phones were dangerous, except Dave Carter. We kept in touch, then, all of a sudden, I didn't hear from him again."

"He died. Last month."

"That's what his secretary said, the last time I called. He knew something was wrong with the phones. People in the group complained of headaches, dizziness, and earaches about a year into the tests. About the same time, a new oil company came to Bastrop. Purchased some land, started developing"

Jack Stevenson began to cough uncontrollably. Monica rushed to get him some water.

"Are you okay? Should I call someone for you?" she asked when she returned with half a cup of water. *Please, Lord, don't let him die*, she prayed. She was afraid he needed medical attention.

"No! No!" he insisted, trying to catch his breath after taking a sip of water. "Need to finish . . ." He took another swallow of water and struggled to continue his story between labored breaths.

"Whole town blamed both oil company and a nearby chemical plant. . . for its medical problems. EPA did a full-blown . . . investigation. Nothing. Townspeople. . . didn't believe it. Lawsuits were filed. People from the study . . . increasingly became ill . . . some died . . . didn't connect phones with health problems . . . "

The paroxysms which wracked his emaciated body

left him so short of breath, he had to hold on to the table as he spoke. He wheezed between every few words.

"We were innocent victims . . . previous cellular customers . . . they put us in four groups. First, farmers. Second and third—doctors, lawyers from Bastrop, Smithville, and La Grange. Last group . . . housewives and a couple of college kids—who drove to Austin daily to attend classes at UT."

"What did they tell you all about the phones?"

"We could use them, whenever we wanted. Long as we wanted. Even long distance. No restrictions."

"What happened?"

"Like children loose in a toy store. Used phones whenever . . . no matter where we were. Some logged as many as five hours a day. The two college kids talked nonstop from Bastrop to Austin—a forty-five-minute trip one way. Same thing on the trip home."

"You were grouped with the doctors and lawyers?"

"Yes. Only veterinarian. Traveled all over the county to treat sick animals." He shook his head ruefully. "At first . . . the phone was a blessing. Allowed me to keep up-to-date on veterinary medicine with researchers at Texas A&M in College Station. Couldn't have afforded it, otherwise."

Monica nodded, encouraging him to go on.

"Ignored initial symptoms, dismissed them as overreacting. Just like everyone else. Longer I talked, hotter the phone became, flush against my head. Got dizzy . . . Soon, headaches—which initially lasted an hour or two—continued . . . No relief. Pain medication didn't help."

Once again he had to stop talking in order to reserve his strength. He held up his index finger in a "Hold up" signal.

169

"Another sip?" Monica lifted his cup. When he nodded his head, she held the cup to his lips.

"One day, Dave came up to Bastrop. Invited him to my house for dinner. We'd become friends. Trusted him enough to finally tell him of my suspicions. He gave me Patch . . . said he was too busy to take proper care of him. That evening, showed Dave X-rays I'd just gotten. Brain tumor above my right temporal bone. Exact spot where phone antenna rested against my head when I used it."

He paused and then slowly removed his cap. Nothing prepared Monica for what she saw. Holding her hand over her mouth, she gasped at the hideous scar that started at the top of the right side of his head and curved around the eyebrow and back behind his right ear. The whole area was a deep, bluish red that had not yet completely healed. She closed her eyes as Jack Stevenson put his cap back on. She kept her eyelids squeezed tight, listening to his voice drone on.

"Other participants . . . same diagnosis. None considered my theory . . . connection between their illnesses and the wireless phones. Too busy filing a lawsuit against the chemical plant and oil company. By the time cases went to court, several of the people had already died." He paused again. "Lost both cases. Too late for another witch hunt against Bayou City Wireless."

"You said Dave knew about the phones being dangerous. How?"

"Epidemiologist at M.D. Anderson Cancer Center. The man had done testing on the effects of electromagnetic rays on humans. Not specifically with wireless phones. Dave pretended he was writing a paper. Gave Dave a copy of the proposal from the scientific group studying cancer/wireless phones. Group was funded by the wireless industry. Contained medical conditions that could evolve from long-term use of radio-frequency radiation. Some of them were the same diagnosis made of my condition.

"Last time I heard from Dave, he believed people at the company were on to him. Told me to use the name John Smith . . . for my own protection. Only called when I was in Houston. He thought his phone was bugged. Said he was going to check on the frequency, power levels of the system. Never heard from him again."

Jack Stevenson stopped talking again to drink some more water. He let out a light snort and Monica noticed a smirk on his face.

"Dave used to joke . . . people were going to think we were both crazy—if our theory ever came out. No way we could convince millions of people those phones were dangerous. Used to laugh about adjoining rooms in an asylum . . . ."

Monica's mind began to race.

*Nut house . . .*

*Gerald . . . mail . . . a sanitarium. . .*

*Port Royal Meadows.*

*Dave Carter's sudden departure.*

*He couldn't be . . . Is it possible?*

"Jack . . ." Monica opened her eyes, wishing she could will away the horrible truth she'd uncovered. "I don't know what to say. What do you expect from me?"

"The truth. No time for another investigation . . . only a few weeks to live."

"Why me?" She put both hands on the side of her head as if its weight was too heavy to hold on her neck. "I'm new to the company. Why haven't you contacted someone else?"

"Dave told me once, when he feared something might happen to him . . . keep looking for another opportunity. Knew there'd be someone else to trust. Last night, I watched you on the news. Saw something different in your eyes . . . not power and greed. Genuine concern for children with Muscular Dystrophy. Saw it in Bastrop, too, when you talked about your friend's dog . . . See compassion right now." He lowered his eyes, then whispered. "Take a good look at me, Taylor. I'm only forty-three years old. After I'm gone, no one else left. Bayou City Wireless will get away with their crimes. Find out what happened to me . . . and the others."

Jack Stevenson looked at that moment as if he were at least ten years older than he'd just confessed. Monica took in a deep breath and slowly exhaled it.

"Don't you have any family, Jack?" Her tone was gentle. "Someone to take care of you?"

He shook his head. "A sister, back in Nebraska. . . divorced with two little boys. She can barely make ends meet. Don't want to worry her."

Monica took her business card from her purse, wrote on the back, and this time, pressed it firmly in his hand. "That's my home number. If you need to get in touch with me for any reason, call me there. If my machine picks up, say you're the mechanic calling with estimates for my car. Leave a number where I can reach you. Now, give me your home number."

After she put the napkin with his number securely in her purse, Monica reached across the table, took his bony fragile hands in hers, and stared deeply into his eyes. "I don't know what I can find out for you. But, believe this: If Bayou City Wireless is responsible in any way for your illness or the deaths of the other people in your

group, I'll make damn sure the company is held account-
able."

# Chapter

# 18

The ringing of the doorbell jolted Cameron out of his sleep. The relentless shrill echoed throughout the house.

"Hold on! Hold on!" he yelled, tightening the belt to his robe, before swinging the front door open to find Taylor standing on the other side.

"This is one part of your road-to-success story you neglected to tell me," she said, brushing past him as she looked around the spacious mansion. "I did a double take at the street address to make sure I had the right house."

"What are you doing here?" Embarrassment plastered his face.

"Sorry to barge in, Cameron, but I need to talk to you."

Making an attempt to explain his luxurious quarters, he fanned his hand languidly. "I didn't tell you Dr. Parnell left me the house in his will because I was afraid it would run you away. I had a hard enough time getting you to talk to me at all about anything other than business."

He looked at her as if he were the one who had just invaded her space.

Monica grinned. "Relax, Cameron. I'm not here to harass you about your humble abode. Although I was shocked as hell when I turned into your driveway."

The stately house on the corner of N. MacGregor and Burkette was at least fifty years old and over five thousand square feet.

"Mind if I fix myself a drink?" She eyed the bar in the corner of the room.

"Help yourself. I'm going to go change and then join you. The ice is in the fridge."

Monica noticed for the first time, he was barefooted and wearing a bathrobe, which exposed his woolly chest.

"Do you always go to bed this early on a Friday night?" Blushing, she glanced at her watch. It was a quarter after nine.

"I fell asleep on the couch after I came in from the gym. Didn't see any reason to get up, since I didn't have plans for tonight."

"Sorry." Monica pulled out a bottle of bourbon. Looking at the label, she said under her breath, "Well, well, Mr. Jack Daniels. You and I keep meeting up in the strangest places."

Monica poured some into a crystal glass—straight— and took a cigarette from her purse. "Mind if I smoke?" she yelled out to Cameron, looking around the impeccably clean room for an ashtray. The entertainment center was impressive, complete with a large screen television and two VCRs.

A few seconds later, returning to the living room dressed in gym shorts and a sweatshirt, Cameron gave her an odd look. "I didn't know you smoked." He brought Monica an ashtray, leaned over to light her cigarette with a book of matches from his collection in a glass dish, then took a seat at the other end of the oyster-colored leather sofa.

"Yeah . . . well, there're a lot of things about me you don't know."

"Apparently. I called you several times today, but never managed to catch you in your office. I can see you're in a great mood. How'd you find out where I lived?"

"That's not important. What matters is what I need to ask you."

"Shoot."

Monica took a long drag from her cigarette and released the smoke in one long stream. "Do you think there's a possibility Dave Carter is still alive?"

His eyes widened in surprise. "What did you put in your glass?"

"I'm not drunk, yet. But I'm getting there fast. Now answer the question."

"Why would you ask me something like that? You know he's dead. I told you that the first day you came to my office."

"You and everybody else." Monica bounded from the sofa and paced the floor, bourbon in one hand, cigarette in the other. She gritted her teeth. "Now I'm going to tell you a few things."

She told him what she knew about the Bastrop Study and her talk with Jack Stevenson. When she finished, Cameron was speechless. Walking over to the bar, he grabbed another glass and the bottle of Jack Daniels. He poured some in each of their glasses. Cameron swallowed hard and then locked eyes with Monica.

She didn't bat an eye.

"How do you know all this?" His voice sounded like gravel rubbing together. "You told me you couldn't find out anything about the study."

"I lied. I wanted to see if you knew what actually happened. But, I can assure you now, all of what I've just told you is the truth."

"I don't know, Taylor." He wiped his face with his hand. "There's got to be another explanation for those deaths. It could be just a coincidence that—"

"Jack Stevenson is not a coincidence," she broke in. "He's a real person who is definitely ill. Deathly ill."

"That doesn't mean he got sick from testing the Excalibur."

"Look, I've been through all this before." Monica remembered her conversation with Michael and Jones, when she had used the exact same words Cameron was using now. The case was getting more complicated by the hour and she had to cut to the chase. She was going with her intuition now that said she could trust Cameron—up to a point. She wouldn't risk blowing her cover by confiding too much in him. But, she damn well intended to come close to the edge.

"Listen to me, Cameron. I have every reason to believe that Dave Carter knew how dangerous the Excalibur was and that Gerald arranged his death to silence him. The only thing I can come up with is that Carter must have documented the true findings of the study and Gerald knows about it, but hasn't gotten his hands on it yet." She then told him about Port Royal Meadows.

"I also checked with the Bureau of Vital Statistics and there's no record of your Dave Carter having died anywhere in the United States. Don't you think that's a little peculiar?"

"How did you—"

"—I got his birth date and social security number

from some old files in the office. Had a friend of mine check it out. No death record. Nothing."

Cameron shook his head, then plopped it onto the back of the sofa and closed his eyes.

Monica went on. "Tomorrow morning, I'm flying to Hilton Head to see if Carter is a patient at Port Royal Meadows." She finished off her drink.

"Oh, no, you're not!" His eyes sprang open, and his voice grew louder with each word. "Are you friggin' crazy? If what you've just said is true, going to Hilton Head is a stupid move. We should call the police and let them handle it."

"And say what? Bayou City Wireless is manufacturing killer phones and the president has stashed a former employee away to keep him from talking? The police would think we were the ones who needed to be committed. We don't have any proof."

"What about this Stevenson guy? He could tell them what he knows."

"Don't you see? Stevenson's illness and the deaths in Bastrop have long been rumored as exposure to a hazardous waste site, not the Excalibur. Nobody would believe him—or us."

Monica went over to the end of the sofa where Cameron was sitting.

"The only way I can help Stevenson," she said softly, "is to get solid proof of what the company has done. Right now, Dave Carter is the only one who really knows. If he is alive, I need to find out."

"I'm coming with you."

"No way. I can handle it on my own. You'd only be in the way, Cameron."

"Listen to you, 'You'd only be in the way,

Cameron.'" He mimicked her in the exact same voice she'd used. "Who the hell do you think you are? James Bond or something?"

Monica laughed. "You sound just like my brother."

"You never told me you had a brother."

"Like I said, there are a lot of things I haven't told you. Look, I'll be gone for less than twenty-four hours, so I'll be back in time for work on Monday. Nobody from the office will ever know."

"Do you actually think you'll be able to just walk right in and ask for Dave Carter? If he's there and Gerald has him confined against his will, don't you think someone is guarding him at all times? And, think about this: you're not exactly a wallflower. This place sounds like a facility for white people. Have you thought about how you're going to get in there without being noticed? This is dangerous stuff you're talking about. And the more I think about it, the more I believe—" pointing his finger for emphasis— "you, Taylor LeBlanc, are crazy as hell!"

"Don't sugar coat it, Cameron, give it to me straight."

"You're nuts!" he countered, attempting to run his fingers through his too-short hair, swearing under his breath.

"Look, Cameron," Monica said, "I'm not going into this blind. I know what I'm doing."

"What I don't understand, Taylor," he said, holding her gaze, "is why you'd go so far on a hunch. Why is this so important to you?"

"We'll talk about that when I get back," Monica heard herself say without warning, as she watched Cameron move closer to her and take her hands in his. She could see the tenderness in his eyes and she began to tremble, wanting to pull back.

179

"Taylor." He hesitated, as though he were afraid that what he was about to say would scare her off. "I care about you. I have from the moment we had our first conversation. I don't want anything to happen to you."

Monica could feel the heat of his breath against her face as he spoke. Her internal alarm was blaring inside of her, warning her to bolt for the door. For the first time in a long time, she didn't want to run away. She mentally disengaged the alarm and moved closer to Cameron. When his full lips touched hers, they ignited tiny fires that burst into flames throughout her whole body. Her skin burnt to the touch of his softly groping hands. Monica shuddered, but didn't want him to stop.

"Taylor." His baritone voice made her tingle inside. Kissing her down her neck, then back up on her lips, he took her in his arms and caressed her back with his hands. He pulled back long enough to say, "I'm fall—"

"Don't." Monica put her finger over his mouth before the words could escape from his lips. She cautiously wrapped her arms around his neck and pulled him closer to her, feeling him grow with desire as he laid her back on the sofa and moved on top of her. Despite the sound of her own heavy breathing, Monica could hear the bricks crumbling inside of her one-by-one, until the whole damn wall came crashing down.

* * *

AT THIRTY-FIVE MINUTES past midnight, Monica quietly put on her clothes, as she watched Cameron's hairy chest move up and down to the cadence of his snoring. She wanted to awaken him and tell him she was leaving, but she knew he would only insist on coming with her to Hilton Head. It was her job to put her life on the line. She wouldn't gamble with his.

Monica placed a note on the nightstand, then leaned over the bed and gently kissed Cameron on his cheek. He stirred, turned over, hugged his pillow, and resumed his breathing pattern. Monica let herself out and drove the twenty minutes to her house.

The red flashing of the message button on her answering machine caught Monica's eye the moment she came in. Assuming the call was from Michael, Monica hit the play button, went into the bathroom to run the water to take a shower, and then walked to her closet and grabbed her large, black leather duffle bag. She instantly dropped it and spun around when the message on the recorder began to play.

"Monica, this is Dad. I just wanted to call to say I hope you're okay. Don't be mad at Michael for giving me your number, he's just trying to help. Monica, I'd really like for you to call me back. Honey, I love you and w—"

Monica punched the stop button and automatically clicked the erase dial, then replayed the blank space of the tape to make sure the message had vanished from the recorder.

"Damn you!" she screamed, as she sat on the edge of the bed, her chest heaving in and out, her nostrils flaring like a bull waiting to charge. *Why can't you leave me alone?* A veil of tears welled up in her eyes. Monica put her arms around herself, fell back onto her bed, and cried.

# Chapter

## 19

"John Smith is Jack Stevenson," Arthur blurted into the phone, as soon as he'd gotten confirmation. "Stevenson was in Houston day before yesterday for treatment. And Gerald . . ." Arthur paused for a moment, ". . . I went over the old phone tapes from Carter's office."

"And?" Gerald yawned, looking at the clock. It was just after one o'clock in the morning.

"Found at least a half dozen calls to Carter from a person with the same name."

"Shit, Arthur! Why didn't you make the connection before?" Gerald shot up from his bed.

"There was no reason to, Gerald." Arthur pleaded his case, his voice faltering. "They were just a handful of calls scattered among thousands."

"Well, damn it, there is now!" Gerald growled. "You fucked this up, Arthur, so you take care of it. I want you to go to Bastrop and shut Stevenson up for good. Then I want you to search his house."

"For chrissakes, Gerald, the man is dying! When he finally does, that'll be the last of them. Everything will be fine, once—"

"Do you know exactly when that blessed event will be, Arthur? How do you know he didn't talk to Taylor later in the day? Or yesterday? Can you assure me that he didn't find another way to get to her, Arthur? I don't give a damn about the status of his health. He's not dead yet and I don't want him having any more opportunities to visit with our Ms. LeBlanc or anyone else."

"I don't think he had a chance to really talk to her, Gerald. I called the *Chronicle* and found out she did have a meeting with one of the reporters there, just like she said. In fact, she was meeting with him when I called."

"That's well and good, Arthur." Gerald sounded unimpressed. "Shut Jack Stevenson up and shut him up for good! You got that?"

"I heard you."

"Another thing, Arthur."

"I'm listening."

"Before you leave, put a man on Taylor. Until Stevenson is taken care of, I want to know everything she does this weekend in case you screw things up again."

*  *  *

AT TEN A.M., SATURDAY MORNING, Jack Stevenson noticed the car in his rearview mirror as he pulled out of his driveway. The dark blue Buick stayed close behind as he drove the short distance from his house on Pecan Street to the Bastrop Post Office. When he reached the front of the building, Jack steered his 1995 Lincoln into the first available parking space and turned off the motor. He watched as the Buick pulled into position three spaces down from him. Waiting until the driver of another car got out in the parking space beside him, Jack quickly picked up the envelope from the seat across from him and weakly opened his door.

With slow, plodding steps, he shuffled inside the post office and walked straight up to the front of the line to the next available postal worker. He pulled the money clip from his pocket, removed $11 in bills, telling the lady it was imperative that the envelope be delivered overnight. He listened impatiently, as she told him the package would not be delivered until Monday morning, watched her stamp the envelope, and then proceed to hand him his tracking receipt and change.

"I won't be needing that." He turned around, ambled to his car, and drove back to his house.

# Chapter
## 20

Sister Theresa walked serenely across the lush green lawn toward the entrance of Port Royal Meadows, her rosary beads dangling from the belt of her long, dark blue habit.

"Hello, Sister," she said in a soft-spoken voice. She gave a slight nod of her head to another Sister who was talking soothingly to a patient in a wheelchair.

The facility was located at the edge of twenty acres of land, lined with water oaks draped in Spanish moss. The back of the building sat on cliffs of huge, black rocks, facing the water. With hands clasped together beneath her scapular, Sister Theresa graciously strode up the long walkway to the veranda of the red bricked, two-story facility that had once been a large plantation house.

Raising her hand to her throat, she inconspicuously tucked her finger into the top of the collar of her cape and moved her head from side to side.

*How can they stand it?* Monica complained to herself, fearing she would strangle from the tightness around her neck. The weight of the habit added another thirty pounds to her tall frame and the pleats in the material made her look much heavier.

"Patience, Sister," Monica said under her breath, repeating the words of the Sister who had dressed her at

185

the Sisters of Charity Convent in Savannah. Monica had remarked that the starched, standout veil made her look like the Flying Nun. When the Bureau had contacted the order seeking their assistance in the investigation, they'd been happy to oblige.

The entry way of Port Royal Meadows was a large area with hardwood floors and dhrurrie rugs. Smaller rooms were lined on each side, colored in various subtle shades of blue and green. Several patients were stationed in each of the rooms. An antiseptic aroma permeated the building.

Monica walked to the desk in the reception area and asked for the director. A broad-shouldered, matronly woman with fair skin and green eyes emerged five minutes later.

"Sister Theresa? I'm Mrs. Hahn." The director had a German accent.

"Pleased to meet you." Monica nodded her head in greeting.

"I'm so glad you called today," Mrs. Hahn smiled. "You are the answer to our prayers. I'm afraid we're a little short-handed. A nasty bout of late-season flu has kept some of our Sisters out sick. I don't know where Port Royal Meadows would be without generous assistance from the Sisters of Charity. Come, let me give you a tour of the facility."

Monica noticed the small patient record room to her right, as she accompanied Mrs. Hahn down the corridor.

"We're a small facility here at Port Royal Meadows," Mrs. Hahn explained. "We have only twenty-five patients in residence. Most of them are with us for an extended period of time, though there are some who do stay for only a short visit. They all have some form of mental disability—a large number are Alzheimer's patients."

She stopped in the doorway of a large room with french windows that captured the waves beating against the rocks. About fifteen patients were situated around the room in front of easels or at small tables in groups of three. Many had paint brushes in their hands. Some simply sat staring out the windows. Soft, classical music played in the background.

"This is our recreation room," Mrs. Hahn said. "The patients who are ambulatory and who retain partial memory come here in the afternoon to paint, draw, or just to sit and listen to music. This approach stimulates the brain and provides opportunity for creativity and expression." Mrs. Hahn paused when she saw Monica's eyes fixed on a woman who had dipped her index finger in bright, red paint and carefully proceeded to smear streaks across her face.

"Don't worry, Sister." Mrs. Hahn sounded assured. "The paint is non-toxic and water soluble. Seldom does anyone enjoy the taste of it."

"Do the families of the patients come to visit?" Monica spoke in a low, unassuming pitch.

"About fifty percent of them have relatives who visit often, usually during dinnertime. Another thirty percent were admitted by family members who never came back. They call two or three times a year, and occasionally, they'll ask about the conditions of their relatives when the payment is sent each month."

"Hmmm." Monica shook her head and clucked her tongue.

"I know it's sad. People seem to think that if a patient is unable to communicate in the conventional sense, then it is futile to visit them at all."

"I can see you don't believe that." Monica heard the tenderness in the woman's voice.

"No, I don't. Behind the blank stares, the glassy eyes, there is some degree of comprehension in even the most severely-damaged brain."

"What about the other twenty percent?"

"They are wards of the court or admitted by doctors who have been given charge over them."

"I see." Monica glanced around the room and studied the faces of the four men who were intermingled among the women. There was no resemblance to the youthful face and smile of the blond-haired man she had seen in the photo Suzanne had shown her. Monica was convinced he was somewhere in the building and she was determined to find him.

When Mrs. Hahn had finished the tour of Port Royal Meadows, Monica calculated that she had seen all of the patients, with the exception of five. She had also noticed that there was a separate wing which had not been on the tour.

After they had returned to the recreation room, Mrs. Hahn pointed to the group of patients. "Would you like to help Sister Bernadette with the activities?" She looked at the clock on the wall. "We have about forty-five minutes left before dinner."

"Wherever you'd think I'd be the most needed," Monica replied.

Sister Bernadette was a petite, soft-spoken woman in her sixties, whose tireless patience Monica admired right away.

"Do you enjoy your work, Sister?" Monica asked, as Sister Bernadette cleaned up a second spill made by the same patient in less than five minutes.

"Oh, yes, Sister," she responded to Monica with a radiant smile. "I consider it a privilege to work with these people. They deserve to be loved and shown kindness just as much as you or I do. Don't you agree, Sister?"

Monica returned her gaze and smiled. Taking a seat next to her, she nodded her head. "Yes, I do. Have you been here long?"

"Just a couple of months. Before that, I worked in one of the local orphanages for almost twenty years. Then one day, I was sent here to take the place of another Sister who was transferred. What I noticed right away was that there were so few people to help out here. As much as I loved working with the children, giving them the love they lacked from not having parents of their own, I realized that our Father had designed a plan for me. My help was needed here more. He always has such divine plans, doesn't He, Sister?"

"He does, indeed." Monica took the hand of an elderly woman beside her and gently placed it around one of the larger brushes. Slowly, with the woman's hand beneath hers, Monica dipped the brush into a dish of brilliant blue paint and drew an arch across the large sheet of paper that sat on an easel. The woman shrieked in delight and motioned for Monica to do it again.

Monica continued in different colors until a bright rainbow covered the whole paper. When she tried to tear the sheet off of the pad to start a new picture, the woman pushed Monica's hand away and just stared at the colors on the page.

"You'd better not take that from her just yet." Sister Bernadette tapped Monica on the shoulder and shook her head in warning. "I'm afraid when Mary becomes fixated on something she likes, she gets pretty disturbed if someone tries to take it away. She'll just stare and stare at that one picture for the rest of the day."

Just as Sister Bernadette had predicted, the woman sat mesmerized by the painting. Several times, she ran her fingers gently across the colors and just smiled, lost in her own world.

"What do you suppose Mary sees when she stares into her pictures?" Monica looked up at Sister Bernadette, as they gathered at the large sink at the back of the room to rinse the brushes and bowls of paint.

"Oh, I don't know. Maybe the angels are singing to her, letting her know in a way she can understand that everything's alright. Whatever she sees, or the others do who stare endlessly into space, it makes them content."

"Where are the rest of them, Sister?" Monica asked casually, dipping another bowl into the sudsy water.

"The rest of whom, Sister Theresa?"

"Mrs. Hahn told me there were twenty-five residents. We passed a few patients who were bedridden when she was showing me around, but I don't think I've seen all of them. I was just wondering where the rest of them were."

"You mean the ones who are in isolation. They can get pretty violent at times and Mrs. Hahn doesn't like for them to upset the other patients."

"How many are there?" Monica couldn't conceal the anxiety in her voice.

"About four or five. They stay in their rooms on the West Wing of the second floor most of the day, and only come together for meals and short, supervised walks outside. Most of the time, they're sedated and manageable, but the medication starts to wear off right before dinner, so they eat upstairs by themselves. The Sisters are allowed to help with the feeding, but not with the walks. The attendants usually accompany them, because they are trained to handle the patients, if they should get out of hand."

"Do you think I could help with dinner?"

"I don't know if that's a good idea. Mrs. Hahn doesn't like the Sisters to work on the West Wing their first day here." Sister Bernadette covered her mouth with her hand and tried to suppress a giggle. "She doesn't want to scare us off."

*I don't frighten that easily,* Monica thought, glancing at the clock on the wall which displayed four fifty-two. She had to find Mrs. Hahn before the others were fed.

Monica located the director as the woman was stepping into the elevator on the first floor.

"Mrs. Hahn, may I speak with you for a moment?" Monica stepped inside before the door closed.

"Yes, Sister?"

"Sister Bernadette told me about the patients in isolation and I was wondering if I could help serve them their dinner today?"

"I don't think that's a wise decision, Sister." The director's face clamped shut. Monica couldn't tell if it was from concern or if she was hiding something from her. "They can be rather overpowering at times, dangerous in fa—"

"I don't mind, really, I don't. You said earlier that there had to be some communication in the darkest of minds. I believe that, too. I'd like to help, if I could."

Monica relaxed when she saw the worried expression on the director's face soften a bit, until finally she offered a smile.

"I did say something like that, didn't I? Okay, Sister, if you're sure."

"Yes, ma'am. Very sure."

Monica sprinted beside Mrs. Hahn until they stopped outside a metal door with barred glass at the end of the West Wing. Taking a set of keys from her skirt pocket, Mrs. Hahn unlocked the door and entered the room with Monica close behind her. A loud, wailing sound greeted them as they walked into the all-white room with locked, barred windows. Large over-stuffed furniture filled the room, much like the furniture Monica had in her home in Atlanta. A mahogany bookshelf lined the wall.

Two male attendants dressed in white short-sleeved shirts and pants struggled to calm an angry young man who had managed to knock his plate from the tray, despite being restrained in his wheelchair.

Monica looked around at the other patients in the room, who seemed to be oblivious to the commotion. One woman laughed uncontrollably, batted her arms at the air to ward off something only she could see. Another woman just sat in a catatonic trance, no trace of life or comprehension. In the right corner of the room, a man with his back to Monica sat quietly in his wheelchair, opening his mouth to accept the spoonful of food the Sister in front of him was coaxing him to eat. Monica watched him as his jaws dropped open on command, chewed the food slowly, and then swallowed almost to a cadence.

"As you can see, Sister," Mrs. Hahn whispered to Monica, "this is not an easy place to work. These patients are the most severely disabled. It is for their own safety, and the safety of everyone else, that they remain isolated from the other patients. I wouldn't blame you if you've had a change of mind about helping in here."

"No, Mrs. Hahn." Monica's eyes were riveted on the man whose back was to her. "I'm sure this is *exactly* where I should be."

"Very well, then. Sister Lorraine will show you what to do. If for any reason you want to leave the room, ask one of the attendants. After I leave, they will be the only ones with keys to let you out." Taking Monica's hand, she pressed it gently. "Bless you, Sister, for your kind heart."

Monica watched as Mrs. Hahn left the room. When the door had closed, she turned back to the man in the corner. His hair was blond and much longer than the neatly-trimmed hair in the photo. He wore a thick, white terry cloth robe over white pajamas and on his feet were black slippers.

Monica eased slowly towards the wheelchair. As she crept up to his side, carefully observing his profile, she spotted the strawberry birthmark on the right side of his forehead—barely visible beneath his hair.

*My God, it's him*, she thought, sucking in a deep breath and trying not to show a change in expression. She'd seen the video camera perched in the top corner of the room when she'd first entered. She hesitated for a brief moment, then smiled at the Sister who had watched her approach.

"Sister Lorraine? I'm Sister Theresa."

"Welcome, Sister." The older nun nodded her head and continued with her feeding.

"He seems to be enjoying his meal," Monica remarked, studying the face that bore only a slight resemblance to Dave Carter.

He was much thinner than in his photo, his eyes

dulled from months of medication. His face was pale, though slightly shaded by razor stubble, and his hair, once clipped short and neat, was stringy and looked as if it had not been washed in several days.

"This is Louis." Sister Lorraine lifted a spoon of oatmeal to his mouth. "He'll eat only if we feed him." She wiped away drool from the corner of his mouth.

"I noticed you talking to him a while ago. Is he able to understand you?"

"I don't know. Sometimes, when his medicine starts to wear off, he babbles a lot. We often read to him and he particularly seems to enjoy looking at that book of dogs over there. He must have owned a dog once, but since his mind is in such a confused state, I've never been able to determine what kind. Louis has Alzheimer's, so it's hard to tell sometimes if what he's saying is true or make believe."

"He's so young, Sister."

"Yes, he is. But we must not question God's will, must we, Sister?" Sister Lorraine gave Monica a stern look and continued. "Besides, Louis doesn't get irritated nearly as often as some of the others. On the other hand—"

Sister Lorraine stopped in mid-sentence as she watched the woman who had been laughing hysterically earlier, approach her and try to dip her fingers in the plate of food the Sister held in her hand.

"You've had your dinner, Cecile." The nun moved the plate out of reach of the woman's determined hand. All of a sudden Cecile stopped, put a finger to her mouth with one hand, yanked a fistful of her uncombed brown hair with the other, and let out a blood-curdling scream. One attendant, who had just returned to the room after removing another patient, rushed to get the deranged woman under control.

"Do you mind taking over, Sister?" Sister Lorraine quickly handed Monica the plate of food. "I need to help with Cecile."

Monica sat down in the chair and watched as Sister Lorraine fled to a near-by cabinet and pulled out a plastic-covered syringe. She picked up a bottle of medicine with the other hand, shook it violently, and stuck the needle into it. As the attendant held Cecile within his grasp, Sister Lorraine jabbed the needle into the woman's arm. Within a few seconds, the screaming stopped and Cecile's body slumped against the nun like a large rag doll's. Monica watched Sister Lorraine gently caress the woman's hair, talking soothingly to her as she and the attendant carried her from the room.

Monica returned her attention to the man in front of her. Unresponsive as a rock, he had not changed his expression or reacted in any way to the disturbance around him. *They must keep him drugged all day,* she thought, raking up a small portion of mashed potatoes and placing the spoon in his mouth. She watched him as he chewed the food slowly, staring through her as if she were invisible.

"That's good, isn't it, Louis?" she asked softly, carefully looking around the room to see if anyone was watching her. The camera at the top of the ceiling slowly moved away from them. With Sister Lorraine and one attendant gone, the other attendant had his hands full with the other two patients.

Monica scooted her chair forward a little, until her knees were just a few inches away from the wheelchair.

"How does that taste, Dave?" She emphasized his

name, studying his eyes for a flicker of recognition at hearing his name. Nothing. Monica sighed and wondered how she was ever going to reach him.

"Talk to me, Dave." Monica spoke in a hushed tone. "I'm here to help you. But, I can't do that unless you help me." Just as she'd spooned up the last of the chocolate pudding and held it to his mouth, a thought struck her. When he had swallowed it, she wiped his mouth with a napkin and moved his tray to another table.

Eyeing the bookshelf, she quickly walked to it and thumbed through the titles until she found the one she was looking for. Clutching the big, hardback book to her chest, she sat back down next to Carter and opened it. The roving camera moved in their direction.

"I want you to try real hard to understand me, okay? You are not Louis or whatever they call you here." She spoke through clenched teeth and smiled, leisurely pointing at the pictures of the dogs on each page. "You're Dave Carter. You used to work in Houston at a company called Bayou City Wireless. You worked on a special phone called the Excalibur that was used in the Bastrop Study. Remember? The phone caused the deaths of many people and I need to know how to prove it. Do you remember the name Gerald Conti?"

Monica searched his eyes frantically and could not see beyond the frozen stare. She drew in another long breath and rapidly turned the pages to the section in the book on Welsh Corgis, praying she would find a picture of a dog that looked like his dog, Patch. When she held the book closer for him to see, her eyes caught the slight tremor in his right hand as he gripped the edge of his chair.

\* \* \*

THE WORDS BEING SPOKEN TO HIM went reeling into the deepest, darkest crevices of Dave Carter's mind, echoing loudly throughout his head. *Excalibur. . . Caused the deaths . . . Gerald Conti! Gerald Conti!* He blinked his eyes and tried to seize the words as they flew into his brain. The blurred figure in front of him moved in and out of focus as he breathed harder to communicate what the concrete slab of a tongue in his mouth prevented him from saying.

Carter rapidly blinked his eyes and tried desperately to latch hold to the words spinning in his head. No matter how hard he tried, how much he willed it, he could not force his mouth to move. He could hear voices in his mind, shouting at him, demanding something of him. But what was it? Try as he might, he couldn't remember. The wrinkles in his forehead furrowed deeply as he tried harder to concentrate.

Suddenly, words reverberated in his brain like an echo on a lake.

*"I know you've hidden the information. Where is it!"*

His body jerked as he remembered the painful, electrical currents that had raced through his body every time he refused to answer. He would not tell them what they wanted to know. He remembered when the shock-treatment eventually stopped and he'd been continuously drugged as punishment for not cooperating. He didn't know how long he could hold on.

*Must . . . get . . . tape.* The words were so clear in his head, but his mouth betrayed him by not releasing them.

* * *

"YOU HEAR ME, DON'T YOU?" Monica whispered, putting the book in her lap and placing both of her hands over his. She looked up and smiled at the attendant who paused to look over her shoulder. "I think he's fond of dogs," she casually commented, as he shrugged his shoulders and walked past her to the back of the room. The camera slowly swept their way again, prompting Monica to talk faster.

"Take it easy," she said under her breath to Dave. "I'm not going to hurt you. I'm here to help you, Dave. You recognized the name Gerald Conti. He's responsible for your being here. I need more to work with."

Monica anxiously picked up the book again and held it closer to his face. She pointed to the small red and white dog. "He looks just like Patch, doesn't he? Patch is safe . . . he's with Jack Stevenson in Bastrop. Help me to get you out of here."

She watched his face scrunch up, his eyes flutter as if he were trying to clear his vision. Without moving his head, Dave scanned the room as though trying to remember where he was.

When the confused pair of blue eyes finally turned back to her, Monica could tell by the way Dave Carter suddenly converged on her that he was really seeing her for the first time. She looked around the room again and swung her chair around beside him, their backs shielding the view from the camera. She lowered her head, made the sign of the cross, and then took Dave's hand in hers again.

"Hail Mary, Mother of God," she began to recite, when she noticed between her slitted eyes, an attendant coming in her direction. He stopped abruptly, then turned around and went back to another patient.

Tightening her hand around Dave's, Monica continued speaking from her prayerful position.

"Dave, I'm not going to hurt you. Move your hand if you can hear me." A long second passed before she felt a weak pressure against her hand.

"Good." Her heart raced in her chest. She was running out of time and could not keep up this charade much longer without drawing attention to herself. "I want you to try to listen carefully. I am going to leave today, but I will come back and get you out of here."

She felt the hand beneath hers ball into a fist. The man's breathing became harder and deliberate, as she talked more quickly.

"I *will* come back, Dave." She made the sign of the cross again and looked up to see that his eyes had widened. His mouth opened and trembled when he tried to speak.

"What is it?" she whispered, as she saw Sister Lorraine come into the room with a man who appeared to be a doctor.

"T—t-tape," Carter said in a voice so low that Monica had to strain to hear.

"What?"

"Get . . . tape!"

This time she heard him.

"Sister Theresa," Sister Lorraine said, unlocking the wheels to Carter's wheelchair. "This is Dr. Blackburn. He's come to give Louis his medication and take him back to his room."

Dressed in a white lab coat, Dr. Blackburn looked coldly over the top of his glasses at Monica, a stethoscope hung from his neck. She smiled nervously up at him, watching how he stood disapprovingly behind his patient, holding a small paper cup in his hand. She then stared back at Carter, whose mouth moved with garbled sounds. As she prepared to stand up, Carter suddenly grabbed her hand and held it tightly.

"No!" he said in a voice that was noticeably stronger. Monica patted his hand and said, "Everything's all right."

"No! No!" he shouted, his eyes bulging and pleading with Monica not to leave.

"Louis, let go of Sister Theresa," Sister Lorraine ordered, reaching down between them to release his fingers.

"No!" he screamed again, as he lunged at Sister Lorraine and gripped both hands around her neck. The assault knocked Dr. Blackburn out of the way with such force that the tiny cup flew from his hand, sending the two orange tablets tumbling to the floor, one of which slid a few inches past Monica.

Amidst the commotion and the persistent shout by the doctor for a syringe, she pretended to lose her balance and fell to the floor where she scooped up the orange tablet and thrust it into her pocket. The attendant grabbed Carter and held him as the doctor injected the needle. Within moments, Carter fell back into his wheelchair and did not resist when the attendant put a straitjacket on him. Monica immediately went to help Sister Lorraine, who leaned against the wall, coughing and holding her throat.

"Are you okay, Sister?" Monica guided the ailing Sister to the nearest chair and sat her down.

"I think so." Sister Lorraine's hands trembled, as she rubbed them over her throat. "Could you get me some water, please?"

When Monica returned with a cup of water, Sister Lorraine swallowed a sip, then shook her head. "He's never reacted so violently, never lashed out at anyone before. What triggered his anger, Sister?"

"That's exactly what I'd like to know," the doctor grumbled, standing directly behind Monica. He was a big man in his late fifties with fading brown hair and a glowing forehead.

"I don't know," Monica lied. "I just said a short prayer and held his hand."

"And what did he say to you?" Dr. Blackburn peered hard over the black-framed glasses perched on his nose.

"Nothing. He mumbled something I couldn't quite understand."

Dr. Blackburn stared at Monica, expecting her to say more. When she did not, he turned to Sister Lorraine and ordered, "From now on, Sister, please keep the new Sisters downstairs with the other patients. I will instruct Mrs. Hahn to do the same."

"Yes, doctor." The Sister pinched her lips together, watching as Dr. Blackburn left the room in a huff.

* * *

A FEW SECONDS LATER, Dr. Blackburn stormed into the observation area behind the mirrored wall of the isolation room.

"I want to see what just happened in there," he demanded, ordering the young, black attendant to play back the video tape.

"The S-Sister was p-praying or something," the young attendant stammered nervously. "And all of a s-sudden, the guy went berserk."

"Where's the audio?" When the tape began to play without the sound, Dr. Blackburn slapped his hands on his thighs angrily. "Turn up the volume!"

The attendant fumbled with the switch, then looked pleadingly at the doctor.

"Uh, one of the p-patients had been screaming just before Louis's outburst, s-so I turned the s-sound down. I must've forgotten to turn it back up again."

"You idiot!" the doctor yelled, veins protruding from his temple.

"He didn't say nothing, Doc. I s-swear it," the young man insisted. "Look for yourself. The Sister prayed over him. That's all that happened. Honest."

"Replay it again. Slowly." Dr. Blackburn adjusted his glasses and leaned closer to the screen. For a moment, he thought he saw Carter trying to speak. The doctor then strained to see the side of Monica's face as she made the sign of the cross. He watched her intently as she kept her head bowed, huddled closely to Carter with her back to the camera, her jaws slowly moving up and down. There was no way for him to know exactly what she was saying.

"Damn it!" He slammed his palm on the desk. "Young man, the next time you do something as asinine as this, you'll find yourself out of a job. I pay you to watch and listen to everything that goes on in that room. Do I make myself clear?"

"Yes, sir." The young man swallowed so loudly, Dr. Blackburn heard him gulp. "It won't happen again, s-sir."

"Make sure it doesn't!"

Dr. Blackburn stormed out of the small room and slammed the door. Still reeling with anger, he stopped for a moment, pulled a handkerchief from his pocket, and wiped his face. He thought of what Gerald's reaction would be to this latest episode.

*How had he gotten himself in such a mess?*

He'd been bought and paid for, that's how, Dr. Blackburn thought in disgust. He removed his glasses and wiped them with the cloth.

This was still *his* facility. *He* decided what Gerald needed to know.

# Chapter
## 21

Jack Stevenson sat in the darkness of his living room and listened to the grandfather clock in the hallway as it struck midnight. Gently swaying his antique rocking chair back and forth to the gongs of the clock, he smiled inwardly. *It won't be long, now.*

He'd sent his weekend nurse home amid protest, telling her he wanted to be by himself tonight. He'd even asked her to take Patch with her. She finally left about a quarter after eight, once he'd changed into his pajamas and silk robe, and taken his medicine.

Since assuming his position in the corner of the room next to the brick fireplace, he had drifted off to sleep twice. He was tired—tired of the excruciating headaches that banged against the brittle walls of his skull, tired of the metallic taste of the chemotherapy that overpowered his taste buds as it dripped through his veins and waged a useless battle against the enemy in his body.

But most of all, he was tired of waiting for his system to wave the white flag of surrender, signaling the end that would finally come. *Yes,* Jack thought, managing a wan smile in an effort to stay awake. *It'll all be over very soon.*

A rattle at the back door prompted him to still the rocking chair and focus on a beam of light that invaded the dark room when the door creaked open. A shadow crept inside the house and hid behind the illumination.

Jack squinted his eyes when he saw the figure reach into the front of his pants and pull out a knife that reflected off the bright light. He wanted to see death when it finally came.

He nodded approvingly.

"Come on in," Jack exhaled softly. "I've been waiting for you."

Shining the flashlight in the direction from which the words rang out, the intruder jumped at the sound of the unexpected voice.

Jack closed his eyes and slowly resumed rocking back and forth in his chair.

# Chapter

## 22

"Michael, wake your ass up! Dave Carter is alive!" Monica shouted ecstatically into the pay phone, as soon as her brother answered. It was one-fifteen Sunday morning and she had just gotten off the plane at Houston's George Bush Intercontinental Airport from her brief trip to Hilton Head.

When Michael only grunted a response, she went ballistic. "Did you hear what I said?"

"Hold on a minute, Monica. Let me get some tooth-picks for my eyes."

Monica could hear the sound of a light being turned on in the background.

Michael groaned. "Geez, girl, don't you ever sleep? Okay, let's have it."

"I found Dave Carter. He's alive and well—okay, maybe not well as in healthy—but alive nonetheless." Monica told him about the visit to Port Royal Meadows. When she had finished, she waited for Michael's response.

"Wait. Let me get a mental picture of this." Michael let out a rip-roaring laugh. "You? Dressed as a *nun*? Habit and all? Boy, I'd love to have seen that."

"Got the job done, didn't it?" She chuckled to herself

as she lit a cigarette. "Listen, the important thing is that Dave Carter is not dead as everyone believes. Which makes me even more curious as to why he wasn't included in the briefing for this assignment. He's obviously at the center of this investigation. Did you ever get around to asking Frasier about him?"

"Yeah. He said he didn't mention him before because the guy had already died and was not important to the case. Jim's been gone for the last week, checking up on another assignment. He'll be back in the next day or so. I'll talk to him again."

"I suppose it doesn't really matter much now that we know Carter is alive and that Gerald is behind it. Still—"

"That's just it, Monica," Michael interrupted. "Why is Gerald keeping him there? It would have been easier for him to just kill him and bury the evidence."

"Not if Carter has something on him, which I believe is the case." Monica then told Michael about her conversation with Jack Stevenson and what Carter had said at the sanitarium.

"What kind of tape was he talking about?"

"I don't know, but believe me, I'm going to find out—even if I have to go through the whole damn company, paper clip by paper clip. Then we get Carter out of that stinking place."

"Wait a minute, Monica." Michael's voice sounded somber. "Let's think this thing through. We can't just go in and get Dave Carter."

"Right—Gerald would know in a flash. He's got the doctor at the facility in his back pocket. If either Carter or Dr. Blackburn suddenly turn up missing, Gerald would become suspicious and cover his tracks. Damn, the whole case would blow up in our faces."

"You said Carter was drugged? Any idea what kind of medication they're giving him?"

"Not exactly . . ." Monica's upbeat mood suddenly soured. "But I was able to get my hands on one of the pills. It's a round, orange-coated tablet. No name, just four letters and two numbers—SKF T79. I'll overnight it to you."

"Is that all he's on?"

"No, the doctor gave him an injection of some kind while I was there."

"Sis, tell me—how did you find him?"

"Just following my hunches. Well, the facility has a patient database—I saw it when I first got there. Dave Carter is registered as Louis Fairchild."

"I'll get one of our technical guys to access it and see what we can find out. In the meantime, Monica," he said, "I'm sending another agent down to help you."

"I don't need any assistance, thank you very much. I'm doing just fine by myself."

"I didn't mean to insinuate that you weren't," he insisted, "but the clock is ticking, Monica. We've got to resolve this thing and fast. If Gerald finds out about you—"

"He won't. I haven't given him any reason to suspect anything. I've gotten this far on my own, I'll make it the rest of the way. I don't need anyone tripping me up."

"Okay . . ." Michael let out a sigh. "It's too late—or should I say too early?—to argue about it now. I'll talk to Frasier again about Carter, then see what I can find out about the medication you're sending me. Take care of yourself and stay out of trouble."

"Always, little brother. Always."

\* \* \*

MONICA PULLED HER FORD EXPLORER INTO the parking space in front of the entrance to the Memorial Park golf course, picked up the water bottle from the passenger seat and got out. She immediately spotted Cameron in his jogging shorts and sweat shirt, engaged in a series of lunges near a cement bench.

"Hi," she said, as she walked up behind him. He turned around, looked at her for a moment, then took her in his arms. Monica returned the hug, inhaling his masculine scent. She felt herself longing for his touch again.

"You look great." He looked her over, head tilted to the side.

She was dressed in a green and white tee shirt, short purple iridescent jogging shorts and running shoes. Her hair was pinned up in a twist with a white headband around her forehead.

"Thanks. You don't look so bad yourself." Her eyes took in his muscular body.

"Do you have any idea how worried I've been? Until you called this afternoon and told me to meet you here, I hadn't left the house all weekend."

"As you can see, I returned safe and sound." Monica crossed her eyes and made circles with her index fingers around both ears.

Cameron laughed and looked more relaxed. "So you really went? To Hilton Head, I mean."

"I told you I was going."

"I know, but somehow I didn't quite believe you would. And what did you find out?"

"Not what. Who." Monica watched Cameron's eyes react to her words.

"You're kidding, right?" He placed his hands on his hips, disbelief on his face.

"Nope. Dave Carter is alive."

"Are you *sure* it's him? You've never even seen—"

"Strawberry birthmark and all."

Cameron stared at Monica with his mouth gaping open. When he continued to stand with his hands on his hips, Monica pulled at his elbow.

"C'mon, let's walk and I'll tell you all about it."

They turned the corner and headed west. Impatient joggers darted around them as Cameron and Monica walked at a steady, but leisurely pace. The air was warm, humid and sticky, the sky a bright blue.

"I can't believe it." Cameron shook his head when Monica finished telling him about her trip. "Now what?"

"Now, I've got to find the damn tape. There's only one little problem: I haven't the faintest idea what kind of tape it is or where to begin looking for it."

"That's not your responsibility. You've done enough already. It's time to go to the police and let them solve this."

"We've been through all that before, Cameron." Monica heaved a sigh. "There's nothing we can tell them without proof."

"You don't think a guy who's been locked up and drugged like a goddamn automaton for months is proof enough?" He stopped his pace so abruptly that the jogger behind him almost collided into the two of them. "I don't like the idea of you playing detective."

"Cameron, trust me. When we find the tape, then we go to the police." She decided that she would think of another excuse to hold him off when the time came. *If* it came.

"And what about Carter in the meantime? He just continues where he is?"

"They're not going to kill him. He's too valuable. What he knows is enough to keep him alive." *For now, that is.*

"I don't like this one bit."

"Neither do I. Let's not talk about it anymore. My brain is exhausted."

Cameron had run out of objections and they walked in silence.

A few minutes later, Cameron spoke up. "You know," he sucked his teeth, "I'm still a little pissed about the way you left the other night. I don't like waking up to notes."

Monica looked ahead and took a swallow of water from her bottle. She could feel his eyes staring at her.

"I know things are happening fast between us." Cameron looked into her eyes. "But I want you to know that I care deeply for you."

"Cameron—"

"Let me finish. I'm attracted to you, and I don't mean just physically. What we shared the other night was more than just sex. It was special. I realized that even more when I woke up yesterday morning and you had left the note saying you were going to Hilton Head. I was crazy with worry. Told myself as soon as you got back, you and I would have a serious discussion. I know you've been hurt by someone in the past. I could tell that the first time I tried to hold a personal conversation with you. Your protective shield is so sensitive that the slightest move- ment toward you flashes a warning signal so bright, it's almost blinding."

"Cameron, I—" Monica couldn't say anything. This conversation terrified her, her heart beat with the boom- ing of a bass drum. She felt her throat clamming up.

"There are a lot of things," Cameron went on, "we

still don't know about each other. One thing I know for sure is that I'm falling in love with you . . . "

"But you don't know me—"

"I know what I feel and I want you to take a chance on me. I'll try like hell not to hurt you." Cameron held his palm up in a "stop" sign. "Don't say anything now. I know you're not ready. And that's okay. As long as you at least think about what I've said." Flashing a devilish grin, he took her hand in his. "There is one condition, however."

"What's that?" Clearing her throat, Monica's voice was barely a whisper.

"No more disappearing acts in the middle of the night. And no more notes."

"That's two things."

"So, I lied. Is it a deal?"

"Deal."

Cameron brought her hand up to his lips and gently kissed it. "How about some pasta and a salad? Cafe Express is just a few minutes away, just off of Post Oak. You can go with me in my car or follow me in yours."

Monica laughed. "I'm right behind you."

As they rounded the corner to head back to Monica's car, she turned her head and looked over her shoulder. Just a short distance behind them, she could see the man who had carefully stayed about thirty feet behind them during their walk. She had spotted him as soon as she had pulled out of her driveway at her house. She hadn't bothered to try and lose him during the drive to the park because she wanted to be certain he was tailing her.

As she opened the door to her car and slid in behind the steering wheel, Monica watched in the rearview mirror as the man dashed to his vehicle across the parking lot.

Gerald Conti was on to her.

# Chapter
## 23

"Tell me again about Stevenson," Gerald grilled Arthur on Monday morning, as soon as the lawyer reported to his office. Puffing on his cigar, Gerald swirled his chair around, crossed his legs, and gazed out the window.

Arthur sighed and shook his head.

"I told you, Gerald, he's dead. It was over in a matter of seconds. He didn't even put up a fight. I ransacked the house and found nothing that linked him to Carter. I'm certain nobody saw me enter and nobody saw me leave. You know how it is in the country, everybody goes to bed early. When Stevenson's body is discovered, if it hasn't been already, it'll look like he got in the way of a burglary. It's over, Gerald."

"It's far from being over, Arthur. We may have silenced him, but we still don't know where Carter hid the information on the Excalibur. What about Stevenson's phone records?"

"There were no calls to Taylor, if that's what you want to know. The only long-distance calls to Houston were made to M. D. Anderson Cancer Center. I don't think he had a chance to talk to her at all."

"Did he go anywhere before you . . . before your little visit?"

"Only to the post office. He stayed home the rest of the day. The only visitor he had was a woman carrying a black medical bag."

"The post office?" Gerald asked, sitting upright in his chair and swinging it back around to face the man. "What'd he mail?"

"He was carrying a small manila envelope."

"Who'd he mail it to?"

"For chrissakes, Gerald. How the hell would I know that?" Arthur snapped, as if realizing he'd made a mistake by not following Stevenson into the building. "I don't have X-ray vision, you know."

Gerald's mind raced as he pondered what Arthur had just said. What was so important in that letter that Stevenson had to personally take it to the post office to send it off? Especially in his condition. He could easily have put it in the mailbox outside his house. Maybe it was an overdue bill, Gerald tried to convince himself. No, it was something more important than that. "What about Taylor?"

Glancing over the pad in his hand, Arthur said, "She was gone all day Saturday and didn't return home until about one a.m. Apparently, she had already left by the time my guy started watching the house that morning at seven." Arthur waited for Gerald to respond. When he didn't, Arthur continued. "She left her house again yesterday afternoon around three-thirty and met Cameron at Memorial Park. They walked for about an hour or so, left the park and went to eat at Cafe Express at the Pavilion on Post Oak. At six-thirty, they left in separate cars. Taylor went back to her house alone. I didn't have Cameron followed."

Arthur looked up from his pad and watched the top of

Gerald's head above the leather chair, billowing blue smoke rising above him. A moment passed before Gerald swirled the chair around again and looked at Arthur.

"Well, well," Gerald said, resting an elbow on the arm of the chair before taking the cigar out of his mouth. "So, Taylor and Cameron have become an item."

"So it seems. My guy said they were holding hands at the park."

"Did he hear any of their conversation?"

"No. He said there were too many people around and he didn't want to risk being seen."

"Maybe she was with him on Saturday."

"It's possible."

"Interesting," Gerald said, as he stubbed out the cigar in the ashtray on his desk.

"Do you want me to take my guy off of her now that Stevenson is out of the way?" Arthur asked.

Gerald didn't immediately answer.

"Gerald?"

"What?"

"I asked if you still wanted Taylor followed?"

"No. There's no need to now that Stevenson is out of the picture. But, just in case he decided to make a deathbed confession to her, check the mailroom to see if she gets anything from Bastrop." Gerald settled back into his chair. "Meanwhile, Bob called this morning. The test results on the Excalibur have been officially approved. I've made some other decisions. Round up senior staff for a meeting this afternoon. Two o'clock. Make sure everybody's there."

\* \* \*

MONICA WALKED INTO the conference room and took a seat next to Peters.

"Any idea why we're meeting today instead of our usual time tomorrow morning?" she whispered to her colleague.

"Nope," he said nonchalantly. "I got back from lunch and had an e-mail that said to be here promptly at two." He cocked his head in the direction of the door and said, "I'm sure we're about to find out."

Monica turned her head to where Peters stared and saw Gerald enter the room. The muffled conversation now diminished to a hush as Gerald took his seat at the head of the table.

"I know you're all wondering why I called this meeting," he said, looking around the room like a farmer surveying his crop.

"I won't waste your time or mine making long-winded speeches." He paused for a couple of seconds, leaned forward in his chair, and simply said, "The launch date for the Excalibur is one week from tomorrow."

Monica's whole body tensed. The bewildered looks on the faces of her colleagues told her they hadn't anticipated the announcement either. Before anyone had a chance to say anything, the door opened and Cameron walked in.

"Just in time, Cameron," Gerald said, motioning for him to have a seat. "I've just made the announcement." Cameron took the available chair next to Fazio, who sat to Gerald's right. "Cameron will be filling in for Vince Simon who underwent an emergency appendectomy over the weekend," Gerald said, staring straight at Monica who met his eyes without a flinch of intimidation.

Gerald continued. "All of you should be prepared.

You've been working on this for months. I want you to drop whatever else you're working on and devote your full attention to making this launch a success. For now, we'll introduce the Excalibur in Houston, Atlanta, and L.A. Since these are our largest markets, we should get a pretty good idea of how it will be received. Two weeks later, we will release it everywhere else in the country. Cameron has assured me that our system is ready to handle the extra load."

Monica's eyes shot to Cameron. He hadn't told her that his group had completed the work on the network. Neither had she asked, Monica berated herself. She had been so preoccupied with Dave Carter, she had neglected everything else. She should have gotten Carter out of Port Royal Meadows. She should have taken Jack Stevenson straight to Washington after her conversation with him. One week and the Excalibur would be out on the streets! She had less than seven days to wrap up a case she was no closer to solving now than when she first began a week ago. That disturbing thought jumbled her mind so that she didn't hear the question being posed to her. When she returned her attention to the present conversation, every eye in the room was on her.

"I asked, Taylor, if you were prepared for the media?" Gerald repeated, impatiently.

"Absolutely," she said, with more confidence than she actually felt. "I just need to get one of the Excaliburs to practice on before the demonstration."

"You and Peters can share one. But it must be returned to me at the end of each day. We've kept this product a secret too long to let one of them suddenly walk out the door. I want to see everyone's plans for the launch on my desk by the end of the day. I know I don't have to remind you that everything we've just discussed is extremely confidential."

Gerald rose from his seat and quickly left the room. Monica fell back into her chair and let out a heavy sigh. She looked at Peters who only shrugged his shoulders as he got up to leave. Cameron immediately slid into the empty chair next to her.

"I saw the look you gave me during Gerald's little speech," he said. "I was just as surprised as you were when he called and told me I was replacing my boss on the team."

"Why didn't you tell me the network was completed?"

"There wasn't time. I just got the report this morning. Right after that, Gerald called."

Monica thought for a moment, then pushed back from the table. "See ya later, Cameron."

* * *

MONICA SLAMMED THE RECEIVER down on the pay phone in the deli downstairs from her office with such force that it missed its slot and dangled at the end of its metal cord against the wall. *Where is he?* She had paged Michael twice and he hadn't returned her call. She hadn't succeeded in reaching Frasier either. Monica glanced at her watch and sighed. It was two thirty. There was nothing else she could do, but go back to her office and try to reach them later.

No sooner had she sat down behind her desk than Jazz hurried in behind her.

"You in trouble or something?" Jazz whispered, hiding in the triangular point between the door and the wall.

*Now what?* Monica thought, as she looked up at him. "Whatta you talking about?"

"Fazio," Jazz whispered. "I saw him walk out of here before you came in."

"Don't you have work to do?" Monica retorted. "We just got out of a meeting. He probably had some last-minute details he wanted to discuss with me."

"Uh, uh, girlfriend," he said, with an incredulous look on his face. "That's not what I mean." He pulled a large envelope from behind his back, tossed it onto her desk, and stepped back behind the door. Monica observed the interoffice envelope, picked it up and turned it over to open it. Just as she did, Jazz blurted out, "Don't do that now!  Lock it in your desk drawer, until I leave."

Monica frowned at him. "*What* is the deal?" she finally said, putting the package into her bottom, right-hand drawer.

"I could get my beautiful ass in big trouble for telling you this," Jazz said, "but I can't resist a good mystery. Fazio came in this morning when I was sorting the mail and asked me where your box was. When I pointed to it, he picked up the stack of letters I'd put in there earlier and started thumbing through them. I acted like I wasn't paying him any attention, but I watched out of the corner of my eyes."

Monica frowned again and asked, "What was he looking for?"

"Let me finish before someone comes in," he snapped. "Whatever it was, he didn't find it because he put every bit of it back in your box, as soon as he'd gone through it all. He then told me if you got anything from Bastrop to take it straight to Gerald.

"That package I just gave you came about two seconds after he'd left. A friend of mine at the downtown post office delivered it." He paused and then said, "It's from Bastrop."

Monica's heart skipped a beat.

"What's this all about?" Jazz asked.

"I don't know, but it's probably nothing," Monica said, trying to sound reassuring.

"Listen," he said, "I know something's going on. Gerald is on the hunt, and you, girlfriend, are the hunted. Later, I want to know every juicy little detail. Right now, I've got to get back downstairs. I don't want them to know I was here."

"What if Gerald or Fazio decides to check with the postal service?" Monica asked, not wanting Jazz to get in trouble because of her.

"Don't worry about that, girlfriend," he winked. "I'll take care of Steve."

"Thanks, Jazz. I really appreciate it."

Monica stared at the door seconds after Jazz had left, then slumped back in her chair. *What the hell is going on?* she asked herself, wondering what was in the package locked in her desk. Monica knew that if it was postmarked from Bastrop, it was probably from Jack Stevenson. But, if she herself wasn't expecting anything from him, how had Fazio known to go to the mailroom? Monica suddenly gasped and rushed to the door.

"Suzanne, come in here a minute, please," she yelled to her secretary.

"You need somethin', Taylor?" the girl said, stepping inside the office door.

"Just a minute," Monica said, rummaging through her files, until she pulled out a legal-sized folder. Handing it to Suzanne, she said, "Make a copy of these papers and then take them to Mr. Conti's secretary. He's expecting them."

"Okay. You goin' out somewhere?" Suzanne asked, watching her boss as she stuffed papers into her brief-case.

"Yeah," Monica answered, without looking up. "I've got a doctor's appointment."

"I don't remember seein' anythin' on your calendar."

"Migraine," Monica said, rubbing her temple for emphasis. "It's been coming on all day. This one's a whopper."

"I hope everythin's alright."

"It will be, Suzanne. Pull my door closed on your way out."

"Sure thin'. See you tomorrow."

Monica waited until the door clicked before unlocking the desk drawer. She pulled out the large, interoffice envelope and held it in her lap. Turning it over, she unfastened the clasp on the back and pulled out the red, white and blue Priority Mail envelope. She hesitated before pulling the tab that opened the package. Her adrenaline raced through her body like a roller-coaster ride at an amusement park. She quickly took out the smaller envelope and held it between her fingers with both hands, running her thumbs meticulously along the edges of the object that bulged from inside.

Monica stopped suddenly and dropped the envelope onto her desk.

# Chapter

## 24

**M**ichael put the receiver back in its cradle and
leaned back into his seat, his face deepened in
a frown.

"Dammit!" he swore under his breath, reaching for
his pager again. The battery had gone dead right after the
fifth digit had come through. He recognized the Houston
area code. It was Monica. But, the prefix was not from
either phone lines at her house. She would not have
dared to call him from her office.

"Double damn!" He slammed his fist on the stack of
papers on his desk. He had tried, to no avail, to contact
Jim Frasier. It wasn't like him to be out of reach without telling Michael where he was going. It was already
four-thirty and he still needed to talk with Frasier about
Dave Carter. Frustrated, he kicked over his waste paper
basket.

Michael picked up the phone again and dialed a number on the interoffice line.

"Chris?" he asked into the phone. "Glad I caught you.
Listen, I need a favor . . . Great. I'll be right down."

Five minutes later, Michael walked into the office of
the Bureau's debriefing division which put together the
profiles for cases to be investigated. Passing the cubicles
of unoccupied computers, he came to the last work space

in the corner of the room.

"What's up, Mike?" A heavy-set black man grinned, staring at his colleague's reflection on his computer screen. "Tired of life at the top and decided to come slumming?" Chris Burgess was one of the Bureau's investigative systems administrators.

"What can I say?" Michael slapped him on the back and pulled up a chair. "It gets lonely up there."

"Give me a minute to finish this. I'll be right with you."

"What 'cha got there?" Michael inched closer to the screen.

"Bank robber in Memphis. Guy held up the same bank five times in the last three weeks. Finally caught him yesterday. Had our guys scratching their heads on this one."

"A slippery fish, huh?"

"Shit, man." Chris finally looked up and grinned from ear to ear. "That's not the half of it. Let me show you something."

Chris punched in a series of strokes on the keyboard and waited a few seconds. Michael watched as individual photos of five beautiful women and one male appeared on the screen. Underneath each photo was the same name.

"Wow!" Michael let out a long, slow whistle. "Aw suki, suki now. This guy is good." He observed each picture, carefully. "You mean, he's—"

"—a white dude who dressed as black women, every time! Don't that beat all?" Chris laughed. "He admitted he stole pancake make-up from his brother's funeral home. Applied layers of it over his entire body, until he was damn near black as me."

"How'd we finally catch him?"

"Listen to this: The guy strolls into the bank, right? He's dressed to the nines in an ankle-length, tight-fitting dress with a scarf around his neck. Nothing but tits and ass, right? Anyway, Sister Boy walks over to the counter with her flowing hair and stilettoes, and strikes up a conversation with a young male teller, who immediately gets the hots for our gal. After she gets him to withdraw a huge amount of cash from an account number she's stolen, Sister Boy tells him she's forgotten how to use the ATM. Asks him to show her what to do. The dumbass doesn't have a clue as to what he's dealing with. When the teller gets to the machine, he asks for her card and pin number."

"Get outta here!" Michael grinned.

"Meanwhile, one of the female tellers from across the room notices a button has popped off the back of Sister Boy's dress. The bra has rubbed against her back so much that the makeup is smeared and pink flesh is exposed.

"When the security guard walks in, Sister Boy pulls a gun from her purse, grabs the young teller, and uses him as human armor as she backs her way out of the bank. The male teller is scared shitless, until he screams out that Sister Boy has gotten a hard-on. That's when Sister Boy throws him to the ground, turns and trips over her own pumps.

"I never laughed so hard in all my life."

"Unbelievable!" Michael laughed, holding his stomach and shaking his head.

"There are some sickos in this world, man. Guys like you and me gotta be careful out there." Chris looked around, lowered his voice and whispered to Michael,

"Between you and me, he would've gotten my attention. Look at the photos, man. He was drop-dead gorgeous!"

Michael looked at the pictures staring back at him and laughed out loud again. "You've gotta point there, brother."

"From now on, I'm doing a background check on any new chick I take out. You better do the same. Now, you said you needed a favor." Chris became serious. "What's up?"

"Remember pulling up some information a few weeks ago when Monica was here?"

"The wireless company in Texas? Bayou something?"

"Bayou City Wireless. That's it. I need to see the list of profiles again."

Chris entered a password into the FBI's on-line case system. Within a few seconds, the wireless company and a list of names showed up on the screen. Michael went down the list slowly, carefully examining each name one at a time. Dave Carter's name was not among them.

"Damn!"

"What's the matter?"

"I don't understand why he's not there."

"Talk English, Mike. Can't help ya, buddy, if you don't tell me who you're looking for."

Michael filled Chris in on the problem, then watched as he pecked on the keyboard again.

"What are you doing now?" Michael asked, peering over Chris's shoulder.

"Looking to see if there's another file on this case. Sometimes, there's a confidential file to the confidential file, know what I mean? Extra security and all that shit." He paused for a moment, looking intently at the screen.

"Bingo! There it is. Only one problem, it's encrypted. Can't get in without an authorized password."

"No problem. Use mine, I'm cleared."

Chris entered Michael's password and then frowned. "Not for this, you're not." He pointed to the blinking message that flashed: ACCESS DENIED.

"What the hell?" Michael exclaimed, staring open-mouthed at Chris. He'd never been denied information during the two years in his position as assistant deputy director. *What was in the file he couldn't see?*

"There must be some mistake," he said. "Enter my password again. S-W-E-E-T-S."

"I can spell, man," Chris remarked, entering the code again. Once more the signal flashed across the screen.

"Who set up this restriction?" Michael scowled, unwilling to believe he was being shut out. If there was something in that file that could help Monica, he was going to find out what it was.

Chris played with the keyboard again. "There's no name," he said. "Only an agent code." He pointed to the screen again, this time to a series of numbers. Michael leaned closer and caught his breath, his mouth flew open again at what he saw.

"Frasier!" Michael spat the name out of his mouth. "I don't believe it!" Suddenly, Michael's mind was clicking, remembering how vague Frasier had been when Michael first mentioned Dave Carter's name.

"What now, Mike?" Chris looked as perturbed as Michael felt.

"Frasier's password. What is it?"

"Are you crazy, man? I can't tell you, even if I did know."

"Don't give me that bull! You can break any code.

Or, have you forgotten that's the main reason we hired you in the first place?"

Michael glared at Chris, daring him to deny his checkered past.

"Type in the password, Chris!" Michael ordered, closing his eyes, trying to keep from exploding.

"Hey, man," Chris protested, "I could get in deep—"

"Do it! I'll take full responsibility."

Chris frowned at Michael for a moment, shook his head, and then finally entered the new code.

"Uh, oh!" Chris said, as soon as the information popped up on the monitor. He propped his elbows on the desk and brought his clasped fingers to his mouth, as he read what was on the screen. Slowly turning his chair around to Michael, he delivered the goods. "No wonder you couldn't find the dude. He's one of ours."

\* \* \*

MONICA LOOKED AT THE LETTER and read it over again—the second time since she got home. The handwriting on Jack Stevenson's stationary was shaky and uncontrolled, but very legible.

*Taylor,*

> *I hope this package reaches you safely. I fear, however, that by the time it does, I will be dead. I've suspected for sometime that I've been under surveillance, but was not certain until this morning when I saw the car parked outside my house. The enclosed tape was given to me for safe keeping by Dave Carter,*

*the last time I saw him. He explicitly told me not to look at it, that it would only make matters worse. I never did. I'm sure I already know the essence of what it says. Dave trusted me with it—and now I'm entrusting you. Look at the tape, Taylor, and make the right decision. Find out the truth about what happened to me—what happened to all of us, who were part of that hideous, senseless study. And when you do, I implore you to expose those persons culpable. This is the only peace I take to my grave. Be safe.*

*Jack*

Monica put the letter down and dried the tears from her eyes. After reading the letter the first time and viewing the tape, she frantically dialed Jack Stevenson's number. A woman answered the phone on the first ring.

"May I speak to Jack?"

At first, the other end of the line fell silent. Then, Monica's ears stung as the woman burst out crying into the phone.

"Ma'am? What's the matter?" Bewildered, Monica didn't know what to do.

Finally, the woman pulled herself together and identified herself as Laura Stevenson, Jack's sister.

Between muffled sobs, she said, "He's dead. My brother's gone. Killed . . ." Then Laura Stevenson proceeded to tell Monica that Jack's nurse had discovered him early yesterday morning when she reported for work. The night before the house had been broken into and someone had murdered Jack. He'd bled to death from several stab wounds. Monica told the woman she was sorry. Laura Stevenson asked if she were a friend of her brother's. Monica said yes, she was his friend. She hung up, her hand still gripping the receiver.

Anger boiled in Monica to the point her ears felt as though they were putting out steam. She stared at the black videocassette in her hand. The dynamics of Dave Carter's words still sang in her mind. *How could Bayou City Wireless have done such a horrid thing?* Not the company, but more specifically, Gerald Conti.

The proof she'd been seeking was right in front of her, yet Monica could not pick up the phone and call the Bureau. If she turned over the information now, the case would be out of her hands forever. But she still had a few more days . . .

Monica picked up her glass and took a big gulp of her bourbon. The drink stung the back of her throat, its warmth stimulating her whole body. She took out a cigarette from the pack of Virginia Slims, thumped the end on the edge of the table, then stuck it between her lips and lit it with a match. Blowing out a long stream of smoke, she then pressed the rewind button on the remote control until the tape stopped, then slowly pressed the play button.

She sat on the edge of the sofa and braced herself for the tape to start again. She had to see it just one more time, before deciding her next move.

# Chapter

## 25

"I'm sorry, Ms. LeBlanc, but Mr. Conti is on an overseas call. In fact, his calendar is booked through the end of the week. If you'd like, I could schedule you an appointment for the first of next week."

Monica gave the secretary a "No-I-would-not-like" glare, adjusted the purse strap on her shoulder and, with both palms firmly planted on the desk, leaned forward against it. She had high-tailed it straight to Victor's office when she learned Gerald had canceled his usual Tuesday morning senior staff meeting and would be out of the office until noon. She was not about to let anyone deter her now.

Noticing the small, gold clock positioned on the corner next to her that showed the time was now eight forty-five, Monica said, "Perhaps you didn't understand me the first time. It's imperative I see Mr. Conti *this* morning. Tell you what, Sandra—" Monica read the secretary's name plate. "—Why don't I just have a seat and wait for him to finish his call?"

"But, Ms.—"

"Maybe I can help, Sandra," Maggie interrupted, walking into the reception area. "Miss LeBlanc? I'm Maggie Wentworth, Mr. Conti's executive assistant. Would you like a cup of coffee?"

"Yes, thank you." Monica followed the lady down the hall. "I didn't mean to cause a scene. But I really need to talk to Victor this morning. I have some information I think he should hear."

Extending a gold-rimmed china cup and saucer to Monica when they had reached the small room, Maggie poured coffee from the silver coffeepot. "Is it something I could help you with?"

"No. I'm afraid not. It's confidential." Monica gave her an adamant stare.

Maggie arched an eyebrow.

"Ms. LeBlanc—"

"Taylor."

"Taylor, Victor Conti is a very busy man. If the matter you wish to discuss with him is indeed as urgent as you say, then I suggest you give me some idea of its nature, so I can assist you in getting in to see him."

Maggie's subtle implication inferred the influence she had over her boss and communicated to Monica that the woman was more than just his trusted assistant.

"All I can say at this point is that I believe there to be a serious problem at Bayou City of which Victor may be unaware. I would like to discuss it with him in private."

"You report directly to Gerald, don't you?" Maggie asked coyly, taking a sip from her cup.

"That's right."

"And have you discussed this 'urgent' matter with him?"

Monica responded without blinking, "No. I have not."

Maggie returned Monica's gaze as if seriously pondering her last remark. Without comment, she rose from her seat and briskly left the room.

Within a span of three minutes, she was back.

"Taylor," she said, "Victor will see you now."

*　*　*

"THIS IS AN UNEXPECTED surprise, Taylor," Victor greeted Monica with a perplexed look. Walking from behind his desk, he extended a hand to her, then led her to a chair directly across from his desk.

"I apologize for barging in like this, Victor. But, as I told Maggie—" Monica looked to her right to see that the woman had closed the door, taken a seat and intended to sit in on the conference. "—this matter is extremely urgent."

Victor sat on the corner of his desk.

"I assure you, Taylor," he smiled, propping his hands on one leg, "whatever you have to say will be held in the strictest confidence. Now, young lady, what seems to be the problem?"

"How much do you know about the Bastrop Study?" She went straight to the point.

Victor reared his head, somewhat taken aback by the question. Frowning, he said, "I'm not sure I understand what you mean."

"Did you know there were complications with the Excalibur during its testing phase?"

"No. I didn't. But if there were initial problems, I'm sure they were minor, since they were never brought to my attention. In fact, I have the report right here."

He walked over to his file cabinet, opened the top drawer and pulled out a folder. He put on his reading glasses and skimmed over the pages. He looked up at Monica.

"There's no mention of any concerns, whatsoever. I think you'd better tell me to what exactly you are referring."

Monica told him about her conversation with Jack Stevenson. Victor grew agitated as he listened to her story.

"That's preposterous!" he shouted, snatching his glasses from his face. "What you're insinuating is that we intentionally used those people as human guinea pigs. An annihilation of sorts. I tell you we would never do such a thing."

"Maybe you wouldn't have, Victor." Monica remained calm. "But what about Gerald?"

Victor weighed her question carefully before responding.

"Taylor, you've only been with us a short time. I understand my brother can be difficult, at times, to work with. If you and Gerald have somehow gotten off on the wrong track, maybe, I can intervene and help—"

"This is not about personality differences," she interjected. "People died from testing the Excalibur and Gerald has known about it all along!"

"Let's get this Stevenson fellow on the phone!" He marched to his desk and picked up the phone. "What's his number? I want to talk to him myself."

"That's not possible, Victor."

"If he's making accusations against this company, I want to hear it from him personally. Now are you going to tell me his number? Or do I have to call directory assistance?"

"Jack Stevenson is dead, Victor. He was killed two days ago in a burglary attempt at his home in Bastrop."

Again Victor stared at Monica, unable to believe what he had just heard. He slowly placed the phone back down on his desk. Clearing his throat, he said, "I'm sorry."

"I don't think his death was just a random act of violence," Monica continued, as though she had not heard his apology. "It's odd that just a couple of days after he contacts me, Jack Stevenson turns up dead."

"Wait just a minute, young lady," Victor charged angrily. "You're not suggesting my brother had anything to do with this man's death, are you?"

Monica glared at him without batting an eye.

"I didn't say that," she said coolly. "You did."

Victor raked a hand through his salt-and-pepper hair and breathed deeply. Before he could catch himself, he blurted out, "This can't possibly be true."

"I had hoped the same thing, Victor," Monica said, breaking into his thoughts, "until yesterday, when I received some information in the mail." Opening the zipper of her purse, she pulled out the manila envelope and handed it to Victor.

"What's this?" He took out the videocassette tape and letter.

"Jack mailed this to me the day he died. Apparently, he knew his life was in danger and wanted me to have proof of everything he'd told me." Monica paused for a moment. "The video was made by Dave Carter."

Victor riveted his eyes to Maggie, who stared back at him with her hand over her mouth. He held her gaze for what seemed like forever.

"But, Dave is—"

"—dead," Monica finished the sentence for him. "Yes, I know. He recorded the tape before leaving the company. Gave it to Jack to keep for him. Just read the letter, Victor, and watch the video."

Victor put his glasses back on, stared down at the letter in his hand, and slowly read its contents. When he had finished, he walked over to the television in the corner of the room and put the videocassette tape into the built-in VCR. His hand trembled as he reached for the remote, and wavered before pressing the play button. When the image appeared on the screen, Victor sucked in his breath, then slid into the chair in front of the television.

* * *

SEATED BEHIND A LARGE desk, Dave Carter was dressed in a white short-sleeve casual shirt with his blond hair neatly combed, his face cleanly shaven. Directly in front of him on the desk was the familiar black tote bag. As the video camera fixed on the healthy tanned face with the piecing blue eyes, Monica closed her eyes and shook her head, remembering the pale sliver of the man hidden away at Port Royal Meadows. Her eyes opened again just as Carter raised his right hand and swore that what he was about to say was God's truth.

"What should have been an adventure into the high-tech world of telecommunications," Carter began, taking the phone in his hand, "suddenly took a wrong turn and became a deadly experiment. Bayou City Wireless deliberately killed members of a group of people in Bastrop, Texas, who were selected to test this product, the Excalibur.

"I have learned that the digital system put in place for the Excalibur boosted the transmission frequency to 1.1 gigahertz—billions of pulses per second—and increased the power to more than 6 watts, exposing the people in Bastrop to lethal dosages of radio-frequency radiation, emitted from the communication device's antenna.

"This gradual process was increased during the two-year study, so that all of the tests could be completed. If the participants had been exposed to the dangerous levels from the start, they would not have lasted the entire experiment. The townspeople already suspected a chemical plant, some twenty miles away, caused the illnesses the people suffered. They believed the emission of coal and carcinogens from the nearby plant was polluting the air and drinking water, resulting in the deaths of many residents of Bastrop from cancer-related illnesses. Children were born with birth defects. The elderly died of respiratory failure.

"To further throw the blame from the Excalibur, a new oil company added fuel to the fire by unearthing a hazardous waste site. I have a document that shows Gerald Conti is the owner of the small oil company, as well. It is my belief that he purposely chose Bastrop as the company's test site for the Excalibur and used this blanket of controversy to conceal himself as the real culprit."

Carter paused for a moment, as he picked up the Excalibur again. Continuing, he said, "Gerald correctly calculated that the people of this little town, unsophisticated in their knowledge of wireless technology, would be so mesmerized, seduced without resistance at being chosen to test such a product, that they would never consider its danger."

Monica eyes were fixed on Victor, as he watched and listened to Carter in silent horror. Carter explained how he first became suspicious of the headaches and dizziness the participants complained about, six months into the study. Many of them had joked that they could not remember a time when they *didn't* have headaches. But, within a year into the study, eighteen of the participants had become ill. Soon, nearly all of them had been diagnosed with various cancerous tumors—most of them, brain tumors. The ironic thing, Carter said with a cynical smile, was that they never once thought that the communications device that they had come to rely on could be the cause of their illnesses. That is, all but Jack Stevenson.

Carter explained how Stevenson's medical background had first alerted him to the possibility of dangerous levels of electromagnetic rays being emitted from the phone. Since Stevenson had read about a team of doctors at M. D. Anderson Cancer Center years ago who studied children whose cancer-related illnesses were thought to have been caused by living near power lines, it was not hard for him to suspect the Excalibur as the source of his problems.

It was not until Carter studied scientific studies conducted on the issue which disclosed side affects—ranging from ringing in the ears to headaches to brain tumors—even changes in the DNA molecular structure from exposure to electrofrequency radiation—that Carter decided to look into the digital system built by Bayou City Wireless. He methodically expounded on how the software installed on NMS/6000 contained the ability to execute background programs, allowing simultaneous readings of the system to run at the same time. Carter found out Gerald had installed the system himself, using the excuse that the intricate project warranted his expertise. He set the NMS screens to display the fictitious readings, while the dangerous data was hidden, recorded, and manipulated daily. Secured by high-level passwords, both the frequency and power levels exceeded the safety standards.

Using the Excalibur, Carter demonstrated how a user would be exposed to electromagnetic rays when the antennae was held in a certain position, flush against the head. This explained, Carter continued, how the participants who were right-handed developed tumors on the left side of the head, and those who were left-handed developed them on the right side. The feed points of the specific absorption rate—or SAR— in all of the participants were near the temporal bone of the forehead and the eye region.

From the scientific studies he referred to, the SAR exposures from human use of wireless devices were almost entirely restricted to the head. The head-to-the-whole-body ratio was as high as 1000 to 1.

Monica shook her head in disgust.

Carter went on to theorize that Bayou City Wireless had not acted alone. Unable to prove it, he suspected Gerald had help from someone at the FCC, most likely, the Chairman. He supported this theory by showing the test results that bore the Chairman's signature of approval and the speedy time line of previous approval processes.

Carter had confronted Gerald with his suspicions. Gerald denied it, threatened Carter's life if he told anyone of his theory. It was the same day of this confrontation, that Carter decided to record his findings on video.

"The innocent people of Bastrop," Carter said at the end of the tape,"were victims of corporate greed, high-level corruption, and public mistrust. It's too late to stop the deaths in Bastrop, but Gerald Conti has to be stopped. It is my intent that this tape will do just that."

The television screen went blue, signaling the end of the tape. The silence in the room was as deafening as a fog-horn, blowing at close range.

* * *

VICTOR SAT STUNNED IN HIS SEAT; his haggard face bore the shock of what he'd just heard. Finally, he raised the remote and turned off the set. He looked to Maggie, who wept silently on the sofa behind him, then he slowly stood up and walked to the chair behind his desk.

"I can't believe it," Victor muttered mostly to himself, shaking his head in disbelief. For months, he'd had a twin's intuition that Gerald was hiding something from him. But, never had he imagined something as diabolical and evil as what he'd just heard.

Victor forcefully tried to control his breathing, which had intensified with every word Dave Carter spoke. Within 15 minutes of viewing that tape, everything he'd worked for came crashing down on him like a skyscraper blown to bits by several tons of dynamite. Victor's whole body trembled with seething anger, his head was a fireball waiting to explode.

It was all clear to him now: Gerald's insistence on controlling the Excalibur project from the beginning; his eagerness to complete the sale to the Indonesians before Victor could analyze the data; the secret meetings with Bob McCormick. And Carter! Had Gerald sacrificed him, as well? It wasn't until Victor felt the stabbing pain in his palms that he realized he'd balled his fists so tight that his short fingernails dug into his skin.

*Gerald is a murderer!*

Taking a white cotton handkerchief from the breast pocket of his suit jacket, Victor wiped the perspiration from his forehead. Maggie stood beside him now, with one hand on his shoulder. Without looking at her, Victor reached for it and ran his thumb across the back of her hand. He then cleared his throat and, in a low voice said to no one in particular, "Believe me. I never knew."

Monica nodded her head. He looked to her like he had aged twenty years in just the last hour. In an equally lowered voice, she said, "I never thought you were a part of all this. That's why I came directly to you, as soon as I knew exactly what was going on."

"Am I correct in assuming Gerald has no knowledge of what you know? Or, about this tape?"

"As far as I know, he has no idea."

Victor nodded his head again. "I see." Nothing was really clear to him anymore. "What do you plan to do with this information?"

"Before I answer that," Monica hesitated, "there's something else I need to tell you. I am an undercover agent for the FBI."

He responded by shaking his head. "It's gone far enough to attract the attention of the government?"

"The FCC is the government, too, Victor. Bob McCormick's shabby cover-up of the deaths is what led us to Bayou City Wireless in the first place. Your company won't be the only one with some explaining to do. The Chairman abused his authority and position. Don't believe for one minute that the Bureau is going to let him go unscathed.

"I can't discuss the specifics of the investigation with you, Victor. But, if it's any consolation, you were never under suspicion. Only Gerald."

"Be that as it may, I'm still guilty by association."

"I have to turn this evidence over to the Bureau. I don't have a choice."

"I understand." Victor sat quietly in his chair and clasped his hands together, his index fingers pointed his chin to the ceiling.

"There is something I haven't been able to figure out." Monica looked Victor squarely in the eye.

"Yes?"

"Why Gerald pushed up the release date of the Excalibur in the U.S. Why did he change his strategy? There's also no record at the Port of Houston indicating a Conti Telecommunications shipment scheduled. Do you know when and where the phones will be exported out of the country?"

At that moment, Victor realized how naive he'd been to let Gerald take charge of the whole project. He let out a heavy sigh. "I honestly don't know what the truth is anymore. I agreed to the early release over the week-end—a mistake, I now realize—after Bob McCormick called and convinced me the product was safe. Since Gerald is general manager of our manufacturing plant, he usually makes all the shipping arrangements. We normally ship out of the Port of Houston. But, if you say there's no record of it, then I don't know what port Gerald is using."

"We'll find out."

"Before you do, Taylor—I suppose that's not even your real name?—I'd like a chance to confront my brother. Maybe I could even convince him to turn himself in."

As if hearing Michael's voice sirening in her head, Monica quickly responded.

"No way, Victor," she said, shaking her head adamantly. "I won't risk blowing this case and letting Gerald get away. He may even try to flee the country, once he knows we're on to him. I'm not willing to take that chance."

"I won't let him, goddammit!" Victor shouted, slamming his fist on the desk, unable to contain his anger for one minute longer. "He has killed innocent people and sabotaged this company. I know he's got to pay for what he's done, but I must find out why he committed such a diabolical act. Everything I've worked for is on the verge of being destroyed. Give me some time, I know I can get him to come forward and confess. You must admit, his cooperation could be essential to the investigation."

He scrutinized her face and saw by her expression that Monica was considering his request.

"How much time?"

Victor consulted the time on his gold Rolex. "It's eleven-fifteen now. End of business day, the day after tomorrow." He saw her wavering. "Let me help clear up this mess. I want to cooperate in any way I can."

"How do I know you won't alert Gerald and the three of you won't run off together?" she asked, involving Maggie for the first time.

"'Touche'," he snorted with a cynical smile. "Can't say that I blame you for thinking that. No, Taylor, I'm not going to run from this. I may have started my company with the fortune my parents left me, but I've built it through the years by being honest and working hard. I'll not start lying now that the company's in trouble. We owe those people in Bastrop."

"Okay, here's the deal: I'll meet you here day after tomorrow, six o'clock sharp," Monica said, getting up from her chair.

"You have my word. And if that's not good enough, Maggie and I will sign whatever you want agreeing to what we've just discussed." Maggie nodded her head in agreement.

"That won't be necessary." Monica unclipped what looked like a pager from the shoulder strap of her purse. Pushing a button, the last few seconds of their conversation replayed on the tiny, micro-cassette recorder. "Just in case," she explained.

"One more thing—" she picked up the remote and ejected the videocassette from the television. "—I'll keep this." She held up Carter's tape. "Gerald must not be told about it or that I was the one who brought it to your attention. I don't want my name mentioned at all. I suspect he's been looking for it for some time."

"Agreed."

Turning to Maggie before leaving the room, Monica said, "Thank you again for your help. I'm sorry we couldn't meet under better circumstances."

As she walked to the door with the tape and Jack Stevenson's letter secured within her purse, Monica heard Victor pick up the phone and very politely tell the person on the other end to tell his brother to get his ass on the line.

\* \* \*

"I GOT HERE AS SOON AS I COULD, Victor," Gerald said, walking into his brother's office at exactly two-fifteen. Arthur Fazio was in step right behind him. "The afternoon traffic in this city is atrocious."

Gerald headed to greet his brother with their usual embrace, but was cut short when Victor ignored him and turned to the lawyer. "Arthur, would you excuse us, please? I'd like to talk to my brother alone."

Arthur Fazio looked uncertainly at Gerald at being dismissed, then back at Victor. "Sure," he replied. To

Gerald he asked, "Do you want me to wait for you?"

"That won't be necessary, Arthur," Victor interjected calmly, before his twin could answer. "Why don't you go back to the office? We won't be needing you for this meeting." Victor had already turned his back to the two men to stare out the window.

"Have Bennett drive you back in the car, Arthur," Gerald added. "I'll take a taxi to the office when I'm done here."

Without another word, the legal counsel turned around and walked out of the office, closing the door behind him. Gerald stared at Victor for a moment, then took a seat on the sofa. Crossing his legs and stretching an arm across the back of the sofa, he asked, "Is something wrong, Victor? You look like you might be ill, though I must say, you have great taste in clothes."

Victor turned and looked at Gerald. Managing a weak smile, he noticed for the first time that he and his brother were wearing almost identical black suits. Every now and then, one of them would buy clothing and find out later that the other had purchased the same thing. *That twin connection,* Victor thought to himself, the smile vanishing from his face.

"No, Gerald," he sighed, "there's nothing wrong with my health. What you see is the day-to-day stress of the job."

"You know I'm always available to help you in any way I can. All you have to do is ask."

Victor looked at his twin and then turned back around, his hands joined together behind his back.

"Tell me, Gerald. How are the plans progressing for the release of the Excalibur?"

"Everything is going smoothly." Gerald gave a sigh

of relief, attributing Victor's sour mood to pre-launch jitters. "The launch date is still on for Tuesday of next week."

"And the shipment to Indonesia? I assume you've made the necessary arrangements with the Port of Houston?"

"It's all taken care of. The first shipment of phones is scheduled to go out day after tomorrow, so that their arrival in Indonesia will coincide with the launch date here. I must have neglected to tell you," he said, looking down to straighten his tie, "but I decided to ship the phones out of Tampico Bay, instead of the Port of Houston."

"Tampico Bay?" Surprised, Victor spun around abruptly. "We've always shipped out of the Port of Houston. What made you decide to change ports?"

"Bob's been doing some relationship building for the U.S. government with Mexican officials down there, helping them with communications guidelines and all. He and I thought it would be good business for Conti Telecommunications, if we used one of their ports, since our manufacturing plant is in Mexico. That's not a problem, is it?"

"You and Bob decided? Without talking to me?"
Gerald sat up in his seat.

"I didn't think it would be a problem."

"I see. And what about your people? Are they prepared for the launch, as well?"

"Damn straight!" Gerald snorted. "Victor, you should see the unveiling we've got planned for the media. We've got commitments from just about every technology reporter of every major television station, newspaper, and technology-related magazine in the country. Not only do we have an award-winning video—highlighting all the functioning capabilities of the Excalibur—but Taylor's arranged to have an area set up for the reporters to test the Excalibur themselves.

"Hell, we've even rented the grand ballroom at the Westin Galleria Hotel to accommodate everyone. I can't wait to see the expressions on their faces when they realize all that the Excalibur can do. The announcement of the product is sure to make front-page news."

Twiddling his thumbs behind his back, Victor asked in eerie calmness, "And what do you think the 'expressions on their faces' will be when they find out the Excalibur killed people in Bastrop?" Turning around at last, Victor glared at his twin with vehement disgust and rage. He saw clearly the nervous smile on Gerald's face.

"You're joking, right?"

"No, Gerald," Victor snapped. "I'm dead serious. Did you think I wouldn't find out? Did you consider it just a minor little detail that would escape my attention? My God, Gerald, how could you have been so stupid?"

"You weren't kidding . . . " Gerald fidgeted in his seat, ". . . when you said earlier that the stress of the job was getting to you. You saw the report. The group loved the Excalibur. It's right there in—"

"Don't play games with me, Gerald!" Victor shouted. "That report is a sham! It fails to mention a few pertinent details: The cancers. The deaths. The increased frequency and power levels. The convenient elimination of Jack Stevenson, the last surviving victim. I know the truth. *I . . . know . . . it . . . all!*"

"Who told you that!" Gerald's eyes widened, the veins in his forehead popped out.

"Never mind how I found out. I'm not going to let

you get away with murder. You had the power to stop all this and you didn't. I won't risk millions of other lives, by releasing a product we know is dangerous. Cancel the press conference, the shipping orders, and the manufacturing of the Excalibur. Cancel everything! It's over!"

"Like hell it is!" Gerald jumped to his feet and marched over to face his twin, his eyes bulging in their sockets. "You're not going to fucking jerk the plug on me after all I've done for this company. After all I've done for *you*. You wouldn't even have Conti Telecommunications, if I hadn't told you about that company years ago that needed financial backing. What happened when I needed help? Instead of selling me fifty per cent of the shares, equal partnership, you offered me a pittance of what was rightfully mine. The president of a subsidiary. What a joke!

"I even helped you when the military asked you to help design communications equipment. But who got all the credit? You did. Yes, you mentioned my name here and there, but you gained the respect and admiration of our peers. You've always wanted everything for yourself. You stole my company, just as you stole Mother's love from me when we had polio."

"What the hell are you talking about?"

"Don't look at me like you don't know. I watched as you lay there, pretending to be an invalid, demanding all of Mother's attention. Nothing I did was ever good enough for her after that, because she was always doting on *you*. When Mother and Father were killed, I thought you and I were finally going to be on an even keel. But, it was your name and accomplishments that kept cropping up on the pages of the business and financial news. Again, I went unnoticed, standing in your shadow. Now, when I'm finally on the verge of distinction from you, when *I* can get some recognition, you want to steal my creation. I won't let you do it. Do you hear me? The Excalibur is mine!"

Gerald's words pierced through Victor like flying glass, spewed by Mother Nature's tumultuous wrath. Victor had never known the depth of Gerald's resentment of him. Looking into his brother's face, seeing in Gerald's eyes that he believed every word he'd just said, Victor could only shake his head. Gerald was demented. But, Victor would *not* bail him out this time.

Victor swallowed hard, then cleared his throat. "Whatever you believe does not condone what you've done. The project can not continue."

"There's no way I'm going to let you halt this project," Gerald warned.

"I don't intend to, Gerald. You are."

"What do you mean?"

"You're going to confess everything to the police and—"

"You're out of your fucking mind! For God's sake, Victor, I'm your own flesh and blood! Alright I admit it. Yes, the people in Bastrop are dead because of the study. But none of them knew the Excalibur was to blame. Only Bob and Arthur—and now you—know the truth. Nobody has to know. Don't you see? I had to increase the frequency and power levels during the testing to be sure the phones were conducive to conditions in Indonesia. There was no other way.

"The American version works fine within the safety standards. It's not a danger to anyone, now. We can just go on with everything as planned. I swear, I didn't know those people were going to die."

Victor stared at Gerald, as though he were really seeing him for the first time. A connoisseur of dissimulation, Gerald was his evil twin, like in the classical tales. He did not know this person who was so cruel and unfeeling, and who, with everything laid out on the table, still wanted to forge ahead, without the slightest regard to human destruction.

There was still one last thing Victor had to know.

"You're lying to me even now, Gerald. Dave Carter warned you. He told you those people in Bastrop were dying."

"That's ridiculous." Gerald laughed, nervously. "Carter couldn't possibly have told you that. Besides, he's dead. There's no way to prove it."

"That's not as convenient as you may think. Before he died, he managed to substantiate everything you've just confessed."

Gerald went stark white.

"I often wondered," Victor continued, walking towards his brother until he was directly in front of where Gerald sat, "why he didn't come to me and tell me about his illness before he left. Why he didn't leave a forwarding address or number where he could be reached. I even asked you about it, remember? You acted so strangely that day in my office when I asked if you'd heard from him.

"I couldn't understand why I had the feeling you knew more about his sudden departure than you were saying. Then, not long after that, you said that you had received a letter stating he was dead. Now that I think of it, you never once bothered to show that letter to me, even though you knew how concerned I was about him. Why? The timing of it all couldn't have been more perfect, if you had planned it yourself. Or did you?"

"Don't be absurd!"

"Answer me, Gerald!" Victor raised his voice. "Did you kill Carter to keep him quiet about the project?"

"No, I did not!" Gerald jumped to his feet, as if the action gave credence to his words. Staring into his brother's angry, but sad, squinted eyes, Gerald let out a heavy sigh and raised his arms in defeat.

"You're right about the Excalibur, little brother. I guess I knew all along that I wouldn't get away with it. What can I say? I'm sorry. I didn't mean to hurt you and I certainly didn't intend for people to die. Oh, but we were this close—" He held his index finger and his thumb within an inch of each other.

Victor stared at him for a long moment, shaking his head. A part of him felt sorry for Gerald, but those sentimental feelings were overshadowed by disgust and outrage. He would be the one who would have to figure a way out of this mess. There was a lot to do and just a short amount of time in which to do it.

"We need to gather all of the data from the study," Victor said, without acknowledging Gerald's apology. "The *accurate* data, as well as the engineering plans for the NMS/6000. I want a written, detailed account of exactly what happened in the study, the names of all the participants, and the exact power and frequency levels used at every stage. We're going to have to compensate the families of those people in Bastrop."

He threw his hands up in despair. "But what price do you put on a life? Once this thing is out in the open—The public will never be able to pick up a cellular or wireless phone again without wondering . . . "

Victor's last thought drifted in the air, as he slowly walked back to his desk and miserably fell down in his seat. The weight of it all was beginning to take effect. He could see the news coverage: CONTI TELECOM- MUNICATIONS SELLS KILLER PHONES. The stock market would go wild. Conti Telecommunications, Inc., would be history.

And what would he say to his employees? He'd preached for years about product reliability, honesty and integrity, of earning the public's trust. How would he ever look them in the face?

Gerald kept his eyes on Victor during his brother's silence.

"Listen, Victor," he started, "maybe it won't be as bad as you think. Remember the Tylenol crisis? Those guys came out and admitted what had happened. Sure sales went down a bit, people were afraid to use that particular brand for awhile. But, right this very minute, there are thousands of Jane and John Does taking Tylenol, without a care in the world for their safety. There may be a way for us to salvage this thing yet. Hell, if not, we can go someplace else and start another company."

Victor looked at his brother and miserably shook his head. *Gerald still doesn't get it.* Always running away from his failures without ever facing where he went wrong. Who the hell did he believe would ever grant them another license?

"It's not the same. That was an accident." Loosening his tie, Victor added, "We might as well start dealing with it now. We've got a long night ahead of us."

"I've got a better idea. Why don't we go to Brennan's and have an early dinner? We could sit down, work out a plan, and go from there. The last supper, you might say."

Victor let out a sigh. "Alright, Gerald, I don't see any harm in that. Do you want to ride over with me or do you want to meet me there?"

"I might as well ride with you, since I'm already here. Just give me a second to call Bennett and tell him to knock off for the day."

Walking towards the door, Victor turned around and faced Gerald. "I'll wait for you outside. I need to let Maggie know that our plans for tonight have changed."

# Chapter

## 26

The thunderstorm that suddenly descended upon Houston was like a bad omen, shadowing an already dismal day. The exact moment Victor steered his black 1997 Mercedes S500 onto Smith Street in the direction of Brennan's restaurant, the darkened sky gave way to torrential rain and impressive streaks of lightning that would have put the annual Fourth of July fireworks display at Eleanor Tinsley Park on Buffalo Bayou to shame. Driving down the rain-pelted streets, Victor's thoughts spun around and around. Neither he nor Gerald spoke during the drive.

Victor could still see the lightning flash outside of the restaurant from the back table where they dined. He was surprised that the dinner conversation had gone as smoothly as it did. He'd expected more protests from Gerald. Instead, his brother's conciliatory mood and agreement to cooperate on Victor's terms had caused Victor to wonder if Gerald were really aware of the seriousness involved.

Victor had been pressed only once during the evening and that was when Gerald insisted on knowing where Victor obtained the information that incriminated him in the first place. Even when Victor firmly said that he had no intention of revealing his source, Gerald backed down and quickly changed the subject to something else.

As Victor listened to him drone on now about the latest semi-conductor chip one of their competitors was rumored to be manufacturing—as if any of that mattered to either of them now—he realized Gerald was drunk. In fact, they'd both had enough to drink and it was time to call it a night. Victor excused himself and went to find their waiter for the check.

"It's only eight-thirty," Gerald protested, squinting his eyes to the dial of his watch.

"I'm tired, Gerald. It's been a long day and we have a lot of work to do tomorrow."

"I assume you'll want Arthur there?"

"Yes. I'm going to make some calls to the legal team tonight, brief them on the situation, and have them join us as well. They need to get started on this right away."

The two men waited just inside the entrance of the restaurant, as a line of cars drove up to be valet parked. The rain had slacked off to a steady drizzle, the thunderstorm quietly rumbled in the distance. But, the conditions still impeded the efforts of the valet attendants who tried to keep the stream of cars with arriving patrons moving along in a timely fashion.

"What the hell is taking so long?" Gerald asked, growing agitated at having to wait.

"The restaurant's crowded tonight, Gerald. It'll only be a few more minutes."

"You'd think they'd melt right here in the street," Gerald said, in the direction of two elegantly dressed women who hurried out of a Lincoln Continental and huddled under an awaiting umbrella.

"Be quiet, Gerald."

"I don't give a damn if they hear me. In fact, I'll get

the keys myself." Gerald staggered over to the valet attendant. "Let's go down the street to Damian's for a drink and then come back and get the car. I'll drive us home."

Victor knew Gerald was in no position to get behind the steering wheel of a car. He grabbed Gerald's arm, only to have his hand slung away. Gerald snatched the keys off the nail and started across the street before Victor had a chance to stop him.

The street lights danced off the rain-slicked, one-way street as cars intermittently sped down past the side of the restaurant. Victor could feel his adrenaline racing through every ounce of his body at the thought of Gerald crossing three lanes of traffic.

"Jesus!" he cried out, as Gerald's first attempt across Smith Street was aborted right before a Suburban swerved around him. Victor ran to where Gerald was standing and tried to restrain him.

"What are you trying to do?" he shouted. "Give me those goddamn keys!"

"You just don't want me to drive your precious car," Gerald sang with a silly grin, ramming the keys in his pockets, as though he were six years old again and they were playing a game.

"Cut it out, Gerald. You're making a scene," Victor said above the roar of cars whizzing past, but out of earshot of the valet attendants and arriving passengers who were now peering through the drizzle at them.

"Who gives a damn what they think? We're Contis. We do whatever the hell we want. C'mon, Victor. Race you to the other side. Oops! Forgot," Gerald broke out in hysterics, "you can't. Your leg would get in the way."

"You're drunk. Now, let's go back to Brennan's and

get out of the rain."

"Not as drunk as I'm gonna be before the night is over. This is the last supper, remember? Eat, drink, and be merry . . . and all that shit. I know," Gerald said with sudden revelation. "If I get across the street before you do, we won't tell anyone about our lil' secret. If you beat me, I'll go straight to 61 Reisner and tell HPD everything I know. How 'bout that?"

"Stop it, Gerald!" Victor struggled to keep his brother from stumbling. "You're coming back with me to the car. Then I'm taking you home."

"I'm not a fucking kid, you sonofabitch! Let go of me!"

With one strong jerk, Gerald broke free from Victor's grasp, causing Victor to lose his balance and tumble to the pavement. A woman's scream was heard in the distance. Gerald turned toward the sound and gave a warning shout to a parking attendant coming towards them.

"Stay away from us!" he shouted, pointing to the man, who stopped on command  some twenty feet away. Victor struggled to his feet, when Gerald returned his attention back to him and knocked him back to the ground.

"This is all your fault, you goddamn sonofabitch," he spat at Victor with such rage that Victor could not fully comprehend what he was saying. Swaggering above him, Gerald looked like a madman. His hair was tousled, dripping with pellets of rain. His clothes were in disarray and drenched clear through to his body. "None of this would have happened, if you had minded your own goddamn business. Now leave me alone!"

Victor rose from the wet pavement and faced his brother's vehement stare. Without another word, Gerald straightened his soaked suit jacket and tie, and turned to walk across the street. Victor shouted a warning behind him, bright lights fast approaching. Gerald paused for a moment without turning around, swayed from side to side as he let cars pass. Then he preceded across the narrow lanes.

Victor ran behind him. A split second later, he heard the sound of burning rubber. He snapped his head around and saw a dark car screeching out of the parking lot across the street next to Damian's, turning onto Smith. He lunged forward and grabbed the back of Gerald's suit, trying with all of his strength to pull his brother back to him. Gerald put up a fight as the two men wrestled in the middle of the street.

\* \* \*

THERE WERE NO SOUNDS of screeching brakes, no crash that should have rumbled the ground like an after-shock. Only a mild thud, as the car made its impact. The valet attendant, who'd backed off earlier at Gerald's command, watched in horror as a silhouette of a man stuck to the front of the car like bonding glue as it was lifted from the street and carried about ten yards before the car stopped, backed up a few feet and stopped again with a jolt that dislodged the man, and then sped off down the street.

The body lay mangled and still. Blood poured out of his head, mixed with rainwater, and was swept away toward the drainage. The attendant, numb with shock, started toward the victim when a weak shout from the man's companion called out for him to call 9-1-1.

The commotion brought patrons out of both Damian's and Brennan's. A man quickly took off his dinner jacket and began waving the on-coming cars to another lane away from the small crowd, which had quickly scurried around the injured men. Shouts for towels, blankets, coats—anything to keep the victims warm and dry— could be heard from blocks away. The howl of the ambulance rang through the air, its shrill growing more prominent as it approached the scene of the accident.

The Conti twins no longer looked like one another. One was disfigured beyond recognition and barely breathing. The other was bloody and held his brother's hand, the only limb that was not battered. He spoke to him in a hushed, but deliberate tone, repeating the same thing over and over.

"I'm so sorry!"

# Chapter

## 27

Michael plunged the accelerator of his Lexus Coupe to the floor, as he turned southward onto I-95 toward Quantico, Virginia. He had streaked out of the J. Edgar Hoover building in Washington, D.C., after finding out Jim Frasier was attending a confidential meeting at the FBI academy.

He would have to make it up to Jim's secretary. After doing everything short of threatening bodily harm to get her to disclose Jim's whereabouts, the frightened woman finally broke down in tears and surrendered the information.

"It doesn't make sense!" Michael shouted into the silence of his car, slapping the steering wheel with the palm of his hand. He tried to keep his mind on the stretch of highway in front of him, but bits and pieces of past conversations kept intruding on his thoughts. Jim had deliberately lied to him. Why? Especially, when Monica's life was at stake.

Michael pulled his car into the entrance of the academy, flashed his FBI badge to the uniformed guard, and sped into the parking lot. He slammed the door of his car and raced into the building. Marching up to the information desk, he flashed his badge again and then demanded to know where he could find Jim Frasier.

When the young man hesitated, Michael was tempted to reach over the desk and snatch him up from his seat. Instead, with extreme calm and control, he identified himself again and explained that there was an emergency in Washington which required his boss's attention.

The marine bought the story, checked his ledger, and directed Michael to a conference room on the second floor. Michael didn't bother to take the elevator. In a flurry of motion, he bolted up the stairs, two at a time, and rushed toward the room where he had attended meetings himself over the years.

When he reached the room, he placed his hand on the doorknob, took a deep breath, and flung open the door. The conversation abruptly came to a halt, as all eyes around the conference table turned in his direction. Michael recognized right away that the people at the table were some of the highest-ranking members in the Bureau. Everyone was there, except him.

The Attorney General of the Justice Department—who had been drawing a diagram on a chart board—froze where he stood, his arm suspended in midair.

"Young man, do you realize—"

"Sorry, sir," Michael interrupted, his eyes searching the room until they locked onto his boss, "but it's extremely important that I speak with Jim Frasier."

"I don't give a damn who you need to speak to, Morgan. We are discussing highly-classified information here. I won't tolerate this kind of intrusion."

Embarrassed, Jim rose with urgency from his seat. Turning to the Attorney General, he said, "Attorney General Fredericks, I asked Michael to interrupt me if there were late developments in one of our cases. I'm sure you'll understand, sir, if I excuse myself for a few moments to take care of the matter."

The Attorney General glanced from Jim Frasier to Michael then back to Jim.

"I'll excuse you this time, Frasier," he said gruffly. "But, next time, teach that young man to knock."

\* \* \*

"ARE YOU OUT OF YOUR MIND?" Jim Frasier lit into Michael, after pulling him into the nearest vacant office. "You pull another stunt like that, Michael, and we'll both be standing on the corner with work-for-food signs. What the hell is so important that you—"

"I *know* about Greg Dumont," Michael managed, his teeth clenched so tight, he could've passed for a victim of lockjaw.

Jim returned the glare, released a deep sigh, and said, "I guess I always knew you'd eventually find out. I'd hoped this conversation would be delayed until Monica completed the investigation."

"Cut the bullshit, Jim," Michael snapped. "You deliberately lied to me. Why weren't Monica and I told the truth? What's the big secret the Bureau's trying to hide?"

Jim didn't answer either of the questions. Instead, he walked to the phone on the edge of the desk, punched in a few numbers, and spoke into the receiver. "He's found out about Dumont . . . Yes, sir . . . I'll tell him."

Jim hung up the phone and pushed it over to the side of the desk. Taking a seat beside it, he removed his glasses and pinched the bridge of his nose. "Have a seat, Michael. Attorney General Fredericks is on his way."

\* \* \*

ATTORNEY GENERAL RANDALL FREDERICKS was a staunch man whose cut-and-dried manner intimidated his subordinates. Michael was anything but inhibited when the AG strode into the office, shut the door behind him, and demanded that Michael take a seat. Without wavering, Michael stood steadfast in his position, as he looked down at the man who ran the Justice Department on a short leash.

"I said sit, Morgan!" Fredericks ordered, meeting Michael's blazing eyes with a scowl that was backed by the power of his position. By comparison, forty-nine-year-old Randall Fredericks looked like a dwarf next to Michael's tall, muscular frame.

It wasn't until Jim latched hold of Michael's shirtsleeve and repeated the order, that Michael finally slumped into the nearest chair.

"Now. Jim said you have questions," Fredericks stated, matter-of-factly.

Michael smirked and shook his head.

"Yeah. *Lots* of questions, Attorney General. Let's start with the pertinent one: Why was I left out of the loop?"

Without flinching, the man answered, "Because you are too close to Monica. I didn't want her influenced by your emotions."

"What do you expect? For God's sake, I'm her brother!"

"Exactly my point. If you had known we'd lost an agent on an earlier assignment to Bayou City Wireless, you would've tried to talk her out of the investigation."

Michael grabbed the sidearms of his chair and threw back his head. "So you threw her to the wolves, without letting her know what she was up against? Jesus!" he muttered under his breath.

The Attorney General looked at Jim Frasier and then said to Michael, "I made that call. Jim wanted to tell you everything from the start. Now, get hold of yourself."

Wiping his hands across his face, Michael leaned forward in his chair and composedly asked, "Why was Greg Dumont sent to Texas in the first place? He was there before the Bastrop Study even started."

"That's right, he was." Attorney General Fredericks paused and began to pace the room. "We believe Gerald Conti experimented with dangerous frequency and power levels in communications devices years ago that caused health problems in some of our military personnel."

"What?" Something triggered Michael's memory. "You don't mean—"

"—The Persian Gulf War," the Attorney General finished for him. "For years, Conti Telecommunications— headed by Victor Conti—designed electronics components for the Defense Department that were superior to any we'd ever seen. Since Gerald was installing communications systems all over Europe, Victor brought him in to set up ours. Gerald's company passed the background check with flying colors.

"When the war broke out in the Persian Gulf, our government got the chance to really test some of this sophisticated equipment. They were small enough to fit inside the headsets worn by our fighter pilots and our ground command."

Stopping to glance at Jim Frasier, the Attorney General continued, "It was not until a year after the war that some of our soldiers began complaining about chronic fatigue, headaches, and dizziness—"

"Persian Gulf Syndrome," Michael interrupted.

"Yes and no." The AG shook his head. "Not all the symptoms were the same. Allied bombing of Iraqi ammunition bunkers were thought to have released dangerous levels of chemical agents that could've exposed as many as 100,000 U.S. troops.

"But we now believe the pilots and the ground patrol—who used the communications system installed by Gerald Conti and who developed cancerous brain tumors—were exposed to high levels of electromagnetic rays."

"Believe? Meaning, you don't know for sure?"

"Not 100 percent. Pilots using older communications models didn't become ill. After the Gulf War ended, all the equipment was still being used in some of our test maneuvers.

"Believing Gerald must've had inside help, we began investigating. We discovered a high-ranking, military technical guy was transferred to work specifically on the communications system, just two weeks prior to the installation. The man confessed to being paid to increase frequency and power levels, and to create false data. He'd been at it a number of years and agreed to name names—once he returned to the States."

"Gerald Conti bought him off?"

The Attorney General shrugged his shoulders.

"The informant's plane exploded in midair, just after takeoff in Iran."

"Jesus!" Michael said, running his hand across his wavy, black hair, his normally fair cheeks burning with anger. "You never questioned Gerald Conti?"

"How could we? What little information we had disintegrated over the Persian Gulf. We never got a full confession. By this time, Gerald Conti's communications company had dissolved and he'd been working with his brother for nearly five years."

"So you started another investigation?"

"Couple of months after the plane crash, the wireless industry was rocked by its first cellular phones/brain cancer link. Though Conti Telecommunications wasn't implicated, we heard rumblings about Gerald shopping a new concept in wireless communications around Europe that required higher frequency and power levels."

"And Greg Dumont?"

"One of our best technical agents. Used the cover of an expert in product development with a background in engineering. He worked directly with Gerald, had access to the NMS/6000, engineering structure and marketing of the Excalibur. Greg went over that place inside out, never found a hair out of place.

"Until the Bastrop people began getting sick. Same symptoms as before. Greg became obsessed. His reports to us became fragmented, less frequent. His telephone conversations vague. That's when we realized the case had ceased being an FBI investigation. Greg was conducting his own operation."

"What happened to him?" Michael turned to Jim to see if they were finally telling him all of the truth.

"He simply disappeared." Jim's face was inscrutable. "We checked the airports, car rentals, bus stations, bank and credit card accounts for activity, car rentals—the usual routine when one of our agents fails to report. Nothing. "

The Attorney General added, "We assume he's dead."

Michael only nodded his head. "And Gerald Conti got away, again?" he asked, cynically.

"We would've found another way in," the AG responded. "But then you brought your friend to us from the FCC."

"Talk about timing." Michael grew angrier at being reminded of Jones's death. The whole conversation made him want to vomit.

"Jim says," Attorney General Fredericks began slowly, "Monica's been asking about Greg—I mean, Dave Carter?"

Michael nodded his head again.

"When was the last time you spoke with her?"

"Couple of days ago," Michael lied. He was not going to jeopardize Monica's safety anymore. "Nothing new to report."

"Now you know everything, Michael. Monica's got a job to finish."

"Yes, sir," Michael said, squelching the desire to call the AG every demeaning word he could think of.

"Good," the AG said, slapping Michael on the back in satisfaction at the response.

An urgent knock at the door interrupted the Attorney General's sentence.

"Come in," he shouted.

"Excuse me, sir," a marine said, walking briskly to the AG. "I was instructed to give you this." He handed the Attorney General a small piece of paper.

"What the hell?" the AG said, glancing over the contents of the note. Crushing it between his fist, he ordered, "Don't just stand there. Turn the television on!" The man scampered to the television across the room and flipped it on.

"What's going on?" Jim Frasier asked, straightening his glasses on his face. Michael walked over to stand beside him.

"Quiet!" the Attorney General ordered.

Flicking the remote to change the channel to CNN, the young man raised the volume and then hurriedly left the room.

Though the reporter was well into the segment, it did not take long for the three men to grasp the content of the breaking story. There, in full color, was a picture of a face they all knew so well.

". . . To repeat the day's top story: Gerald Conti, president of Houston's Bayou City Wireless, and brother of multi-billionaire mogul Victor Conti, has died from massive injuries sustained in a hit-and-run last night in Houston, Texas. Victor Conti, who was with his brother at the time of the incident, was treated for cuts and bruises. He was released from Houston's Ben Taub Hospital late last night. The late-model Oldsmobile, that mowed down the oldest of the Conti twins, was found abandoned early this morning. The identity of the driver and his whereabouts remain unknown. We will be back in a moment with more on this shocking story that has stunned the telecommunications industry . . ."

"Goddamn sonofabitch!"

"Shut up, Morgan," AG Fredericks snarled, clicking off the television angrily. He didn't need to wait for an update. "Don't either of you say another word!" he ordered, crossing his arms as he stood in silence.

Jim Frasier was the first to speak.

"Surely, Attorney General Fredericks, this means—"

"That monster's death means absolutely *nothing!*" he shouted at Jim. "The investigation will continue. And you," he pointed a chubby finger at Michael, "will not say a word to Monica about what we've discussed here today. I am not going to look like a laughing stock in front of the President again. I plan to get every goddamn person involved in those experiments!"

# Chapter

## 28

"Suzanne," Monica said into the phone, massaging her fingers in a circular pattern on her left temple, "could you please bring me a glass of water? I've got a headache that just won't quit."

The news of Gerald's death spread across the country like a California brush fire. By 10 a.m., Monica had appeared on camera with more than twenty reporters and Suzanne had faxed the press release Monica had written to another fifty.

The calls were still pouring in by noon, when Monica decided she needed to take a few minutes break or else her head would explode.

"Thanks," she said, taking the glass from her secretary to wash down the two Tylenol gelcaps she had just popped into her mouth.

"Can I get you anythin' else, Taylor?"

"No—just hold down the fort for a few minutes. Be sure you get the names and numbers of everyone who calls and tell them I'll get back to them shortly. I just need a few minutes to catch my breath."

"Don't worry. I'll take care of everythin'."

Monica slumped in her chair, threw her head back, and closed her eyes. What in the hell was she going to do now? There had been so much to do to prepare for the onslaught of media requests. This was the first time, since the 5 a.m. call from Victor with the news of Gerald's death, that she'd had a chance to contemplate the investigation. She'd been too stunned, Victor too distraught, to pose the question at the time. Instead, she called Cameron to meet her at the office, gotten dressed, and headed straight for Bayou City Wireless to draft a statement to the press.

Monica took in a deep breath and slowly let it out. Gerald's death had not been part of the plan. It cheated her out of delivering the goods—that is, Gerald Conti—much like winning by default. The Excalibur would be halted and the evidence turned over to the Bureau. The FBI would get Dave Carter from Port Royal Meadows. Her work would be done. Now, if she could just get through the day, all she'd have to do was check in with Michael to see how the Bureau wanted her to proceed.

Monica positioned herself in her seat and waited for the Tylenol to attack the throbbing in her head. Just as she was about to drift, a knock at the door jolted her back to reality.

"Sorry to bother ya, Taylor," Suzanne said, sticking her head in the door, "but Cameron called a second ago. Said he needed to speak with you. I told him you were busy and that I—"

"That's okay, Suzanne." Cameron startled the blonde as he appeared in the doorway behind her.

"Gosh, Cameron. You scared the stew out of me."

"Sorry." Cameron stepped past her, taking the doorknob in his hand. "I decided to come by, instead."

"It's okay, Suzanne," Monica said with concern. Looking back to Cameron, she asked, "What's going on?"

"Get your things. Arthur Fazio is gathering all of senior staff in the conference room. Victor has called a press conference at his home. It's supposed to air in about ten minutes. Arthur said Victor wants all of us to watch it together."

"Uh-oh!" Monica pushed her chair back and reached beneath her desk to find her shoes. When she'd slipped her feet into the leather pumps, she asked, "Why didn't Victor call me himself? He told me this morning that if he decided to address the media, we would go over it together first."

"I don't know." Cameron shook his head. "Apparently, he decided to do it without you. C'mon, let's go."

* * *

ARTHUR FAZIO SOLEMNLY walked into the conference and, without saying a word, he turned on the television. Monica could tell by the shadow across his face and the sagging, dark bags under his eyes that he had not been to sleep all night She turned her attention to the television, and watched the camera zoom in as Victor appeared outside the doorway of his heavily-wooded, sprawling Memorial-area home.

Dressed in a pair of charcoal slacks, white shirt, and a buttoned-down navy cardigan, Victor leaned onto the cane in his right hand and slowly limped to the crowd of reporters. His face grimaced with pain as he took each step, almost dragging his right leg that had once been riddled with polio. He'd told Monica that morning that his leg had been severely bruised in the accident. A white bandage appeared over his right temple.

Monica leaned onto her elbow on the table and placed

her hand over her mouth as she watched Victor put on his reading glasses and pull a prepared statement from the breast pocket of his sweater.

Clearing his throat, he read, "My brother, Gerald Conti, and I were victims of a tragic hit-and-run last night. Gerald sustained the brunt of the impact. He died shortly upon arrival at Ben Taub Hospital."

The reporters waited in silence as Victor paused to blink back tears and regain his composure. After a beat of a moment, he continued.

"I would like to thank the paramedics and medical personnel who worked tirelessly to save my brother's life. His injuries were just too severe to overcome. I would also like to thank the public for the numerous calls, telegrams, and flowers I have received since the news of Gerald's death was first reported. Your kindness is deeply appreciated."

Victor's voice cracked, and when he swallowed, his Adam's apple moved up and down. In a blink, his tone changed to a brisk, business-like one.

"For those of you who are wondering how Gerald's death will affect the operations of Conti Telecommunications, Inc., and Bayou City Wireless, let me offer some reassurance. Though Gerald's presence will be sorely missed, let me assure you there will be no delays, no hesitation in our production or quality of service.

"I will personally see to it—as I have in the past—that Conti Telecommunications, Inc., remains on the cutting edge of technology. It will continue to offer the latest, most innovative, wireless products and services. I will also assume the responsibilities of president of Bayou City Wireless, until a suitable replacement can be found. The press conference scheduled for next Tuesday to unveil our newest product will proceed as planned. I promise you will not be disappointed. Now, if you would allow me some privacy to grieve, I will issue another statement at a later time."

Monica sat stunned in her seat, her eyes were the only parts of her body that dared to move as they followed Arthur Fazio when he got up to turn off the television. The room was silent, tension high in anticipation of what lay ahead for a company that had just been dealt a devastating blow. But Monica didn't harbor such sentiments. She wondered if Victor was suffering from a concussion that had gone undetected.

He couldn't be serious about continuing the launch of the Excalibur? *After the discussion we had the day before?* Monica looked to Cameron who returned her questioning look.

"Arthur," Monica interjected, as the lawyer was dismissing the staff. "Surely, Victor didn't mean—"

"He meant *exactly* what he said, Taylor," he answered curtly. His narrowing eyes cut through her as he exuded confidence in Victor's statement.

Monica felt the pressure of Cameron's size twelve foot bearing down on her toes underneath the table. A signal for her to refrain from questioning the lawyer further. Taking the hint, she smiled apologetically at Arthur and waited for him to leave the room.

When everyone had left, Monica turned to Cameron and said, "I've gotta talk to Victor. He's knows he can't go through with that launch."

"There's no law that says he has to delay the project because of a death in the family," he responded sarcastically. "It's his company."

"Cameron, have you forgotten about Jack Stevenson

and the others in Bastrop? About Dave Carter?"

"You know something you're not telling me." His voice was calm, but sure. "I can tell by the urgency in your voice. Your whole body tensed when Victor made the announcement, as if you expected him to say something different. Don't deny it, because I saw you. You usually do a much better job of masking your feelings, baby, but not this time. You're really scared. Why?"

*He's beginning to read me like a book,* Monica thought to herself. *I've got to tell him. I may need his help.* Her feelings for him were getting in the way. She had to keep her mind clear. *But can I trust him?*

Cameron grabbed her shoulder firmly with his hand.

"Let me tell you something, baby," he said gently. "You stopped me once from telling you how I feel. Now, I'm gonna say it, without interruption. I don't know who hurt you so badly in the past that you've wrapped yourself tightly in that cocoon of yours, and you won't give anybody else a chance to get in. But I love you and I will *not* hurt you. If you're in trouble, let me help. Tell me what it is."

"Cameron, I—" Monica didn't dare trust herself to finish. The blockage in her throat felt as she imagined a boa constrictor's would when devouring a white mouse. Releasing herself from his grip, she turned her back to him as she tried to compose herself. *Pull yourself together, girl,* Monica commanded herself. *You still have a job to do.* She also knew that she loved him, too. She decided right then she would tell him everything—but not now.

"Cameron," she began again, turning around to face him. "Let me meet with Victor first."

"Didn't you just hear what I said?"

"Yes." Running her hand down the side of her neck

and resting it above her breast, she flashed a sultry smile. "Every word. And I promise we'll talk *after* my meeting with Victor. I'll call you when I get back to my office. We can have dinner tonight and talk about everything."

"I won't let you change your mind."

"I don't plan to."

"Then, it's a deal."

* * *

"DID YOU SEE THE PRESS CONFERENCE?" Jim Frasier asked, walking into Michael's office.

"I was just about to come see you."

"What do you make of it?"

Michael shrugged his shoulders. "Apparently, Victor's still planning to release the Excalibur."

"Have you talked to Monica?"

"Not yet. But I will."

"We're running out of time, Mike. Tell her to put a move on it."

Michael stared after Jim as his boss left the room. Things were moving too fast. *Think, man,* he told himself. Monica was deliberately avoiding him. *What's she up to?* She could be in a lot of danger if she's not careful. There's got to be something he could do on his end to help her.

He hesitated, then picked up the phone and dialed a number.

"Hello?"

"Dad? It's Michael."

"How's it going, son? I was planning to call—"

"Dad, listen to me. It's Monica. She might be in danger."

275

Without missing a beat, Ben said, "I'm catching the next flight to Washington."

# Chapter
## 29

**M**indful of the altercation she'd had the day before with Victor's secretary, Monica prepared for battle again, as she straightened her chartreuse Adrienne Vittidini suit and held her head high as the elevator ascended to the top floor. Maggie was waiting for her as soon as she stepped out.

"Maggie?"

"Hi, Taylor." Maggie looked behind her towards Victor's office. "Sandra told me you were on your way over. Victor just got in. I thought you and I could have a cup of coffee while we give him a few minutes to get himself together."

"Alright." Monica noticed that Maggie looked distracted and a bit worried.

In the small formal room, Monica poured herself some coffee from the silver serving set and took a seat in one of the wing-back chairs. She watched Maggie put a teaspoon of sugar and a dab of cream into her cup, pour coffee, and then begin to repeat the process. Before the woman had a chance to put in the second creamer, Monica stepped forward and took the cup from Maggie's hands.

"Are you having coffee with your sugar and cream?" Monica set the cup on the table. "Why don't we just sit for a moment?"

"I don't know what I'm doing," Maggie said, taking a lace handkerchief from the sleeve of her dress. Wiping her eyes, she turned to Monica. "I'm so worried about Victor."

"Are his injuries more severe than he's saying?"

"No. It's a miracle he escaped with only cuts and bruises."

"Then what's the matter?"

"He's so distraught over Gerald's death, that he's beside himself with grief—and guilt. I've never seen him like this."

"Like what?"

"He feels he's to blame for what happened. He's always felt responsible for Gerald, even though Gerald was the oldest. Victor believes he should've been able to stop Gerald before . . . before . . . "

Maggie turned her head and wept softly into the handkerchief.

"Maggie . . . " Monica crooked an arm around her. "That's a normal reaction. Twins have a special bond that's different from normal siblings."

"I understand that. I really do. It's just that Victor's so distant, acting so strangely that I don't even know him. Did you hear him say during the press conference that he plans to head up Bayou City Wireless?"

Monica nodded her head.

"That's what I'm talking about," Maggie continued. "He could promote any one of the vice presidents. He's said so numerous times in the past. Another thing, why on Earth would he release the Excalibur after what you told him yesterday? He's just not thinking clearly, Taylor."

"I admit I was surprised. That's why I came straight over to talk to him."

"He's never pushed me away before. I don't know how to help him."

Monica hesitated before she spoke. In a soft tone, she said, "You really love him, don't you?"

Maggie nodded her head.

"I know I shouldn't tell you all this." Maggie wiped the corners of her eyes. "But Victor and I have shared each other's lives for years. Gerald's death has driven a wedge between us, locked a door I don't have the key to open."

"Give him time, Maggie. He just needs a few days to absorb it all."

"I'm not so sure." Maggie's almond-colored eyes flooded with sadness. "Last night, after I brought him home from the hospital, he told me it would be best if I went back to my house. Maybe even for a few days. Taylor, Victor and I have never spent a night apart in more than seven years."

"But you just said—"

"—When I moved into Victor's house, he bought the condo on San Felipe I was leasing. He knew I wanted a place of my own, even if it was left unoccupied most of the time.

"When he suggested I leave the house in Memorial last night, I told him I had no intention of leaving him at a time like this. Every time I tried to comfort him, he said he wanted to be alone. It's heartbreaking not being able to help him."

"How is he this morning?"

"He gave me a quick kiss on the cheek when he arrived a few minutes ago. When I asked if there was anything he needed, he just walked into his office and closed the door."

"He just needs time to accept Gerald's death, Maggie," Monica repeated. She wished she could think of something more comforting to say. No matter how devastated Victor was over the death of his brother, there was no way Monica would let him release the Excalibur.

"I'll talk to him, Maggie. Victor's an intelligent man. He knows how perilous the Excalibur is. He's just too overwhelmed now."

"Thank you, Taylor." She gathered her composure. "Forgive me for breaking down like this."

Monica smiled and watched as Maggie ran her manicured fingers over her short, curly hair. *Victor is lucky to have someone like Maggie.* And then, a more disturbing, unsettling thought struck Monica. How is it she could understand how Maggie and Victor—an interracial couple—felt about each other, when she had condemned her own parents?

"Maggie," Monica said slowly. "I know it's none of my business, but why didn't you and Victor ever marry?" Monica knew she was prying.

Maggie wrapped her arms around herself, rose from her seat, and walked to the other side of the room.

"There were so many reasons at the time, Taylor," she said. "I don't know if any of them make sense now. The prejudices against a mixed-race couple—however subtle—are still there. There were people who knew I had taken care of his wife before she died, and I didn't want . . . well, I didn't want to be perceived as an opportunist. That's why I insisted on having my own house.

"It would have been different if I came from the same socio-economic background as Victor, but I didn't. I was

280

from a poor Trinidadian family. I knew I would never be accepted as Mrs. Victor Conti."

Maggie paused and then smiled. "I guess I didn't have the courage."

Monica felt a tug at her heart. In this day and age, Maggie could've easily lived more openly with Victor. How sad that it had taken Monica all this time to give her parents credit for meeting the challenge.

"Maggie," Victor's secretary broke the silence. "Mr. Conti is ready to see Miss LeBlanc now."

"I'll bring her right in, Sandra." Maggie wiped her eyes again before stuffing the handkerchief back into the sleeve of her dress.

When the girl had gone, Maggie and Monica both rose from their seats and embraced.

"Thanks for listening, Taylor," Maggie said softly.

"No, thank you for sharing something so personal. It's meant more to me than you'll ever know. If you need to talk again, you have my number." Monica patted Maggie's hand.

Walking into Victor's office a few minutes late, Monica instantly noticed the stress that Maggie had eluded to. Victor met Monica with his usual courteous manner, shaking her hand as he offered her a chair. To Maggie he flashed a brief smile, but unlike the meeting that had taken place the day before, Maggie returned his gesture with a sad smile of her own and closed the door behind her as she left the room.

"Could I offer you some coffee or soda?" Victor eased into his chair with some difficulty. Though the darkness under his eyes was more prominent than it had been on television just an hour or so ago, Victor was impeccably dressed in a dark gray suit, and a white shirt

281

with a tie in shades of gray and black.

"No, thank you." Monica noticed from the crystal high-ball glass on his desk that he was drinking something stronger than the beverages he'd offered her.

"Surely, you must know how difficult a time—"

"Yes, Victor," Monica interrupted. "I'm sorry about Gerald. Everyone at Bayou City Wireless is in shock about it."

"Thank you," he responded softly, taking a drink from his glass. "You didn't have to come all the way over here to express your condolences, Taylor."

Monica looked at him and instinctively cocked her head to the side.

"Actually, Victor," she said, "I was more than a little surprised when you announced plans to move forward with the press conference for the Excalibur."

Victor picked up his glass and turned his chair around to face the window.

"I thought after our discussion yesterday," Monica continued, "it was perfectly clear that we halt all plans for its release."

Monica watched from behind as Victor adjusted his body in the leather chair and lifted the glass to his mouth.

"Our discussion?" he asked, as though his thoughts were miles away.

"I know Gerald's death has been a strain on you." Monica was growing more irritated at his aloofness. *He must be drunk*, she thought to herself. "After watching Dave Carter's tape yesterday and listening to what actually happened to the people in Bastrop, you assured me you were going to stop the project. You gave me your word that you would voluntarily take the evidence to the police."

Victor slowly swung his chair around. Meeting Monica's questioning gaze, he squinted his eyes and stared at her as though he were looking at an apparition. He fumbled for his cane and steadied it on the floor. Putting his weight against it, he slowly rose to his feet and began to walk to the bookshelf, dragging his injured leg behind him.

Monica waited for him to speak. When he did not, she too stood up and walked to him. Standing beside him, she said, "I understand your wanting to—"

"You understand nothing," he retorted in a chilling voice that made the hair on Monica's neck stand erect. She watched him pour himself another drink from the crystal decanter that rested on top of a brass platter. Taking a sip, he turned around to face Monica who continued to stare at him in utter confusion.

"That tape is the reason Gerald is dead," he said, unable to control the twitching in his eyes. "If I had not confronted him, he would be alive today. He couldn't believe that I would betray him, that I would even consider turning on him because of someone else's word over his. He even begged me to reveal how I had gotten the information in the first place."

"Did you tell him?"

"No," he answered.

He lifted his glass, offering her a drink which she refused.

"It was just between you and me. It doesn't matter now, does it?"

"Don't forget about—"

Something about the way he looked at her now froze the words in her mouth. The piercing black eyes that stared back at her did not match the suave charm and calmness of his demeanor.

"Don't forget about *whom*?" he repeated, waiting for her to continue her sentence. "You were about to name someone else?"

"I just meant Dave Carter," she said quickly. "But I guess he doesn't really count now either."

"No. He doesn't. Nothing matters but the evidence. You kept your word, didn't you? You didn't tell anyone else about the tape or about our conversation yesterday?"

"No. I promised I wouldn't go to the authorities until you had a chance to talk to Gerald and gather the rest of the information about the NMS\6000."

"Good. Good," he said, sipping his drink in satisfaction. "Where is the tape now?"

"I took it home. Thought it would be safer there instead of in my office. Why?"

"Bring it to me in the morning. I should review it again before we turn it over to the police. I also think it best if we keep all of the evidence together. Don't you agree?"

"Yes, I do," she said. "I'll bring it here on my way to work tomorrow, around seven-thirty. Then you haven't changed your mind?"

Victor hesitated a moment and then spoke.

"No," he said wearily, releasing a deep sigh, his composure once more intact. "You're right, I don't know what came over me this morning. Of course, we can't release it. You and I will prepare a retraction to the media in the morning If you don't mind, Taylor, I'm scheduled to meet with Arthur Fazio now. I'll see you at seven-thirty tomorrow morning—with the tape."

"See you then," she said, adjusting the straps of her purse on her shoulder. Walking toward the door, Monica abruptly stopped and then turned around.

"I almost forgot," she laughed nervously. "Do you want me to bring Dave Carter's journals with the tape? You may want to review those again, as well."

Monica thought she saw a twitch in his eyes.

"Yes. Thank you for remembering them, Taylor." He smiled. "Please have Sandra send Arthur in now."

Monica relayed the message to Victor's secretary and then took the elevator to the parking garage. Once she pulled her truck out of the covered building, she picked up her car phone and dialed a number.

"Cameron Maxwell's office," a lady's voice answered.

"Hi. This is Taylor LeBlanc, is he in?"

"No, Taylor. Cameron's in a meeting. Do you want to leave a message on his voice mail?"

"No!" Monica screamed, without thinking. There was no way she was going to leave a message someone else could retrieve.

"Sorry to shout in your ear," Monica continued. "There's crosstalk on my line. Just ask Cameron to stop by my office when he gets a chance. I need to talk to him right away."

"I'll give him the message."

"Thanks."

Monica tried to put the mobile phone back in its position as she steered her car onto Memorial Drive out of downtown, but her hands were shaking beyond control.

"Shit!" she said, as the phone tumbled onto the floor in front of the passenger seat. Monica didn't try to reach for it. Instead, she pressed down on the accelerator and flew right past two blue-and-whites parked at the HPD Memorial Monument. She didn't even bother to look in her rear-view mirror to see if they were chasing her.

\* \* \*

ARTHUR WALKED INTO the office and closed the door behind him. He waited for Victor to turn around from where he stood looking out of the window. When he didn't, Arthur moved forward.

"You wanted to see me, Victor?" he asked.

"Have a drink, Arthur. Given the circumstances, we both need a little something to calm our nerves."

At first Arthur hesitated. Then he walked toward the bar after seeing the glass in Victor's hand when the man finally turned around.

"Thank you. I will."

"I'll get straight to the point, Arthur." Victor watched the lawyer help himself to the brandy. "I know about the deaths in Bastrop."

Arthur's hand slipped as he returned the top to the crystal decanter and missed the circular opening. The decorative container toppled over onto the brass tray beneath it, sending the brandy sloshing out as it spilled over the side of the bookshelf. Nervously, he fumbled to set the decanter upright without looking around.

"I-I don't know what you mean, Victor." He wiped away the traces of alcohol.

"You've always worked closely with Gerald, Arthur. Surely you know what really happened with the Bastrop Study."

"Victor, I—"

"Don't bother denying it, Arthur. I know everything. Go ahead and fix your drink. You and I have some talking to do."

Victor slid into his chair behind his desk and waited for Arthur to sit down across from him. When the lawyer settled into his chair, Victor continued.

"What do you think I should do about it, Arthur?"

"I, uh, don't know." He stared straight ahead with eyes that appealed for leniency.

"I'll tell you what I'm going to do." Victor leaned forward in his chair, holding Arthur's gaze, daring him to turn away. "Not a damn thing!"

Victor slapped the desk with his hand, fell back into his chair, and roared with laughter.

The smack against the wooden desk jolted Arthur in his seat. He looked at Victor as though the man were crazy.

"C'mon, Arthur," Victor laughed, getting out of his chair without the use of his cane. Walking erectly now toward the shaken lawyer, he said, "Get a grip. You look like horse shit. It's me, *Gerald*."

Arthur's mouth opened in disbelief, the glass slid right out of his hand and shattered as it hit the delicate Persian rug. Gerald doubled over with laughter again as Arthur scrambled to his feet as if he had seen a phantom in the night.

"Gerald?" he whispered, taking a step backwards, his face blanched as white as fine, granulated sugar. He looked as if he didn't know whether he should laugh with relief or drop dead from fright.

Gerald raised his hand in mock salute.

"In the flesh," he grinned. "Back from the dead. Fooled you, didn't I? Hell, I fooled the whole goddamn world! Here, Arthur." He stooped with no evidence of pain and picked up the shards of broken glass. "Let me fix you another drink. Hell, you could use a double, don't you think? Damn, man, if you could see your face, it's downright hilarious. "

Arthur grabbed the back of his chair for support and slowly sat down, his eyes never losing sight of Gerald, who strutted back to the bar like a peacock on parade.

"But you were—" Arthur stammered, taking the glass with both hands this time and swallowing a long, hard drink.

"Not me. *Victor,*" Gerald winked, settling into his chair again. "Poor Victor never saw what hit him. Hell, if I hadn't pushed him off me when I did, I'd be in the slab right next to him with a tag dangling from my big toe. Close your mouth, Arthur. You're drooling all over that Armani suit."

Arthur took another gulp of brandy and wiped his mouth with the back of his hand. "You arranged the . . . the . . . ?"

"Accident, Arthur. That's what the police report says. Practice saying the word, you'll have to use it again. I didn't have much to do with the weather, but, yeah, I planned it. It went off without a hitch."

"But . . . *why?*"

"Because that sonofabitch brother of mine found out about those hicks in Bastrop and threatened to turn me in to the police, that's why."

"I don't understand. How did you—"

"Drink up, Arthur. I'll tell you what happened."

Arthur took another sip and sat back in his chair as Gerald began his tale.

"You know that information we were looking for that Carter alluded to before he began his extended vacation at Port Royal Meadows? Well, Victor found out about it. More specifically, our little Ms. Public Relations found the videocassette tape and brought it straight to him. There's something familiar about that little bitch. I can't put my finger on it, but I've felt all along that I'd seen her somewhere before."

Gerald stopped and frowned. Not being able to place where he'd run across Taylor nagged at him like a splinter embedded under his skin.

"Anyway, I don't know where she got it or how she found out about it—it really doesn't matter at this point. Once Victor viewed it, it was over—or so he thought. I knew when he gave his 'responsibility-to-society speech,' I had to do something to stop him."

"But, to kill your own brother, Gerald . . ." Arthur could not hide his repulsion.

Gerald waved his hand in dismissal. "Why should this be any different? We've killed before. I told you I wouldn't let anything get in the way of selling this product to the Indonesians and releasing it in the States, and I meant it. Unfortunately, Victor didn't take me seriously. So, I took matters into my own hands.

"Victor didn't suspect a thing," Gerald continued, eyes glazed with glee at pulling off his crime. He rubbed his palms together, as if he got excited just relating what happened.

"I suggested we go to Brennan's for an early dinner. He probably thought I was being gracious by suggesting his favorite eatery. Little did he know that I had phoned one of my boys and instructed him to wait in the parking lot next to Damian's across the street. It had to look like a hit-and-run. Smith Street was the perfect place, since it would give my guy access to the Southwest Freeway where he could disappear into oblivion. The thunderstorm was a stroke of luck that played out like a scene in a movie. Couldn't have planned it better if I had ordered it myself.

"Once we got to the restaurant, I pretended to get drunk. How would Victor know the difference? I always drink. When he thought I had consumed too much, he decided that it was time to call it a night. That's when he made his first mistake. He excused himself and went to find the waiter for our check. I took it upon myself to switch our jackets—which were the same color and style—while he was gone. He'd already removed his wallet, so I carefully replaced his coat with mine.

"He was too busy trying to get me out of the restaurant without causing a scene, that he didn't even notice he wasn't wearing his own jacket.

"When we got outside the restaurant, I carried on like a drunk on a tear. I told Victor that I was going to walk the few, short blocks to Damian's for a nightcap. He insisted that he drive me home. That was his second mistake. I knew Victor would do anything—including follow me blindly into the street—to keep me from going anywhere in my condition. Always trying to save me from myself, the stupid fool." Gerald chortled, then snorted.

"Tony was watching from his stakeout in the parking lot. I'd told him to watch for two men quarreling in the middle of the street. Then he was to pull out and plow the one closest to the middle—"

"But how could you count on it not being you?" Arthur asked.

"You're forgetting, Arthur. I had a slight advantage. I knew what was going to happen. Victor didn't. Therefore, all I had to do was make sure Victor was in the right spot at precisely the right time. I saw the car come screeching out of the parking lot. It was heading toward us like a freight train picking up steam on an open track. It took every ounce of my strength to push Victor off of me before it struck. Next thing I knew, Victor lay dead. I had a small gash on the side of my forehead, a few scrapes and bruises on my leg. The rest you know."

Gerald paused for a moment to take a drink. His pride would not let him tell Arthur that when he'd finally reached Victor, he'd had second thoughts. Looking at his brother's mangled body and his bloodied, disfigured face had evoked tears and uncharacteristic feelings of sorrow in Gerald. He felt nauseated now just thinking about it.

Gerald took another sip of his brandy to still the chill that ran through his body. He then reached for his cane and held it up.

"*This* is for special effect," he continued. "Aside from self-mutilation, I had to come up with some way to mimic Victor's limp."

"You can't use that thing forever. You're bound to slip up. Somebody will notice."

Gerald's voice rose higher and higher as he spoke. "You oughtta know by now, Arthur, that 'can't' is not a part of my vocabulary. I can do anything I damn well please. And, I've just proven that very fact with the whole world watching. Why do you think I didn't let you in on my little plan before now? You know me better than anyone. Hell, if I fooled you, I can fool just anybody."

"What about Maggie? She's bound to learn the truth."

Gerald flipped his hand in the air as though he were batting away an irritating gnat.

"I'll take care of her. She only wanted Victor for his money, *my* money. The little whore. For now, I've kept her at bay by convincing her that I'm too overwhelmed by my brother's death to deal with our relationship. Eventually,

I'll pay her off and send her packing."

"That won't be so easy," Arthur commented. "She loves Victor."

"Shut up, Arthur!" Gerald snapped. "Let me worry about that. Right now I need to know if you're still with me. We have business to take care of."

Gerald tapped his foot, eyes narrowed into caverns of impatience.

Arthur's lips finally curled upward.

"I'm in. What's the plan?"

# Chapter

## 30

"Suzanne!" Monica shouted over her shoulder, as she threw her purse onto the desk.

"Hey, Taylor," the secretary said. "I didn't see you come in."

"Never mind that," Monica snapped. "Has Cameron been by?"

"No. Were you expectin' him?"

"I wouldn't have asked if he'd been by, if I weren't expecting him. Now would I?"

As soon as the words flew out of her mouth, Monica wished she could take them back. The hurt on Suzanne's face didn't make the situation any better. Monica put one hand on her hip and ran the other through her hair. She let out a sigh and went to Suzanne and pulled her into her office.

"Look, Suzanne," Monica said with sincerity. "I'm sorry. I shouldn't have talked to you like that. I'm under tremendous pressure right now, but that doesn't give me the right to take my frustration out on you. I'm sorry, okay? It was a stupid thing to say. Please accept my apology."

Suzanne blinked back the tears that were filling her azure eyes, and slung her hair out of her face. A reluctant smile formed on her lips as she slowly nodded her head.

"Good girl," Monica said, giving her a quick hug. "You know I couldn't get anything done around here without you. You're my right arm." A definite exaggeration, but it made Suzanne feel better.

Monica called out to her, "If you see Cameron, send him—"

"Did I hear my name?" Cameron winked as he walked in, his jacket flung over his shoulders.

"You did." Monica came from behind her desk to where he stood. "Suzanne, hold my calls, please," she yelled, before closing the door.

"What's the deal?" Cameron tossed his coat on the back of a chair and sat down in the other. He leaned forward, clasping his hands together. "I got the message you wanted to see me. If you've changed your mind about our date tonight, I'm warning you in advance, I won't be a gentleman about it."

"No. I'm not canceling, but there is a problem."

Monica rose from her chair and walked around her desk. Taking a seat on the edge, she said, "I haven't been entirely honest with you."

"Confession time, is it?"

"Don't interrupt, Cameron." She held her hands in her lap. "I don't have much time. I need you to listen to me."

Monica paused for a moment.

"Gerald did not die in that accident last night. Victor did."

Cameron sat back in his chair, staring intently at her.

"What are you talking about? You heard the news report. We both saw Victor's press conference this mor—"

"That wasn't Victor, Cameron. It was Gerald. I know

294

how crazy this sounds, but I'm telling you the truth. I wasn't entirely sure myself until my meeting with him a half hour ago. I just this minute got back from his office."

"Wait a minute." Cameron looked shocked. "Are you saying what I think you are?"

"That's right. Gerald is impersonating Victor. I don't know how he pulled it off, but I think I know why. Remember this morning when you said you felt I was keeping something from you?"

Cameron nodded.

"You were right. I met with Victor yesterday to show him evidence that the deaths in Bastrop were the direct result of Gerald's manipulation. He didn't want to believe it at first, but the proof was right there in front of him. Victor was supposed to confront Gerald yesterday evening. I don't know what happened in that meeting but both you and I know how it ended—with Victor dead and Gerald taking his place."

"This is too much." Cameron shook his head. "Even for Gerald. What 'evidence' did you have?"

Monica went to her bookshelf and picked up the red Webster's II dictionary she'd brought from home. Opening it, she took the black videocassette from within the neatly cut-out inlay and handed it to Cameron.

"My safe-deposit box," she explained.

"What's the other stuff in there? Is that a picture of you in your wild days?" he asked, before Monica snapped the book shut.

"That's the only thing you need, right now," she said, pointing to the tape in his hand.

"What's on it?" he asked, turning it over, looking for an identifiable label.

"Dave Carter. Jack Stevenson mailed it to me. He had it all the time and never told a soul. Carter documented everything about the Bastrop Study including the increased frequency and power levels, the deaths, the phony data from the NMS\6000, and Gerald's involvement. There's something I should warn you about."

Monica paused again.

"Now that Gerald knows about the tape, he'll do anything to get it back. He had Jack Stevenson killed because of it."

"Incredible." Cameron rubbed the dark wrinkles on his forehead. "Why didn't you tell me all this before?"

"I couldn't. Not until I was sure about everything. This morning when I talked to Victor—Gerald—I asked him if he wanted Carter's journals that we went over yesterday. He just smiled and said yes."

Cameron shrugged his shoulders in puzzlement.

"That's just it." Monica spoke in a rush. "Victor and I never discussed any journals. They don't exist. I made them up because I wanted to be sure of my suspicions. And another thing, he seemed to have forgotten that Maggie sat in on that meeting as well. Don't you see? Victor would have known all that. Gerald didn't."

"This is dangerous, baby. I hope you know Gerald's not going to let you get away with what you know. For God's sake, he killed his own brother!" Cameron slapped his palm to his forehead. "What do you think he's going to do to you? You've got to go to the police."

"I plan to do more than that," she said. "First, I've got to give him what he wants." She looked at the tape in Cameron's hands.

"You can't give him this!" He waved the tape in the air.

"No—but I can give him a copy, and buy myself some more time. I need your help, Cameron. I noticed you had two VCRs at your house. Can you take this home and make a copy for me and have it ready by the time I get there this evening?"

"I don't like the sound of this."

"Cameron, please. I don't have much time. I have to secure a copy of this tape tonight."

"Why do I get the feeling there's still more to this you're not telling me?"

"There is. I'll explain everything tonight. Listen, you told me this morning you wanted me to trust you. I do. I've been afraid to do that, because of something that happened between my parents. But I'm not anymore. I care for you, too, and now, I'm asking you to trust me. We can't talk anymore now. I'll sit down with you this evening and explain everything. I promise."

Cameron stood up and took Monica in his arms, her body trembling against his as he held her tight.

"Nothing like a little murder to bring a woman to her senses," he joked, stroking her hair with his hand. He held her in his embrace for a moment, then stepped back and took her face in his hands.

"Better late than never, don't you think?" Monica murmured, inhaling his now familiar scent.

"Absolutely." Cameron kissed her on the lips, before finally releasing her and opening the door. He reached for his jacket and placed the videocassette inside the breast pocket. "I'd better go and get started on things. Two steaks on the grill, one—make that two—chilled bottles of Kendall-Jackson Pinot Noir, and one copy of our after-dinner movie, coming up."

Before leaving, he leaned his head back into

Monica's office. "Get out of here as soon as you can. I warned you before about Gerald. That cat is dangerous."

"I've got another hour and a half—five o'clock at the latest. I'm going to run home, change clothes, then be at your house about six-thirty. How does that sound?"

"Can't wait." He kissed his finger and brought it gently to her lips. "I love you, baby."

Monica kissed it back, her eyes pools of longing.

"See ya soon."

She watched as Cameron headed down the hallway and turned the corner toward the elevator, before going back into her office. *No turning back now,* she thought to herself, surprised at her feelings of euphoria.

* * *

NEITHER SHE NOR CAMERON were aware of the spying pair of eyes that watched them from behind a cubicle a few feet away.

* * *

FOUR FORTY-FIVE DID NOT come quickly enough. Monica put the phone on the hook after talking to a reporter from *Wireless Marketing Magazine* who was trying to make a five o'clock deadline on a story about Gerald's death. She found it increasingly difficult to appear bereaved, knowing that Gerald was indeed very much alive and had taken over Victor's domain at Conti Towers. Watching the news segments on the accident sickened her. All the time, a guilty pang gnawed at Monica, because she could not yet tell Maggie that Victor was dead.

Monica was just about to reach for the phone again to transfer her calls to voice mail when it rang. Glancing at the display to see if it were Suzanne buzzing to say she would be leaving for the day, Monica saw it was an outside call. Fearing another reporter on deadline, she let out a heavy sigh.

"Taylor LeBlanc."

"Ms. LeBlanc? This is Troy Nelson with *Inside Wireless*. I was wondering if you could provide some information on Gerald Conti's business background for a story we're working on?"

Recognizing the name, she said, "Mr. Nelson, I believe our office sent you a statement this morning."

"You did. But there are a couple of things I need to go over before my deadline this evening. Do you have a few moments?"

*Damn*, Monica mouthed into the phone, as she looked at the clock–already five minutes past five. *Inside Wireless* was a West Coast magazine—which meant there was a two-hour difference. The telephone interview had the potential of going on forever.

"Okay. Shoot."

Monica leaned back into her chair, massaged her temple, and kicked off her shoes as the man began rattling off questions. When the last detail had been confirmed and the last question answered, Monica threw down the phone and looked at the clock again.

It was six-thirty. With rush hour traffic, it would take her another hour and a half to go home, take a shower and change, and then drive to Cameron's house.

"Dammit," Monica whispered to herself as she dialed his home number to tell him she was on her way. When there was no answer by the fourth ring, she discontinued the call, then dialed his cell phone number.

Although she found it odd that he did not answer the phone—which he normally wore clipped to his belt—Monica casually dismissed the thought. She transferred her calls to voice mail, threw the fake Webster's Dictionary into her briefcase, and locked the door to her office. She'd call him from her car.

# Chapter
# 31

The scent of charcoal permeated the cool, humid night when Monica stepped out of her truck in front of Cameron's house. She bounded up the walkway, dressed in denim jeans, beige scoop-neck sweater, and a navy silk jacket tied around her waist. The seductive wail of Kirk Whalum's saxophone flowed from the back of the house, prompting Monica to abandon her course to the front door and follow the hypnotic notes.

Monica grabbed the metal handle on the cedar fence, unlatched it with her thumb, and walked through the narrow walkway. She reached behind her to break the force of the door's clang as it swung back into place. She eyed the gray smoke coming from the cylinder chimney of the smoker and smiled.

"Smells good," she called out toward the living room's french door that was propped open by a potted Aloe Vera plant. The dimmed light that radiated from inside the room provided a romantic touch to the soulful music blaring from the stereo. Dropping her purse on a chaise lounge, Monica lifted the top of the grill and gazed over the sizzling rib-eye steaks and baked potatoes wrapped in tin foil.

"How do you like your steak, Cameron?" Monica

yelled over her shoulder above the jazz, turning the meat over with the long, two-pronged fork that rested in a metal pan. "Medium well or well-done? No e-coli for this girl."

Monica stopped prodding the meat and turned around, tilting her head to the side when she didn't get a response from inside the house. Closing the grill's lid, she placed the fork back in the pan and grabbed her purse, surveying her surroundings as she adjusted the straps on her shoulder.

"Cameron?" she called out again. She slowly placed her hand inside her purse where she formed her fingers around the Sig Sauer as she walked through the door.

Monica gasped once she stepped inside the room, stopping dead in her tracks. She drew her gun out in the open, spinning around to the four corners of the room.

For the first time since she'd arrived, Monica got a good look at the inside of the house. Everything was in shambles. The light that shone through the door was from a lamp on the floor beside an over-turned end table. Potted plants were knocked over, with dirt strewed over the light-colored carpeted floor. The metal bar stools lay on their sides next to broken glass, and red wine-stained chips of ice that had been knocked from a bucket on top of the bar.

Monica crept through the room, her gun pointed in front of her with both hands, her heart thudding in her chest. Swaying the gun from side to side as she took each step, Monica's breathing became short and labored. From the corner of her eye, she caught a glimpse of something on the floor just inside the kitchen doorway.

Trembling, she looked around her as she approached it. Monica stopped abruptly. Her left hand quickly flew to her mouth to stifle a cry, while the gun quivered in her right hand.

She blinked back tears as she looked down at Cameron, whose cold, open eyes stared back at her. He lay on his back in a pool of blood that streamed from a single gunshot to his forehead. Leafs of lettuce, sliced cucumbers and tomatoes, and shattered pieces of a glass salad bowl were scattered on the tiled floor around him. She knew instantly that he was dead.

Monica dropped to her knees beside him. Wiping tears from her eyes, she reached for Cameron's wrist—which was still warm—and desperately felt underneath the sleeve of his jogging suit for a pulse she knew would not be there. The pain in her heart was inconsolable. She'd finally found love again and now it was gone.

After several minutes, Monica got control of herself enough to go to the phone to dial the police. As she reached for it on the kitchen wall, her hand recoiled in mid-air with the swiftness of a cobra after making a surprise attack on its victim. Suddenly, Monica turned around and looked for Cameron's suit jacket he'd worn earlier in the day and found it thrown on the floor. The inside pocket where he had put the tape was empty. She flew to the VCRs and pressed both eject buttons. There was nothing inside either of them.

Cameron was killed because of her.

Someone had watched Cameron put the tape in his pocket earlier today. Now, both the man she loved and the only piece of evidence she had linking Gerald to the murders in Bastrop were gone from her. She had killed Cameron just as sure as she had pulled the trigger herself. Her heart constricted with guilt. The pain was almost too much for Monica to bear.

*Gerald's behind this!* Monica cried to herself, her guilt supplanted by rage that plagued her whole body. *That bastard is not gonna get away with murder this time.*

Monica walked back to Cameron's body and knelt down beside him again. Slowly, she lifted her shaking hand and closed his eyes, careful not to touch the blood that seeped down the side of his head. She then kissed her index finger and gently brought it to his lips. This time, he would not kiss her back as she had done just a few hours before. In the background, the last jazz note sounded sour.

Monica rose to her feet and took one last look at Cameron before turning to leave. She used the sleeve of her jacket to wipe her fingerprints from the VCR. Then she went outside to the grill and wiped the handle and the fork she'd used to turn the steaks when she'd first arrived. Using her jacket again, she opened the fence latch and wiped the handle from the outside.

Quickly, Monica headed to her truck and got in, frantically looking around in all directions for someone who might have seen her. The neighborhood was quiet, no sounds of stirring. Monica started the car and pulled off, traveling some yards before turning on her lights. She headed west on N. MacGregor until she reached the entrance to 288 South and gunned the accelerator as she entered the freeway. She changed lanes several times, her eyes alternating from the rear-view mirror to the side mirrors to see if anyone was following her.

Monica knew she had to report the murder. The thought of Cameron lying dead on the kitchen floor made her nauseous. She couldn't call from her mobile phone. Even though the police wouldn't be able to trace the call,

she knew Bayou City Wireless could check their billing
records to see if she had placed the call. She had to get
to a pay phone, somewhere with lots of people.

As she raced past the cars on the freeway and turned
onto the 610 West Loop, she remembered the movie theater in Meyer Park, just a few miles away. It would be
brightly lit, with hordes of people streaming in and out.

Monica exited at West Bellfort and turned into the
parking lot. Parking her truck several parking aisles from
the building, she hurriedly walked to the nearest line and
purchased a ticket for the same movie as the couple in
front of her. Handing the ticket to the attendant inside
the entrance, Monica searched around the busy lobby for
a pay phone. Spotting one near the restrooms, she dug in
her purse for a quarter as she approached it.

Monica looked around and hesitated before picking
up the receiver, concentrating on what she would say.
She had less than a minute to make the report before the
call would be traced back to the theater. Taking a deep
breath, she picked up the phone.

"9-1-1. Is this an emergency?" the lady's voice on
the other end asked.

"Yes." Monica struggled to speak in a low steady
voice, her back to the phone as she looked around the
congested area. "I heard gunshots at 321 N. MacGregor."

"Could you speak up, ma'am? I'm having difficulty
hearing you."

"There's been a shooting at 321 N. MacGregor. Please
send an officer over to check it out. Someone may be
hurt." Monica's voice cracked, wishing her last statement
weren't true.

"May I have your name, please?"

"Just get the police over there in a hurry," Monica

snapped, careful not to raise her voice. She slammed the phone down before she could be asked anything else.

Monica closed her eyes for a moment and took deep breaths. Picking up the phone again, she redeposited the quarter and dialed directory assistance.

"Houston . . . Margaret Wentworth, please . . . on San Felipe."

\* \* \*

THE FLASHING RED, WHITE AND BLUE lights lit up N. MacGregor in front of Cameron's house like decorations at Christmas, as Monica slowly cruised by the crime scene. Cracking her tinted window a couple of inches to get a better view, she heard voices echoing into the night from the police radios and saw the flurry of activity as she got closer.

She strained to see past the curious neighbors who lined the street in front of the house, talking among themselves as they watched the police put up the yellow tape around the estate. As Monica came directly in front of the house, she slowed almost to a stop when she saw Cameron's body being wheeled on a gurney, his muscular form zipped within a black body bag. After the body was loaded into the hearse, Monica drove the car forward, warm tears splashing down her cheeks and dripping under her chin.

\* \* \*

MONICA PLOTTED HER NEXT STEPS as she went through her house like a mighty hurricane blowing in from the Gulf. Stuffing a few clothes and personal items into the black duffle bag, she kept her ears tuned to every sound. There was no time to give the house a thorough going over. She hoped she hadn't forgotten anything important. It would be just a matter of time before Gerald came after her, too.

"Come on, you bastard," she yelled out loud. There was only one thing left for her to do, and she would blow Gerald's goddamn head off if he tried to get in her way.

Sitting on the side of the bed after everything was packed, Monica picked up the phone and paged Michael, prepared for the tongue lashing she'd get for not checking in before now. Monica answered the phone on the first ring a few seconds later.

Taking a deep breath, she picked it up.

"Yes?"

"Where the hell have you been?" Michael yelled into the phone. "I was beginning to think you were dead."

"I'm not in the mood for that bullshit tonight, Michael," she lashed out. "I just wanted to tell you my plans."

"No, Monica. You listen to me. There are a lot of things going on here you don't know about. Get your ass on the next plane and come in."

"I can't, Michael. There's something I've gotta do first." She took in a deep breath and released it. "Gerald is alive. It was Victor who was killed in the accident last night, and now Gerald's got the only evidence that proves he was knowingly responsible for the deaths in Bastrop. My only choice now is to go to Port Royal Meadows and get Dave Carter out before Gerald has him killed, too."

"You can't go back to that place by yourself!" Michael shouted. "It's too dangerous." He ordered, "Get out of the house now, Monica. Go to a motel, some-place safe. Call me as soon as you get there. I'm coming down to get you."

"No!" Her voice rose. "I'm going to do this my way. It's my fault everything's screwed up. I had the evidence in the palm of my hand and I gambled it away. Dave Carter is the only chance we've got to prove what's going on and I'm going to get him before Gerald does."

"I don't know what the hell you're talking about," Michael screamed. "But, other than what you've just told me about going to Hilton Head, it really doesn't matter. You can't go on the run by yourself. Dave Carter is not who you think he is. He's—"

"Goodbye, Michael!" She didn't wait for him to finish his sentence. "Stay outta my way. I'll call when I've got him." Monica slammed down the phone.

* * *

"COME IN, TAYLOR," MAGGIE said, with a per-plexed look. "I haven't been able to sit still since you called. Have a seat while I turn the television down. There's brandy on the table."

"Thanks," Monica said, taking off her jacket and lying it beside her on the Duncan Phyfe antique sofa. The room was elegantly decorated with delicate pieces of antique American and European furniture.

She took a sip of her drink, then set the goblet on the marble-topped coffee table. There was no easy way to soften the blow.

"Maggie," she started, "it was Victor who died in the accident last night."

The woman looked intently at Monica, both hands

firmly grasping the crystal glass in her lap.

Monica continued. "I believe Gerald had him killed. And that's not all." Then in a trembling voice, she told Maggie about Cameron and the missing tape.

"Oh, my God! Will nothing stop him?"

"Don't think for one minute that I'm going to let him get away with any of this," Monica said angrily, lighting one of her cigarettes. "Do you mind?" She said it more as a formality, because she was already puffing.

Maggie shook her head and wiped the tears from her eyes. "A part of me knew," she said, trying to compose herself, "that the man I was with today was not Victor. You don't love a man for as long as I've loved Victor and not know him inside and out. I knew something was wrong. So very, very, wrong . . ."

She held her face in her hands and silently wept, her shoulders shuddering with emotion. Monica went to get one of the linen napkins from the dining room table and took it to her.

"I'm so sorry, Maggie," she said, patting her back. "I feel responsible. If I hadn't brought the tape to Victor and told him what I'd found out about the deaths in Bastrop, he'd still be alive today."

"It's not your fault," Maggie said, wiping her eyes. "Gerald would've killed him eventually. He's evil. I've never liked him. In fact, I loath him. He was the main reason I never married Victor. He always believed I was only after Victor's money."

Maggie picked up her drink and took a large swallow. Turning to Monica, she said, "I guess Gerald had the last laugh."

"How so?"

"Today, he asked me to make final arrangements for

Gerald—I mean, Victor. He told me his brother had wanted to be cremated. I was happy to help—I thought Victor was finally reaching out to me. I called the funeral home he recommended, chose one of their most expensive caskets, and arranged for them to transfer the body.

"Gerald wanted the body cremated as soon as possible. No expenses spared. Now, I understand his urgency. The funeral director called back this evening and confirmed the cremation had been completed."

Maggie drank the last of her brandy, then strode over to the tea table to pour another glass.

"Gerald must've enjoyed his sick little joke."

Smoothing out her gown, Maggie turned around and explained.

"Victor and I had burial plots together. I didn't even get a chance to say goodbye. It was a cruel thing to do. He'll kill you, too, Taylor," she warned. "He's probably looking for you right this minute."

"You're in just as much danger as I am, Maggie."

Monica took a pen and piece of paper from her purse. "I want you to call someone. Michael Morgan. He's the assistant deputy director of the FBI in Washington and he's also my broth—"

"Oh, no!" Maggie interrupted, covering her mouth with her hand, as she stared past Monica to the muted television set encased in an antique armoire.

"What's the matter?" Monica spun her head around as Maggie flew to the TV. She gasped as she saw the company photo of herself flash across the screen. Maggie turned up the volume as a man identified as a homicide detective with the Houston Police Department made an urgent plea.

"Ms. LeBlanc," the detective was saying, "is wanted for questioning in the death of Cameron Maxwell, a Bayou City Wireless engineer who was found murdered at his home less than an hour ago. Bayou City Wireless President Victor Conti confirmed that Mr. Maxwell had recently starting dating Ms. LeBlanc.

"We're not sure whether Ms. LeBlanc actually met with the victim tonight, but clearly Mr. Maxwell was expecting someone. Food was still cooking on the grill when we arrived. Also, an unidentified woman placed a 9-1-1 call and reported the shooting. HPD would like to question Ms. LeBlanc. Anyone knowing of her where-abouts should notify HPD immediately."

A seven-digit number boldly flashed across the screen.

"Gerald's trying to frame *me* for Cameron's murder!"

"What are you going to do?" Maggie's face grew ashen with fear.

"Don't worry about me." Monica scribbled Michael's pager number on a piece of paper. "Page Michael. He's my brother. Do you have someplace safe you can stay for the night?"

Maggie nodded. "A friend, who lives close by. Gerald doesn't know her."

"Good. We'll leave together. Does your friend have a garage?"

Maggie nodded again, as she rushed to her bedroom.

"We'll drive two cars." Monica's mind was churning, picking up speed like an avalanche of snow crashing down from the highest mountain. "I'll need to leave mine in her garage and borrow yours."

"She can be trusted, Taylor," Maggie yelled from the other room. A few minutes later, she came back into the living room carrying a small overnight bag.

311

"You have the number I gave you?" Monica asked.

Maggie patted the left side of her chest.

"As soon as you're safe, dial Michael's pager. When he calls you back, tell him you're a friend of mine and explain what's happened. He'll take care of you."

Maggie hugged Monica, then took her hands in hers. "Thank you. Be careful."

"I'll be fine." Monica smiled, feeling a kinship to this woman she'd only known for a short time. "I know someone who'll help me. As for Gerald, I'll get his ass if it's the last thing I do."

* * *

MONICA KNOCKED FRANTICALLY on the Montrose-area apartment door, her head lowered as she moved it slightly from side to side to see if anyone was watching her. The front of the apartment faced the street and it was just her rotten luck that the door she now stood in front of was in clear view of anyone passing by.

She rapped at the door again.

"Hold your horses!" a voice shouted from behind the door. Swinging it open, the young man said, "There'd better be a fire—Taylor!"

"Jazz, I need your help!" Throwing her head back, Monica stared at the young man who had white cream all over his face and a bath towel wrapped around his head.

Without saying a word, Jazz grabbed her arm and pulled her inside. Then he crooked his neck back out the door, eyes scanning the area, to see if anyone had witnessed Monica's arrival.

"You've got yourself in a pickle, girlfriend. Have you seen the news? Your picture's been plastered all over the television for the last hour. Did you really kill Cameron?"

"Don't be ridiculous. You know I didn't." Monica took her pack of cigarettes from her purse, refusing to let images of Cameron's dead body resurface in her mind. "I'm being setup."

"If you're going to light that filthy thing in here, let me open the windows. I don't want cigarette stench in my clothes."

Monica smiled, as she watched him go through the two-bedroom apartment, lifting each window about two inches high. With the cold cream on his face, hair wrapped in a towel, and the silk bathrobe he wore belted around his narrow waist, he looked more feminine at the moment than she did. The room where she stood was sparsely furnished with a sofa, chair, and glass coffee table. Monica could see a small kitchen in the background.

"You caught me in the middle of my beauty treatment," Jazz said, when he came back into the room, the cream washed from his face.

"I see." Monica laughed, dropping her purse to the floor as she sat down in the chair.

"Wanna drink?" Jazz sashayed into the kitchen. "All I have is gin, of course. You could use a little calming down."

"Not too strong, Jazz. I can't afford to get drunk tonight."

Jazz handed her a glass and plopped down on the sofa. "Okay now, tell Jazz about the fix you're in. Why do the police say you killed Cameron?"

Monica took a sip of her drink, then sadly shook her head. "Cameron is dead, but I didn't kill him. He was already dead when I got to his house."

"Any idea who'd want to kill that luscious creature?"

"Yes. But I can't tell you now and I definitely can't go to the police. I need a place to stay tonight, Jazz. Then I've gotta get out of the city and I need your help. Think you could loan me one of your outfits? Maybe even one of your wigs?"

Jazz leaned forward. "Does this have to do with that package I gave you?"

Without blinking, Monica replied, "Yes."

"Say no more, girlfriend. It's Jazz to the rescue. This is so exciting, just like an old-fashioned slumber party!"

# Chapter

## 32

"Good thinking, Gerald," Arthur Fazio congratulated his friend, as he took a drink from his glass. The police had long since left Victor's house where Gerald had conveniently taken up residence. The two men had cooperated with the Department in its investigation of Cameron's death.

"Yeah, I seem to be on a roll. Those in-case-of-emergency cards Victor had senior staff carry around in their wallets with all his numbers printed on them came in handy."

"Where do you suppose Taylor is hiding? Tony said she hasn't been back to her house since you told him to stake out the place."

"She won't get very far. Now that she's the prime suspect in a murder case, it buys us some time to get rid of Carter and get the shipment safely to Jakarta. Let the police find her ass and drag her in."

"What if they believe her story?"

"Who's going to take her word against mine? They'll slap handcuffs on her wrists so fast, she won't know what hit her."

Waving that thought off as if it were already a done deal, Gerald changed the subject. "Is the shipment ready to leave tonight?"

"It's scheduled to pull out about midnight, cross into international waters in twenty-four hours. Then we'll be home free. Once the guys in Jakarta secure the shipment, you'll get your money."

"That's all I need to hear."

"Bob's still a little surprised that 'Victor' is going along with the plans."

"Forget about Bob. Anytime there's a hint of a problem, he wrings his hands like a nervous old lady. Right now, all we have to do is take care of Miss Taylor LeBlanc."

"What if she knows about Carter and leads them straight to the police?"

Gerald leaned back into his chair and propped his feet up on the matching ottoman.

"I've been thinking about that." Comfortably wrapped in one of Victor's smoking jackets, he puffed on his Cuban cigar. "If she knew about Carter, why didn't she tell Victor when she showed him the tape?"

Fazio shrugged his shoulders. "Maybe she did and Victor just didn't mention it."

Gerald snorted and shook his head, squinting his eyes as if he were trying to bring a blurred picture into focus. "Oh, no. My dearly departed brother wouldn't have bypassed the chance to point out another one of my shortcomings. No, she doesn't know."

"Sure?"

"We're the only ones who know Carter's there. Blackburn keeps him so doped up, he can't even speak. Other than the nuns and the staff—"

*The black nun.* Gerald suddenly remembered an incident in one of the doctor's weekly reports. An incident between Carter and a new nun. A *black* nun.

"Taylor's a clever broad," he said, sitting up in his chair. "She got in to see Carter by pretending to be a nun."

"Why didn't she tell Victor?" Fazio repeated.

"Maybe she thought that was her ace-in-the-hole, her trump card against me."

Suddenly, Gerald's face lit up. "I'll bet that's where she's headed, to collect her star witness. It's too late for her to pay a visit to him tonight, but I can bet you she'll try to get in tomorrow. Get Blackburn on the phone."

"But, Gerald, he thinks you're dead."

"I know that, you idiot! Just tell him you've decided to transfer our patient to another sanitarium. He's paid not to ask questions."

"But what if he does?"

"Will you just get him on the phone? Use your cell phone. I don't want that call traced back to this house. We'll delete the number from your phone records later."

Getting up from his seat, Gerald walked to the bar. "Another drink?"

Fazio nodded his head as he pulled the small digital phone from his pocket and dialed the number to Port Royal Meadows. He spoke only briefly, before hanging it up.

"Blackburn's away in Atlanta, at a two-day seminar. He'll be back tomorrow evening. I left a message for him to call me tomorrow morning."

"You won't be here." Gerald handed Arthur his drink. "You're going to Port Royal Meadow to take care of Taylor as soon as she gets there."

Arthur put his drink on the table beside him and looked Gerald squarely in the eyes.

"Look, Gerald," Arthur said slowly, "can't we just

dispose of Carter? Now that you've got the tape, we don't need him anymore."

"That's exactly the plan. To take care of Carter *and* Taylor, kill two birds with one stone."

"What if we just leave Tay—?"

"Hell no! We wait for Blackburn to get back to the facility, have him sign the release papers, then move Carter out. It's gotta look legitimate or the staff will get suspicious. Then, you wait for Miss Nosey. And when she shows up, get rid of her!"

* * *

MONICA LEFT THE SAVANNAH AIRPORT and headed north on Interstate 95 for the fifty-mile drive to Hilton Head. She had caught the 6 a.m. Delta Airlines flight out of Hobby Airport and, after changing planes in Atlanta, she'd landed in Savannah at eleven o'clock.

She had no problem getting past airport security and HPD, who swarmed over the airport in Houston like bees looking for honey. The queen bee they'd been searching for had shed the corporate look of Taylor LeBlanc for the more alluring, sensual look of a Jazz original.

Outfitted in a teal, three-piece silk pants suit, Jazz had added a multi-colored silk scarf and high-heel pumps. The long, dark-brown straight wig, with wispy bangs, bounced naturally against the back of her shoulders as she strode through the airport. She'd flashed her Monica Sinclair identification to the agent, purchased her ticket, and then breezed through the security check, the Sig strapped against her ankle.

*The task ahead would not be as easy,* Monica thought to herself, as she now sat inside the rented car. She fastened the fanny pack around her waist, securing her gun inside. Lighting a cigarette, her eyes roamed in every direction for the slightest indication that someone might be watching her, before driving the car out of the Savannah Airport parking lot.

The sun shone brightly in the sky, competing for sole dominance against puffs of clouds being chased by a light wind. Though the temperature was about seventy-four degrees, a trace of coolness hung in the air as a reminder that winter had not yet hung its hat for the season.

It was not until she turned from Montgomery onto Bay Street in Savannah's historic district that Monica noticed a white mid-sized car following close behind her. Driving past the Days Inn where she had reserved a room, she maintained her speed and kept going straight until she spotted a seafood restaurant with lots of cars scattered about the parking lot.

Whipping into an open parking space next to a group of people who were getting into their vehicle to leave the restaurant, Monica watched the white car slowly drive past her. She got out of her car and quickly went inside. She talked into the pay phone near the restroom at the back of the restaurant and stared out the window. Her eyes alternated from the entrance door to the parking lot to Bay Street.

Monica spotted the white car again as it drove into the lot and crept slowly down the aisle—pausing briefly behind the one she'd just gotten out of—before leaving the lot completely. She stretched her neck to see if she could get a glimpse of the driver—who talked into a mobile phone—and his passenger in the front seat. Though she could not identify them, she knew they were looking for her.

As soon as they pulled out of the parking lot, Monica dashed to her car and grabbed her bag from the front seat.

Ten minutes later, a black-and-white cab drove up to the entrance and Monica stepped outside, before the driver had a chance to blow the horn, and quickly slid into the back seat.

"Where to, lady?" the driver asked into the mirror, before spitting out a mouthful of tobacco into a tin can that rested in his lap. He wore a red bandana tied around his head, a thinning gray ponytail snaked down his back. A tattoo with the name "Tiger" was scrawled in green ink on his arm, just above his right elbow.

"Quick tour of the district, Eddie." Monica noted the man's name tag dangling from the mirror.

"No better tour guide than me. Been living here all my life, which will be exactly forty-eight years this December. I kin show you some things that ain't on any tour map."

"I'm counting on it." Monica stared out the back window for the white car and the two men, before settling down in her seat.

As the driver pointed out revolutionary war sites and shared gossip about the people who lived in the mansions he drove past, Monica was alert to her surroundings.

Monica listened to Eddie and pretended to be interested for another fifteen minutes, before instructing him to pull over to the curb.

"You don't want to shop here, lady," Eddie protested, as he pulled the cab in front of a thrift store called "Hidden Treasures." It was the only storefront on the block of commercial warehouses. "They got nothing but musty old clothes that's been sitting in closets a hunerd years. Let me take ya to the mall where you can find something more suitable for a young lady like yourself."

Monica got out of the car. Leaning her head into the front passenger window, she said, "You know what they say, 'One man's trash is another's treasure.' Besides, I want to get something 'vintage' for my grandmother. I'll only be ten minutes."

"Suit yourself, but my meter's running."

Exactly ten minutes later, Monica swung open the back door of the cab and tossed her packages on the seat.

"What'd I tell ya, Eddie?" she said, grinning, holding up the bags for him to see in his rear-view mirror. "I got my grandmother some clothes that'll look great on her."

"If I were you, I'd air out the mothball smell and wrap them in a fancy box before giving 'em to her."

Monica laughed and lit a cigarette. Blowing the smoke, she pointed with her cigarette. "Just a couple more stops, Eddie. Then on to the Days Inn on Bay Street."

* * *

THE MOTEL WAS A FLURRY of activity, with college students on spring break and families with small children, when Monica checked in at a little after three p.m. It was exactly the type of atmosphere where she could blend in and not draw attention to herself.

Monica locked the door to her room on the second floor, opened the draperies about a foot, and peeked through the sheers. Below her, swimsuit-clad bodies, layered with suntan oil, stretched out on chaise lounges and lined the outer area of the swimming pool. A guy in blue jeans, tee shirt, and a baseball cap turned backwards, leisurely talked on the pay phone near the entrance leading to the recreation area. Monica turned her head in the direction of squealing coming from the swimming pool, just in time to watch a young man pull his reluctant female companion into the water.

The ringing of the telephone on the nightstand by the bed brought her attention back inside the room. Frowning, Monica looked at it for a moment before deciding to pick it up on the third ring.

"Hello?" she said suspiciously. She'd told no one where she was staying.

Monica could hear the sound of breathing on the other end, though the caller did not say a word. "Who is this?" Her eyes darted to the chain lock on the door, her hand slowly unzipping the fanny pack around her waist that contained her gun.

"Joyce?" the man asked in a low voice. Monica could hear low murmuring in the background.

"You must have the wrong number," Monica said, without acknowledging the name she'd used when she checked into the motel. Joyce McIntyre was a character out of one of her novels, whose name only Michael knew she often used when traveling. The man on the phone was definitely not her brother.

"Be careful, Joyce. The hawk is after the mouse. Watch your step closely tonight." The sinister-sounding voice was unfamiliar.

"Who is this?" Monica shouted, before she heard a click, followed by a dial tone. The man was gone.

She stood holding the phone to her ear, the hairs on the back of her neck standing up, as a chill ran through her. She slowly put the receiver down and went to look through the curtains again. Not much had changed from a few moments before.

*Gerald knows I'm here!* She took her gun out and placed it on the nightstand.

Taking a bottle from a small paper bag, Monica poured some Jack Daniels into a glass and took a drink. She opened the other bags and spread the clothing across the bed. Studying them, she lit a cigarette, placed one hand on her hip, and tilted her head to the side as she blew smoke through her nostrils. She rearranged the clothing and accessories again until, finally, everything was in place. Standing back, Monica stared at the bed and smiled.

"Okay, Miss Lucy. It's just you and me."

\* \* \*

"WHAT DO YOU MEAN you lost her?" Michael yelled into the phone, wiping the perspiration from above his lips. He thought he would lose his mind waiting for the call. "Sam, all you had to do was keep an eye on her once she left the air—"

"Wait a minute, boss," the man on the other end protested. "We followed her from the airport just like you said, until she got to the historic district here in Savannah. She must've spotted us, because she passed up the motel, then turned into the parking lot of a seafood restaurant and went inside. By the time we circled the block and doubled back—it took awhile because there was a lot of traffic—she'd ditched the car and split.

"We went back to the motel and waited a couple of hours. She pulled up in a cab a little while ago. I'm calling you from a pay phone out by the pool."

"Did she see you?" Michael knew his sister well. She'd casually mentioned the motel on her first trip to Hilton Head. After their conversation last night, he'd had a hunch she would go back there.

"Don't think so. The place is swarming with kids on spring break. What do you want us to do now?"

Michael let out a deep sigh and ran his hand through his hair. Sitting in his office waiting by the phone was the last place he wanted to be. The acid churning in his stomach told him things were going to get rough for Monica from now on out.

"Sit tight for awhile. I don't think she'll leave before dark. Just keep an eye on the place. I'm warning you now, she's sly as a fox. She's got eyes in the back of her head. Follow her wherever she goes." Michael paused. "And, Sam, give her some rope. I believe she's headed for a place on Hilton Head Island called Port Royal Meadows. When she gets there, back off. I've got it covered from there."

"Okay, boss."

After the agent hung up, Michael rested the receiver on his shoulder and listened to the hum of the dial tone. Slowly, he punched in a long-distance number, took another deep breath, and shifted gears.

"How's my favorite girl?" he asked cheerfully, when his grandmother answered the phone on the other end.

"Michael, is that you, darling?"

"Unless you've got a beau you haven't told me about."

"Go on, you," Sweets laughed in her high-pitched shrill. When she finally caught her breath again, she said, "You and Monica must have ESP."

Michael held his breath.

"You talked to Twig? Today?" He measured his breathing, to keep his tone even.

"I hadn't long hung up with her when you called. That girl's always on the go. Said she was on the road and just wanted to check in. Asked about Sneakers, of course. She wanted to know if I was feeding him too much. You'd think that dog was her child."

"I guess he is, in a way."

"Is she okay, Michael?"

"Yeah, sure. Why do you ask?"

"She sounded too cheery. Like she was hiding something. Like you're doing now. What's wrong, Michael?"

Michael hesitated a moment. He and Monica were never able to fool their grandmother. It was like Sweets had a radar to their souls.

"Michael?"

"I'm here, Sweets. Listen, everything's fine. You know Monica always gets a little jumpy when she's on assignment. We've had a few unexpected twists and turns, but she's okay. It'll all be over soon, so don't worry your pretty little head."

"Just the same, I'm going to have a little talk with the Lord when I hang up the phone, until I hear back from her."

"Did she say when she would call again?" Michael straightened up in his seat, wondering what his sister was up to now.

"No, she didn't. She asked about Big Red, then we chatted for a few minutes before she hung up."

"She obviously has something on her mind. Do me a favor, Sweets. Call me the minute you hear from her, okay?"

"Okay, darling. Look out for your sister, Michael.

You kids and Ben are the only family I have."

"Don't worry. Everything will be fine. Talk to you soon, sweetheart."

"Bye, darling."

As soon as Michael hung up the phone, it rang again. "Yeah."

"There's someone here in my office I think you'd like to talk to," Jim Frasier said.

"Be right there."

Five minutes later, Michael swung open the door to Jim's office. Sitting across from his boss's desk, with legs crossed and head lowered, was Bob McCormick. Michael slammed the door behind him.

"What's the matter, McCormick?" he glared, walking closer to the man, growing angrier with each step. "Did the rock you finally slithered out from under suddenly get too heavy for you?"

Bob McCormick did not make eye contact.

"Calm down, Michael," Jim said. "He's confessed to his role in the Bayou City Wireless cover-up. The Coast Guard is already in pursuit of the shipment of phones to Indonesia. I think we'll get it in time. Thought you might be interested in the last statement he just made. Tell him, Bob."

Bob McCormick finally looked up at Michael with strained, red eyes and the tired, worn face of an old man.

"Well?" Michael said.

With his voice strained with emotion, the older man said, "Gerald's alive. He had Victor killed. Assumed his identity to go ahead with the plans to release the Excalibur."

"Tell me something I don't know," Michael said, unimpressed by the man's declaration.

Jim Frasier took off his glasses, his mouth gaped open in surprise.

"You knew and didn't tell me?"

"That's right. Just like you kept a few things from me, Jim," Michael snapped at his boss. "Monica only recently found out. If I had told you, you would've sent our guys charging down to Houston, interfering with her plans."

Frasier winced. "I'm already organizing agents to bring Gerald Conti in."

"Call 'em off!" Michael shouted, pointing to the phone. He and Jim had hit a turning point in their relationship. Michael was not willing to sit back and take orders anymore, especially where Monica's safety was concerned.

"Are you outta your mind? What if he tries to flee?"

"He's not going anywhere. Gerald doesn't know McCormick's here. He's not gonna leave the country without terminating the last person he thinks has the goods on him. And that's Greg Dumont. That's right, Jim, Monica's found him alive. She's on her way to get him. There's a good chance Gerald is aware of this and will try to stop her. So, call off the bloodhounds, Jim. Now!"

Jim Frasier's face turned scarlet with fury. Michael knew he had never spoken to him in this manner before, but he didn't care.

Michael watched as Jim hesitantly picked up the phone and muttered into the receiver. Hanging it back up, he looked at Michael sternly.

Michael turned back to Bob McCormick. There was still one more question he needed answered.

"Who killed Jarrett Jones?"

The man did not answer. He simply buried his head

in his hands.

"Answer me, goddammit!" Michael shouted, snatching the man up from his chair by the front of his shirt. "Was it you?"

"Michael!" Jim hollered, running from behind his desk to pry Michael's hands away from the other man.

"One of Gerald's men shot him!" McCormick cried openly. "I never meant for him to get hurt. That's why I transferred him out of the division." Slobbering, he broke down in tears again as he told Michael how Jones had died.

When McCormick finished, it took every ounce of self-control Michael had left in him not to attack the man again.

"You're pathetic," Michael spat at him, turning to leave the filth behind him. "You're one of his father's closest friends. God help you when Mr. Jones learns that you could've prevented his son's death."

"Where's Monica, Michael?" Jim ordered, sternly. "Tell me, so I can help her."

"You didn't help her when she needed you, Jim." Michael stood in the doorway. "Now, stay out of her way."

# Chapter

## 33

The cab arrived promptly at the Days Inn at 5 p.m. Monica stepped outside the front door, a large black patent leather purse swaying from side to side in the crook of her left arm, as she gripped a rubber-tipped wooden cane with her gloved right hand. A motel employee walked beside her carrying her duffle bag.

Eddie, the cab driver, got out of the front seat, walked around the car, and met her just as she reached the back door.

"Let me help you with that, ma'am," he said, taking her arm and helping her into the cab. Monica smiled and sweetly said in a slightly higher-pitched voice than her own, "Thank you, young man. It's so nice to see a gentleman these days."

She laid her cane on the seat beside her and crossed her feet, as Eddie gently closed the door. When he opened the truck to put her bag inside, Monica chuckled to herself. Just as she'd anticipated, he didn't recognize her. She'd specifically asked for him by name, when she'd placed the call to the cab company.

Before he got back into the car, Monica quickly took off one of her gloves, ran her hand over the theatrical makeup she'd applied to her face and neck, and stole a glance at herself in the driver's rear-view mirror. It would take a lot of scrubbing to remove the thick, dark makeup from her skin. The wrinkles on her forehead, around her eyes and mouth—induced by the make-up—made her look older than Sweets.

A soft black hat with a turned-up front flap sat on top of the short gray wig that covered Monica's forehead and stopped in the back just above the double-strand of pearls around her neck. On the center of her nose sat a tiny oval pair of silver wire-rimmed glasses with bifocal lines across the middle of each lens.

After padding her body with pillow stuffing to give her a more full-figured look, the gray tweed, two-piece suit she'd purchased from the thrift shop fit her perfectly. The black lace-up shoes with low heels were a little snug.

"Where to, ma'am?" Eddie said, as he pulled from the curb and turned right on Bay Street.

"You can call me Miss Lucy, dearie. All of my friends do."

"Okay, Miss Lucy. My friends call me Eddie. So where're you headed this evening?"

"I'm going to pay a visit to my boy, Louis. He's a patient at a place over in Hilton Head named Port Royal Meadows. Do you know where that is, Eddie?"

"Sure do. But that's gonna cost you a bundle."

"Don't worry about the money, young man," Monica pretended to scold. "I've got enough to cover the fare. But don't go getting any silly ideas in your head about robbing me. I'm warning you now, I've got old Sally with me." Monica patted her purse with her gun inside. "She just might get a notion to do something foolish."

"No ma'am," Eddie laughed. "I wouldn't think of hurting you. I'm as gentle as a pussycat."

"That's what my granddaughter said. Though I'm not as trusting as she is."

"Your granddaughter?"

"I believe you took her sightseeing this afternoon."

Eddie's face brightened.

"That's right, I did. She sure is a nice lady."

"She's a sweetheart." Monica kept a straight face. "She bought me this lovely new suit, so I could look my best when I see Louis. She even went to the trouble of wrapping it in a white box with a great big red bow. Wasn't that thoughtful of her?"

Eddie rubbed the back of his neck and cleared his throat.

"Yes, ma'am. Like I said, she sure is a nice lady."

* * *

"PULL OVER IN THE parking lot, dearie," Monica said, when they'd reached the entrance of the lane leading to the facility. "My granddaughter left a car for me to drive back after my visit. You can put my bag in the trunk before I get out."

"I know the car. I took her to the airport this afternoon to pick it out and followed behind her when she brought it here."

"You're such a nice boy, Eddie. Your mother should be very proud of you."

"Yes, ma'am," he said, pulling up behind the dark blue Illumina. "I'll tell her you said that."

Taking the keys from Monica, Eddie got out and transferred the bag from the cab into the back seat of the car. Monica reached into her purse, pulled out a small compact, and took one last glance at her appearance in

331

its small mirror. Pressing her red-stained lips together, she smoothed out her suit, and then tucked her gun inside the front of her skirt. If she could pull off this last performance, she would be home free.

Eddie pulled up to the entrance of the facility and walked around to help Monica out of the car.

"Here you go, Miss Lucy. Safe and sound, just like I promised."

"Thank you, dear," she said, taking his hand for support, as she got out of the cab. Opening her purse, she paid the fare and steadied her cane on the pavement.

"You want me to walk you to the front door?"

"No, sirree. I might look old and decrepit on the outside, but on the inside, I feel like a girl half my age."

"Well, you be careful driving back to Savannah, Miss Lucy." Eddie climbed back into the cab.

Monica waved as he drove off, then turned and slowly walked up the sidewalk, her shoulders hunched forward. It was six-fifteen. Relatives and friends of the patients sat outside on the veranda ahead of her. She knew Mrs. Hahn would not be far away.

Monica slowly maneuvered her way up the front stairs and stopped at the top, pretending to catch her breath. Taking a deep breath, she hobbled through the front door to the information desk in the front lobby.

"May I help you?" the receptionist asked.

"I hope so, dear. My name is Lucy Jones. My friends call me Miss Lucy. I'm here to visit my boy, Louis Fairchild."

The young lady picked up a chart and skimmed the pages. Sitting behind the desk, she looked like a Buddha dressed in a white uniform and appeared to be in her early thirties.

"I'm sorry, ma'am, but Mr. Fairchild is not well enough to receive visitors."

Monica frowned, the make-up pulled at her face.

"Oh, dear," she said in a quivering voice. "I've come such a long way to see him. You see, I used to work for his family. Raised him from an infant. I've just got to see him before I . . . before . . . I . . . "

Monica's eyes began to tear as she took a handkerchief from her purse and pressed it slightly against her face. She looked through the narrow slits of her eyes and saw the woman's confused expression.

"Mrs. Jones—"

"Call me Miss Lucy, dear." Monica choked back tears.

"—Miss Lucy, why don't you wait right here. I'll go get Mrs. Hahn, the director. Have a seat in this chair next to my desk. I'll be right back. Can I get you a glass of water?"

"Thank you, dear. That's so kind of you."

A few minutes later, the receptionist returned with Mrs. Hahn. Monica propped both her hands on top of the cane and looked up at the German woman.

"Mrs. Jones," the woman held out her hand, "I'm Mrs. Hahn, the director of Port Royal Meadows."

"Call me Miss Lucy, dearie. All my friends do."

Mrs. Hahn smiled.

"Miss Lucy, Jennifer tells me you've come to visit Louis Fairchild."

"That's right. You see, he's like my own son, all the family I have left. I'm getting on in years. I just want to see him one more time before I pass on. You understand, don't you, dear?"

"Yes, ma'am. But, as Jennifer informed you, Louis is

too sick to have visitors. In fact, you're the first one he's had in all the months he's been here."

"Oh, I've been suffering something terrible with my arthritis. Sometimes I can hardly move. My heart's not that strong, either. There are times when I don't know if I'm going to make it through the day."

Monica could see Mrs. Hahn wavering. "Well, Dr. Blackburn has issued strict orders for Louis not to see anyone. The doctor is the only person who can authorize visitations and he hasn't returned from a seminar in Atlanta. He's not expected until later tonight."

"Oh, goodness. I've just got to see Louis today. I leave tomorrow on an early train. You won't deprive an old woman of her last wish?"

Monica looked innocently up at Mrs. Hahn, who bit her bottom lip and then dismissed the receptionist.

"I'll take responsibility, Jennifer." She bent down to take Monica's elbow and helped her from her chair. "Come with me, Miss Lucy. I'll take you up to see Louis, just for a few minutes. He really is very sick. He's on a lot of medication, so don't be upset if he doesn't recognize you."

"He won't upset me none." Monica chuckled. "In my lifetime, I've seen practically every kind of illness there is."

Mrs. Hahn led Monica from the elevator on the second floor and walked toward the room at the end of the hall. The familiar smell of sterilized cleansers filled Monica's nostrils. She casually looked into some of the opened doors as she passed, televisions playing low in the background. She stared at the bright red exit sign over the door leading to the stairs at the end of the hall. Just as Mrs. Hahn paused outside of the closed door of

Carter's room, Monica turned her head slowly and noted another exit at the opposite end of the floor with a large window in the corner.

"Louis's bed is the one at the far end of the room," Mrs. Hahn said in a low voice, before opening the door. "He has a roommate. Mr. Byers is an amnesia patient. Nothing to worry about, though. He's as docile as a lamb. I'll be back for you in about ten minutes."

Monica nodded her head up and down, then side to side, as she'd seen elderly people do. Leaning on her cane, she limped into the room. The curtains were drawn over the large, barred windows and the room was dimly lit by a light that shone through the sheer white curtain that separated the two beds. Monica slowly walked past the old man in the first bed. Smiling, he waved to her. He appeared to be in his late seventies or early eighties, dressed in a navy terry cloth robe and light blue pajamas.

Monica nodded her head and continued to the side of Carter's bed that was closest to the wall. Although his eyes were closed, his face did not look as gaunt and pale as it had the last time she'd seen him. He lay straight on his back with his arms on top of the covers that were tightly tucked around him. Monica put her cane and purse gently in the chair beside the bed, then leaned over the guard rail and ran her hand across his forehead.

"Carter?" she whispered, taking one of his hands in hers. "Can you hear me? Open your eyes, if you can hear me."

She continued to rub his head as his eyes slowly opened. Blinking, he turned in the direction of Monica's voice and stared at her. Though his eyes appeared clearer than she remembered, he didn't say a word.

"Listen carefully, Carter, we don't have much time.

We're leaving tonight. Do you understand?" Carter looked at her with the same blank expression.

*I wish you could understand me.* She was going to have one hell of a time getting him out of the facility. "It's too late to turn back now," she heard herself whisper aloud.

"What's too late?" the man said, standing behind the curtain. Monica jumped as he drew back the curtain and stepped over to Carter's bed.

"Mercy," she said, placing her hand over her heart. "You scared the life outta me."

"You said it was 'too late.' What did you mean?"

Monica looked at him for a moment, her head cocked to the side. There was a familiarity about his voice, though she was sure she had not met him before.

"Just thinking out loud, dear," she said. "I'm getting up in age and I was telling my boy here I might not get another chance to see him before I pass on to my glory."

Mr. Byers looked at Monica. His eyes were gentle and he smiled with understanding. His hair was dark and he had a full gray beard and mustache; his eyebrows were bushy and came to a point in the middle of his forehead. Somehow, Monica felt no fear of him.

"Are you his mother?" the old man asked shyly.

"You might say that. I raised him from a young pup."

"I don't remember my mother."

Monica smiled and walked around to him. Taking his hand, she led him back to his bed. "You get back in bed, young man. You're going to be all right."

She tucked the covers around him. When she looked back into his eyes, Monica felt as if she'd looked into them before.

"Thank you for being so nice to me," Mr. Byers said.

Monica stared at him a few minutes longer, then patted his hand. "You take care of yourself. I'm going back over to talk to my baby."

She turned away slowly and began to close the curtain. Before she'd closed it all the way, Mr. Byers waved again. Monica managed a faint smile, nodded her head, and walked back to Carter's bed.

She stopped in front of the closet and pulled on the handle. Just as she'd expected, aside from a pair of slippers on the floor, it was empty. She was glad she'd gone with her intuition and bought Carter some clothes and shoes from the thrift shop.

Monica closed the closet door and quickly moved to Carter's side, when she heard the sound of approaching voices outside the room. Whispering into his ear, she said, "I'll be back to get you."

Mrs. Hahn walked into the room and paused briefly to speak with Mr. Byers. When she walked around the curtain, she found Monica sitting in the chair beside Carter's bed, humming a tune.

"It's time to go now, Miss Lucy."

"My, my. Where did the time go?" Monica gathered her cane and purse as she pulled herself to her feet. "I was singing him his favorite hymn. 'Bringing in the Sheaves.' Do you know it?"

"I don't think so."

Turning to Carter, Monica bent down and kissed his cheek. She stared into his eyes again and smiled before Mrs. Hahn took her elbow and led her away.

"Come back again." Mr. Byers waved at Monica, as the two ladies passed his bed.

"Oh, I will, dear."

* * *

MONICA SAW ARTHUR FAZIO as soon as she and Mrs. Hahn stepped off the elevator into the lobby. He stood anxiously beside the receptionist's desk, looking at his watch and then turning his head around to case the room. Monica faltered when the receptionist pointed towards them. In a quick glimpse, she saw the bulge just inside the left side of his suit jacket as Arthur turned and started in their direction. The receptionist ran behind him.

"I'll walk you to the door, Miss Lucy." The director held Monica's hand in hers.

"Don't trouble yourself, dear. You've been so kind." Monica turned to leave before Arthur reached them, but it was too late.

"You the director of this facility?" Arthur demanded with authority.

Monica lowered her eyes and pulled at her gloves as she turned to walk away.

"Mrs. Hahn," Jennifer said, taking deep breaths as she ran around the man, "this gentleman wants us to release one of our patients. I've already explained to him Dr. Blackburn is not on the premises."

"If you'll wait one moment, sir," Mrs. Hahn said to him disapprovingly. "I'm going to walk this lady to the door. Then, I'll be right with you."

When the two women reached the front door, Monica shook Mrs. Hahn's hand again and started down the front steps. The sun faded in the distance as Monica turned the corner of the building and headed for her car. Once inside, she stared intently at the front door, waiting for Arthur Fazio to come out.

Five minutes later, she saw him walk hurriedly down

the steps, get into a dark Lincoln driven by another man Monica did not recognize, and ride off. She knew he would be back. She took out a cigarette, lit it, and blew the smoke out the window. Looking at the dainty, antique-looking watch on her arm, Monica settled into her seat. It was a few minutes before seven. *Just a couple more hours.*

# Chapter
## 34

"**D**amn!" Gerald shouted, slamming down the receiver so hard that it flew over the side of his desk and bounced up and down like a bungee jumper. For the fourth time that day he'd tried calling Maggie at her home, only to get her answering machine. She had not reported to work that morning, nor called with an explanation.

"Where the hell can she be?" he asked out loud. He shuffled through papers until he found the ones he wanted and stuffed them into his briefcase. Gerald stomped over to the bar to fix himself another drink.

It was time for him to leave the country. Victor's corporate jet was already fueled and waiting at George Bush Intercontinental Airport to fly Gerald to Jakarta, Indonesia. He'd transferred large sums of money from Victor's account into a Swiss account opened months before. He left a memo on his secretary's desk that stated he would be in Indonesia for a couple of weeks. Once his dealings with the Indonesians were completed, Gerald would go on to Switzerland to start a new life.

But there were still a few loose ends. Maggie was one of them. It was 6:15 p.m. If he did not locate her by the time he planned to leave, a few hours from now, he'd just take his chances.

Taylor LeBlanc was another piece of unfinished business. Their paths had crossed before, Gerald was sure of it. *Where?*

Gerald halted the glass in his hand before it reached his mouth, the cognac splashed over the sides. Why hadn't he thought of it before? Instantly, he put the glass down on the brass platter, walked to his desk, and picked up the phone.

"Don't do anything before you hear back from me," he said into the phone to Arthur, while putting on his jacket. "There's something I gotta check out . . . Go back to Port Royal . . . She'll show up . . . I know what I said . . . just do what I'm telling you now!"

* * *

AT NINE O'CLOCK, MONICA crept from the storage closet in the kitchen and looked around for signs of activity. She'd learned during her first visit to Port Royal Meadows that the kitchen door to the outside was not locked until after the last dose of medicine was administered. The attendants had just left to make their rounds.

Still dressed as Miss Lucy, Monica figured if she were caught during Carter's escape, it'd be much easier to pretend to be a disoriented old woman, than a young one with no reason for being there. She had memorized every detail of the first floor when she had spent that first day at Port Royal Meadows as Sister Theresa. An hour earlier, the attendants had come to get the last round of medicine for the patients before they were settled in for the night. Now, all was quiet.

Monica tip-toed out of the kitchen and headed for the stairs. Just as she placed her hand on the door to push it open, she heard footsteps on the stairwell. *Shit!* Frantically, she spun around in search for a place to hide. Dr. Blackburn's office was the nearest room to her.

She remembered that Mrs. Hahn had told Arthur Fazio earlier this evening that the doctor was not expected back until tonight. *Here's hoping it's later tonight.* Monica held her skirt up and sprinted across the hall. Once inside the office, which was lit by a lamp on the desk, she quietly closed the door and pressed her ear against it. Her breathing was hard, her heart thumped wildly in her chest. She heard the stairwell door open and close. The footsteps grew louder, then faded away.

Monica relaxed her whole body against the door and let out a long sigh. Shifting the padding inside her dress back into place, she started to turn to leave. Suddenly, something across the room caught her eye and stopped her dead in her tracks. There, on Dr. Blackburn's desk, was an Excalibur. A mound of papers sat beside it. *What the . . .?*

Monica checked her watch. She had only twenty minutes to get Carter before the kitchen door was locked for the night and the alarm activated. *Damn!*

She hurried to the desk and moved the phone aside. She picked up the top sheet of paper and scanned its contents. A second later, she gasped.

*Oh, my God!*

For the first time, she heard a faint swooshing to her left that caused her to snap her head around. It reminded her of the sound made when stoking a fire. It came from a narrow, slightly ajar door that looked like a closet. Monica put the paper down and walked towards it. She felt for her gun, tucked away in the waistband of her skirt, as she used her right hand to tug on the doorknob.

As she descended down the dimmed stairway, the sound grew louder. The rubber-soled shoes she wore barely made a sound. When Monica reached the opened door at the bottom of the stairs, she held onto the knob and peeked inside the brightly lit room.

It was then she saw what generated the noise. Her eyes widened in terror as she looked at the body on the hospital bed across the room. It was hooked up to a respirator that pumped the chest up and down. There were tubes protruding from both the mouth and the bladder. A large tube stuck out from the shaved head. Monica could not tell whether the patient was a man or a woman.

A flicker of movement to her right caught her eye. Dr. Blackburn sat on a four-wheeled stool, hunched over a small table in the corner of the room. She watched him roll the stool to the side and pick up a writing pad.

As he did, Monica saw the microscope.

* * *

DR. BLACKBURN PUT ON a pair of latex gloves from the box on the surgical tray next to the patient's bed. He pulled a syringe from his pocket, pulled off the protective cover with his teeth, then spat it on the floor. He then unscrewed the bottom of the plastic bag—which contained cerebrospinal fluid that dripped from the epithelial cyst in the patient's brain—and withdrew 10ccs of the clear liquid.

He reached into his other pocket, took out a vial, stuck the needle into the vial, and transferred the liquid. Once he had finished, he placed the vial into a tube, then placed the tube into the centrifuge.

Dr. Blackburn stepped back and took the gloves off.

He turned to look at the patient whose chest bellowed up and down to the cadence of the respirator. He took off his glasses, crossed his arms, and hoped that this time, he'd made the discovery of a lifetime.

* * *

"CARTER, WAKE UP!" Monica covered his mouth with her hand just in case he awoke with a scream. Instead, he blinked his eyes and stared at her as he had just a few hours before.

"I'm gonna put your shoes on. Then, we're gonna get outta here."

Monica removed her hand. When he didn't utter a sound, she sat him up and swung his feet over the edge of the bed. She stooped over and slipped the house shoes on his feet. When she turned around, she was startled to see the curtain between the two beds drawn back. Mr. Byers sat on the side of his bed, staring at her.

Monica opened her mouth to say something, but closed it again when the old man got out of his bed and came to help her with Carter. Smiling, he lifted Carter from the bed and stood him up as Monica hesitated before sliding Carter's arms through the sleeves of the robe.

"You will be tossed by the wind." The old man's eyes were transfixed on her face. "But you will not fail. You are not alone."

She nervously smiled back and nodded her head. *He thinks this is a game!* Monica watched in astonishment as Mr. Byers stuffed pillows beneath the sheets of Carter's bed and covered them up. Carter stared ahead as she tied the belt around his waist. Just as Monica turned to lead him out of the room, she saw that the door was standing wide open. Mr. Byers was gone.

"Shit!" she said, propping Carter against the wall. Monica caught sight of the man from the doorway as he ran to the end of the hall. *Dammit! He's gonna turn me in!*

Just as she turned to go back to Carter, she heard a loud crash and the sound of shattering glass. Monica stuck her head out the door again and watched in horror as Mr. Byers swung at the small panes of the french window with his bare fists. He screamed like a wild man.

"Let me out! Let me out!" Several attendants rushed from a nearby room to restrain him. Monica watched for a second longer until the bloodied old man was given a shot, then led into a nearby bathroom. Gathering Carter, she quickly walked him to the door, slipped out of the room, and headed down the stairs.

* * *

IT WAS NOT UNTIL she had crossed the bridge leading out of Hilton Head that Monica realized she was shaking and her teeth were chattering. She could not wipe the images from her mind of the bloodied old man striking out the window. She wondered if he knew just how much he'd helped her.

Monica blew the smoke from her cigarette out the window, then turned to look at Carter. In the darkness of the car, she could see the light of the passing cars reflecting off of his eyes as he stared out the window. He hadn't so much as mumbled a sound since they'd left Port Royal Meadows.

There was something else besides Mr. Byers's raging fit that troubled Monica. Dr. Blackburn was a part of the

Bastrop experiment. The scope of the investigation was expanding to epic proportions.

Monica had been prepared to confront Arthur Fazio at some point during her escape. Why hadn't he shown up to stop her? Where was he? *It was all too easy. Too damn easy.*

* * *

"SHE'S GOT HIM," Arthur Fazio said into his mobile phone, turning his car onto Bay Street. "She's dressed in some old lady getup. Walked right out the back door of the facility. Nobody even saw her."

"Where is she now?" Gerald sat in the plush leather seat of his jet. A wide grin spread across his lips as he crossed his legs and ran a cigar under his nose. He had to hand it to her, the broad was smart.

"She's turning into a motel in Savannah. You want me to dispose of them now?"

"Let 'em go."

"Are you crazy, Gerald?" Arthur yelled. "Didn't you hear what I said? Taylor's got Dave Carter. If I don't stop them right this minute, they're gonna get away."

"I've got something a little more entertaining for our little Miss Nosey before she's terminated. Go to the Savannah airport. I'll pick you up in an hour. You and I have a pit-stop to make before we head on to Jakarta."

Gerald hung up the phone and looked down at the piece of paper in his hand. Taking a sip of his drink, he tapped the cigar on the tray table to his side and winked his eye. "Now, let's see if you really want to play games."

\* \* \*

MONICA DIALED MICHAEL'S pager number. A few seconds later, he answered the phone on the first ring. She could hear Michael screaming her name before she even said hello.

"Everything's fine, Michael." She looked over at Carter who dozed off to sleep as soon as she helped him into the bed.

"I should wring your little neck!" he shouted. "Do you know how worried I've been? I was just about to send out the goddamn calvary!"

"Relax, Michael. I got Dave Carter. We're in a motel in Savannah. We've gotta early morning flight to Washington."

"I'm tired of this crap. Stay where you are, Monica. I'm sending some—"

"I don't need an escort, Michael." Monica was livid. "Things don't always go according to plan. I screwed up once. I wasn't going to let that happen again. Dave Carter was my last shot and I'm bringing him in by myself."

"Monica—!"

"I'm tired, Michael, so listen up. Gerald has probably shipped the phones out by now. Check the Ports in Mexico. The manufacturing plant is down there. And send someone to pick up Dr. Blackburn at Port Royal Meadows. He's got the last Bastrop participant in an induced coma. Conducting his own medical experiments. I'll call you in the morning when we change planes in Atlanta."

"Monica, *listen!* There's something I need to tell you be—"

"Save it, Michael. I'll call you tomorrow."

Monica hung up the phone. After a moment of thinking how her brother had turned into a bureaucrat, she took the receiver off the hook.

# Chapter

## 35

The plane touched down on the runway at Hartsfield International Airport and roared like a mighty lion. Monica unclenched her fingers and exhaled a deep breath. *I'll never get used to this.* She looked over at Carter who was unfazed by the flight. He had struggled to speak a couple of times during the night, but his words were sporadic and confused.

Whatever damage he'd sustained to his brain, she hoped it was reversible. Everything was riding on him now.

Monica pushed the button above her head for the flight attendant. She wanted to make sure the electric cart was waiting at the gate when they deplaned. Unfastening her seat belt, she turned to Carter.

"Head . . . hurts." He rubbed his forehead with a trembling hand. "Can't r-remember w-what's happened to me."

"Don't worry." Monica took two Tylenol from her purse and handed him the bottle of water she'd brought from Savannah. "Just hang on. We'll be home soon."

Carter nodded his head. He wrapped both hands around the water bottle and brought it to his mouth. Monica looked at her watch. They had another hour before the departure of their next plane.

When they exited the plane, the cart and driver were

there. Monica checked the monitor for departing flights.

"Gate #10." She threw her duffle bag into the cart, before helping Carter aboard.

"Where're you headed?" The young lady spoke in a southern accent, shifting the cart into gear. The beeping sound warned travelers who walked in front of it.

"Washington, D.C. Our plane leaves at 9:58."

"You've got plenty of time. The gate's just down the way a bit."

Monica spotted a pay phone through the multitude of travelers and remembered her promise to call Michael.

"Can you stop at that phone over there?" she pointed. "I need to make a quick call."

Just as Monica stepped off the cart in front of the phone, her pager went off. She recognized the number instantly. Frowning, she dug into her purse, pulled out her calling card, and dialed the operator. Monica waited for the call to be connected.

"Hello?" Sweets answered before the ring had been completed.

"Sweets? Hi, it's Monica."

"Hi, darling."

An alarm went off in Monica's head when she heard the quiver in Sweets's voice.

"I'm changing planes in Atlanta. Is everything alright?"

"I'm fine, darling. There's someone here who wants to talk to you."

Monica pushed the phone closer to her ear with her shoulder, her chest heaved up and down from panic as she heard her grandmother's muffled voice talking to someone in the background. *Who is she—*

"You've got a nice little grandma here, Taylor," a

man's voice said. "She just cooked me the most delicious breakfast."

Monica closed her eyes and swallowed to keep from vomiting. Her heart beat so loudly in her chest, she could hear it in her ears. It was Gerald! And he had her grandmother.

"If . . . you . . . hurt . . . her, Gerald," Monica hissed, through lips that barely moved. She could have passed for a ventriloquist. "I'm warning you, I'll—"

"You're in no position to threaten me, you little bitch. I'm giving the orders. Now, you listen to me and do exactly as I say. Get yourself on the first plane to Lynchburg. Don't stop at go, don't tip off any of your little comrades at the FBI—and yes, Monica Sinclair, I know you're an agent—come directly to this house. And don't forget our catatonic friend. The party won't be complete without him."

Monica felt as if the life had been sucked out of her. She was sure her rubbery legs would buckle at any moment. The crowded airport terminal seemed to spin around her. She gripped onto the metal phone cord for support.

"Did you hear what I said?" Gerald yelled into the phone.

"I . . . I heard you. I need time to check the schedule. I don't know when the next flight to Lynchburg leaves," Monica stammered, stalling to give herself time to think. She was too far away to play games with Gerald. Her grandmother's life was at stake.

"Just so happens, I have the schedule right here in front of me. Figured since you were flying Delta, you'd have to pass through Atlanta. Now, let's see here . . . "

Monica heard paper rattling in the background.

"Next plane leaves at 9:22. Atlantic Southeast Airlines. You've got less than twenty minutes to make that flight."

Monica pushed back the sleeve of her jacket and looked at her watch. It was five after nine.

"We can't make that! I've gotta buy the tickets and get to the—"

"—And I've got a gun pointed at your sweet little grandmother's head and she's not too happy about it. I'd hate for her to have a heart attack or something while you make up your mind. Now, get moving. You're wasting time."

"Okay, okay. Just let me speak to her again."

"No funny stuff or she's dead. Oh, I'm sending an entourage to pick you up in Lynchburg to make sure you get here safe and sound."

He handed the phone back to Sweets.

"Don't worry about me, darling," she said, sounding calmer than she had before.

"Listen carefully, Sweets." There was one phone in the house. Monica gambled that Gerald was not listening next to her grandmother.

"Is Red there?"

"No, I said not to worry. But I do have some distressing news, dear. His father died a couple of days ago. They're burying him today at the old farmhouse—"

"Enough small talk," Gerald got back on the phone. "Make sure you get on that plane or there's going to be one more funeral."

"Don't you—" Monica managed before the line went dead. Holding onto the phone, her mind went back to what Sweets had said. Red's father died over twenty years ago. The cemetery was nowhere near the farmhouse.

*The farmhouse!* Sweets was giving her a signal. Monica frantically punched in another number and prayed that it was still connected. Nobody had lived in the house for years.

"Who is it?" Red answered, annoyed, as if he were in the middle of doing something important.

"Red? It's Monica."

"Well, I declare. How'd the hell you know Big Red would be here? Hey, I thought of a new word yester—"

"Not now, Red," Monica snapped. "Sweets is in trouble. She needs your help."

"What? Seen her just this mor—"

"Be quiet and listen, Red. Only got a second. Here's what I want you to do . . ."

# Chapter
## 36

Michael was crazy with worry. The agent he'd assigned to watch Monica's hotel in Savannah had called from the airport more than an hour ago. Monica and Dumont had boarded the plane without incident. Michael checked the time. *She should've called from Atlanta by now.*

"Where the hell are you, Monica?" He questioned the phone on his desk, as if it were patched through to his sister. He rubbed his hands together so hard his skin began to burn. A sudden knock at his office door made him jump.

"Come in!" Michael looked up just as Ben swung open the door and walked into the room. He abruptly pushed back his chair and went to embrace his father.

"Thanks, Dad," Michael's voice trembled with emotion.

Ben smiled and nodded his head. "She's my daughter, remember?" He released his son and sat down opposite the large desk.

"You okay?" Michael noticed the bandages on his hands. "They didn't hurt you, did they?"

"Nah." Ben chuckled, holding up his injured hands. "I overplayed my part just a bit. The injection they gave me left me a bit groggy, but other than that, I'm in pretty good shape. Any word yet about Monica?"

Michael sighed and wiped his face with his hand. "She made it out of Savannah. She was supposed to call me when she got to Atlanta, but I haven't heard from her."

Michael paused when he saw the troubled look return to Ben's face, the lines on his forehead seeming to multiply right before his eyes. Michael hated getting him so deeply involved, but he knew his father would have it no other way.

"Quite frankly, Dad, I'm worried."

"Relax, son. She'll call."

Michael shook his head.

"It's not just that. She doesn't check in half the time she's supposed to. When the adrenaline's pumping, quick decisions have to be made—sometimes you just can't turn it off just to make a simple phone call.

"But this is different. Monica *always* calls when she's on her way in. Something must've gone wrong in Atlanta. The only thing that keeps me from going out of my mind is that I had the Atlanta field office send one of its agents to the airport to watch her until she boards the plane to D.C. He's supposed to call me when the plane takes off."

"When's it scheduled to leave?"

"Nine fifty-eight. She has another in—" Michael glanced at the large clock on his wall—"twenty minutes or so."

"That's a big airport, son. And, remember, Monica's not traveling by herself."

"Dad, she's had almost an hour's layover. She could've gone from one end of the airport and back by now."

"We've done all we can do, Michael. Now, we wait.

She'll call. If she doesn't, she'll probably walk through that door in a couple of hours like no big deal—that is, until she sees me."

Sadly, Michael knew his father's last statement was probably true.

* * *

THE TINY PLANE SHOOK against the turbulence as it made its ascension through the clouds. Monica placed her hand on her chest and leaned her head back against the seat, taking deep breaths to keep from hyperventilating.

When she and Dave Carter had finally reached the gate of Atlantic Southeast Airlines for their flight and purchased the two tickets, she'd nearly fainted when she saw the small, twin-engine prop parked outside the terminal. The tiny plane seated less than twenty-five passengers. There were no flight attendants.

Now, as she checked her watch for the fifth time since they'd taken off, she wished she could trade mental states with her companion.

Monica looked from her seat on the third row down the aisle that led into the doorway of the cockpit. Drawn curtains separated the two pilots from their six passengers who were sporadically seated. Through the crack of the curtains, she could see the men with headsets on, checking their instruments and talking among themselves. Being that close to them made her physically ill.

Monica reached into her purse and fumbled around for the container of Altoids, hoping the strong peppermint flavor would ease the nausea that consumed her.

*You're gonna be okay.* She sucked on the tiny mint as

she closed her eyes and tried to concentrate on Sweets. How Gerald had found his way to Amherst and knew about her FBI status, she couldn't fathom.

She had to think of a plan. There would be no surprise attack. Gerald's men were waiting for her at the airport.

Monica gripped her armrest as the plane hit an air pocket. It shook like a car hitting a pothole in the road. She opened her eyes again when she felt a hand on her arm.

"Are you okay?" An elderly woman leaned across the aisle and gently stroked Monica's arm.

"Yes, ma'am. Just a little nervous."

"This little plane is more durable than you think. Gets over those huge mountains like a champ. Take a little nap like your young man over there. Before you know it, we'll be safely on the ground. I'm Hazel Bing."

Monica shook the woman's wrinkled hand.

"Joyce McIntyre." Monica smiled weakly at the woman whose skin tone was the same shade of brown as Sweets's, though Hazel Bing was probably ten years older. She was a distinguished-looking woman who wore pearl earrings and a large pearl ring surrounded with diamonds on her left hand. Her hair was pulled back into a neat bun.

Monica felt a wave of nausea again. She popped another Altoid into her mouth and closed her eyes again. Then, as suddenly as they closed, Monica's eyes sprang open and flickered as if a piece of lint had just become embedded beneath her lids.

Her mind cleared like a ship maneuvering its way through a thick fog. The details of her plan came into view.

She looked at her watch again. There were only about

forty-five minutes left in the flight. With a new burst of energy, she unbuckled her seatbelt, stood up, and reached into the storage bin above her head to get her bag. She then turned cheerfully to the woman across the aisle. "I feel better already."

# Chapter
## 37

The plane pulled up at the gate in Lynchburg at precisely 10:20 a.m. Monica turned to Hazel. "You remember what you're supposed to do?"

The woman winked her eye and smiled approvingly at the transformation Monica had gone through right before her eyes. Hazel pointed her bony finger against her temple and tapped it lightly. "There's still some mileage left here."

"Thatta girl." Monica winked back, as she unbuckled Carter and looked him over. The make-up she'd smeared on his face, neck and hands didn't do much to distort his appearance, but it helped him blend in with Hazel and Ms. Lucy. Monica lowered the front of his cap, handed him a dark pair of sunglasses to hide his blue eyes, and rushed through the plan again in her mind.

During the flight, she had changed into the old tweed suit with accessories and hurriedly applied the theatrical make-up to her skin as she brought Miss Lucy back to life. Monica explained to a mesmerized Hazel that she was actually an actress, running away from an abusive husband who might show up at the airport to drag her back to Atlanta. Monica also told the woman that her husband had drugged her lover—Carter—before they both escaped.

Hazel eagerly agreed to help. The other three passengers looked at them as though they were crazy.

With the door to the plane opened and the stairs mounted for the passengers to descend, Hazel clambered off first with Carter right behind her. Monica followed a few steps behind him.

At the bottom of the stairs, Monica watched as Hazel linked her arm in Carter's, stopped briefly to speak with an airport employee with a walkie talkie in his hand, then proceeded across the pavement toward the terminal door.

"Oh my," Monica mimicked her best Miss Lucy impression and struggled with her luggage. "This bag is so heavy."

"You should've checked it at the gate, ma'am." The man took Monica's bag and frowned at Carter for not assisting the old woman.

"No, sirree. Sister and I always keep our jewelry in our possession. Don't want our bags sent on a wild-goose chase across the country. Isn't that right, Sister?"

Monica looked down at Hazel, who stood no more than five feet tall. Standing next to Monica, she looked like an acorn next to a tree.

Hazel laughed. "You always know what's best, Lucy."

"Young man," Monica's eyes roved the terminal entrance in search of Gerald's men, "please call for one of those electric contraptions to take Sister and me to the baggage claim. Our brittle old bones can't walk that far."

The man spoke into the two-way radio as they stood outside the terminal door. Monica instantly spotted two men in dark suits a few feet away. They scrutinized each passenger.

One of them was Dr. Blackburn. The other man, she did not know. When he put his hand inside the breast pocket of his suit jacket, she immediately saw the bulge of a gun. Blackburn talked into a cellular phone.

Monica linked one arm through Carter's and urged him forward. She nudged Mabel with her elbow.

"Oh dear, Sister." The back of Hazel's hand trembled against her forehead. "I'm starting to get one of those spells again. Everything's going black. I need one of my pills."

"Help us!" Monica cried out, right before Hazel's body faltered. "My sister's ill. We need a cart." The ticket agent rushed toward them from behind the counter. People crowded around. A motorized cart drove up and stopped in front of them.

As Monica placed an Altoid in Hazel's mouth and cradled the woman's head in her lap, she watched Dr. Blackburn talk into the phone and look in their direction. She could see by the way he waved his hand in the air, that he was frustrated at not being able to locate them. He stared her way as the cart pulled off, then dismissed the disturbance and walked over to the airline counter to talk to the ticket agent.

\* \* \*

DAVE CARTER LOOKED UP from under the flap of his cap and locked his eyes on the man at the counter like a fighter pilot locked onto his target right before launching a missile. He'd seen that man before. He was afraid of him, though he did not know why. Fragmented memories filled his mind as Dave tried to make sense of them. Darkness swallowed up reality. He remembered a dark, empty parking lot and a black haze that approached him. The closer it got, the more it multiplied. One by one, they hit and kicked him. The entire time, he'd struggled to protect himself with his arms.

Carter's breathing increased. He squirmed in the electric cart as he recreated the scene in his mind. Though the darkness blurred his vision, he saw the shadow of a huge hand move closer to him. A syringe spurted drops of liquid.

The last thing he'd remembered before the stab of sharp pain was a demented face of evil.

* * *

"HE'S THE ONE!" Carter pointed to the man. Monica grabbed him and pulled him down beside her. She turned around and saw Dr. Blackburn and the other man running after them at the end of the long hallway.

"Can you please hurry?"

"We're going as fast as we can." The nervous driver looked at Carter as if he were going to be attacked.

Carter's outburst jolted Hazel from her "attack."

"Is he okay?" She held onto the cart.

"My husband's spotted us. We're gonna have to get off soon. Are you sure someone's meeting you?"

"Don't worry about me. My son's probably getting my luggage now."

"In case I don't get a chance to later, thanks so much for helping us."

Hazel smiled and patted Monica's hand. "Good luck to you, dear."

Monica stretched her neck to see how much farther they had to go before they reached the baggage claim area. She then looked back. The men were gaining on them. She couldn't wait any longer. She and Carter were going to have to make a run for it.

"Let's go, Carter." She took her bag in her arm. "We've gotta go—now! Stop the cart," she said to the driver. "We need to get off."

"We're almost there," the man protested.

"Stop this thing, now!"

Monica jumped from the cart as it slowed down and pulled Carter with her. He struggled to control his weak legs. She turned to get her bearings and rushed Carter through the automatic glass doors of the airport. She scoured the line of parked cars, until she saw the black truck in the distance. Big Red leaned against it, puffing on his pipe.

"Just a little farther." Monica dragged Carter toward the truck. She turned her head and saw the men exit the building several yards behind. One of them held a gun in front of him.

Big Red looked up. A red feather stuck out from the side of his black felt hat, two long braids hung in front of his chest.

"Hold on now, lady," he said, pulling the clay pipe from his mouth. He walked from the front of the truck when Monica yanked open the passenger door and pushed Carter into the front seat.

"Hey? You can't just get into Big Red's truck without me inviting you."

"Get in, Red!" Monica took her gun from inside the waistband of her skirt and jumped into the truck.

"How you know Big Red's name?" The Indian eyed her suspiciously.

"For God's sake, Red! It's me, Monica. Now, get your ass in this truck and haul ass like the moon-shining sonofabitch you are!"

A broad grin broke out on Big Red's copper-colored face. He moved like greased lightning around the truck and hopped inside. Besides members of his family, only Monica, Sweets, and Michael knew that Red had hauled whiskey for his father across the county line more than fifty years ago.

"I taught you well!" He beamed proudly. Pulling the truck from the curb with a loud screech, he frowned. "How come you dressed like that?"

Monica didn't answer right away. She ripped off the jacket of her suit without bothering to unfasten the buttons. Laying her Sig across her lap, she pulled out the tail of her shirt and then turned to look out the cracked back window of the truck. The two men following them jumped into a parked black Lincoln.

"We're gonna have company pretty soon, Red," she announced. As she checked the bullets in her gun and removed the safety latch, she explained what was going on. When she'd finished, she asked, "You think this piece of shit can still live up to its reputation?"

"Watch what you say, little girl," Red grinned, stroking the tattered vinyl dashboard. "This old gal is still the fastest thing this side of the Mississippi. I've made sure of that. Show some respect. She's got feelings, you know."

"We'll see how she holds up with a couple of bullets in her. Those guys back there won't be shooting blanks." Monica turned to Carter and lit a cigarette. "How're you doing?"

"Okay," he said, inhaling deeply. "Just a little tired."

"Don't konk out on me now. We've got a bumpy road ahead of us."

Red sped onto 29 North and shifted the black truck

into fourth gear.

"Hold onto ya hats," he yelled to his companions. He looked into the rear-view mirror, his eyes gleaming like shiny new pennies. "They're right behind us."

Monica and Carter turned around at the same time. The black Lincoln changed into the lane three cars behind them. Red swerved into another lane, then sped up to pass a large mobile home pulling a car behind it. The black Lincoln swerved in and out of lanes, until it was almost right behind them.

"We've gotta lose 'em before we get to Sweets's house," Monica yelled above the creaking of the old truck. "Keep 'em busy, Red. Don't give 'em time to call ahead."

"Just sit back, little girl. Let Big Red do his thing." The old man chuckled wickedly, darting in and out of the lanes like a race car driver competing in a national championship. "Nobody knows these parts like Big Red."

It was as if fifty years had dropped off Big Red, he was so exhilarated. He gave out a couple of whoops as he careened around curves. He hollered out to Carter, acknowledging him for the first time. "You mighty quiet, boy. Reach into that there glove compartment and hand Big Red some fuel for his engine."

Carter did as he was told and took out a brown, glass jug of liquor. Pulling out the cork, he handed it to the Indian. Red turned it up to his mouth and gulped it down like it was cool, spring water.

"Ah-h." He wiped his mouth with the back of his hand. "This'll cure whatever ails you." He shoved the jug at Carter. "Don't be afraid, boy, take a sip."

"Give me that." Monica reached across Carter and took the container from Red. "He doesn't need any of this, but I sure as hell do." Monica took a long swig and immediately grabbed her throat. "I'll never get used to the first sting," she said, bouncing up and down on the seat when Big Red turned onto Old Coolwell Road. She swiveled her head around again. The black Lincoln was right on their tails.

"Show me whatcha got, Red." She flicked the cigarette out the window. "They're hanging tough back there."

Red stepped on the gas. The truck sped up, hanging with each curve as they tackled the steep hills. The road was a two-lane stretch that led to the turnoff to Sweets's land. As they rounded another hill, a shot rang out.

"Get down!" Monica screamed, pulling Carter down in the seat by the sleeve of his shirt. The bullet struck the cab of the truck. She leaned out the side of her window and fired a shot. The Lincoln swerved to the side, then immediately straightened.

"We're leading 'em straight to the house! What about the old turnoff to your people's land, Red?"

"You reading my mind, little one," Red hollered back. "Hold on, now. This old gal's gonna turn on two wheels."

Monica saw the grand old oak tree a short distance ahead that marked the turn-off spot that led into the woods. It was the secret entrance into Cherokee territory. Its hidden road was the one the Indians used as an escape route to haul liquor in the late hours of the night when eluding the law.

She gripped the door handle, as Red suddenly steered to his right onto the dirt road and entered the heavily-wooded area. The truck tilted so far, Monica thought they would turn over. When they righted again, she looked back through the dust.

"They're still back there."

"You wanna follow this old Indian, you fuckers?" Red yelled out the window, grinning like the devil himself. "I've got something for ya, alright. You'll follow me straight to hell!" He leaned forward in his seat and gripped the big steering wheel even tighter.

Then he started to moan. It sounded soft at first, like someone tone deaf trying to hum a tune. Then Big Red sang out even louder and startled his passengers. They stared at him in puzzlement as he over-articulated words only he knew so well. Monica recognized it as one of the Indian chants he had taught her and Michael when they were children.

"What the hell you doing, Red? This is no time for—" Her mouth gaped open in recognition. It was the chant his people believed summoned the spirits for protection. She looked at Big Red, then turned her head to where he was staring. Her eyes widened with fear.

"Have you lost your goddamn mind?" she screamed. "That old bridge rotted out when I was a kid. Those planks won't hold this heavy truck. We'll never make it!"

The skeletal remains of the Cherokee bridge were less than a mile in front of them.

Red didn't even look at Monica. He sang louder. His body twitched and jerked with each syllable, much like the old truck he was driving. Another shot fired from the Lincoln and shattered the back window. Glass flew into the truck as Monica covered Carter with her body. The old man pressed the gas pedal all the way to the floor.

"Red! Red!" Monica shouted at him. "Don't try it, Red! It won't hold! Turn off! We'll find another way!"

"Concentration is all it takes. It's all in the way you hit it." He sang out without fear, tuning out everything around him. He gripped the steering wheel so tight his knuckles turned chalk white. "I'll make a believer out of you yet, little one."

Monica screamed and covered her eyes with her arm right before they hit the bridge. The truck bounced up and down, the wood beneath them crackled like freshly-cut wood burning in a roaring fireplace. When she opened her eyes again, they were safely on the other side.

"Alright!" She shouted at the old man, who then brought the vehicle to an abrupt stop. The three of them bounced around like lottery balls jumbled right before a Saturday night drawing.

"Why the hell are you stopping here?" Monica flailed her arms hysterically. She glared at the old man as if he'd suddenly become senile. "They're gonna catch up to us."

"Watch," he winked, ". . . and learn." Then he leaned his head against the back of the seat. He closed his eyes and started his chanting all over again.

Monica and Carter looked out the broken window behind them. The Lincoln slowed down, then stopped completely in front of the entrance to the bridge. The driver gunned his engine as if he were trying to intimidate an opponent at the start of a drag race. With screeching tires, the car shot onto the bridge like an object exploding from a cannon. It got halfway across, before the dilapidated planks gave way.

The car plunged head first into the forty-foot drop below. The screams of the men inside echoed through the trees.

Monica turned around and fell back into her seat. When she looked at Red, the old man smiled at her and nodded his head in satisfaction.

"I'll never question you again, you old fart," she conceded. The old man took a drink from his jug before he handed it to her. He started the car again and put it in gear. Monica swallowed long and hard. When she finished a second drink, she said, "Now, let's go get Sweets."

# Chapter

## 38

Gerald paced the floor like a nervous old hen, the gun close to his side and held firmly in his hand. Arthur Fazio stood posted at the window.

"What the hell's taking them so long?" Gerald muttered out loud. "They should've been here by now. Arthur, try the cell phone again."

Sweets rocked in the wooden chair in front of the wood-burning stove, her hands folded on top of the black leather Bible in her lap. Sneakers curled up at her feet.

"You wouldn't be so worried," she said calmly, without looking at Gerald or breaking her cadence, "if you weren't up to the devil's work."

"Shut your mouth, old woman!" Gerald shouted. He stood in front of her and waved his gun in the air as a reminder that he was still in control. "You're lucky I didn't kill you a long time ago."

He stared at her long and hard, his hair flung down into his face. He whipped off his tie and pulled out his shirttail. He'd shed the jacket to his suit an hour ago.

"Don't you have anything to drink in this house?"

"Made some fresh lemonade just yesterday. It's in the refrigerator. Help yourself."

"I'm not talking about any goddamn lemonade," Gerald sneered. "I mean liquor."

"The good Lord clearly warns, plain and simple in the good Book, against getting drunk on wine or—"

"Enough of that religious talk! You've done nothing but try to reform me ever since we got here and I'm sick of it. I don't wanna hear another word about it, you understand me?"

Sweets shrugged her shoulders. "You don't mind if I read to myself, do you?"

"As long as you're praying your granddaughter gets here real soon."

"Still no answer, Gerald," Arthur interrupted.

Sneakers raised his head and began to growl. His large, fox-like ears stood erect as he looked around the room. Sweets lifted her eyes from the pages of her Bible and looked over her glasses.

"Quiet, Sneakers," Sweets murmured. The little dog cocked his head to the side and suddenly rose up on all fours. He barked loudly as he took off down the hall to the front, of the house. Gerald and Arthur both raised their guns.

"What's he barking at?" Gerald asked Sweets.

"No telling. That silly dog can hear a cat a mile down the road."

Gerald motioned to Arthur. "I didn't hear a car. Go take a look."

Arthur tucked in his shirt and followed in the direction where Sneakers ran. He opened the screen door. Before he could step outside, Sneakers bolted out the door, scampered down the front stairs, and rounded the corner of the house.

Monica heard him from her crouched position next to the rear wheel of Gerald's car, parked in the driveway to the left of the house. She'd come alone, ordering Carter and Big Red to stay in the truck off the road. With her gun drawn, and both hands in front of her, she heard Arthur slowly walk down the stairs.

Sneakers reached the back of the house, stopped and began sniffing the ground as he turned around and retraced his steps. Monica held her breath and prayed he wouldn't pick up her scent. The prayer came too late. The dog's radar locked onto her. Ears perched back on his head, he ran in her direction like a child whose parent had suddenly returned from a long trip. Monica grabbed him, locked an arm around him, and tried to squelch his whimpering.

"Drop your gun and get up where you are," a deadly voice said from behind her.

Sneakers snarled at him, as Monica rose slowly to her feet. She turned around to face Arthur. She hesitated, then threw the gun in front of her and raised her hands above her head.

"Turn around slowly, and walk into the house," Arthur ordered. "You'd better calm that mutt of yours down before I shut him up myself."

As Monica turned to walk away, she suddenly swung her arms around like a baseball bat and knocked the gun from Arthur's hand. He lunged for it and she kicked him hard in the crotch. He screamed in pain as Monica delivered a sharp blow to his head with her hands locked together.

He fell unconscious to the ground. She ran to get his gun, tucked it underneath her shirt inside her skirt, and crept up the stairs toward the front door. She held the Sig out in front of her.

She opened the door and let Sneakers in before slipping in behind him, holding the screen door behind her so it wouldn't slam.

Sneakers ran excitedly down the hall to where he'd left Sweets. Monica tiptoed stealthily behind him. She paused briefly to glance inside the doorway of the front room of the house. Just as she passed it, she heard a noise and spun around. Gerald stood with one arm firmly around Sweets, who was positioned as a shield in front of him. He held a gun to the side of her head.

"Put the gun down," he ordered, tightening his grip around Sweets. "Or Granny here dies."

Monica froze with her gun still drawn, her eyes shifting from the frightened look on her grandmother's face to the gun held next to her head.

"You think I'm joking?" Gerald shouted. "I said put the goddamn gun down. Now!"

"Alright, alright. Just don't hurt her." Monica lowered her arm and then bent down to place the gun on the floor beside her. "You okay, Sweets?"

Her grandmother nodded her head. "I'm—"

"Shut up! I'll decide when it's time to talk. Now, turn around slowly and walk into the next room. Remember, my gun's loaded."

Monica turned around and walked to the large family room. She turned her head slightly to the side and saw out the corners of her eyes that Gerald still had his gun at Sweets's head.

"Sit down over there." He pointed his gun to the oversize chair next to the window. Grabbing the back of the rocker, he pulled it in front of him and pushed Sweets down into the seat. "I'll keep Granny over here next to me."

Sneakers stood in front of Monica and barked ferociously at Gerald like a dog twice his size.

"Shut him up or he'll be the first to go."

Monica grabbed the little dog. "Be quiet, Sneakers. Sit."

The dog whimpered, then sat down on the floor beside the chair, growling softly under his breath.

Gerald leaned onto the back of the rocker and smiled.

"Well, now," he said, looking Monica over for the first time. "I see the job at Bayou City Wireless has taken its toll on you, Taylor. Oh, silly me." He slapped the palm of his hand to his forehead. "It's really Monica Sinclair, isn't it? You almost got away with it. But not quite."

"How'd you find out about me?"

Gerald winked. "All in due time. I think you're going to enjoy that little story. But, first, where's my package? Where's Dave Carter?"

"Dead. Shot by one of the goons you sent to the airport."

Gerald eyed her suspiciously.

"I don't believe you. Now where is he? And where are my men?"

"I told you," Monica said with a serious face. "Carter is dead. I had someone else pick us up from the airport. We managed to get past your men, but they followed us until we pulled onto Old Coolwell Road. They fired several shots through the back window of the truck. Carter was hit, died instantly. Your men crashed trying to cross a dilapidated bridge. They didn't make it."

"And the driver of your car. Where's he?"

Monica looked directly at Sweets.

"I'm sorry, Sweets. Big Red had a heart attack and died shortly after that. The excitement was too much for him."

"Oh, my Jesus!" Sweets cried out, her hand flew over her mouth with horror. "Are you sure?"

Monica closed her eyes and shook her head, as her grandmother cried softly.

"Well, I don't believe a word of it." Gerald stalked towards Monica, his gun aimed at her.

"You think I'd come here by myself if I had help?"

"There's no car out front." Gerald eyed her suspiciously. "How'd you get here?"

"Couldn't restart the truck after the chase. It's about a mile down the road. I ran the rest of the way. If you don't believe me, I'll take you to it."

Gerald looked at her and then shook his head.

"You must think I'm a fool. Nobody's stepping one foot out of this house. We're all going to stay right here until our little chat is over. Then . . . " His voice trailed off as he turned around and slowly walked back to his post behind Sweets's chair.

"How'd you find out about me?" Monica asked him a second time.

A grin broke out on Gerald's face.

"Ah, yes," he said. "That's where you underestimated me. You had me stumped for awhile, the dark contact lenses threw me off. I knew the first time I saw you at Bayou City Wireless you seemed familiar, but I couldn't quite place where we'd met."

He pulled a piece of paper from his shirt pocket, walked back over to Monica, and handed it to her. Looking curiously at him, she reached up and took it. Unfolding it, she glanced at the front of the program and gasped.

"That's right," Gerald grinned with satisfaction. "The poetry reading in London. 1978. Remember?"

"How . . .?" Monica mumbled, crumpling the program in her hand. It was the same photo Cameron had spotted when she gave him the videocassette tape that day in her office. Her first encounter with Gerald was all coming back to her now.

"How did I figure it out?" Gerald's smile broadened, obviously relishing the shock on her face. "It came to me when I implicated you in Cameron's murder. Arthur Fazio saw him leave your office with the tape. Pretty clever, wouldn't you say?"

Monica's whole body tensed as she recalled the last image of Cameron lying dead in a pool of blood. Hearing Gerald boast about the killing made her blood curdle, then simmer to a slow boil.

"That doesn't explain how you knew to look for *this*." She held up the piece of paper in her hand.

"Chalk it up to an excellent memory," Gerald answered matter-of-factly. "You see, Dr. Blackburn casually mentioned that a young, black nun upset Carter during her visit to the facility a few days ago. One of the things he said about her—you—was that the woman had striking hazel eyes. It wasn't until Arthur saw you leave Port Royal Meadows with Carter, dressed as an old woman, that it hit me. You forgot your contacts that time, my dear. It suddenly dawned on me that I, too, once met an old woman with those same memorable eyes.

"On a hunch, I searched your house. The police overlooked the phoney dictionary. I did not."

He grinned before speaking again.

"I can see from your face you know what I'm about to say. The pub in London, remember? You dressed as an old woman and read poems about the days of slavery.

"Like having a little chat with Miss Jane Pittman herself. It wasn't just your dramatization that got my attention. It was those fabulous hazel eyes. So electric. Still are, now that I see them again. I flipped through the program to find your picture and biography. So determined to meet you, I left my date after you'd finished reading and came over and offered to buy you a drink. But, you were hardly appreciative."

"Stop." Monica held up her hand in front of her face, the memory of that evening rushing to the forefront of her mind, as if it had just recently happened. "I don't want to hear anymore."

She remembered now the disgusting young man who approached her that night, when she was an exchange student at University College London. He'd reeked of alcohol and had forced himself on her as he held a fistful of hundred dollar bills. Before he was thrown out of the pub, he had called her a "nigga bitch." It was the only time during her year abroad that Monica had been reminded of why she'd left the racial prejudices in the States.

"Granny," Gerald addressed Sweets, his eyes blazing with anger, "you should've taught this granddaughter of yours better manners. She threw whiskey in my face."

"You thought you could buy me!" Monica spat out.

"Can't imagine why she'd do such a thing," Sweets answered sarcastically.

"Neither could I," he said, gently stroking his gun over the top of Sweets's head. "I had every intention of repaying your courtesy." Gerald continued talking to Monica. "I kept tabs on you. Until one of the trustees of your prestigious college—who was a business associate—informed me a year later that you'd entered the FBI academy.

"By that time, I had other things to occupy my time.

So now, after all these years, we meet again. Don't know what prompted the FBI investigation into Bayou City Wireless, but you must not have much to go on because here we both sit. No arrests. No warrants."

"You won't get away with this, Gerald." Monica's tone was unflinching, firm.

"I already have. The shipment of phones is already in international waters. As soon as the transaction in Indonesia is made, I—Victor Conti—will simply disappear. Only two things stand in my way. And you just told me one of them has been eliminated. "So, now there's only you."

Gerald walked over and stood in front of Monica. A low growl began to rumble in Sneakers's throat until it escalated into full-blown barks of hysterics, as he danced around Gerald's feet.

"I am *sick* of this goddamn dog." Gerald pointed his gun down at Sneakers.

"No!" Monica lunged for the weapon in Gerald's hand. "Run, Sweets!" she yelled to her grandmother, who bolted from her chair behind him and ran towards the kitchen.

Monica heard the slam of the back door as she struggled to get the gun from Gerald. An explosion thundered through the house. Gerald elbowed Monica in the chest with a blow so hard, it nearly knocked the wind out of her. She fell to the floor. Beside her, Sneakers lay bleeding from a gaping hole in his side.

"Oh, God! No!" Monica held her aching chest and reached for the little dog. She watched Sneakers flicker his eyes once more in her direction as if to say goodbye. Then his panting stopped, his tongue hung out the side of his mouth.

"Get back in that goddamn chair!"

"Let me help him!" Monica cried.

Gerald fired off another shot that blew a hole in the wall behind her. "That was just a warning. Now, get your ass back in that chair!" His eyes swelled in size, veins bulged from his neck, his face turned crimson with anger.

Monica hesitated before moving away from her precious dog, tears burned down her face like battery acid. There was no fear inside her anymore. Only rage.

"No matter where you go," she warned, pulling herself onto the seat of the large chair, "I'll hunt you down and kill you myself."

Gerald ran his hand through his disheveled hair, his breathing hard and irregular. A scowl crossed over his face. He stepped forward and slapped Monica hard across her face with the back of his hand.

"You'll never get the chance." The gun wavered in his hand as he slowly raised his arm in her direction. "You've caused me nothing but trouble ever since you came to Bayou City Wireless. Victor is dead because of you. So are Cameron and Carter. And, now, your time has finally come. I'm going to enjoy watching you die."

He aimed his gun at Monica's face and pressed his finger around the trigger.

"Drop the gun, Gerald!" a voice boomed behind him.

Gerald spun around and fired off a shot. But it was too late and off center for the marksman standing in front of him. Carter fired a shot and hit Gerald in the shoulder. Monica plowed into Gerald's side with her body and knocked him to the floor. The gun flew from his hand and slid a few inches across the hardwood floor, spinning out of his reach. Monica quickly grabbed it and ran to where Carter stood, his gun still aimed at his target.

"You!" Gerald stared up in disbelief. "Should've killed you when I had the chance."

Carter crept closer to Gerald, both of his hands wrapped tightly around the gun to keep it steady. He looked down at the man who had once held his life in his hands. Monica stood next to him.

"Don't do it, Carter," she warned softly. "It's not worth it. He can't hurt you anymore."

"No! You don't understand . . ." He shook his head furiously, without taking his eyes off of Gerald. His lips trembled. Beads of sweat formed around his mouth, his face turned a pale pink. His chest heaved in and out as he concentrated on speaking words that had almost been erased from his memory.

"You don't know what he's done to me. I remember clearly now what he did to those people. How he let them die when he could've saved them. He stole eight months of my life, and now, I'm going to take the rest of his."

"Give me the gun," Monica said firmly, reaching for Carter's weapon. "He's gonna pay for what he's done. I promise you that. Now, let go of the gun and give it to me."

"You don't have the guts to pull the trigger," Gerald goaded, clutching the wound to his shoulder, as he lay slumped on the floor. Blood seeped profusely through his fingers like water flowing downstream.

"He wants you to kill him, Dave," Monica insisted. "Can't you see that? He wants the easy way out."

Carter stood in position, his eyes squinting as if indecision and determination battled in his mind. A loud crash came from the kitchen and the sound of footsteps made Monica swing her gun around.

"It's all over, Dumont!" Michael rushed into the room

with his gun drawn. Three other agents with weapons ran to Gerald and yanked him to his feet. His screams of agony went unnoticed.

"You okay?" Michael asked.

Monica shook her head. "How did you know we were here?"

Michael smiled. "You're not the only one with a few tricks up your sleeve. Though you're a hard one to keep up with, big sister. I'll take over from here."

Monica stepped aside and let out a heavy sigh. Her chest ached with pain as she went over to her little friend. With tears in her eyes, she pulled one of the quilts Sweets had made from off the back of the chair and placed it over his limp body.

At the same time, Michael walked over to Carter and gently placed a hand on his shoulder. His arms were still extended in front of him with his gun aimed at Gerald.

"Give me the gun, Dumont," Michael slowly reached for his gun. "It's okay, Greg. It's over."

Carter blinked tears from his eyes, bit his bottom lip, and closed his eyes. Turning to Michael, he nodded his head and placed the gun in his hand.

Monica looked from one man to the other in total confusion.

"Michael, what the hell's going on? This is Dave—"

"No, Monica," Michael put his arm on the man's shoulder. Staring him straight in the eye, he said, "*This* is Greg Dumont, FBI undercover agent."

*"Undercover agent?"* she exclaimed.

Michael nodded.

"Well, I'm goddamn glad you finally got around to telling me."

"I'll explain everything as soon as we get rid of this

scumbag." He then walked over to Gerald and met his vehement glare.

"It took a long time, Conti," Michael said, "but we finally got you. That little cargo you were shipping to Indonesia? We got that, too. The plant in Mexico's been shut down. The equipment confiscated. And last, but, not least, there's a little canary in Washington, D.C., by the name of Bob McCormick, who's singing his head off as we speak. With the exception of Dr. Blackburn—"

"—Who's at the bottom of Cherokee pit." Monica interjected.

Michael continued. "All of the killing and experimenting you did was for nothing. Where you're going, we're gonna make damn sure you can't hurt anyone else again."

Gerald smiled demonically and tilted his head back. He looked like he was ready to froth at the mouth.

"Think you have it all figured out, don'tcha, agent man?" he spat out. "That shipment's just small potatoes. I've been at this a long time, made sure wireless technology got into the hands of millions of people. At this moment, they're chatting their heads off on communications devices designed by me."

"And?" Michael asked.

"Do you think the Bastrop Study was the first? Thousands of little towns all over this country were only too eager to test our products and too naive about the technology to know they were being used as laboratory rats."

Gerald winked an eye at Michael and then flashed a chilling grin. "How will you know for sure which studies were legitimate and which ones were for my own pleasure? Tell me, agent man. You can lock me away, but I'll have the satisfaction of knowing you'll be out there spinning your investigative wheels, clawing your way through millions of haystacks, trying to find out just how much damage I've really done."

Gerald roared with the satanic laughter of a deranged man.

Michael drew back his fist and punched Gerald hard in the stomach. Gerald doubled over as two agents on each side of him held him up. Michael wound up for another shot when Monica pulled him back. Sirens wailed just outside the house.

"Stop it, Michael!"

"Get him out of here, before I beat the crap out of him!" Michael ordered the paramedics when they stormed into the room carrying medical supplies. Several Amherst County sheriffs fell in step behind them.

Michael motioned to his men who pushed Gerald onto the stretcher.

"Go with him in the ambulance. Strap him down. Make sure he doesn't do anything stupid, like try and kill himself. I want him alive to stand trial for all he's done. There's another one locked in the car. Take him, too."

Sweets and Big Red pushed through the huddled men and rushed to Michael and Monica.

"Thank God, you're both all right." Sweets hugged her grandchildren. "I left this house on the wings of an eagle. Didn't know this old body could move so fast. Nearly died from fright when Red stepped from behind a tree. We called 9-1-1 and prayed they'd get here in time."

"Sorry I had to lie about Red being dead, Sweets," Monica said.

"I understand, darling."

"I tried to keep him in the truck just like you told me, Monica." Red pointed a finger at Greg Dumont, who sat with his head in his hands. "But the damn fool took my pistol and threatened to shoot Red with his own gun if I didn't show him the way here. Was on my way to my house to call the sheriff's department when I heard Sweets running through the woods, screaming for help."

"You both did just fine," Monica smiled sadly. "Sneakers was shot."

"Oh, baby." Sweets took Monica in her arms again. "Where is he?"

Monica looked down to the spot where she'd left her trusted friend. Wiping her eyes, she turned to Big Red.

"Red, take him outside for me, will you? I can't bear to see him like that. I'll be along in a few minutes."

"Don't worry, little one." The old Indian picked up the bundle. "Big Red will take good care of him."

Sweets reached for her apron off the corner of the sofa. "Red, I suppose we could all use a drop of your whiskey. Lord knows, after all this excitement, we need it."

Monica watched Big Red take Sneakers away, then walked to where Michael stood, finishing his conversation with one of the sheriffs.

"You think Gerald's telling the truth?" She saw by the anguished look on Michael's face that he was considering the validity of Gerald's statement.

"I don't know." He shook his head. "I just don't know. Hundreds of thousands—even millions—of people around the world may be affected. It could be years before we'd know for sure."

Michael's voice filled with despair. "I've gotta call Frasier." Before turning to leave, he said, "Maggie's

384

safe. I sent one of the agents in Houston to guard her as soon as she contacted me. Said to tell you thanks. Are you okay, Monica?"

Monica rubbed his shoulder and nodded her head. "Go make the call. We'll talk later."

She watched him stare at the phone for a couple of seconds, before finally picking up the receiver. *What do we do now?*

# Chapter

## 39

"Jim wants us back in Washington first thing tomor row morning." Michael straddled a seat between Monica and Greg Dumont at Sweets's kitchen table. For the past two hours, he'd talked intermittently on the phone with Jim Frasier, who stood within inches of the Attorney General. All three were patched through to the President.

Sweets and Big Red scrubbed away at the blood stains on the hardwood floor in the family room. It was nearly 5:30 p.m. and the sun still hovered between the clouds.

Michael sighed heavily as he removed the cork from Big Red's whiskey jug and poured some into his tea. Monica lit another cigarette and looked down into her lap, where Sneakers lay sleeping. She had completely broken down, when Big Red brought the dog back to her—alive, but weak—washed of blood and tightly bandaged.

The old Indian had only smiled when Monica asked how he'd brought her dog back to life, when she'd watched Sneakers take his last breath—or so she thought—moments after being shot. Ancestral spirits, herbal concoctions—however he did it, she was grateful.

Monica pushed her tea cup over to Michael for some

more whiskey. Dumont drank his tea straight.

"I'm surprised Frasier didn't order us back tonight," she said, blowing smoke out the corner of her mouth.

"He's scared. So is the AG." Michael took a long swallow of his drink. "They assumed—as we all did—that once Gerald was captured and the shipment seized, our problems would be over. Another time bomb has been set, waiting to be detonated.

"Speaking of explosions," he continued, "you know that patient you saw in Blackburn's secret operations?"

"Yeah."

"He was dead when our guys raided Port Royal Meadows. Blackburn was experimenting on him. Wanted to find at what point noncancerous cysts became cancerous from exceeded levels of electromagnetic rays. Thought the discovery would gain him admissions into the Academy of Neurological Surgeons, an elitist group of 100 of the world's most powerful neurosurgeons."

Monica blew out a long whistle.

"Guess I was pretty lucky, huh?" Greg Dumont shook his head

"What about the patient's family?" Monica asked.

"According to Blackburn's journal, they think he's already dead. When the guy slipped into a coma, Blackburn used his position as chairman of neurosurgery at University to recommend his facility at Port Royal Meadows for terminal care. After a month or so, he notified the family the patient was dead and convinced them to have the body cremated. Then, he sent home an urn of bogus ashes."

"Well, he's the one eating ashes, now," Monica bristled. "In Cherokee pit!" She leaned back in her chair and asked, "Whadda ya think Frasier and Fredericks's recommendation to the President will be?"

Michael shook his head.

"They're still discussing it. Then all three will meet formally with the National Security Council to devise a strategy. No easy way to break news like this to the public. That's why Jim wants us there to present the facts before the plans are announced." Michael turned to Dumont. "Especially you."

Greg Dumont looked from Michael to Monica, then lowered his head. "I just hope I can help. I let the Bureau down . . . If Monica hadn't . . . "

"Hey," Monica said softly. "Happens to the best of us. I screwed up and lost the tape you made. Got Cameron killed in the process." She looked away, trying not to let them see the pain in her eyes.

She'd told them earlier about her stint as Taylor LeBlanc, including her role in Cameron's death. The only part she'd excluded was how much she'd loved him.

"Enough with the screw-ups, okay?" Michael spoke up. "You both did what you were sent to do. We finally got Gerald, that says it all. Now, we prepare a written brief that'll help the NSC make an informed decision tomorrow."

"As for you, Greg," Michael addressed his colleague, "we don't need the videocassette. Your memory's getting sharper by the minute. Whatever's still hazy, Monica can fill in. We're just lucky we were able to stop the medication you were being given. Otherwise, you'd still be out there in the Twilight Zone."

Michael hummed the theme song of the popular television series.

"You're hopeless, l'il bro." Monica threw her

cigarette lighter at Michael, who ducked just in time.

"Yeah, but you love me anyway, right?"

"Just a little. But tell me something: How'd you do it? Stop the medication, I mean."

Michael took another sip of his drink, then glanced at his watch.

"Gotta plane to catch, Michael?"

"There's something I haven't—"

"—Did you just hear a car drive up?" Monica instinctively reached for her Sig on the table. She laid Sneakers in her chair and went to the window and looked out. She heard the slam of a car door.

"Who could that be?"

"I asked someone to join us." Michael hesitated.

Monica turned around and raised a suspicious eyebrow. "Who?"

"Me, Monica," a voice said, from the doorway of the kitchen. Monica looked up into the eyes of her father, Sweets stood nervously beside him. For the briefest moment, Monica felt she would suffocate from being so near to him.

"How could you, Michael!" Her words filled with the venom of a rattlesnake. She placed the gun on the counter and turned to rush out the back door. Michael bolted from his chair, grabbed her arm, and swung her around. Sweets quickly moved to get Sneakers out of the chair.

"You're not running away this time, Monica." He flung his sister down into the chair with a loud thud and held her shoulders firmly in his strong grasp. "You're going to stay your butt right here and listen for a change."

"Let her go if she wants, Michael," Ben said wearily.

"No! No, no, Dad." Michael defiantly shook his head. "This has gone on way too long. Monica, I'm gonna take my hands away. But, I'm warning you straight up, if you try to leave this chair before we're through talking, I'll be right on your heels. You know I'll do it."

Michael let go of his sister and walked around to face her. Monica tried to compose herself, the bile rose from her stomach and strangled her throat.

"Why do you insist on making this your business?" This is not about you."

"The hell it's not!" Michael screamed back. "You weren't the only one affected by Mom's death. Do you have any idea how I've felt all these years, knowing deep down you resented me because I looked white? For being the reason you decided it made a difference between us?"

"That's not true! I've always loved you!"

"I know, but I've carried the guilt inside, just the same. Much like the anger you have for Dad. He's done everything he could for you—"

"—Until he decided he didn't want me!" Monica shouted directly to Ben. "I was too dark for his lily-white world, just like Mama was!" She was beyond the point of no return. At that moment, she was a child again, spilling out the hateful, hurtful pain that set her insides on fire.

"Monica, I love—"Ben pleaded.

"Don't you dare try to deny it!" The legs of her chair rumbled across the floor, as she scooted her chair back from the table and stood from her seat. Michael unfolded his arms and started forward to make good his earlier threat. He halted only when Monica put her palms on the table and leaned forward.

"I went through my whole life trying to be the best, trying to camouflage my color. I did everything Sweets

390

ever asked—didn't I Sweets?—so you'd come back for me and Sweets.

"The highest grades, the most awards and achievements—I took up acting because it was one of your passions. But nothing I did was ever enough. You turned your back on me. What did you ever do to really show me how much you loved me? What did you ever do?"

Ben lowered his head. He looked as if his heart was breaking from his daughter's words.

"I'll tell you what he did." Michael spoke up angrily, diverting the daggers away from his father. "He risked his life for you. When I told him you were on the run to Port Royal Meadows and in danger, he insisted on helping you.

"Wanna know how he showed his love for you?" Michael came within inches of his sister's hostile glare. "Look at him closely, Monica. Especially around the eyes. See anything familiar?" He grabbed her chin and turned her face around to look at Ben. "I said look!"

Monica lifted her eyelids and, reluctantly, looked at her father.

"Dad was in my office when you called about losing the tape. I knew you were going to try to get Greg Dumont. We'd learned that if the Thorazine Greg was being given were discontinued, his memory would gradually come back, making it easier for him to cooperate with you during your escape. Someone had to be planted inside the facility to do that. We didn't know who was on Gerald's payroll.

"Remember Mr. Byers? The old man who caused such a ruckus? That was Dad."

Greg Dumont took a step forward from where he'd silently been in the background. "That was you?" he asked Ben. "I thought I was hallucinating when the medicine suddenly tasted like candy."

Ben smiled sadly and nodded.

Michael continued, talking faster with each word he spoke, moving in for the kill while he had Monica's attention. "I just knew that razor-sharp instinct of yours would recognize your own father, no matter how much we altered his appearance."

Monica looked at Ben and slowly slid down into her chair. Closing her eyes, she brought the image of Mr. Byers into focus. Michael was right, she had noticed something familiar about him. Her shoulders quaked now, as she started to cry.

"Dad told me he even telephoned you at the motel. That was a risk in itself. We checked him into the facility as a bonafide patient. No one knew it was a hoax until we went back to get him out.

"You were there to see his love for you, Monica." Michael crouched down beside her chair and took her hand in his. He wiped the tears from her eyes. "Give him a chance, Twig."

Michael waited and held his breath. Sweets took a handkerchief from her apron pocket and pressed it to her mouth. Finally, Monica miserably nodded her head.

Michael kissed the top of her head. He went to Sweets and embraced her, turning his head slightly to smile into Ben's tear-stained face. With Greg Dumont, they eased out of the room to leave father and daughter alone.

When they had gone, Ben cleared his throat to break the silence and wiped his face with his bandaged hand. Speaking in almost a whisper, his voice cracked with emotion. "I've regretted separating you and Michael every minute of every day since I made that promise to Sarah.

"But, Monica, I swear to you, if I'd known things would turn out this way, I wouldn't have done it, no matter how much your mother wanted it. Sarah was my whole life. The only reason I didn't die right along with her was because of you and Michael.

"It was never about color, Monica. It was about keeping my children safe in a racist world. I've always loved you. Look at me, Precious. Please."

Monica lifted her eyes to his. She had not heard him call her that, since she was a little girl. Suddenly, the floodgates inside of her opened, old memories and buried feelings rushing through like raging water violently breaking through a dam.

Ben wiped his own eyes, then reached into his hip pocket and took out his wallet. Opening it, he pulled out a worn piece of paper whose edges were jagged and had yellowed with time.

"I've carried this around with me all these years," he continued. "Read it now." He paused, cleared his throat again, then reached across the table and handed the paper to Monica, his eyes never leaving her face. In a tender voice, he said, "It's from Sarah."

Monica caught her breath as soon as her mother's name left his lips. She looked at the paper in his hand. Her hand trembled as she took it, summoning the courage to open it.

Taking a deep breath, she carefully opened the letter and began to read her mother's beautifully-scripted words:

*My darling Monica,*

*Leaving you is the hardest thing I've ever had to do. But you are so lucky to have Sweets, your father, and Michael to help you through this difficult time. And these are troubled times, my darling, not just because of this unmerciful illness that is taking me away from you.*

*But because of the cruel prejudices in today's world that will mount against you, your father, and Michael if you all continue to live together. We've kept our family safe so far, but as you and Michael grow up, there may be trouble. Virginia doesn't tolerate mixed-race marriages. Let alone children.*

*The only solution that makes sense is for Michael to go back to Hartford with Ben and you stay here with Sweets. Please understand, you are being separated only because it's the safest living arrangement for all of you.*

*Your father will always be there for you. If it were his choice alone—and it is not—he would take you both. He loves you just that much. But, in the end, my darling, his love alone would not be enough to fight the ignorance of this world. Another time, another decade . . .*

*In the meantime, sweetheart, be kind to one another. And take good care of Daddy. He's going to need you after I'm gone. He's been my rock, my strength, my light through a dark and winding tunnel.*

*I leave you now, my darling. Not because I want to, but, because it is God's will. Be a big girl for Mama, Monica. I love you with all the love a mother has to give—and more.*

*Sarah*

"Mama." Monica pressed the letter to her chest as if it were the glue that would hold her breaking heart together. Ben put his arms around her. For the first time in many years, Monica's body did not flinch, nor did it constrict from his closeness. Instead, she let herself bask in his loving arms, just as she did when she was a child.

"Your mother left a similar letter for Michael." He whispered in her ear, savoring the moment like a rare vintage wine tasted for the very first time.

Monica whirled around and wrapped her arms around her father's waist, burying her head against him. "Oh, Daddy!" She sobbed uncontrollably. "Forgive me. I didn't really mean to hurt you."

"Sh-h-h, Precious." He comforted her, rocking her like a baby. "Everything's okay, now."

Sweets stood in the doorway, silently observing the scene unfolding before her. She clasped her hands together and brought them to her lips. Raising her head, she closed her eyes and sent up a prayer.

"It's taken some time, Sarah," she whispered, smiling as tears streamed down her rounded cheeks. "God is good . . . all the time."

# Chapter
## 40

onica, Michael, and Greg Dumont sat stoically around the Washington office, waiting for the decision that was being made in the large conference room down the hall. Each one had presented their findings on the Bayou City Wireless investigation, in both oral and written form, which took almost two hours. And now, there was nothing more they could do, but wait.

Michael loosened his tie as he sat behind the desk and looked at his watch—again. It was 10:30 a.m., and they had been waiting in insolation for over an hour.

Greg Dumont rubbed his fingers across his forehead as he sat at the small table in the center of the room, flipping through the pages of his report, rechecking its contents to see if there was something more he could have added.

Monica leaned her left hip against the sill of the window to the right of Michael's desk, one arm crossed underneath the other, as she blew the smoke from her cigarette. Her mind kept drifting to the night before when she had begun her reconciliation with her father. It felt good to be relieved of the hatred she'd once felt towards him.

Love was rekindled in its place. The pain was still

there, only now, it was less intense. In time, Monica smiled, it may even disappear for good. She felt like a hole in her heart was slowly being healed. At least, now, she was hopeful.

"How do you think they'll make the announcement?" She looked at Michael, her thoughts returning to the dire situation at hand.

Michael shrugged his shoulders.

"How would I know?" he snapped nervously. "Put that thing out. You know you're not supposed to smoke in here."

"Whoa! Bad day at the office, Mike?" she said sarcastically, taking a last drag off her cigarette before putting out the butt in a tissue.

Michael looked at her and then chuckled, running his fingers through his hair.

"Sorry."

The door to the office flung open and three pairs of anxious eyes focused on Jim Frasier, as he walked into the room and closed the door behind him. The grim expression on his face said it all, though Monica couldn't stop herself from asking the question they all wanted to know the answer to.

"Well?"

Jim ran two fingers across his thick mustache. After a long pause, he spoke. "They decided not to alert the public and declare a national state of emergency. The best we can hope for is stricter laws governing the wireless industry."

"Shit!"

"I don't fucking believe this!" Michael slammed his fist on his desk as he stared at his boss in bewilderment. "Did they think we made up this crap just for their entertainment? To add some excitement to their ho-hum existence?"

Greg Dumont propped both elbows up on the table and sank his head in his hands, as though the outcome of the decision was all his fault.

"It's not that they didn't believe you guys, Michael," Jim insisted, holding his hands up in front of him in defense.

"Oh, really?" Monica scoffed. "Then what the hell was it, Frasier?"

"This thing is just too big," he simply said. "Involves too many people—about *forty-five* million people in the U.S., more than *100* million worldwide with another twenty-eight *thousand* subscribers signing up every day."

"That's a cop-out and you know it."

"I agree, Monica, but you tell me what else we can do? If we told the public about the Bastrop Study, there'd be mass hysteria—honest-to-God, worldwide panic! You said yourself, there's no way to know for sure if Gerald is telling the truth about experimenting on other people. What if we issued an alert and we were *wrong*? Think about it. What would our recourse be? And what about the industry? It pumps more than twenty-three billion dollars annually into the economy."

"If we don't expose the truth, Frasier, we're doing the same thing McCormick did—covering up the whole mess. What are the three of us to do now? Stand by, twiddling our thumbs, while there's a damn good possibility people are dying from lethal levels of electromagnetic rays? Don't you realize how large the Conti Telecommunications market is? Are you telling us that we're supposed to keep our mouths shut and act like everything's fine with the world and nothing horrible is going on?"

Frasier looked at Monica without batting an eye. "That's about the size of it. You are instructed to say nothing more about this investigation. It never happened."

"What about Gerald Conti?" Michael glared at Frasier. "I guess he never killed anyone either?"

"He'll be brought up on charges, but they won't be linked to the Excalibur."

"And Jarrett Jones?" Michael's tone indicated he already knew the answer.

"His death was ruled a homicide. That's the way it'll remain."

"Well, that's just peachy, Frasier," Monica snorted, shaking her head in disgust. "Just fucking peachy," she repeated, as she walked toward the table where a distraught Greg Dumont sat, and snatched her purse.

"Don't leave, Monica," Michael asked. "You can't just walk out now.

"Why not? Frasier just said the final decision's been made. You and I both know there's nothing else we can do. We're just little peons.

"I'm gonna drive back to Amherst, check on Sneakers—who, by the way, Frasier, is giving an Academy-Award winning performance of a dog recovering from a gunshot wound. Then, I'm gonna hang out all night with Big Red and drown myself with shots of his fabulously wonderful whiskey. And, if I'm lucky as hell, I'll reach that blissful state where I won't remember what happened here today."

Monica swung open the door. "And another thing, Frasier," she said, standing in the doorway without looking back, "the next time you get the urge to call me in on another terrific assignment . . . *don't!*"

## EPILOGUE

Six months after the Federal Bureau of Investigations, the National Security Council, and the President of the United States rendered the joint verdict, the Earth continued spinning around the moon without a care in the world.

Greg Dumont testified before a closed, special committee of Congress, about the dangers of radio-frequency radiation from wireless phones. His account was instrumental in the ordering of new epidemiology studies. Government agencies, like the EPA and FDA, in accordance with the National Institutes of Heath, were ordered to participate in existing studies conducted on the issue. Dumont later resigned from his duties as an undercover agent with the FBI and started his own engineering firm.

FCC Director Bob McCormick was charged and convicted of bribery, a second-degree felony, and given a maximum sentence of twenty years without parole. One week after arriving at a federal penitentiary, he hung himself in his jail cell.

A new chairman was appointed head of the Federal Communications Commission and recommended a more stricter standard to which the wireless industry would adhere. It was passed by Congress and signed into law by the President of the United States.

Gerald Conti was charged on two counts of solicitation of capital murder, in the deaths of Victor Conti and

Cameron Maxwell. After being found not guilty, by reason of insanity, Gerald was sentenced to consecutive life sentences to be served in a maximum-security facility for the criminally insane.

Arthur Fazio was not as "lucky" as his friend, Gerald Conti. He was charged and convicted of murder in the first degree, for the death of Cameron Maxwell. He was given the death penalty by lethal injection and bides his time on death row in a federal penitentiary.

Under the terms of Victor Conti's will, Conti Telecommunications, Inc., was left to his sole beneficiary, Maggie Wentworth, who, subsequently, sold the conglomerate to its competitor. As an anonymous benefactor, she donated twenty-eight million dollars—one million dollars each—to the families of the participants of the Bastrop Study. Maggie moved from Houston and lives quietly in Bastrop, Texas, where the urn containing Victor's ashes—which she had exhumed—is prominently, and lovingly, displayed on the mantle of her living room fireplace.

Jasper—Jazz—Lopez quit his job as mail clerk at Bayou City Wireless and moved to New York to start his own designer label of women's evening wear. The move was made possible by the financial backing of one of his most ardent fans, Monica Sinclair.

Jim Frasier remained with the Justice Department as Director of the FBI.

Michael Morgan continued as an assistant deputy director with the FBI after a one-month leave of absence.

Monica Sinclair returned to her secluded life in Atlanta. Her latest novel, *A Woman of Determination*, became a best-seller just two weeks after its release. She and Sneakers frequently visit Sweets and Big Red at their home at the foot of the Blue Ridge Mountains in Virginia where Benjamin Morgan is a welcomed guest.

# Order Form

Milligan Books
1425 West Manchester, Suite B,
Los Angeles, California 90047
(323) 750-3592

Mail Check or Money Order to:
Milligan Books

Name _____ Date _____

Address _____

City_____ State ____ Zip Code_____

Day telephone _____

Evening telephone_____

Book title _____

Number of books ordered ___ Total cost .............. $ _____

Sales Taxes (CA Add 8%) ............................. $ _____

Shipping & Handling $4.50 per book.....................$ _____

Total Amount Due................................ $ _____

_ Check _ Money Order  Other Cards _____

_ Visa _ Master Card  Expiration Date _____

Credit Card No. _____

Driver's License No. _____

_____        _____
Signature                              Date